FILTHY

THE FIVE POINTS' COLLECTION

SERENA AKEROYD

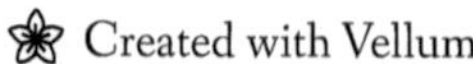 Created with Vellum

PLAYLIST

IF YOU'D LIKE to hear a curated soundtrack, with songs that are featured in the book, as well as songs that inspired it, then here's the link:

https://open.spotify.com/playlist/oiQB8qZUK6CjFg5AQRtKuu

THE CROSSOVER READING ORDER WITH THE FIVE POINTS

FILTHY
FILTHY SINNER
NYX
LINK
FILTHY RICH
SIN
STEEL
FILTHY DARK
CRUZ
MAVERICK
FILTHY SEX
HAWK
FILTHY HOT
STORM
THE DON
THE LADY
FILTHY SECRET
REX
RACHEL

FILTHY KING
REVELATION BOOK ONE
REVELATION BOOK TWO
FILTHY LIES
FILTHY TRUTH

RUSSIAN MAFIA
Adjacent to the universe, but can be read as a standalone
SILENCED

FOREWORD

You're about to meet Finn O'Grady and Aoife Keegan.

Before you get started, just FYI: Aoife is pronounced Ee-Fah.

Ah, the joyous marvel that is Irish Gaelic... I loved it so much that I had no choice but to write a sequel series: FILTHY FECKERS.

I hope you love these Feckers as much as I love writing them.

Much love,

Serena

xoxo

Triggers:

- Blackmail,
- Dubious consent,
- Gun violence/mass shooting,
- General violence

Amazon:
www.books2read.com/FilthySerenaAkeroyd
Apple:
https://books.apple.com/us/audiobook/filthy-the-five-points-mob-collection-book-1-unabridged/id1606275073

PART 1

SCREW YOU

1

———

FINN

OBSESSIVE HABITS WEREN'T alien to me.

They were as much a part of me as my coal-dark hair and my diamond-blue eyes. Ingrained as they were, it didn't mean they weren't irritating as fuck.

As I rifled through the folder on the table in front of me, staring down at the life of one pesky tenant, I wanted to toss it in the trash. I truly did.

I wanted not to be interested in her.

Wanted my focus to return to the matter at hand—business.

But there was something about her.

Something. . .

Irish.

I was a sucker for my own people. When I was a kid, I'd only dated other Irish girls in my class, and though I'd become less discerning about nationality and had grown more interested in tits and ass, I'd thought that desire had died down.

But Aoife Keegan was undeniably, indefatigably Irish.

From her fucking name—I didn't know people still named their kids in Gaelic over here—to her red goddamn hair and milky-white skin.

To many, she wouldn't be sexy. Too pale, too curvy, too rounded and wholesome. But to me? It was like God had formed a creature that was born to be my downfall.

I could feel the beast inside me roaring to life as I stared at the photos of her. It wanted out. It wanted her.

Fuck.

"I told you not to get those briefs."

My eyes flared wide in surprise at my brother, Aidan O'Donnelly's remark. "What?" I snapped.

"I told you not to get those briefs," he repeated, unoffended. Which was a miracle. Had I been speaking to Aidan Sr., I'd probably have lost a finger, but Aidan Jr. was one of my best friends, as well as a confidant and fellow businessman.

When I said business, it wasn't the kind Valley girls dreamed their future husbands would be involved in. No Manhattan socialite, though we were wealthy as fuck, would want us on their arm if they truly knew what games we were involved in.

My business was forged, unashamedly, in blood, sweat, and tears.

Preferably not my own, although I had taken a few hits for the Family over the years.

"My briefs aren't irritating me," I carried on, blowing out a breath.

"No? You look like you've got something up your ass crack." Aidan cocked a brow at me, but his smirk told me he knew exactly what the fuck was wrong.

I flipped him the bird—the finger that I'd have lost by showing cheek to his father—and he just grinned at me as he leaned over my glass desk and scooped up one of the pictures.

That beast I mentioned earlier?

It roared to life again when his eyes drifted over Aoife's curvy form.

"She's like your kryptonite," he breathed, tilting his head to the side. "Fuck me, Finn."

"I'd rather not," I told him dryly. "Now her? Yeah. I'd fuck her anytime."

He wafted a dismissive hand at my teasing. "I knew from that look in your eye, there was a woman involved. I just didn't know it would be a looker like this."

I snatched the photo from him. "Mine."

My growl had him snickering. "The Old Country ain't where I get my women from, Finn. Simmer down."

Throat tightening, I grated out, "What the fuck am I going to do?"

"Screw her?" he suggested.

"I can't."

He snorted. "You can."

"How the fuck am I supposed to get her in my bed when I'm about to bribe her into selling off her commercial lot?"

Aidan shrugged. "Do the bribing after."

That had me blowing out a breath. "You're a bastard, you know that, right?"

Piously, he murmured, "My parents were well and truly married before I came along. I have the wedding and birth certificates to prove it." He grinned. "Anyway, you're only just figuring that out?"

I shot him a scowl. "You're remarkably cheerful today."

"Is that a question or a statement?"

"Both?" The word sounded far too Irish for my own taste. My mother had come from Ireland, Tipperary to be precise—yeah, like the song. I was American born and bred, my accent that of someone who'd been raised in Hell's Kitchen but, and I hated it, my mother's accent would make an appearance every now and then.

'Both' came out sounding almost like 'boat.'

Aidan, knowing me as well as he did, smirked again—the fucker. "I got laid."

Grunting, I told him, "That doesn't usually make you cheerful."

"It does. I just never see you first thing after I wake up. Da hasn't managed to piss me off today."

Aidan was the heir to the Five Points—an Irish gang who operated out of Hell's Kitchen. It wasn't like being the heir to a candy company or a title. It came with responsibilities that no one really appreciated.

We were tied into the life, though. Had been since the day we were born.

There was no use in whining over it, and Aidan wasn't. But if I had to deal with his father on a daily basis? I'd have been whining to the morgue and back.

Aidan Sr. was the shrewdest man I knew. What the man could do with our clout defied belief. Even if I thought he was a sociopath, he had my respect, and in truth, my love and loyalty.

Bastard or no, he'd taken me in when I was fourteen and had made me one of his family. I'd gone from being his kids' friend, the son of one of his runners, to suddenly being welcome in the main house.

All because Aidan Sr.—though I was sure he was certifiable—believed in family.

I shot Aidan Jr. a look. "Was it that blonde over on Canal Street?"

He rubbed his chin. "Yeah."

Snorting, I told him, "Hope you wore a rubber. I swear that woman has so many men going in and out of her door, it should be on double-action hinges."

He scowled at me. "Are you trying to piss me off?"

"Why? Didn't wear a jimmy?" I grinned at him, my mood soaring in the face of his irritation. "Better get to the clinic before it drops off."

Though he flipped me the bird as easily as I'd done to him—I was his brother, after all—he grumbled, "What are you going to do about little Aoife?"

I squinted at him. "She's not little."

That seemed to restore his humor. "I know. Just how you like them." He shook his head. "You and Conor, I swear. What do you do with them? Drown yourself in their tits?"

Heaving a sigh, I informed him, "My predilection for large tits is none of your business."

"And whether or not I wore a jimmy last night is none of yours."

"If it turns green and looks like a moldy corn on the cob, who you gonna call?"

"Ghostbusters?" he tried.

I shook my head, then pointed a finger at him and back at myself. "No. Me."

Grunting, he got to his feet and pressed his fists to the desk. "We need that building, Finn."

"The business development plan was mine, Aid. I know we need it. Don't worry, I won't do anything stupid."

He snorted. "Your kind of stupid could go one of two ways."

That had me narrowing my eyes at him, but he held up his hands in surrender.

"Fuck her out of your system quickly, and then get started on the deal," he advised. "Best way."

It probably was the best way, but—

He sighed. "That fucking honor of yours."

I had to laugh. Only in the O'Donnelly family would my thoughts be considered honorable.

"If I'm fucking someone over, I want them to know it," was all I said.

"That makes no sense."

"Makes for epic sex, though," I jibed, and he shot me a grin.

"Angry sex is always good." He rubbed his chin, then he reached over again and flipped through the photos. "Who's the old guy to her?"

"To her? Not sure. Sugar daddy?" The thought alone made the beast inside rage. I cleared my throat to get rid of the rasp there. "To us? He's our meal ticket."

Aidan's eyes widened. "He is?"

I nodded. "Just leave it to me."

"I was always going to, *dearthàir*." He tilted his chin at me, honoring me with the Gaelic word for brother. "Be careful out there."

"You, too, brother."

Aidan winked at me and, with a far too cheerful whistle for someone whose dick might soon be 'ribbed for her pleasure' without the need for a condom, walked out of my office leaving me to brood.

The instant his back was to me, I stared at the photos again. Flipping through them, I glowered at the innocent face staring back at me through the photo paper—if only she knew.

Hers was a building in Hell's Kitchen. Five Points Territory. One of many on my hit list.

Back in the 70s, Aidan Sr., following in his father's footsteps, had bought up a shit-ton of property, pre-gentrification, and it was my job to either sell off the portfolio, reconstruct, or 'improve' the current aesthetics of the buildings the Points owned.

This particular one was something I'd taken a personal interest in.

See, I was technically a legitimate businessman.

This office?

I had views of the Hudson. I could see the Empire State Building, and in the evening, I had an epic view of the sunset setting over Manhattan. This office building, also Points' property, was worth a cool hundred million, and I was, again technically, the CEO of it.

On paper?

I looked seamless.

The businessman who sported hundred thousand dollar watches and had a house in the Hamptons. No one save the Points and my CPA knew where the money came from. I liked that because, fuck, I had no intention of switching this pad for a lock-up in Riker's Island.

Still, this project cut close to home, and the reasoning was fucking pathetic.

I'd never admit it to any of the O'Donnellys. The bastards were like family to me, and if I admitted to this, they'd never let me hear the end of it.

Extortion?

I usually doled that out to someone else's to do list. Someone with a far lower paygrade than me, someone expendable. But the minute I'd heard of the troublesome tenant who was refusing to sell her lot to us? After not one, not two, not even three attempts with higher prices?

Five outright refusals?

The challenge to convince her otherwise had overtaken me.

See, I liked stubborn in women.

I liked fucking it out of them.

Throw in the fact the woman's name was Aoife? It had been enough to get me sending someone out to follow her.

If she'd been fifty with as many chins as she had grandchildren, she'd have been safe from me.

But she wasn't.

She was, as Aidan had correctly stated, my kryptonite. All milky flesh with gleaming auburn hair that I wanted to tie around my clenched fist. Her soft features with those delicate green eyes that sparkled when she smiled and were like wet grass when she was mad, acted like a punch to my gut.

Now?

My interest hadn't just been piqued.

It had fucking imploded.

Yeah, I was thinking with my cock, but what man, at the end of the day, didn't?

I'd just have to be careful. Just have to make sure I put pressure on the right places, make sure she'd bend and not break, and the old bastard in the pictures was my key to just that.

See, every third Tuesday of the month, Aoife Keegan had a habit of traipsing across Manhattan to the Upper East Side. There, at three PM on the dot, she'd enter a discreet little boutique hotel and wouldn't leave until nine PM that night.

Five minutes after she arrived and left, the same man would leave, too.

At first, when Jimmy O'Leary had told me that Senator Alan Davidson was at the hotel, I hadn't thought anything of it.

Why would I?

Senators trawled for donations in fancy hotels every fucking day of the week. It was the true luxury of politics. Sure, they made it look real good for the press. Posing in derelict neighborhoods and shaking hands with people who did the fucking work . . . all while they lived it up large with women half their age in two thousand dollar a night suites.

My mouth firmed at that.

Was Aoife selling herself to the Senator?

The thought pissed me off.

I couldn't see why she'd do such a thing. Not when I'd looked into her finances, had seen just how secure she was. But maybe that was why. Maybe the Senator was funneling money to her.

The only problem was that the lot Aoife owned—did I mention it was owned outright? Yeah, that was enough to chafe my suspicions, too, considering she was only twenty-fucking-five years old—was a teashop in a small building in a questionable area of HK.

I mean, come on. I loved Hell's Kitchen. It was home. But fuck. Where she was? What kind of Senator would put his fancy piece in *that*?

My jaw clenched as I studied the Senator's and Aoife's smiling faces as they left the hotel. Separately, of course. But whatever they'd been doing together, it sure put a Cheshire Cat grin on their chops– that was for fucking sure. Jimmy being a dumbass, hadn't put the two together, had just remarked on the 'coincidence,' but I was no fool.

How did I know they were together in the hotel?

Jimmy had been trailing Aoife for four months—told you I was obsessive—and every third Tuesday, come rain or shine, this little routine had jumped out, and when Jimmy had picked up on the fact Davidson had been there each and every time, I'd gotten my hands dirty, bribed one of the hotel maids myself—and fuck, that had been hard. Turned out that place made even the maids sign NDA agreements, but everyone had a price—and I'd found out that my little obsession shared a suite with the old prick.

My fingers curled into fists as I stared at her. Butter wouldn't fucking melt. She was the epitome of innocence. Like a redheaded angel. Could she really be lifting her skirts for that old fucker? Just so she could own a teashop?

Something didn't make sense, and fuck, if that didn't intrigue me all the more.

Aoife Keegan had snared one of the biggest, nastiest sharks in Manhattan.

She just didn't know it yet.

2

———

AOIFE

"WE NEED MORE scones for tomorrow. I keep telling you four dozen isn't enough."

Lifting a hand at my waitress and friend, Jenny, I mumbled, "I know, I know."

"If you know, then why the hell don't you listen?" Jenny complained, making me grin.

"Because I'm the one who has to make them? Making half that again is just . . ." I sighed.

I loved my job.

I did.

I adored baking—my butt and hips attested to that fact—and making a career out of my passion was something every twenty-something hoped for. Especially in one of the most expensive cities in the world. But sheesh. There was only so much one person could do, and this was still, essentially, a one-woman-band.

With the threat of Acuig Corp looming over me, I didn't feel safe hiring extra staff. I'd held them off for close to six months now. Six months of them trying to tempt me to leave, to sell up. They'd raised their prices to ten percent above market value, whereas with everyone else in the building, they'd just offered what the apartments were truly worth. Considering this place wasn't the nicest in the block, that wasn't much.

Most people hadn't held out because, hell, why wouldn't they want to live elsewhere?

Those who were landlords hadn't felt any issue in tossing their tenants out on the street. The tenants grumbled, but when did they ever have any rights, anyway?

For myself, this was where my mom and I had worked to—

I brought that thought to a shuddering halt.

Mom was dead now.

I had to remember that. This was on me, not her.

My throat thickened with tears as I turned to Jenny and murmured, "I'll try better tomorrow."

The words had her frowning at me. "Babe, you know I'm not the boss here, right?"

Lips curving, I whispered, "I know. But you're so scary."

She snickered then peered down at herself. "Yeah, I bet I'd make grown men cry."

Maybe for a taste of her. . . .

Jenny was everything I wasn't.

She was slender, didn't dip her hand into the cookie jar at will—the woman had more willpower than I did hips, and my hips seemed to go on forever—and her face looked like it belonged on the cover of a fashion magazine. Even her hair was enough to inspire envy. It was black and straight as a ruler.

Mine?

Bright red and curly like a bitch. I had to straighten it out every morning if I didn't want to look like little orphan Annie.

I'd once read that curly-haired women straightened their hair for special events, and that straight-haired women curled theirs in turn, but I called bullshit.

Curly-haired women lived with their straightening irons surgically attached to their hands.

At least, *I* did.

"I think grown men would cry," I told her dryly, "if you asked them to."

She pshawed, but there was a twinkle in her eye that I understood. . . . She agreed with me, knew it was true, but wasn't going to admit it. With anyone else, she might have. She had an ego—that was for damn sure. But with me? I think she figured I was zero competition, so she felt no need to rub salt in the wound, too.

I plunked my elbows on the counter and stared around my domain as she bustled off and started clearing the tables. It was her last duty of the day, and my feet were aching so damn bad that I didn't even have it in me to care.

This owning your own business shit?

It wasn't easy.

Not saying I didn't love it, but it was hard.

I slept like four hours a night, and when I wasn't in bed, I was here. All the time.

Baking, cooking, serving, and smiling. Always smiling. Even if I was so sleep-deprived I could sob.

Jenny's actually a life saver.

My mom used to be front of house before. . . .

I sucked down a breath.

I had to get used to thinking about it.

She wasn't here anymore, but just avoiding all thoughts of her period wasn't working for me. It was like I was purposely forgetting her, and, well, fuck that.

She'd always wanted to have a teashop. It had been her one true dream. Back in Ireland, when she was a little girl, her grandmother had owned one in Limerick. Mom had caught the bug and had wanted to have one here in the States. But not only was it too fucking expensive for a woman on her own, it was also impossible with my feckless father at her side.

I didn't want to think about him either, though.

Why?

Because the feckless father who'd pretty much ruined my mother's life, wasn't the only father in my life. My biological dad hadn't exactly cared about her happiness, but once he'd come to know about me, he'd tried. That was more than could be said for the man who'd lived with me throughout my early childhood.

"You look gloomy."

Jenny's statement had me blinking in surprise. She had a ton of dishes piled in her arms, and I'd have worried for the expensive china if I hadn't known she was an old pro at this shit. Just as I was.

We could probably earn a Guinness World Record on how many dishes we could take back and forth to the kitchen of *Ellie's Tea Rooms*. I swear, I had guns because of all that hefting. My biceps were probably the firmest part of my body.

More's the pity.

I'd have preferred an ass you could bounce dimes off of, but, when it boiled down to it, there was no way in this universe I could live without cake.

Just wasn't going to happen.

My big butt wasn't going *anywhere* until scientists could make zero calorie eclairs and pies.

"I'm not glum."

"No? Then why are your eyes sad?"

Were they? I pursed my lips as I let the 'sad eyes' drift around the tea room. I wish I could say it was all forged on my own hard work, but it wasn't. Not really.

"I was just thinking about Mom."

"Oh, honey," Jenny said sadly, and she carefully placed all the dishes on the counter, so she could round it and curve her arm around my waist. "It was only seven months ago. Of course, you were thinking of her."

"I just—" I blew out a breath. "I don't know if I'm doing what she'd want."

"You can't live for her choices, sweetness. You have to do what you think is right for you."

I gnawed at my bottom lip again. "I-I know, but she was always there for me. A guiding light. With Fiona gone and her, too? I don't really know what I'm doing with myself."

This business wasn't something that made me want to get up on a morning. It was my mom's dream, her goal. Every decision I made, I tried to remember how she'd longed for a place like this, but it wasn't my passion. It was hers, and I was trying to keep that dream alive while fretting over the fact my heart wasn't in it.

"I think you're doing a damn fine job. You have a very successful teashop. Your cakes are raved about. Have you visited our TripAdvisor page recently? Or our Yelp?" She squeaked. "I swear, you're making this place a tourist hotspot. I don't think Fiona or Michelle could be more proud of you if they tried."

The baking shit, yeah, that was all on me, but the other stuff? The finances?

I'd caved in.

I'd caved where my mom had always refused in the past.

With the accident had come a lot of medical bills that I just hadn't been able to afford. Without her help, I'd had to take on extra staff, and out of nowhere, my expenses had added up.

Mom had been so proud of this place, so ferociously gleeful that we'd done it by ourselves, and yet, here I was, financially free for the first time in my life, and I still felt like I was drowning because my freedom went entirely against her wishes.

"Is this to do with Acuig? I know they're still pestering you."

Jenny's statement had me wincing. Acuig were the bottom feeders who wanted to snap up this building, demolish it, and then replace it with a skyscraper. Don't get me wrong, the building was foul, but a lot of people lived here, and the minute it morphed into some exclusive condo, no one from around here would be able to afford to live in it.

It would become yuppy central.

I'd rejected all their offers to buy my tea room even though I didn't want the damn thing, not really. Mostly I wanted to keep mom's goals alive and kicking, but also, it pissed me off the way Acuig were changing Hell's Kitchen. Ratcheting up prices, making it unaffordable for the everyday man and woman—the people I'd grown up with—and bringing a shit-ton of banker-wankers and 1%ers to the area.

So, maybe I'd watched Erin Brockovich a time or two as a kid and had a social conscience . . . Wasn't the worst thing to possess, right?

"Aoife?" Jenny stated, making me look over at her. "Is Acuig pressuring you?"

I winced, realizing I hadn't answered—Jenny was my friend, but she also worked here and relied on the paycheck. It wasn't fair of me to keep her hanging like that. "They upped the sales price. I guess that isn't helping," I admitted, frowning down at my hands.

Unlike Jenny who had her nails manicured, mine were cut neatly and plain. I had no rings on my fingers, and wore no watch or bracelets because my wrists were usually deep in flour or sugar bags.

I spent most of my life right where I wanted it—behind the shopfront. That had slowly morphed where I was doing double the work to compensate for Mom's loss.

Was it any wonder I was feeling a little out of my league?

I was coping without Fiona, grieving Mom, working without her, too, and then practically living in the kitchens here. I didn't exactly have that much of a life. I had nothing cheerful on the horizon, either.

Well, nothing except for next Tuesday, and that wasn't enough to turn my frown upside down.

The money was a temptation. I didn't need to sell up and start working on my own goals, but that just loaded me down with more guilt and made me feel like a really shitty daughter.

Jenny squeezed me in a gentle hug. But as I turned to speak to her, the bell above the door rang as it opened. We both jerked in surprise—each of us apparently thinking the other had locked up when neither of us had—and turned to face the entrance.

On the brink of telling the client we were closed for the day, my mouth opened then shut.

Standing there, amid the frilly, lacy curtains, was the most masculine man I'd ever seen in my life.

And I meant that.

It was like a thousand aftershave models had morphed into one handsome creature that had just walked through my door.

At my side, I could feel Jenny's 'hot guy radar' flare to life, and for once, I couldn't damn well blame her.

This guy was . . . well, he was enough to make me choke on my words and splutter to a halt.

The tea room was all girly femininity. It was sophisticated enough to appeal to businesswomen with its mauve, taupe, and cream-toned hues, and the ethereal watercolors that decorated the walls. But the tablecloths were lacy, and the china dishes and cake stands we used were the height of Edwardian elegance.

Moms brought their little girls here for their birthday, and high-powered executives spilled dirt on their lovers with their girlfriends over scones and clotted cream—breaking their diets as they discussed the boyfriends who had broken their hearts.

The man, whoever the hell he was, was dressed to impress in a navy suit with the finest pinstripe. It was close to a silver fleck, and I could see, even from this distance, that it was hand tailored. I'd seen custom tailoring before, and only a trained eye could get a suit cut so perfectly to this man's form.

With wide shoulders that looked like they could take the weight of the world, a long, lean frame that was enhanced by strong muscles evident through the close fit of his pants and jacket, then the silkiness of his shirt which revealed delineated abs when his bright gold and scarlet tie flapped as he moved, the guy was hot.

With a capital H.

"How can we help, sir?" Jenny purred, and despite my own awe, I had to dip my chin to hide my smile.

Even if I wanted to throw my hat into this particular man's game, there was no way he'd choose me over Jenny. Fuck, I'd screw her, and

I wasn't even a lesbian. Not even a teensy bit bi. I'd gone shopping with her enough to have seen her ass, and I promise you, it's biteable.

So, nope. I didn't have a snowball's chance in hell of this Adonis seeing *me* when Jenny was in the room.

Yet. . . .

When I'd controlled my smile, I looked over at the man, and his focus was on me.

My breath stuttered to a halt.

Why wasn't his gaze glued to Jenny?

Why weren't those ice-white blue eyes fixated on my best friend's tits, which Jenny helpfully plumped up as she preened at my side?

For a second, I was so close to breaking out into a coughing fit, it was humiliating. Then, more humiliation struck in a quieter manner, but it was nevertheless rotten—I turned pink.

Now, you might think you know what a blush is. You might think you've even experienced it yourself a time or two. But I was a redhead. My skin made fresh milk look yellow, and even my fucking freckles were pale. Everything about me was like I'd been dunked into white wax.

But as the heat crawled over me, taking over my skin as the man looked at me without pause, I knew things had rarely been this dire.

See, with Jenny as a best friend, I was used to the attention going her way. I could hide in the background, hide in her shadow. I liked it there. I was comfortable there. Sometimes, on double dates, she'd drag me along, and even the guy supposed to be dating me would be gaping at Jenny. As pathetic as it was, I was so used to it, it didn't bother me.

But now?

I just wasn't used to being in the spotlight.

Especially not a man like this one's spotlight.

When you're a teenager, practicing with your mom's blush for the first time, you always look like a tomato that's been left out in the sun, right?

I was redder than that.

I could feel it. I could fucking feel the heat turning me tomato red.

When Jenny cleared her throat, I thanked God when it broke the man's attention. He shot her a look, but it wasn't admiring. It wasn't even impressed.

If anything, it was irritated.

Okay, so now both Jenny and I were stunned.

Fuck that, we were floored.

Literally.

Our mouths were doing a pretty good fish impression as the man turned back to look at me.

Shit, was this some kind of joke?

Was it April 1st and I'd just gotten the dates mixed up again?

"Ms. Keegan?"

Oh fuck. His voice.

Oh. My. God.

That voice.

It was. . . .

I had to swallow.

Did men even talk like that?

It was low and husky and raspy and made me think of sex, not just mediocre sex, but the best sex. Toe-curling, nails-breaking-in-the-sheets sex. Sex so fucking good you couldn't walk the next day. Sex so hot that it made my current core temperature look polar in comparison. Sex that I'd never been lucky to have before, so I pined for it in the worst way.

Jenny nudged me in the side when I just carried on gaping at the man. "Y-Yes. That's me." I cleared my throat, feeling nervous and stupid and flustered as I wiped my hands on my apron.

Sweet Jesus.

Was this man really looking for me while I was wearing a goddamn pinafore?

Even as practical as they were, I wanted to beg the patron saint of pinnies to remove it from me. To do something, anything, to make sure that this man didn't see me in the red gingham check that I always wore to cover up stains.

And then I felt it.

Jenny's hand.

Tugging at the knot.

I wanted to kiss her. Seriously. I wanted to give her a fucking raise! As I moved away from the counter and her side, the apron dropped to the floor as I headed for the man whose hand was now held out, ready for me to shake in greeting.

There are those moments in your life when you know you'll never forget them. They can be happy or sad, annoying or exhilarating. This was one of them.

As I slipped my hand into his, I felt the electric shocks down to my core. Meeting his gaze wasn't hard because I was stunned, and I needed to know if he'd felt that, too.

From the way those eyelids were shielding his icy-blue eyes, I figured he was just as surprised.

It was like a satisfied puma was watching me. One that was happy there was plump prey prancing around in front of him.

Shit.

Did I just describe myself as 'plump prey?'

And like that, my house of cards came tumbling down because what the hell would this man want with me?

I was seeing things.

God, I was so stupid sometimes.

I cleared my throat for, like, the fourth damn time, and asked, "I'm Ms. Keegan. You are?"

His smile, when it appeared, was as charming as the rest of him. His teeth were white, but not creepy, reality-TV-star white. They were straight except for one of his canines, which tilted in slightly. In his perfect face, it was one flaw that I almost clung to. Because with that wide brow, the hair so dark it looked like black silk that was cut closely to his head with a faint peak at his forehead, the strong nose, and even stronger jaw, I needed something imperfect to focus on.

Then, I sucked down a breath and remembered what Fiona had told me once upon a time. When I'd been nervous about asking Jamie Winters to homecoming, she'd advised me in her soft Irish lilt, "Lass, that boy takes a dump just like you do. He uses the bathroom twice a day and undoubtedly leaves a puddle on the floor for his ma to clean up. I bet he's puked a time or two as well. Had diarrhea and the good Lord only knows what else. Just you think that the next time you see that boy and want to ask him out."

Yeah. It was gross, but fuck, it had worked. Her advice had worked so well I hadn't asked anyone out because I could only think of them using the damn toilet!

Still, looking at this Adonis, there was no imagining *that*.

Surely, gods didn't use the bathroom.

Did they?

"The name's Finn. Finn O'Grady."

My eyes flared at the name.

No.

It couldn't be.

Finn O'Grady?

No. It wasn't a rare name, but it was a strong one. One that suited him, one that had always suited him.

I frowned up at him wondering, yet again, if this was a joke of some sort, but as he looked at me, *really* looked at me, I saw no recognition. Saw nothing on his features that revealed any ounce of awareness that I'd known him for years.

Well, okay, not *known*. But I'd known his mother. Our mothers had been best friends. And as I looked, I saw the same almond-shaped eyes Fiona had, the stubborn jaw, and that unmistakable butt-indent on his chin.

At the reminder of just how forgettable I was, my heart sank, and hurt whistled through me.

Then, I realized I was *still* holding his hand, and as he squeezed, the flush returned and I almost died of mortification.

3
———

FINN

GOD, she was perfect.

And when I said perfect, I meant it.

I'd fucked a lot of women. Redheads, blondes, brunettes, even the rare thing that is a natural head of black hair. None of them, not a single one, lit up like Aoife Keegan.

Her cheeks were cherry red and in the light camisole she wore, a cheerful yellow, I could see how the blush went all the way down to the upper curve of her breasts.

She'd go that color, I knew, when she came.

And fuck, I wanted to see that.

I wanted to see that perfectly pale flesh turn bright pink under my ministrations.

Even as I looked at her, all shy and flustered, I wondered if she was a screamer in bed.

Some of the shyest often were.

Maybe not at first, but after a handful of orgasms, it was a wonder what that could do to a woman's self-confidence, and Jesus, I wanted to *see* that, too. I wanted a seat at center stage.

My suit jacket was open, and I regretted it. Immensely. My cock was hard, had been since we'd shaken hands, and her fingers had clung to mine like a daughter would to her daddy's at her first visit to the county fair.

Fuck.

Squeezing her fingers wasn't intentional. If anything, I'd just liked the feel of her palm against mine, but when I put faint pressure on her, she jerked back like she'd been scalded.

Her cheeks bloomed with heat again, and she whispered, "Mr. O'Grady, what can I do for you?"

You can get on your fucking knees and sort out the hard-on you just caused.

That's what she could fucking do.

I almost growled at the thought because the image of her on her knees, my cock in her small fist, her dainty mouth opening to take the tip. . . .

Shit.

That had to happen.

Here, too.

In this fancy, frilly, feminine place, I wanted to defile her.

Fuck, I wanted that so goddamn much, it was enough to make me reconsider my demolition plans.

I wanted to screw her against all this goddamn lace, which suited her perfectly. She was made for lace. And silk. Hell, silk would look like heaven against her skin. I wouldn't know where she ended and it began.

When her brow puckered, she dipped her chin, and that gorgeous wave of auburn hair slipped over her shoulder.

If we'd been alone, if that brassy bitch—who was staring at me like I could fuck her over the counter with her friend watching if I was game—wasn't here, I'd have grabbed that rope of hair, twisted it around my fingers, and forced her gaze up.

Some guys liked their women demure. And I was one of them. I wasn't about to lie. I liked that in her, but I wanted her eyes on me. Always.

It was enough to prompt me to bite out, "Can we speak privately?"

She jerked at my words, then as she licked her bottom lip, turned to look at the waitress. "Jenny, it's okay. I can handle the rest by myself. You get home."

Jenny, her gaze drifting between me and her boss, nodded. She retreated to a door that swung as she moved through the opening, and within seconds, she had her coat and purse over her arm.

As she sashayed past—for my benefit, I was sure—she murmured, "See you tomorrow, Aoife."

Aoife nodded and shot her friend a smile, but I wasn't smiling. There were dishes on every table. Plates and saucers and tea pots. Those fancy stands that made any man wonder if he could touch it without snapping it.

Aoife was going to clear all that herself? Not on my fucking watch.

When the bell rang as the waitress opened the door, I didn't take my eyes off her until it rang once more upon closing.

Aoife swallowed, and I watched her throat work, watched it with a hunger that felt alien to me, because, God, I wanted to see my bites on her. Wanted to see my marks on that pale column of skin and her tits.

Barely withholding a groan, I asked, "Do you often let your staff go when you still have a lot of work to do, so you can speak to a stranger?"

Her cheeks flushed again, and she took a step back. "I-I, you're not—" Flustered once more, she fell silent.

"I'm not what?" Curiosity had me asking the question. Whatever I'd expected her to say, it hadn't been that.

She cleared her throat. "N-Nothing. You wished to speak with me, Mr. O'Grady?"

My other hand tightened around my briefcase, and though seeing her had made my reason for being here all that more necessary, I was almost disappointed. There was a gentle warmth to those bright-green eyes that would die out when I told her my purpose for being here. And her innocent attraction to me would change, morph into something else.

But I could only handle *something else.*

Some men were made for forever.

But those men weren't in my line of business.

I moved away from her, pressing my briefcase to one of the few empty tables. I wasn't happy about her having to do all the clearing up later on, and wondered if Paul, my PA, would know who to call to get her some help.

There was no way I was spending the rest of the night alone in my bed, my only companion my fist wrapped around my cock.

No way, no fucking how.

I paid Paul enough for him to come and clear the fucking place on his own if he couldn't find someone else.

I wanted Aoife on her knees, bent over my goddamn bed, and I was a man who always got what he wanted.

In this jungle, I was the lion, and Aoife? She was my prey.

I keyed in the code and opened my briefcase. The manila envelope was large and thick, well-padded with my documentation of Aoife's every move for the past few months.

It had started off as a legitimate move.

I'd wanted to know her weaknesses, so I could put pressure on her and make her cave to my demands.

Now, my demands had changed. I didn't just want her to sell the tea room we were standing in, I wanted her in my bed.

Fuck, I wanted that more than I wanted to make Aidan Sr. a fucking profit, and Aidan's profit and my balls still being attached to my body ran hand in hand.

Aidan was an evil cunt.

If I failed to deliver, he'd take it out on me. Whether I was his idea of an adopted son or not, he'd have done the same to his blood sons.

Well, he wouldn't have taken their balls. The man, for all his psychotic flaws, was obsessed with the idea of grandchildren, of passing it all on to the next generation. He'd cut his boys though. Without a doubt.

I knew Conor had marks on his back from a beating he refused to speak about. Then there was Brennan. He had a weak wrist because his father had a habit of breaking *that* wrist.

Without speaking, I grabbed the envelope and passed it to her.

She frowned down at it and asked, "For me?"

I smiled at her. "Open it."

"What is it?"

"Leverage."

That had her eyes flaring wide as she pulled out some of the photos. A gasp fell from her lips as she grabbed the photos when she spotted herself in them, jerking so hard the envelope tore. Some of the pictures spilled to the ground, but I didn't care about that.

Leaning back against one of the dainty tables once I was satisfied it would take my weight, I watched her cheeks blanch, all that delicious color dissipating as she took in everything the photos revealed.

"Y-You've been stalking me. Why?"

The question was high-pitched, loaded down with panic. I'd heard it often enough to recognize it easily.

I didn't get involved in wet work anymore. That wasn't my style, but along the way, to reach this point, I'd had no choice but to get my hands dirty. Panic was part of the job when you were collecting debts for the Irish Mob. And the Five Points were notorious for Aidan Sr.'s temper.

He wasn't the first patriarch. If anything, his grandfather was the founder. But Aidan Sr. was the type of guy that if you didn't pay him back, he didn't give a fuck about the money, he cared about the lack of respect.

See, you owed the mob and didn't pay? They'd send heavies around, beat the shit out of you, and threaten to do the same to your family, and usually, that did the trick. You didn't kill the cash cow.

Aidan Sr.?

He didn't give a fuck about the cash cow.

Only the truly desperate thought about borrowing money from Aidan, because if you didn't pay it back, he'd take your teeth, and your fingers and toes as a first warning. Then, if you still didn't pay—and most did—it was death.

Respect meant a lot to Aidan.

And fuck, if it wasn't starting to mean a lot to me. The panic in her voice made my cock throb.

I wanted this woman weak and willing.

I wanted it more than I wanted my next breath.

Ignoring her, I reached for my phone and tapped out a message to Paul.

Need housekeeping crew to clean this place.

I attached my live location, saw the blue ticks as Paul read the message—he knew better than to ignore my texts, whatever time of day they came—and he replied: *Sure thing.*

That was the kind of reply I was used to getting. Not just from Paul, but from everyone.

There were very few people who weren't below me in the strata of Five Points, and I'd worked my ass off to make that so.

The only people who ranked above me included Aidan Jr. and his brothers, Aidan Sr. of course, and then maybe a handful of his advisors that he respected for what they'd done for him and the Points over the years.

But the money I made Aidan Sr.?

That blew most of their 'advice' out of the window.

The reason Aidan had a Dassault Falcon executive private plane?

Because I was, as the City itself called me, a whiz kid.

I'd made my first million—backed by the Points, of course—at twenty-two.

Fifteen years later?

I'd made him hundreds of millions.

My own personal fortune was nothing to sniff at, either.

"W-Why have you done this?" Aoife asked, her voice breathy enough to make me wonder if she sounded like that in the sack.

"Because you've been a very stubborn little girl."

Her eyes flared wide. "Excuse me?"

I reached into the inside pocket of my suit coat and pulled out a business card. "For you," I prompted, offering it to her.

When she turned it over, saw the logo of five points shaped into a star, then read Acuig—in the Gaelic way, ah-coo-ig, not a butchered American way, ah-coo-ch—aloud, I watched her throat work as she swallowed.

"I-I should have realized with the Irish name," she whispered, the muscles in her brow twitching as she took in the chaos of the scattered photos on the floor.

Watching her as she dropped the contents on the ground, so she was surrounded by them, I tilted my head to the side, taking her in as her panic started to crest.

"I-I won't sell." Her first words surprised me.

I should have figured, though. Everything about this woman was surprisingly delicious.

"You have no choice," I purred. "As far as I'm aware, the Senator has a wife. He also has a reputation to protect. I'm not sure he'd be happy if any of those made it onto the *National Enquirer's* front page. Not when he's just trying to shore up his image to take a run for the White House next election."

She reached up and clutched her throat. The self-protective gesture was enough to make me smile at her—I knew what the absence of hope looked like.

There'd been a time when that had been my life, too.

"But, on the bright side," I carried on, "this can all be wiped away if you sell." As her gaze flicked to mine, I added, "As well as if you do something for me."

For a second, she was speechless. I could see she knew what that *something* was. Had my body language given it away? Had there been a certain raspiness to my tone?

I wasn't sure, and frankly, didn't give a fuck.

There was a little hiccoughing sound that escaped her lips, and she frowned at me, then down at herself.

"Is this a joke?"

"Do I look like I'm the kind of guy who jokes, Aoife?" Fuck, I loved saying her name.

The Gaelic notes just drove me insane.

Ee-Fah.

Nothing like the spelling, and all the more complicated and delicious for it.

"N-No," she confirmed, "but . . ."

"But what?" I prompted.

"I mean . . . you just can't be serious."

"Oh, but I am." I grinned. "Deadly. You've wasted a lot of my time, Aoife Keegan. A lot. Do you think I'm normally involved in negotiations of this level?"

Her eyes whispered over me, and I felt the loving caress of her gaze as she took in each and every inch of me. When she licked her lips, I knew she liked what she saw. I didn't really care, but it was helpful for her to be eager in some small way—especially when coercion was involved.

Aidan had called it bribery. I preferred 'coercion'. It sounded far kinder.

"No. That suit alone probably cost the mortgage payment on this place."

I nodded—she wasn't wrong. I knew what she'd been paying as rent, then as a mortgage, before some kind *benefactor* had paid it all off. Free and clear.

"I had to get my hands dirty, and while I might like some things dirty . . .," I trailed off, smirking when she flushed. "So, as I see it, we have a problem. I want this building. You don't want anyone to know you're having an affair with a Senator. Or, should I say, the Senator doesn't want anyone to know he's having an affair with someone young enough to be his daughter . . ."

If my voice turned into a growl at that point, then it was because the notion of her spreading her legs for that old bastard just turned my stomach.

Fuck, this woman, the thoughts she made me think.

Because I was startled at the possessive note to my growl, I ran a hand over my head. I kept my hair short for a reason—ease. I wasn't the kind of man who wasted time primping. It was an expensive cut, so I didn't have to do anything to it. Even mussing it up had it falling back into the same sleek lines as before—a man in my position had to look pristine under pressure. And very few people could even begin to understand the kind of strain I was under.

The formation of igneous rock had less volcanic pressure than Aidan Sr.

She licked her lips as she stared down at the photos, then back up at me. "And you want me to sell the place to you, even though this is my livelihood and the livelihood of all my staff, and then sleep with you?"

Her squeaky voice, putting suspicion into words, had me crossing my legs at the ankle. "We wouldn't be doing much sleeping."

Another shaky breath soughed from her lips, then, those beautiful pillowy morsels that would look good around my cock, quivered.

"This is crazy," she whispered shakily.

"As far as I'm concerned, all of this could be avoided if you'd just sold to me a few months back. Now you have to pay for my time wasted on this project."

"By spreading my legs?"

Another squeak. I tsked at her question, but in truth, I was annoyed at her using those same words I had to describe her with that old hypocrite of a Senator.

I didn't move, though. Didn't even flex my arms in irritation, just murmured, "Small price to pay. And, even though it's ten percent above market price, I'll stick to the last offer Acuig gave you. Can't say anything's fairer than that."

She shook her head, and there was a desperation to the gesture as she cried, "I need this business. You don't understand—"

"I understand that some very powerful and very dangerous businessmen want this building demolished. I understand that those same powerful and dangerous men want a skyscraper taking up this plot of land. I understand that a four hundred million dollar project isn't going to be put on hiatus because one small Irish woman doesn't want to go out of business . . ." I cocked a brow at her. "You think I'm coming in hot and heavy? These kinds of men, Aoife, they're not the sort you fuck around with.

"Take my check, and my other offer, before you or the people you care about are threatened." I got to my feet and straightened my jacket out. "This suit? These shoes? That briefcase and this watch? I own them because I'm damn good at what I do. I'm a financial advisor, Aoife. Take my word for it. You're getting the best deal out of this."

She staggered back, the counter stopping her from crumpling to the floor. "You'd hurt me?"

"Not me," I repudiated. Not in the way she thought, anyway. "But the men I work for?"

Her gaze dropped to the one thing she'd retained in her hand— my card. "Acuig," she whispered. "Five in Gaelic."

My brows twitched in surprise. She knew Gaelic?

"The Five Points." Her eyes flared wide with terror. "They're behind this deal."

I hadn't expected her to put one and one together, but now that she had? It worked to my advantage.

Nodding, I told her, "Any minute now, there'll be a team of housekeepers coming in here to clear up for the night." When she gaped at me, I retrieved the contract from my briefcase, slapped it on the table, and handed her a pen as I carried on, "I suggest you let tonight be your last night of business."

What I didn't tell her, was that my suggestions weren't wasted words. They were like the law.

You didn't break them, and, like any lawmaker, I expected immediate obeisance.

4

______

AOIFE

SO, the beautiful man just happened to be an absolute cocksucker of
a bastard.

Still, this couldn't be real, could it?

The dick could have anyone he wanted. Jesus, Jenny was panting
after him like a dog in heat. She would have gone out with him if he'd
so much as clicked his fingers at her.

But he'd had eyes for me.

Like he wanted me.

He thought he'd bought me. Or, at least, bought my silence, and
yeah, to some extent he had. But . . . why buy me, why not just drop
the price on the building if he wanted me to pay for the time he'd
wasted on me?

The arrogance imbued in those words was enough to make me
pull my hair out, but that was inwardly. I was a redhead. I had a
temper. But that temper was mostly overshadowed by fear.

Senator Alan Davidson wasn't my boyfriend, my lover, as this
dick seemed to believe. He was my father, and as Finn O'Grady had
correctly surmised, he was aiming for the White House.

How could I put that in jeopardy?

My dad was a good man. He'd made a mistake one summer when he'd come home from college, one that only some careful digging by his campaign manager had uncovered. Dad himself hadn't known of my existence, not until his CM had gone hunting for any nasty secrets that could come out and bite him in the ass.

This had been five years ago when he'd run for Senator. Now, Dad's goal was the presidential seat, and I wasn't going to be the one who put a wrench in the works.

When Garry Smythe had approached me back then, I'd thought he was joking. I was out on the street, heading home from work. At the side of me, a black car had driven in from the lane of traffic, just to park, or so I'd thought. As he'd held out his hand with a card, one of the car doors had opened up, and I'd been 'invited' inside.

Had I been scared?

At first.

But when Garry had told me my country needed me, I hadn't been sure whether to laugh or tell him to fuck off. He hadn't shuffled me into the car, though, hadn't tried to coerce me. He'd just asked if I'd voted for Senator Alan Davidson in the elections, and because he was one of the only politicians out there who wasn't a complete douche, and that was the name printed on the card in my hand, I'd shuffled into the back of the car.

Where the Senator himself had been sitting.

Now, when I thought about that day, I realized how fucking naive I'd been to get into the back of a limo for such a vague reason. But I'd been fortunate. Alan *had* been waiting for me. Waiting to tell me a story that still shook me to my core.

I'd made a promise to my dad that I wouldn't tell anyone. He'd offered me money, and I hadn't accepted it. I guess I should have, but back then, I'd been haughty and proud, and because the good guy I'd thought him to be hadn't been so good when he tried to buy my silence, I'd told him to fuck off. I'd been disappointed in him, frightened by the lifelong lie I'd been living, and equally hurt that the man who'd sired me was just concerned that I was a threat to his campaign.

I'd walked out of that car never expecting to see my dear old Dad ever again.

Then, the day after he'd been elected, he'd been sitting in the booth of the cafe where I worked part-time to get me through culinary school.

Seeing him, I'd almost handed that table off to one of the other waitresses, but I hadn't. Not when every time I'd passed the table, he'd caught my eye, a patient smile on his lips, one that said he'd wait for me all day if he had to.

Ever since that second meeting, I'd been catching up with him every three weeks.

And this bastard thought he could use our limited time together against my father? The one politician who could make a difference in the White House? One who didn't have Big Oil up his ass, a pharmaceutical company sucking his dick, or any other kind of corporation so far up his rectum that he was a walking, talking lie?

No.

That wasn't going to happen.

Which meant I was going to have to sleep with this stranger.

Before this conversation, hell, that hadn't been too disturbing a prospect. Because, dayum, what woman wouldn't want to sleep with this guy?

Even with an ego as big as his, he was delicious. Better than any cake I could bake, that was for fucking sure.

More than that, I knew him.

And I now knew that the life Fiona would never have wanted for her son was one he'd been drawn into.

The Mob.

The Five Points were notorious in these parts. Everyone was scared of them. I paid protection money to them, for God's sake. I knew to be scared of them, and having been raised in their territory, it was the height of stupidity to think paying them wasn't just a part of business.

Still, Fiona had never wanted that for Finn, and her Finn was the same as the one standing before me here today. In my tea room, which looked far too small to contain the might of this man.

She'd be so disappointed. So heart-sore to know that he was up to his neck in dirty dealings with the Five Points, and as he'd pointed out, the cost of his shoes, his clothes, and his jewelry, was enough to speak for itself.

If he wasn't high up the ladder in the gang, then I wasn't one of the best bakers of scones in the district.

Like Jenny had said, I had five star ratings across most social media platforms for a reason. I was good. But apparently, this man wasn't.

Before I could utter a word, before I could even cringe at how utterly sorrowful Fiona would be about this turn of events—not just about the Five Points but what her son was making me do—the door clattered open.

Like he'd predicted, a team of people swarmed in.

Finn motioned to the floor. "Want anyone to see those?"

With a gasp, I dropped to my knees and collected the shots, stuffing them back into the envelope with a haste that wasn't exactly practical.

Two shiny shoes appeared before me, followed by two expensively clad legs, and I peered up at him, wondering what he was about. He held out his hand, but I clasped the photos to my chest.

"You're making more of a mess than anything else, Aoife." His voice was raspy, his eyes weighted down by heavy lids.

For a second, I wondered why, then I saw *why*.

He had an erection.

An erection?

I peered around at the staff, but they were all men. Not a single woman in sight, well, save for the seventy-year-old with a clipboard who was barking out orders to the guys in what sounded like Russian.

So that meant, what?

The erection was for me?

The blush, the dreaded, hated blush, made another goddamn appearance, and to cover it, I ducked my head, then pushed the photos and the envelope at him.

For whatever reason, I stayed where I was, staring up at him as he calmly, coolly, and so fucking collectedly pushed the photos back into the torn envelope—it was some coverage. Better than none at all, I figured.

Being down here was. . . .

Hell, I don't know what it was.

To be looked at like that?

For his body to respond to me like that?

It was unprecedented.

I'd had one sexual experience with a boy back in college, and that had not gone according to plan. So much so I was still technically a fucking virgin because, and this was no lie, the guy had *zero* understanding of a woman's body.

Craig had spent more time fingering my perineum than my clit, and every time he'd tried to shove his dick into me, he'd somehow managed to drag it down toward my ass.

I'd gotten so sick of him frigging the wrong bits of me, that I'd pushed him off and given him a blowjob. It had been the quickest way to get out of that annoying situation.

Yeah, annoying.

Jenny, when I'd told her, had pissed herself laughing, and ever since, had tried to get me to hook up with randoms, so I could slough off my virginity like it was dead skin and I was a snake. But life had just always gotten in the way, and I'd had no time for men.

Shortly after *that* had happened, we'd lost Fiona. Then, I'd graduated, and after, Mom and I had set up this place thanks to some insurance money she'd come into after her husband had died. It had been crazy building the tea room into an established cafe, and then mom had passed on, too.

So, here I was. Still a virgin. On my knees in front of the sexiest man on Earth, a man I knew, a man whose mother had half raised me, one who wanted me in his bed as some kind of blackmail payment.

Was this a dream?

Seriously?

I mean, I'd been depressed before Finn O'Grady had walked through my doors. Now I wasn't sure whether to be apoplectic or worried as fuck because he wasn't wrong: you didn't mess with the Five Points.

God, if I'd known they'd been behind the development on this building, I'd have probably signed over months ago.

The Points were. . . .

I shuddered.

Vindictive.

Aidan O'Donnelly was half-evil genius and half-twisted sociopath. St. Patrick's Church, two streets away, had the best roof in the neighborhood and the strongest attendance because Aidan, for all he'd cut you into more pieces than a butcher, was a devout Catholic. His men knew better than to avoid Sunday service, and I reckoned that Father Doyle was the busiest priest in the city because of Five Points' attendance.

"I like you down there," he murmured absentmindedly.

The words weren't exactly dirty, but the meaning? They had my temperature soaring.

Shit.

What the hell was I doing?

Enjoying the way this man was victimizing me?

It was so wrong, and yet, what was standing right in front of me? I knew he'd know what to do with that thing tucked behind his pants.

He wouldn't try to penetrate my urethra—yes, you read that right. Craig had tried to fuck my pee-hole! Like, *why?*

Finn?

He oozed sex appeal.

It seemed to seep from every pore, perfuming the air around me with his pheromones.

I hadn't even believed in pheromones until I scented Finn O'Grady's delicious essence.

It reminded me of the one out of town vacation we'd ever had. We'd gone to Cooperstown, and I'd scented a body of water that didn't have corpses floating in it—Otsego Lake. He reminded me of that. So green and earthy. It was an attack on my overwhelmed senses, an attack I didn't need.

With the envelope in his hand, he held out his other for me. When I placed my fingers in his, the size difference between us was noticeable once more.

I was just over five feet, and he was over six. I was round and curvy, and he was hard and lean.

It reminded me of the nursery tale Mom had sung to me as a child—Jack Sprat could eat no fat, and his wife could eat no lean.

Did it say a lot for my confidence that I couldn't seem to take it in that he wanted *me*? Or was it simply that I wasn't understanding how anyone could prefer me over Jenny?

Even my mom had called Jenny beautiful, whereas she'd kissed me on the nose and called me her 'bonny lass.'

Biting my lip, I accepted his help off the floor. My black jeans weren't the smartest thing for the tea room, but I didn't actually serve that many dishes, just bustled around behind the counter, working up the courage to do what Mom had done every day—greet people.

I wasn't a sociable person. I preferred my kitchen to the front of house, hence the jeans, but I regretted not wearing something else today. Something that covered just how big my ass was, how slender my waist *wasn't*.

Ugh.

This man is blackmailing you into his bed, Aoife. For Christ's sake, you're not supposed to be worrying if he likes the goods, too!

Still, no matter how much I tried, years of inadequacy weighed me down as I wiped off my knees.

"Do you have a coat?" he asked, and his voice was raspy again. "A jacket? Or a purse?"

I nodded at him but kept my gaze trained on the floor. "Yes."

"Go get them."

His order had me shuffling my feet toward the kitchen, but as I approached the door, I heard his strong voice speaking with the old woman with the clipboard: "I want this all cleaned up and boxed. Take it to my storage lot in Queens."

With my back to him, I stiffened at his brisk orders. *Was I just going to let him do this? Get away with it?*

My shoulders immediately sagged.

Did I have a choice?

If it was just him, just Acuig, then I'd fight this, as I'd been fighting it since the building had come to the attention of the developer. But this wasn't a regular business deal.

This was mob business, and it seemed like somehow, I'd become a part of that.

FML.

Seriously, FML.

5

———

FINN

SHE WASN'T AS fiery as I imagined.

Did that disappoint me?

Maybe.

Then I had to chide myself because, Jesus, the woman had just been *coerced* out of her business. What did I expect? For her to be popping open a champagne bottle after I'd forced her to sign over her building to me?

Sure, she'd made a nice and tidy profit on her investment—I hadn't screwed her that way. But this morning, she'd gone into work with a game plan in mind, and tonight? Well, tonight she was out of a job and knee deep in a deal with the devil.

Of course, she hadn't actually agreed to my other terms, but when I guided her out of the tea room and toward my waiting car, she didn't falter.

Didn't utter a peep.

Just climbed into the vehicle, neatly tucked her knees together, and waited for me to get in beside her.

Like the well-oiled team my chauffeur and car were, they set off the minute I'd clicked my seatbelt.

The privacy screen was up, and I knew how soundproofed it was —not because of technology, but because Samuel knew not to listen to any of the murmurs he might hear back here.

And if he was ever to share the most innocent of those whispers he might have discerned? We both knew I'd slice off his fucking ear.

This was a hard world. One we'd both grown up in, so we knew how things rolled. Samuel had it pretty easy with me, and he wasn't about to fuck up this job when he was so close to retirement. If he kept his mouth shut, did as I asked, ignored what he may or may not have heard, and drove me wherever the fuck I wanted to go, Sam knew I'd set him and his missus up somewhere nice in Florida. Near the beach, so the moaning old bastard's knees didn't give him too much trouble in his dotage.

See?

I wasn't all bad.

Rapping my fingers against my knee, I studied her, and I made no bones about it.

Her face was tilted down, and it let me see the longest lashes I'd ever come across on a woman. Well, natural ones. Those fucking false ones that fell off on my sheets were just irritating. But as with everything, Aoife was all natural.

So pure.

So fucking perfect.

Jesus, Mary, and Joseph.

She was a benediction come to life.

I wasn't as devout as Aidan Sr. would like me to be, but even I felt uncomfortable thinking such thoughts while sporting a hard-on that made me ache. That made my mental blasphemy even worse.

"Why did you let him touch you? Was it for money?"

I hadn't meant to ask that question.

Really, I hadn't.

It was the last thing I wanted to know, but like poison, it had spewed from my lips.

Who she'd fucked and who she hadn't, was none of my goddamn affair.

This was a business deal. Nothing more, nothing less. She'd fuck me to make sure I kept quiet, and I fucked her so I could revel in the copious curves this woman had to offer.

Simple, no?

She stiffened at the question, and I couldn't blame her. "Do I really have to answer that?"

I could have made her. It was on the tip of my tongue to force her to, but I didn't really want to know even if, somewhere deep down, I did.

"You know why you're here, don't you?" I asked instead of replying.

Her nostrils flared. "To keep silent."

I nodded and almost smiled at her because, internally she was furious, but equally, she was lost. I could sense that like a shark could scent blood in the water. This had thrown her for a loop, and she was in shock, but she was, underneath it all, angry.

Good.

I wanted to fuck her tonight when she was angry.

Spitting flames at me, taking her outrage out on me as she scratched lines of fire down my spine as she screamed her climax. . . .

I almost shuddered at how well I'd painted that mental picture.

"When you're ready, you have my card."

"Ready for what?" she asked, perplexed. Her brow furrowed as she, for the first time since she'd climbed into the car, looked over at me.

"To make another tea room. I've had them move all the stuff into storage."

She licked her lips. "I want to say that's kind of you, but I'm in this predicament because of you."

A corner of my mouth hitched at that. "Honestly, be grateful I was the one who came knocking today. You wouldn't want any of the

Five Points' men around that place. Half that china would be on the floor now."

Her shoulders drooped. "I know."

"You do?"

"I pay them protection money," she snapped. "Plus, I grew up around enough Five Pointers to know the score."

That statement targeted my curiosity, hard. "You did, huh? Whereabouts?"

Her mouth pursed. "Nowhere you'd know," she muttered under her breath.

"I doubt it. This is my area, too."

She turned to me, and the tautness around her eyes reminded me of something, but even as it flashed into being, the memory disappeared as I drowned in her emerald green eyes. "Why are you doing this?"

"Why do you think?" I retorted. "You're a beautiful woman—"

"Don't pretend like you couldn't have any woman under you if you asked them."

I wanted to smile, but I didn't because I knew, just as Aidan had pointed out to me earlier that day, that Aoife wasn't exactly what society considered on trend.

She'd have suited the glorious Titian era. She was a Raphaelite, a gorgeous and vivacious Aphrodite.

She wasn't slender. Her butt bounced, and when I fucked her, I'd have some meat to slam into, and her hips would be delicious handholds to grab.

If I smiled, I'd confirm that I was mocking her, and though I was a bastard, and though I was enough of a cunt to blackmail her into this when it hadn't been necessary—after all, before I'd told her who I was, I could have asked her out and done this normally—there was no way I was going to knock this glorious creature's confidence.

"Some men like slim and trim gym bunnies, some men like curves." I shrugged. "That's how it works, isn't it?"

Her eyes flared at that. "But Jenny—"

"Would you prefer she be here with me?" I asked dryly, amused when she flushed.

"Of course not. I wouldn't want her to be in this position."

I laughed. "Nicely phrased."

"What's that supposed to mean?"

Leaning forward, I grabbed her chin and forced her to look at me. "It's supposed to mean that you can fight this all you fucking want, but deep down, you're glad you're here. Your little cunt is probably sopping wet, and it's dying for a taste of my dick. So, simmer down. We're almost at my apartment."

And with that, I dipped my chin, and opening my mouth, raked my teeth down her bottom lip before I bit her. Hard enough to make her moan.

6

———

AOIFE

THE STING of pain should have had me rearing back.

It didn't.

It felt. . . .

I almost shuddered.

Good.

It had felt good.

The way he'd done it. So fucking cocky, so fucking sure of himself, and who could blame him? He'd taken what he wanted, and I hadn't pulled away because he was right. My pussy *was* wet, and even though this was all kinds of wrong, I did want to feel him there. To have his cock push inside me.

Jesus, this was way too early for Stockholm syndrome, right?

I mean, this was . . . what was it?

It couldn't be that I was so horny and desperate for male attention that I was willingly allowing this to happen, was it?

Fuck. How pathetic was I if that was true? And yet, I didn't feel desperate for anything other than more of that small taste Finn had given me.

As a little girl, I'd watched Finn. It had been back in the day when his old man had been around and Fiona had lived with her husband and son. He'd beaten her up something rotten. Barely a week went by when Fiona, my mom's friend, didn't appear with some badly made-up bruise on her face.

I was young, only two, but old enough to know something wasn't right. I'd even asked my mom about it, wanting to understand why someone would do that to another person.

I couldn't remember what my mother had said, but I could remember how sad she'd been.

For all his faults, my dipshit stepfather had never beaten her, he'd just taken all her tips for himself and spent every night getting drunk.

Well, Finn's dad had been the same, except where mine passed out on the decrepit La-Z-Boy in front of the TV, Gerry had taken out his drunk out on Fiona.

And eventually, Finn.

Even as a boy, in the photos Fiona kept of him, Finn had been beautiful.

I could see him now, deep in my mind's eye. His hair had been as coal dark then as it was now, and not even a hint of silver or gray marred the noir perfection. His jaw and nose had grown, obviously, but they were just as obstinate as I remembered. Fiona had always said Finn was hardheaded.

When I was little, I hadn't had a crush on him—I'd been a toddler, for God's sake—but I'd been in awe of him. In awe of the big boy who'd been all arms and legs, just waiting for his growth spurt. Sadly, when that had happened, he'd disappeared.

As had his father.

Overnight, Fiona had gone from having a full house to an empty nest, and my mom had comforted her over the loss of her boy.

To my young self, I'd thought he'd died.

Genuinely. The way Fiona had mourned him? It had been as though both men had passed on, except we'd never had to go to church for a service, and there'd been no wake.

As kids do, I'd forgotten him. I'd been two when he'd disappeared, so I only really remembered that Fiona was a mom and that she was grieving.

We'd barely spoken his name because it could set her off into bouts of tears that would have my mom pouring tea down her gullet as they talked through her feelings.

As time passed, those little scenes in our crappy kitchen stopped, yet Fiona hung around our place so much it was like her second home.

One day, my stepfather died in an accident at work. The insurance paid out, Fiona moved in with us, and Mom had started scheming as to how to make her dream of owning a tea room come true. With Fiona living in, I'd heard Finn's name more often, but the notion he was dead still rang true.

Yet, here he was.

Finn wasn't dead.

He was very much alive.

Had Fiona known that?

Had she?

I wasn't sure what I hoped for her.

Was it better to believe your son was dead, or that your son didn't give enough of a fuck about you to contact you for years?

I gnawed on my bottom lip at the thought and accidentally raked over the tissue where Finn had bitten earlier.

"We're almost there," the man himself grated out, and I could sense he was pissed because the phone had buzzed, and whatever he'd been reading had a storm cloud passing behind his eyes.

"O-Okay," I replied, hating the quiver in my voice, but also just hating my situation.

This was. . . .

It was too much.

How was it that I was sitting here?

This morning, I'd owned a tea room. Now, I didn't.

This morning, I'd been exhausted, depressed about my mom, and *feeling* lost.

Now?

I was the *epitome* of lost.

A man was going to use me for sex, for Christ's sake.

But all I could think was: *did I still have my hymen?*

God, would he be angry if he had to push through it?

Should I tell him?

If I did, it would be for my benefit, not his, and why the hell was I thinking like this? I should be trying to convince him that normal people did not work business deals out by bribing someone into bed.

But, deep down, I knew all my scattered thinking was futile.

I wasn't dealing with normal people here.

I was dealing with a Five Pointer.

A high ranking one at that.

It was like dealing with a Martian. To average, everyday folk, a Five Pointer was just outside of their knowledge banks.

Sure, they thought they knew what they were like because they watched *The Wire* or some other procedural show, but they didn't.

Real-life gangsters?

They were larger than life.

They throbbed with violence, and hell, a part of me knew that Finn was cutting me some slack by asking to sleep with me.

Yeah, as fucked up as that was, it was the truth.

He could have asked for so much more.

He'd have a Senator in his pocket, and to the mob, what else would they ask for if not that?

Yet Finn?

He just wanted to fuck me.

My throat felt tight and itchy from dryness. I wanted some water so badly, but equally, I wasn't sure if it would make me puke.

Not at the thought of sex with this man—a part of me knew I'd enjoy it too much to even be nervous.

No, at what else he could ask of me, that had me fretting.

Was this a one-time deal?

How could I protect my dad from the Five Points when . . .?

I shuddered because there was nothing I could do. There was no way I could even broach any of those questions since I wasn't in charge here.

Finn was.

Finn always would be until he deemed I'd paid my dues. Whether that was tomorrow or two years down the line.

Shit, it might even be forever. If my dad hit the White House, only God knew what kind of leverage Finn could pull if my father tried to carry on covering up my existence. . . .

"We're here."

Something had *definitely* pissed him off.

He'd gone from the cat who'd drank a carton full of cream, to a pissed off tabby scrounging for supper in the trash.

"We're going to go through to the private elevator, and I'm going to head straight down the hall to my living room. You're going to slip into the first door on the right—that's my bedroom."

"O-Okay," I told him, wondering what the hell was going on.

"You're going to stay quiet, and you're going to try to not hear any fucking thing I say, do you hear me?"

"I hear you."

"You'd better," he ground out, his hand tightening around his cellphone. "Coming to Aidan O'Donnelly's attention is the last thing a little mouse like you wants."

A shiver ran through me.

Aidan O'Donnelly was in his apartment?

Fuck, just how high up the ranks was he?

7

———

FINN

TO SAY I was annoyed at the delay was an understatement.

I wanted Aoife underneath me the second I made it to my penthouse. Instead, I was going to have to deal with my cranky boss—because guys like me answered to three people. The boss, the IRS—from time to time—and God himself.

Which meant even though I wanted to fuck Aoife more than I wanted my next breath, I had to deal with Aidan and whatever hissy fit he was going through right now, when all I wanted to deal with was my aching cock.

I felt like I'd endured hours of foreplay already.

Just the time spent with this woman had built to this moment, like a towering crescendo that had soared and soared, just waiting for everything to come tumbling down.

My skin felt taut, my body too hot as I helped Aoife out of the car. She was so fucking small and dainty that everything inside me wanted to protect her. I hadn't felt like that about a woman since my mother, and there was no way I was thinking about that stupid bitch right now. Talk about a way to make my cock deflate.

Still, Aoife was fragile. Not just in body but in mind. I couldn't say I'd broken her because I hadn't. I guess I'd broken her will. But at least shit was straight between us.

I could have fucked her, enjoyed the fuck, and then revealed my intentions. Instead, I'd been relatively open and honest.

The only thing I hadn't declared outright?

How long she'd be in my bed.

I couldn't put a time frame on something I didn't have an answer to.

If she was crap in bed, then I'd let her go after one screw. But if, as I suspected, things were awesome between us, no way was I doing away with my leverage. Not if these sparks between us could morph into an out-an-out inferno.

See, ironically enough, I liked Senator Alan Davidson. Or I had until I'd learned the bastard was schtupping my woman.

He was good for my business with his policies, and as such, the news of just how I was using Aoife for my own gain would never come to light.

Having a politician in my pocket would make me look like the golden boy in Aidan Sr.'s eyes, but I wasn't tempted.

I made the man enough money to have his respect—more than that, I laundered nearly sixty percent of his capital with Conor's help. We were both the financial brains behind Acuig, but we were a team. We bounced off each other, always had.

Aidan would love to have a Senator, one who wanted to rise to the White House, in his back pocket, but I didn't want that.

It wasn't that I had a conscience.

I didn't.

Leverage was leverage, and business was business.

But I knew, in my gut—and I trusted my gut. It had saved my life too many times to ignore—that blackmailing a man like Davidson would go nowhere.

There was a reason I'd liked the dick before today. That reason? He was a career Army man, who'd served during Desert Storm and had served his dues to this country. Any man deserved respect for that alone. More than that, as a politician, he'd seemed inviolate.

Sure, every man had some secrets, especially after getting into the down and dirty game of politics, and I didn't even begrudge the man for having a little something-something on the side. I only begrudged the fact it was this woman.

Possessive and stupid?

Sure.

Was I thinking with my cock?

Definitely.

Still, there was a reason Davidson was where he was. Until now, his reputation had been lily white. I was under no illusion that Aidan would want to get his claws into the Senator, but a guy like Davidson? He'd bite back.

There was not a single doubt in my mind, no matter what Aoife thought, the politician would never allow himself to be manipulated into doing anything he didn't want. So, no, I wasn't about to use the Senator's sticky side boo as a means of getting an in with the future President of the USA. I was too fucking smart to do that. Aidan, not so much, and the last thing I needed was Aidan and Aoife in the same fucking place.

Aidan resented the fact that none of his boys were married. It was a point of contention, one that we all narrowly avoided by never bringing the subject to his attention. But taking home a woman? Yeah, that would have him leaping down my throat, and no way in fuck did I want that conversation.

I was stressed as we walked down the darkened parking garage toward the elevator. In the background, the exhaust on Samuel's beat-up car made a racket as he set off and headed home for the night—on the proviso that if I needed him, he'd be back here within thirty minutes. I always made that stipulation, but I rarely asked him to come back unless business with Aidan made it imperative.

Tonight, unfortunately, Aidan had brought business to me.

He said we had a problem, and Aidan's problems were rarely

things like a leaky roof or a bathroom faucet that was dripping and driving Magdalena, his wife, nuts.

I was hoping that whatever his issue was today, it would be dealt with after a half-hour's conversation, one that was liberally lubricated with half a bottle of good Irish whiskey, then he'd fuck off home and I could, well, fuck.

The elevator whirred as we silently climbed the floors to the penthouse. I had private access to it, and that came as one of the perks of being the developer behind the building. I'd had the penthouse designed with my personal tastes in mind.

I said it was a perk, but it was one Aidan gave us.

This was my 'bonus' for hitting an all-time high almost five years ago—thirty million dollars in profit, and five laundered through the system Conor and I had drafted that year.

Conor had the other penthouse in the building's twin across the way, and so far, only the two of us and Eoghan had been given such a bonus. I knew Aidan Jr. was pissed about that, too. As the oldest of the brothers, it normally figured that he'd be the golden boy and would receive all the perks first.

Not in the O'Donnelly household.

Everything was earned.

Every-fucking-thing.

Take Eoghan. He was the youngest. That was why his name started with an 'E.' The brothers often joked that their mother was so unimaginative, she'd named her children after the alphabet, but then, they also joked how it was fate that I become her sixth son considering my name began with the letter 'F.'

Still, he might be the baby, but where wet work was concerned?

He made a Navy Seal look soft core.

It helped that he'd been through all kinds of military training. Back in the day, when he'd rebelled about becoming a part of his father's 'corporation,' he'd headed out to serve his country, only coming back when he was dishonorably discharged.

See, Eoghan wasn't like regular people.

In his own way, he was a decent man.

He knew the difference between right and wrong, but to him, right and wrong was skewed.

Take his battalion commander.

He'd been fucking one of his female soldiers.

Against her will.

So, what did Eoghan do?

Didn't keep his mouth shut. Didn't even report said battalion commander to the MPs. No, he blew out his knee caps. Five Points' style.

Aidan Sr. had had to pull a shit-ton of clout to get Eoghan out of prison, and only by using a crap-ton of leverage and a fucking mountain of favors, had he managed to make it so.

In the end, it had been a worthy investment.

Uncle Sam had trained Eoghan to be one of the world's best snipers, and lookie here, wasn't that just a nice way to shore up his daddy's empire.

Eoghan had earned his penthouse after killing a cartel leader down in Mexico. Or, that's to say, he'd been paid to shoot the cartel leader, but he got the penthouse because he'd made it look like the Colombians were behind it.

Cue gang war in their Central *and* North American territories.

Cue a nice surge in our profits in the city.

"Remember what I said?" I bit off as my floor approached.

I wasn't really giving her much attention, but when I looked at her, I saw she was white as a sheet, and looking like she could either faint from fright or piss herself.

Disturbed by both prospects, I murmured, "Just go down the hall and slip into my bedroom. Ignore what you think you hear and forget about it. Do you understand me?"

She whimpered, but that wasn't enough of a response for me. I grabbed her chin and forced her to look at me. When our eyes clashed, it was like. . . .

Fuck.

It was like I could hear my fucking soul sing as I drowned in the crystal pools of her eyes. It was like my heart was beating double time, and it wanted to soar out of my chest just to get some space.

I'd never felt anything like this before, and I couldn't afford to feel it, either.

Some men might dream of meeting Mrs. Perfect, settling down, having two point four kids, and driving a people carrier.

I wasn't one of those guys.

This was my life.

Violence went hand in hand with the expensive suits I wore. My life had a price tag. That wasn't the kind of shit you brought a woman into. Not unless you were a selfish cunt like Aidan Sr.

I sucked in a shaky breath and pulled my hand from her jaw. Turning back to face the doors, I tried to get my breathing steady, my heartbeat back to its regular pace.

I wanted to screw her.

That was all this was.

Nothing more.

Nothing less.

Just screwing.

8

———

AOIFE

THERE WAS something about Finn's temperament that had me on edge.

I wasn't exactly thrilled at the prospect of going to his penthouse. I wasn't thrilled by the knowledge that Aidan O'Donnelly was in there doing only God knew what.

But 'not thrilled' morphed into outright terror when I sensed Finn's edginess.

Until that moment, Finn had been so cool, he'd made a cucumber look like grilled cheese.

He'd emanated it. Seemingly from his very pores. So collected, so rational, and logical that arguing with him had seemed ridiculous.

He'd approached me having weighed up the facts, and knew which pressure points to push. It helped that I remembered him. Helped that his mom had talked about how methodical he was as a boy.

Even as I was reeling at the fact he'd learned I had a connection to Senator Alan Davidson, I was stunned more by the prospect that there was no way out of this.

No way, no how.

If there was, Finn wouldn't have come to me.

He'd have waited. Found more shit to stick against the walls that were my life, and he wouldn't have stopped until I was dancing to his tune in the way he wanted.

So, if I seemed like a pushover, I was.

I'd been trained to be a pushover when it came to the Five Points.

We all were.

Meggie O'Leary had been raped by one of the Pointers, and hadn't gone to the cops, because no one went against the gang.

Of course, Aidan O'Donnelly Sr. had blown out the bastard's brain when he'd learned one of his men had raped a fifteen-year-old girl, but that didn't take away Meggie's pain, did it?

And when you saw the Pointers doing anything in my neighborhood, you looked the other goddamn way and hoped to Christ they hadn't realized you'd seen them.

I couldn't even begin to count how many damn drug deals I'd seen going down. I'd witnessed a stabbing, which might even have morphed from assault with a deadly weapon to murder, and I'd even seen someone being shot, too.

Had I gone to the cops?

Did I look crazy?

Of course, I damn well hadn't.

We all knew to stay out of Points' business if it was feasibly possible. Sometimes, it just wasn't. Their work meshed with our lives, but we had to ignore it, and remember that they worked to their own weird code.

It was half Catholic, half Old Testament, and half Aidan-O'Donnelly crazy.

In fact, the more my conditioning came into play, the more centered I became. I was doing this to protect my father, but I was also doing it to please a Points' man, because that was what we did.

We pleased them.

My mom had told me once that if I was unlucky enough to come to the attention of one of the runners, she'd forgive me if I gave my virginity to them.

Yeah.

Fucked up, right?

Mom was devout Catholic though, and she was naive enough to think that I was willing to wait until marriage before I got laid.

Of course, things had worked out in her favor until now. But unintentionally.

Still, that was how it worked.

She'd known I couldn't say no. That if I did, I'd get hurt, and being hurt wasn't worth closing your eyes and thinking of England for however long some punk with a gun pumped between your legs.

To be honest, the only advantage to my plus size had always been, in my mind anyway, that I'd always coasted under the radar.

Jenny hadn't, but she got off on the bad boy thing. She liked being a gangster's moll as she teasingly labeled it. I always told her she'd watched *Once Upon a Time in America* too many times.

But here I was, my time had come to lock horns with the devil, and there was no way I wasn't about to do exactly as my mom had taught me all those years ago.

I'd just never thought I'd be close to Finn O'Grady when it happened.

I'd never thought he'd be the one extorting me into his bed, and I'd sure as hell never imagined that I'd be going somewhere where Aidan O'Donnelly, the head of the terrifying gang that ruled the roost that was Hell's Kitchen, was in the same vicinity.

By the time we made it into the elevator, I was freaking out. Then, Finn touched me, and it was—no lie—like the sun, the moon, and the stars had suddenly come into alignment.

I'd never felt anything like it before, had never thought I'd experience something that I'd only ever read about in books or seen in movies. And yet, when I'd stared into those eyes of his, wide blue pools that I could drown in—how apt—everything had centered itself again.

I'd taken a moment to calm down, to breathe, and had known that just as was the case with my mom's dictates, if I followed Finn's, I'd be okay.

Of course, as we were spat out into a very impressive foyer, things went to shit almost immediately.

Before I had a chance to even take in the wide open spaces, the golden amber marble on the floor, the decor that looked like it belonged in a magazine—and I was in the frickin' hallway, of all places—I saw him.

I didn't know who he was, but he was terrified.

A bag was over his head, taped around his throat, so I couldn't see his face, but the way his lungs were working? He was close to hyperventilating.

Even from this distance, I could see the stains on his pants where he'd obviously urinated, and I couldn't blame him. I'd be peeing my pants, too, if I was surrounded by Aidan O'Donnelly and only God knew who else.

The man in charge was waving a gun in his hand as he paced from one side of the large living room to the other. He didn't seem to realize there were new people here, he was just ranting about some shit or other as he wafted that damn weapon about.

At my side, Finn swore under his breath and, waiting until Aidan disappeared out of sight for a handful of seconds thanks to a wall that hid us from him and him from us, he stormed down the corridor and dragged me with him.

I didn't even have it in me to argue. I just let him drag me along, so fucking grateful when he shoved me through a doorway and didn't take me down to that gorgeous salon, which would always be spoiled thanks to the fact someone just had the piss beaten out of them.

My whole body quivered as I rushed inside the bedroom.

A quick glance told me it was sartorial elegance in the flesh. There was a California King bed that seemed to go on for miles and miles, and it was covered with a crisp comforter the color of Finn's eyes. With the plump pillows, and the soft white cotton under sheet, which was revealed thanks to the way the comforter had been folded, I really wanted nothing more than to bury myself under that duvet and hide my head under the squashy down.

There were stylish rugs placed in artful angles that brought a rich color to the tapestry of the room. Expensive oil paintings with an almost Middle Eastern theme decorated the walls, and combined with the lighting, it was, I realized, as colorful as a souk. Like a little Arabian tent in the middle of Manhattan.

It was cozy and comfortable, and even better, had several doors leading from it to other rooms.

I had no desire to hear what was going on. Not even one ounce of me was curious. We learned not to be curious in my neighborhood. That kind of stupid logic got you killed, and as everyone was taught from a young age, if we were stupid around the Points, our moms would be attending our funerals.

To be fair, I didn't know if the Five Points *had* killed any kids. I doubted it, Aidan O'Donnelly was a God-fearing man, and even if he went to confession to be absolved of all his sins, killing kids just didn't seem like his kind of remit.

At least, I hoped so.

Not that it helped me at the moment.

My mom was no longer around to attend my funeral, and I was an adult. Aidan, I felt certain, would have no compunction about getting rid of me if I caused too much of a stink for him and his men.

One of the doors led to a sleek bathroom that was done in all black. The tiles, the vanity, the sink, the shower stall . . . totally black. All done in marble so shiny, I could see my reflection in it. Only the mirror and the faucets gave any relief to the color scheme, and over-head, there was a huge skylight that brought in a shit-ton of light as well as brightening up the room with the gorgeous sky that was so pretty, it made my eyes water.

Well, it was either that or fear.

Would that be the last beautiful thing I'd see before Aidan shot me between my eyes for sneaking around?

My throat closed.

No. Finn wouldn't have brought me here if he'd wanted Aidan to kill me.

Finn wanted to fuck me, not murder me.

I realized then how stupid I'd been not telling him my link to him, my link to his mom. The truth was, I'd been so stunned by not only his beauty, but the photos, and the fact that, well, I'd not only believed Finn was dead, but the knowledge that if he'd lived all these years and had never told Fiona of his whereabouts–that spoke of a hatred that I didn't really need to align myself with.

The bathroom was useless. I'd stick out like a sitting duck with my pale skin and red hair, so I ducked into another door and found a closet.

I didn't care if it made me look like a child. I pulled the door, and dropped to my knees. There were shoes there, but I didn't give a fuck. I clambered above them, uncaring that the expensive accessories dug into my ass as I huddled in the corner and, for the first time in five years, prayed.

Our father who art in heaven, hallowed be thy name,
Thy kingdom come, thy will be—

Then, like something from my nightmares, I heard it.

The gunshot.

And like it hadn't interrupted, I continued with a harried, terrified inner voice,

–done, on Earth as it is in heaven. . . .

9

———

FINN

TO SAY I was pissed that Aidan had entered my apartment without permission was an understatement.

To say I was pissed that he'd also brought a fucking John to my home?

Yeah. I was raging.

Any other fucker would know how disrespectful that shit was, but the trouble was, Aidan wasn't like 'any other fucker.' And you couldn't approach him mad.

Getting my temper under control was difficult.

There were so many goddamn wrongs going down in my fucking home that I wasn't sure which to process, and as I stepped toward my fucking living room and saw the puddle of piss and blood staining my rug, my nostrils flared in rage.

Eoghan cleared his throat, caught my eye, and shook his head.

I knew why he was warning me off.

Aidan was never very rational.

But clashing with him when he was pissed off?

I'd be asking for the same five-star service the poor bastard tied to one of my dining chairs was getting.

Christ.

Why had I even tried to make this place nice?

I'd spent a fucking fortune on it. Trying to make myself a goddamn home.

Why fucking bother?

"About damn time," Aidan snarled as he finally sensed I was here.

In the corner, I saw Aidan Jr. leaning against the wall, phone in his hands. He looked bored, and from the way his fingers were flying over the screen, he was either sorting out a hook up tonight or he was playing some stupid game.

Unlike his da, Jr. hadn't inherited the same zeal, and even though we all knew that Aidan's heart wasn't in the work, he was the eldest, and he'd inherit when Aidan Sr. died.

Truthfully, I couldn't wait for that day.

I loved Aidan Sr. I did. Fucked up, yeah, but when he wasn't off in his crazy head, he was a great guy. Knew more about the Knicks than any man still breathing. I swear, he was like one of those didacts. Knew so many statistics–could reel them off–that sometimes, it was like talking to Rain Man.

On Sundays, after church—which I only attended because it was required for those of us on Aidan's inner council—we all headed back to the house, and Magdalena would have a huge Sunday roast ready for lunch.

We'd shoot the shit, chill out in front of Aidan's big screen, which was on par with a screen at a cinema, and eat until we were blue in the face.

Magdalena was awesome.

She was a fighter, and I loved that about her.

Back in the day, word was that Aidan had been handy with his fists. Coming from his background? I didn't outright blame him. You did what you'd been taught, after all, but Magdalena knocked that fucking lesson right out of him.

He had a huge ass scar marring the back of his skull to prove it, too.

He'd gotten handy with his fists, *she'd* clomped him over the head with a rolling pin.

It was the one occasion where Aidan had looked set to serve jail time, until Magdalena had turned a leaf and had told the cops Aidan hadn't been beating her, but she had, in fact, thought he was an intruder.

The cops had been head over heels with the notion of getting the notorious Aidan O'Donnelly behind bars on a domestic violence charge. It was Al Capone all over again, but Magdalena? She'd left it just close enough to make Aidan sweat.

What a woman.

See, that was what a wife and mother should do.

She gave shit back when it was reaped on her. She didn't just fucking take it. Not like my mother. She didn't stand there and watch as her piece of shit husband beat on her boy.

Though Aidan had definitely laid a few scars on his sons, me, and the rest of the Points, he was under no illusion that if Magdalena ever found that out, he would wake up screaming one night as she snipped off his balls.

With a dull pair of kitchen scissors.

Maybe rusty ones, too. Just to make sure he got tetanus while she was at it.

Magdalena was a multi-tasker like that.

We knew not to share any of those salient facts about the scars on Conor's back, or Brennan's weak wrist, with the small woman whose might was bigger than her brawn.

The only person Aidan O'Donnelly was scared of, ironically enough, was his wife. And I fucking loved him for that.

But the day when he couldn't darken my door again would come as a relief.

The older he was, the more bat-shit he became.

Fucked up nonsense like this was getting to be a habit that none of us knew how to break without him taking it out on us.

I wasn't scared of him. I respected him, even. But I knew, as did we all, that in those moments where Aidan was lost in whatever fucking headspace wet work drove him to, we might as well have been Cartel foot soldiers for all the attention Aidan paid us.

We could have been enemies.

Not trusted and beloved sons.

That was the danger.

Twelve years ago, I could have asked him what the fuck he was doing, and he'd have clipped me around the ear.

Now?

I wasn't sure if I'd wake up after being pistol whipped.

That kind of erratic behavior was difficult to monitor, to be around, so we were all like chickens in a henhouse that was set on a minefield.

Clucking around blindly, just hoping someone else was stupid enough to stand on the trigger.

"I got here as soon as I could," I stated, my voice as calm as I could make it.

"Not soon enough," Aidan growled, but he wasn't looking at me.

Jr. sighed. "You literally texted him five minutes ago, Da. Cut the man some slack. You know what traffic is like at this time of night."

I shot Jr. a grateful look, but he didn't take his focus off his cell.

Aidan grumbled, "I guess."

"Who's the stiff?" I asked, because I was under no illusion that although the guy was alive now, he wouldn't be for long.

The bag over his head wasn't to protect our identities, to stop him from revealing us to the cops. It was because he was a dead man, and Aidan was more comfortable keeping his victims out of sight, and out of mind, until he was ready to do the deed.

"Architect," Eoghan rasped, and I tilted my head to stare at him.

"Architect?" I mouthed.

Eoghan pulled a face and sliced a finger along his throat. Well, that wasn't *very* informative.

"This bastard thought he could short change me," Aidan growled, and said bastard began to moan behind his gag.

I'd heard it often enough to translate the muffled apologies and pleas for forgiveness.

It wasn't going to work.

Aidan might believe in atonement and confession for himself and his boys, but for those who crossed him?

No such luck.

"How did he do that?" I asked, trying to keep my tone soothing. Not that it was easy, considering I was feeling anything *but* calm.

"I wanted that wrap around pool, do you remember? On Acuig Heights?"

I mentally flipped through the manifest for the project that had brought Aoife Keegan into my life, and recalled the pool.

Aidan had seen a hotel in Asia that had a pool on the side of the building. The base was glass, so when you were swimming, you were looking down to your death.

It was the kind of sick shit he found amusing, and ever since I'd rummaged through the Points' property portfolio and had come up with Aoife's building as a nice location ready for gentrification, he'd been rambling on and on about the pool.

"Yeah, I remember," I told him warily, wondering how we'd gone from that to this.

"Bastard only says it isn't possible now he promised it to me. Says it goes against the permit we have."

My nostrils flared, and I caught Aidan's gaze with mine. "We can get new permits, Aidan. Getting a new architect isn't exactly easy."

The gushing sounds coming from the gagged man were noisy. He was agreeing and pleading for his life simultaneously.

I rolled my eyes at the noise.

Seriously, didn't people realize how fucking annoying they were?

Didn't they know that pissing off someone with a loaded gun was only going to get them shot fucking sooner?

Christ.

"Architects are ten a penny," Aidan countered, the lilt of our home land coming out.

None of us had even set foot in Ireland, well, none save for Brennan and Magdalena, and especially not Aidan, but the accent came out every now and again. Usually, when he was at his most enraged.

Taking the lilt for the warning it was, I murmured, "You know that's not true, Aidan. We're building the Heights to be one of the largest skyscrapers in the city. Greaves and Potters are the best on the East Coast with that kind of engineering."

"Then we get the best in from the West Coast," Aidan growled.

"And that will add time to our schedule."

"Schedule?" Aidan snorted. "You can't even clear the building, so we can pull the bastard down to make way for the Heights."

I pursed my lips. "That's where you're wrong. I finally managed to clear the building today. By next month, we'll be breaking ground on the Heights if everything goes according to plan, and you butchering our architect—" My words were interrupted by some noisy sobs and more piss puddling on my fifty thousand dollar rug. "—then that's going to drag shit behind, isn't it?"

Sometimes, when Aidan was like this, you had to explain things to him rationally. Almost as if he were a boy.

As he processed my words, he began to slow his pacing, until finally, he demanded, "Why didn't one of you dipshits remind me I needed the architect?"

Jr. snickered. "Da, there's no reminding you your fly's down when you're in one of your mads."

Shit, that was true. Aidan's *mads*, as his wife called them, were infamous, but it was a little too close to the line for Jr. to be making jokes at his Pa's expense.

In one of his lightning swift moods swings that were coming more and more frequently these days, Aidan tipped his head back and roared at that.

Then, as we all chuckled because the bastard had one of those infectious laughs that you couldn't help but laugh with, he raised his gun, which was tipped with a silencer, and shot the architect in the leg.

The scream was muffled by the gag, but it still went through the air, as did the scent of more piss and shit this time as the guy let everything loose.

"That's for not getting the right permits," Aidan informed the bound man. "And that's for thinking you could jerk me around."

10

———

AOIFE

"AOIFE?"

It was Finn's voice, but I was too freaked out to even look outside the closet. One of his shoes was digging into my left butt cheek, and I swear, I felt like my chest was absorbing my legs through osmosis I was so tightly squished in the space, but that didn't mean I was about to leave the relative safety of this little haven I'd made for myself.

Of course, havens never lasted forever.

The brisk clip of Finn's expensive shoes against the marble tiles sounded loud to me, and I braced myself for him to open the door.

I didn't want him to.

I wanted to stay in here, pretend like I hadn't come to the attention of the Five Points, but that was futile when he opened the door and was staring down at me as though I'd just discovered the way to Narnia in here.

"They're gone."

My stomach twisted. "Did he kill that man?"

"Do you really think you should ask me that question, little girl?"

If my stomach had twisted before, now, it went diving into a somersault.

"No. I shouldn't be asking that question. No, I know it's the most stupid question I could ever ask, but seriously, I don't know if I can stay in an apartment with a dead body."

He snickered. "And you think I could?"

At his amusement, I glowered up at him, squinting when I saw that perfect fucking smile that made my ovaries do a happy dance.

I gnawed at my bottom lip before I whispered, "I don't know, do I? It's part of business for you."

He pursed his lips at that, those morsels of sin that made me think of kissing him, of drowning in his mouth. "Well, many may consider me a monster, but I'm not a fucking freak. The man walked out of here. With help."

"Aidan O'Donnelly let him go?" I'd have reared back, but there was no space to move.

"He does have reason, sometimes. Especially when there's a profit to be made."

I knew better than to let a whisper of judgment pass my lips, but in my mind, I was sad for Fiona. Sad because she'd never have imagined her boy was involved in these kinds of doings, and if she'd known, it would have broken her heart.

"What is it?" he ground out, making me wonder what he'd seen in my face.

"Nothing. Just a cramp," I lied, and he tutted then leaned down, grabbed my hands and hauled me to my feet.

Immediately, I staggered as one foot went numb.

Even as he went for me, I wrapped my hands around his waist and hugged him tight.

"I was so frightened," I whispered, and I didn't know why I made that admission of weakness to him when I couldn't to anyone else, but it was the truth.

The unpalatable truth.

A ghost of a kiss came down on my head, and then he rested his chin against my crown, and sucked down a sharp breath. "I wouldn't have let him harm you."

"N-No, maybe not, but if he'd have caught me . . .," I let my words trail off. He'd been right earlier. The last thing I needed was to come to the attention of the ringleader of the band of not-so-merry men.

"No need to fret about that now," he hummed under his breath, and it drove me crazy because I didn't know why I was responding like this—with relief and wonder and comfort.

His arms gave me something I'd never felt before.

Mom and I had loved one another, but we'd just never been all that tactile. I couldn't even tell you the last time I'd kissed her good-night or goodbye. We didn't even hug all that much. Fiona had been more affectionate, I guess. Yet, to settle into this man's warm arms, to feel safe when he was the reason I was in danger in the first place was the height of lunacy, but it was how I felt.

It's weird but sometimes, without even knowing it, you find yourself back on a path you should never have left.

As crazy as it sounded, I had a feeling that Finn and I had been destined to meet all these years later.

Maybe it was a feeling in my blood or maybe it was just my fright from earlier talking, but somehow, as wrong as the reasons were for Finn's bringing me here . . . This felt too damn right to ignore.

11

FINN

THE FEEL of her in my arms was like nothing I could have imagined.

I'd seen pictures of her before today. Enough to pique my curiosity and ask for more. The two original pictures Jimmy had taken for me had been like an entree. Then, I'd had to head back for an appetizer.

Dessert would be on the cards, shortly, but after the clusterfuck that had just gone down in my living room? It felt good to hold onto something that wasn't stained or tainted by my life.

No, there wasn't a dead body out in my salon, but there were blood marks on the rug, sofa, and floor. As well as piss and goddamn shit stains.

Aidan's team would be coming shortly, and I knew they'd get rid of any evidence, making my apartment so clean, only the memory of coming back here and seeing how Aidan had infiltrated my home would linger.

Still, as I tugged Aoife closer, I told myself it was for her benefit. Not mine.

She was right to be scared.

From her profile, a profile I intended on adding to, I knew that she'd been raised in Five Points' territory. But then, that wasn't hard considering how big our territory was, and growing.

The Irish Mob might be dying out in other cities, but in Manhattan and New York? We had the biggest presence in the nation, mostly because we had the capital.

Aidan Sr.'s daddy, as well as the man himself, had purchased a shit-ton of land back in the fifties, sixties, and seventies. Old buildings that had been ready for demolition back then, warehouses and big plots of land where factories had once pumped out pollution as well as the products they created.

Little by little, we'd been transforming the neighborhood with our version of housing projects, and as a result of the gentrification of the area, we'd also improved our demand.

Living in the city wasn't exactly good for the soul. It had a 'work hard, live harder' vibe, and without something to make that easier to handle, it was a shitty place to be.

Ever since we'd cleaned up the area, taking up half our territory with elegant skyscrapers that were filled with bankers and traders, socialites and bored wives who sat on charitable foundations, our sales of cocaine and speed had shot through the roof.

A molly to come down, some pot to mellow you out.

The best part of it?

The dealers lived in.

It was like a fast food service. You didn't have to drive anywhere to get your hit, you just got in the elevator and got off at the appropriate floor.

Even though I knew they were good for business, I hated drugs. Always had. The brothers and I'd had a best friend back in school who'd overdosed. Some fucker had spliced his baggy of coke with weed killer of all things.

We preferred the legit side of the biz, but I'd admit to getting a kick out of supplying the city's finest residents.

So, with our territory taking up so much space, it was no wonder Aoife knew to be scared of me as well as the rep of my Family.

The beast inside that had urged me to bring her here, to my home, to my bed, reared its head again.

It was a metaphorical beast.

The creature that had helped me shoot out kneecaps, deal drugs even when I loathed everything they stood for, when I'd slept on the streets those first few weeks when I'd run away from home . . . it was that fire inside me that kept me going, kept me fighting, struggling for more.

Well, now, that beast wanted Aoife.

Anyway I could fucking get in her.

My adrenaline was high after brushing against Aidan. Handling him sometimes was like taking a leap out of a plane. Restful it was *not*. But I knew exactly what would help burn off my edginess.

I moved my hands down from her hips and cupped her ass through her black jeans. When she jolted at my touch, I half hid a smile in her hair as I drew her hips against mine until I had a nice rhythm and she was rubbing against me in a way that had my cock standing to attention.

She didn't roll her hips back though, not until I left one hand there and grabbed her loose hair in a makeshift pony tail with the other, winding it around my fist as I'd dreamed. Then I dragged her head back so that I could press my mouth to hers and plunge my tongue between her lips.

I was under no illusion that she was still feeling the fright that had her hiding in my wardrobe of all damn places, but I didn't care.

I wanted her.

I needed her.

And I always got what I wanted.

When she didn't kiss me back, I grabbed her lip between my teeth and dug down again. She hissed but, interestingly enough, didn't try to pull back. Considering that was instinctive, I had to wonder why she hadn't. Then, I wasn't left to wonder much longer because, finally, her hips began to roll against mine.

The move was edgy. Unpracticed.

I didn't care, though. It just felt too fucking good to have some friction against my cock that wasn't thanks to my own fist.

I released her lip and she, in turn, released a whimper. That sound lit me up inside. It was keyed to everything about me that was instinctual. Like the caveman part of me had just woken up by triggering that atavistic side of her.

Fuck, I was speaking bullshit, but this was just so beyond normal for me that I didn't know what the fuck was happening. I simply knew that from her unskilled movements, I could goddamn climax.

I pulled back from her and put space between us. She looked confused, her eyes wide and hungry, her lips parted as she pulled in ragged breaths. Her tits jiggled, and I wanted nothing more than to have my cock pillowed between those delicious mounds, and to have her naked on the floor, all of her glorious creaminess out on display.

"Strip," I grated, and she jerked at my tone. Narrowing my eyes at her when she didn't move, I bit off, "What the fuck are you waiting for?"

She jumped again, her tits bouncing with her, and then she reached for her camisole. As was the way with women, she crossed her arms in front of her, grabbed the hem, and then lifted it over her head. And what that simple move did to her tits had my tongue feeling too heavy for my mouth—I could have panted at the sight of all that flesh just waiting for my touch, my teeth.

Her hands were shaking as she reached behind her to release the snap of her simple, white cotton bra. There was no artifice about her, nothing that screamed she was a politician's fancy piece of ass. When she undressed, she didn't make it into an art form. A dance. She was utilitarian with her movements, and fuck, if that didn't get me even hotter.

As she dragged the tight jeans down her legs, revealing a pair of mismatched panties from her now-discarded bra, her bottom lip quivered as she hooked them down, too.

When she toed out of them, standing there before me like something from a Renaissance painting, I couldn't contain the growl as I snarled, "Get on my bed."

With a little squeak, she hurried over to the bed, and her fear? Fuck, it got me hot.

I usually fucked women who knew what they were getting into when they got into my bed.

Some women? They liked the bad boys. They liked thinking they were fucking someone who knew what it was like on the other side of the tracks. Some of them probably had husbands who came home every night at six and kissed them goodnight while making love to them in their double bed.

That wasn't me.

They came to me for a fuck, and I fucked them. Using them as much as they used me.

But Aoife wasn't like that, and maybe that was why she got to me so fucking much.

I watched her ass jiggle as she retreated to my room, and when she planted herself on my bed, her skin clashed with the blue comforter, and it made her look like one big bowl of peaches and cream that I wanted to lap right up.

My mouth watered with need for a taste, but instead, I stayed the bastard I was and murmured, "Spread your legs and show me your pussy."

Her eyes widened, a whimper escaped her, but God love good Irish women, she obeyed. She parted her thighs, slipped her hand between her legs and showed me her pussy.

I looked at her for endless moments, our gazes trained on one another until I broke it, broke the stare to grab a chair from the side of my dresser. I dragged it over to the foot of the bed and took a seat before the show in front of me.

"Are you Catholic, Aoife?"

She blinked at me. "My mom was. I was b-baptized."

I tilted my head at that. "Do you go to church?"

"Sometimes."

"When was your last confession?" I half-mocked.

She swallowed. "About five years ago."

I tsked under my breath. "Do good girls touch themselves, Aoife?"

I didn't know why I was asking the question but fuck, it made my cock pound and from the sight of her dilated eyes, I knew she was wound up tighter than a spring, too.

"It's a sin," she half-mewled.

"I know. That's why I asked."

I reached over, pressed my hand above hers and began to move her fingers. As we moved them together, she whimpered, her eyes fell closed, and her lips parted.

"That's a sin, Aoife," I told her gravely, watching the slick lips of her pussy, seeing the juices that were gathering there.

I couldn't believe how wet she was.

I'd known, when I walked into her teashop, she was attracted to me. I'd known that I could have gotten her here, in this room, with no coercion whatsoever. But that she was here, despite my coercion, and that she was dripping onto my coverlet like I'd been tongue fucking her for the past thirty minutes?

Well, it had me reaching down, unfastening my zipper and pulling my cock through the fly. The relief was instantaneous, and I gripped my shaft as we both worked her sweetly wet little cunt.

Her head moved from side to side, slowly at first, slowly. Then faster, faster, until it became a thrashing motion. Then, just when her thighs tensed, I pulled my hand back.

This time, her head shot up, and confusion and fear and panic threaded together in those emotive emerald eyes of hers. "W-Why did you stop?"

Because I'm a bastard?

I didn't say that, though, just motioned at my cock. Her eyelids fluttered at the sight, but what was all the more delicious was the way her skin turned bright pink like it had back in her tea room.

"Roll over and rest your neck against the edge of the bed."

She looked confused, her brow puckered with uncertainty as she moved. Her submissiveness satisfied something in me, pleased some integral part of me. But what made me fucking burn was how, when she moved, and her thighs rubbed together, she paused, dipped her head to moan at the sensation, then like she'd been drugged, carried on with my orders.

There was something about her that got to me.

It was like she hadn't done this before. Like her body wasn't used to these sensations, but I knew that to be bullshit.

Was this all an act, then?

Fuck, if the thought didn't infuriate me.

I wanted to snarl at her to hurry up, but she was already in position. Her head tilted back against the side of the bed so that I could dip my shaft into her mouth when I wanted to.

"Spread your legs again," I directed. When she'd obeyed, I murmured, "You can touch your hungry little cunt, you can even come, but you have to take everything I give you. Do you understand?"

She nodded, but I knew, deep down, that she didn't. What the fuck?

With her hands between her legs, I muttered, "Make your mouth wet, work up some spit, and when you have enough, open up for me."

Though she frowned, she did as bid.

When I sank my cock into her wet, slick mouth, I almost shot off like I'd pushed into her cunt.

Jesus, Mary, and Joseph.

I swore at the ceiling as I gazed up at it, I cursed at the picture she made when I began to thrust my dick into her greedy mouth.

Fuck.

She took me so perfectly.

Like she was made for my cock.

I was slow at first. I wasn't packing a ten-inch hammer, but I was above average, and I wanted to make sure she was comfortable. Then, when we both worked out a rhythm, when I saw her body relax, her features flush, every part of her getting off by her touching herself, as well as the way I was fucking her mouth, I began to move faster.

Harder.

Deeper.

The little gagging sounds she made were like manna from heaven, and one of her hands moved from between her thighs, and her wet fingers grabbed at my hip—not to stop me, to urge me on.

That she was getting off on me using her mouth was an electric shock to the back of my neck. And trust me. I'd been tazered a few times in my misspent youth, I knew how that shit felt, and this was like that.

I was so close to coming in her mouth, so close to jetting my seed down her throat, but I couldn't. Just couldn't.

I needed my first load in her pussy.

Needed it like I needed my next breath.

With a groan of disappointment, I pulled out of her mouth, and even as she moaned her own annoyance, I strode to the side of the bed, opened one of the drawers on the nightstand and pulled out a condom.

Sheathing myself, I climbed onto the bed, slotted myself between her thighs, grabbed her legs and pinned them high against my chest, then I fisted my dick and began to push into her.

A panicked squeak escaped her at the brisk roughness of my caresses, but I ignored her as I sank the first inch into her.

"Jesus, you're so tight," I bit off, feeling the sweat pop out of my pores as she clamped down around me.

Her panting breaths sounded overly loud in the room as I dipped my chin and pressed my forehead to the side of her calf which was propped up against my pec.

I tried to fuck another inch into her, but shit, she was like a vise.

It was my turn to pant. "Relax."

"I'm trying," she whimpered, and I opened my eyes to look at her. She was white again, not pink with arousal, and though her cunt was fucking sloppy from all her juices, she was constricting around me in a stranglehold to maim, not to caress.

I frowned down at her then parted her legs. Grabbing her ankles, I dragged her up against me, tilting her hips and pelvis up. I ignored the faint squeal she made, enjoyed the show as her tits moved in the opposite direction she went, and then spread her legs once more, this time so that each ankle was either side of my neck.

Resting my shaft against her sweet, slick folds, I popped the head in, and she released a deep, guttural moan that resonated inside me.

Slowly, in minute increments, I pushed home, and only when I felt it did I realize what the fuck I was touching.

Her hymen.

12

———

AOIFE

OH, *God; oh, God; oh, God.*

It had been so good. So, so, so good and now? Now, it just hurt.

As he rearranged me on the bed, pressed the tip of his shaft to my gate and slipped inside, I had to release a deep breath loaded with relief as this time, it was easier. I didn't feel like he was tearing into me, and he managed to get what had to be at least two inches into my body.

Did this mean I wasn't a virgin anymore?

Fuck, I should *not* have been as excited about that as I was. . .

Famous last words.

My excitement drained when he came up against something, and he nudged it, and it fucking hurt.

"What the hell?" he ground out, gaping down at me like he wasn't sure if I was insane or just an apparition of Mother Mary herself. "Are you a virgin?"

That was the last thing I'd expected him to ask. I mean, surely with all the fumbling Craig had done, he'd managed to take that tiny piece of flesh away?

But nope. Apparently Craig hadn't even managed to do the decency of making *this* less mortifying.

I covered my face with my hand, and tilted my head to the side. Refusing, physically, to answer.

His fingers grabbed my chin, though, and he urged me to look at him, swatting my hand away as he did. "Aoife," he ground out. "Are you, or are you not, a fucking virgin?"

For a second, my mouth quivered.

How had this gone from the sexiest thing I'd ever done to *this*?

It was almost as bad as trying to dissuade Craig from penetrating my urethra. Assuring him that, nope, that particular hole was not about to get any damn bigger.

Yeah.

That was how mortified I felt.

Because I couldn't speak, I dipped my chin.

A flood of curses escaped his mouth, but what stunned the hell out of me even more was the glitter in his gaze.

He stared at me for endless seconds, his eyes trained on mine, refusing to let me look away, almost like he was the predator and I, as his prey, needed to know just who was in charge here.

My boobs shook with my heavy breaths and my body was strung up with the intensity of the sensations coursing through me.

His cock was there, in me, but not. So close, but not. And the way he looked at me, the way his nostrils were flared like some sort of stallion ready to mount a mare in heat? I wasn't sure whether I liked it or wanted to run screaming from the room.

Then, he thrust into me, and the word that escaped his lips seared itself to my eardrums. It ricocheted through my body. Rattling around inside my skull because even though it was only one simple word, it made no sense.

"Mine," he whispered as he pushed into me. I released a sharp scream as he finally forged all the way inside me, the pain and pleasure was so intense, I didn't know where it began and ended, where *I* began and *he* ended.

Then, he grated it.

Mine.

And he pulled out of me.

Then, he grunted it.

Mine.

And he thrust into me.

He repeated it again and again, a one-word litany as he fucked me. Hard.

He didn't take my virgin state into consideration, and that was actually *more* consideration than I could have asked for.

For some stupid reason, I didn't want him to treat me like I was a delicate flower. I wanted him to fuck me. I wanted him to fuck that word into me.

His?

I wasn't his.

And yet, as he screwed me, as he fucked me hard, long, and wet, a part of me would always be his, and I knew that like I knew my face in the mirror.

13

FINN

WHEN AOIFE CAME around my cock, the first cock ever to be inside her, it was lights out for me.

There was no way I could hold back my own release, no way I could stop it to carry on reveling in the tightness of her cunt, of the snug, wet heat that was mine and mine alone.

She clamped and clutched at me, her body curling upward, her tits jiggling as she released a shrill scream that nearly burst my ear drums as ecstasy poured through her.

Then, because I couldn't stop myself, I reached down and pinched her clit.

Her gaze clashed with mine, and for half a heartbeat, she looked at me as though I'd hurt her, as though she were asking why I'd be so mean, and then I knew why.

Her spine arched, her hips thrust up, and she almost pushed me back on my ass as she used me as support to let the joy of her second release flood her veins.

I'd never seen an orgasm like it.

Never seen someone own their pleasure like this innocent had, and it fired my blood like nothing else could.

Her sweet tits, those milky mounds, that bright-pink flush that crested in myriad points around her fleshy body, and the bright scorch of auburn hair that swirled around her form against my navy comforter, was the prettiest thing I'd ever seen.

I'd never called someone mine before, but Aoife was.

There was no way in fuck I was letting her go now I knew she'd only ever taken my cock.

Shit like that in my world was sacred.

Virgins weren't women you fucked and left behind. You didn't pull a coyote ugly on them and sneak out of their bed the next day.

You put a ring on their finger.

You made them your wife, and you put your babies in their bellies.

It was nothing I'd ever expected for myself. Nothing I'd ever particularly wanted. Not until her.

Until Aoife.

When I climaxed, it was, as everything else had been, extraordinary.

I felt like I'd been punched in the side of the head—just in a good way. Sensations pulled at my nerve endings, making me realize that sex had never been this fucking epic in all my life.

As my cum boiled out of my balls and slalomed into the condom, I resented that piece of latex like nothing else in this world.

Nothing, ever again, would be between this woman and me.

That was a fucking fact.

When I finally got my breath back, when I'd stopped seeing stars, and I had feeling back where it should be, I pulled out of her tight little slit.

When she whimpered, guilt flooded me, and she curled onto her side like she was ashamed.

That made me mad, but I didn't take it out on her.

I'd treated her like a common slut, and now it was time to make amends.

The sight of the blood on the condom was like a red rag to a bull.

It would be so easy to get hard again. Just thinking of her being mine, uniquely mine, pummeled my skull.

Trying to force those thoughts away, I shucked out of my clothes quickly, my eyes on her fetal form as I headed for the bathroom, I finally turned away when I slipped inside. Running the water as I disposed of the condom, I stared down at her blood and felt like some kind of elemental tie joined me to her.

When the water was hot, I grabbed a cloth from the vanity, soaked it through, and then grabbed a towel. Seeing her on the side of the bed, listlessly dressing, had more rage swirling inside me.

"Get back on the bed. Now," I snarled. I didn't care that I'd made her jump, I just wanted her to obey.

I could only imagine what she was thinking, but at my bark, she did as bid.

Fuck, she got to me. I loved her like this, but I wanted the fire that was on her head as well as on her pussy to come to the fore, too.

I liked a woman bare down there. Nothing to get in the way of my teeth, lips, and tongue. But Aoife? I liked her trimmed. I wanted proof that I was fucking a genuine redhead, and my mouth watered, knowing I'd be tasting her as soon as she was ready.

"Spread your legs," I commanded, watching as she did so with a wince.

I knew she wasn't ready again, so did she, but she had to think I was going to use her for a second round, yet she still obeyed.

Then, as I neared, her eyes widened as she saw what was in my hands. The cloth dripped, but I didn't care. I kneeled against the side of the bed then climbed onto it. Spreading the cloth flat out, I pressed it to her core and pushed the flexible material into each crevice of her sex I could reach.

She released a keening sound as the heat got to her, working into sore and poorly used tissues. Though I did feel guilty, I also felt hot, knowing that she was sore because of me.

Fuck, could I sound more like a Neanderthal?

In apology, I crooned to her, "Let it soothe you."

She whimpered, but relaxed when I made no move other than to cleanse her. I kept the hot cloth there until it grew chill, then I asked, "Do you want more?"

"Another washcloth?" she replied carefully, making me laugh.

"I didn't mean more cock."

When her cheeks flushed, I had to laugh again. She was so easy to rile, so easy to embarrass. A part of me wondered where this woman had been.

She was a New Yorker, born and bred. Had been raised in Hell's Kitchen, knew the deal with the Five Points—enough to know that hiding in the fucking wardrobe wasn't too stupid an idea—and yet, she flushed and blushed and cringed like she was a debutante coming out two hundred years ago.

"Please," she whispered huskily. "The heat helped some."

I nodded and maneuvered off the bed. As I did, her eyes drifted over my body. I didn't preen, but I let her look her fill before I told her, "Don't move an inch. I'll know."

She flared her eyes wide, looking like a cat in headlights. "O-Okay."

Because I knew she would obey, I just dropped the used cloth on the ground, knowing my maid service would clean up after me. Returning to the bathroom, it took me less than thirty seconds to get another cloth as the water was already piping hot.

When I returned, she was exactly where I'd left her. Legs splayed, her pussy bright pink from my use. Her belly wasn't firm like a model's, her hips weren't as taut, but I didn't need that. Sure, it was nice to bang. Variety was good for the soul, after all. But what had Paul Newman said?

"Why go out for a burger when you've got a steak at home?"

For the first time in my life, I saw the sense in that.

She had hips meant for carrying a child, not that she'd appreciate that particular acknowledgment. But more important than that, they were perfectly ripe for my fists. I could and would, at some point, grab a hold of her there and tug and fuck her how I wanted her. I could bounce my pelvis against her ass without our bones rattling. Her body was soft and padded, perfect for fucking.

I shuddered, knowing she was out for the count tonight, so getting myself riled up wasn't smart.

I'd been a bastard to her, and I had no doubt I'd be a bastard again —it was in my nature—but I wasn't about to use her hard on this, her first time with me.

The trouble with this day and age?

Women had a say.

Well, women outside of the life.

Magdalena had come from another Family, one out in Hoboken. The marriage between her and Aidan had been to cement some kind of agreement between two families. There were other daughters that would make smarter choices for wives, and I knew if I asked Aidan, he'd contract one for me.

Because yeah, that was how this world worked.

Contracts.

Arranged marriages.

It was very second world. Very Victorian. But it worked. Women outside of this way of life didn't understand. Aoife? She did. Maybe she hadn't learned it like Magdalena had, but she'd learned it from living in the territory.

She was dozing, I realized, when I made it back to her side, and I smirked down at her, ridiculously proud that I'd worn her out. From this angle, her tits were fucking epic. Better than a swimsuit model's. These weren't goddamn apples, but fucking melons. Jesus, if I stayed away from them tonight, I deserved a goddamn medal.

I shuddered, forced my gaze away from them, and then carefully placed the cloth over her sore cunt. It was a mixture of pink from exertion, the heat of the washcloth, and her natural coloring down there. I liked seeing it, wanted to see my cum spill from her pussy even more.

Next time, I promised myself.

Next time.

She stirred when I pressed my finger carefully inside her, swirling it gently to try and soothe her inside. When she winced, I retreated, knowing I was trying to help but could be making it worse.

Instead, I left the cloth there and climbed atop her. My cock settled against the fabric, too, separating us, and though she stiffened with me directly above her, she stared up into my eyes with no fear.

She was a bewildering mixture.

Trepidatious, yet also, confident.

It was a concoction I was pleased to decipher.

"Why didn't you warn me?"

My voice was raspier than I'd intended. When she flinched, I knew she thought I was angry. She dipped her chin and turned her gaze from mine, but I reached up and forced her to look at me.

"I ask because I could have been kinder to you."

That had her tensing beneath me. "I wouldn't have changed what happened if you asked me to."

Her tone was husky, and it sent shivers down my spine. I heard the lilt of home in her words, and it made me need her all the more.

"I wouldn't hurt you like that," I chided her. "There are ways I *will* hurt you . . ." I curved my teeth about her bottom lip, nipped again, just enough to hurt. When she moaned, I knew I'd made my point. "But I wouldn't have hurt you during your first time."

"I-It's okay," she whispered shyly.

I sighed. It wasn't okay, but she was obviously not going to agree with me.

Instead of arguing, I slipped my tongue between her lips and kissed her. Fuck, just the meeting of our mouths was enough to stir my cock to life. She tensed in response to it, but it was like the upper half and the lower half of her body were at war.

I kissed her, nipping and biting at her lips, fucking her mouth like I couldn't fuck her cunt.

"Relax," I cooed at her. "Nothing else is going to happen tonight."

She released a shaky breath, and as I stared at her face, I saw the disappointment there.

"Do you know what a pearl necklace is?"

Her eyes widened. "You don't mean a necklace of pearls, do you?"

"No, smartass," I mocked, but I had to laugh at her when her nose crinkled as she hid a chuckle. It was the first real side of her I'd seen all evening—my own fault considering I'd threatened and maneuvered her here.

Still, I had time to learn more of her.

Time to get to know every inch of this gorgeous fucking body.

"You mean," she broke off to clear her throat, "you want to come on my throat."

"I do," I told her. "I want to slide my cock between your tits. Can you manage that tonight?"

She huffed. "I'm not entirely hopeless."

"No? Your pussy is off limits to me tonight. That means it's disabled for all intents and purposes. Unless you feel like trying. . . ."

She shook her head swiftly, and I had to hide a grin.

I tapped her bottom lip. "Don't bait a tiger by pulling his tail. Literally." With a wink, I leaned over to the nightstand again and opened the top drawer where I stashed the condoms and some lube. I didn't use the latter often, but it made fucking my fist a more bearable prospect.

I preferred to get my dick wet in a cunt, but I'd settle for my hand when time was short, and I really needed to blow my load.

Grabbing the bottle, I sat up on my heels, one of my knees on either side of her hips. Opening the lid, I poured some onto my hands, and then I poured some onto her tits. They gleamed like wet silk and I watched, my mouth watering, as the lube spilled over the mounds.

I realized I'd barely tugged and sucked at the perfect cherries cresting each tit, but I could do that later.

Coating my cock with my slick fist elicited a moan from her. I grinned at her. "Like that, huh?" I did it again, twice more, and watched as she licked her lips at the sight.

Fuck, I needed her.

Not just her tits, but her cunt.

Christ.

Grabbing the gorgeous swells with either hand, I pushed them together and made a tunnel for myself. She whimpered as she felt my cock against her skin, then slowly, I began to fuck her there. I manipulated her skin, knowing that I pinched her in some points, squeezed to the point of pain in others as I screwed her tits.

She didn't seem to mind.

Her breathy pants told me she was eager for this, eager for more, and I had no doubt that her once virginal, little pussy wanted more action than it was ready for.

Mouth watering at the prospect of tasting her tonight, I used her tits. I'd never been a fan of titty fucks. I found them boring. But as I stared down into her eyes as I did this, there was nothing boring about it.

Shit, what the hell was happening to me?

There was a whole world of delight in her gaze, and I found myself falling into it like I'd just uttered the password to Ali Baba's cave.

When my orgasm approached, I tilted my head back, unable to look at her as I climaxed. My thrusts grew shaky, staccato, as I found my pleasure. I roared as I came, my seed spattering the upper slopes of her tits, her nipples, her throat, her chin, even her mouth and cheek.

Fuck, that was a lot of cum, and while I'd thought she was beautiful, I wasn't sure I'd seen a more beautiful sight than I did at that moment.

Releasing my taut grip on her tits, I let them fall aside, but I left my cock there, in the welcome haven of her body. Then, with slow and sure movements, I began to rub the cum into her skin. Languidly, dreamily, I guessed. Not stopping until my cum had merged with the lube and she was a shiny mess.

Wiping my hands on the bed cover, I reached up for the cum on her face. Scooping some up, I carried it to her mouth.

"Lick my fingers," I ordered her.

Her tongue popped out, and she sucked them clean. Before I could groan, I saw her nose wrinkle, and though I smiled, I told her, "Get used to tasting it. I want you to swallow every drop next time."

Her eyes flared wide. "Next time?"

I nodded. "Next time."

If she thought I was going anywhere, if she thought *she* was going anywhere, she was fucking crazy.

With a hum, I did the same as I had earlier.

I rubbed my seed into her cheeks. Coated her upper lip with it and ran it around her lips. "Don't lick them," I warned her. "Leave my cum there. Above your lip."

She tensed. "I-I can't."

"You can," I told her, the warning clear in my voice.

Aoife shifted restlessly on the bed, and I moved away, knowing she was fighting several urges.

I had no doubt that she needed to come again. I also had no doubt that she was fighting my dominance.

Some women were born submissive. They just didn't know it.

Aoife was, but she undoubtedly had a lifetime of women's lib being deep-throated down her fucking gullet, and she thought she shouldn't like the way I bossed her around.

I'd show her differently.

Unlike many men in my line of work, I didn't actually want a totally compliant wife. In the bedroom was one thing, in other aspects of our life, it was another.

Women in this world needed backbone. Grit. I figured Aoife had that in spades if she'd felt strong enough to try to fight Acuig's purchasing of her lot. It was there, but she was still being cautious.

I had time to show her how I wanted her to be.

Before she could complain anymore about the cum on her face, which had her skin gleaming like she'd put some of that shitty highlighter stuff I'd seen my bed-warmers in the past apply to their cheekbones to make them gleam under the light, I maneuvered to the foot of the bed.

This time, I got to my knees as I moved to the floor. I grabbed her legs and dragged her toward me. She released a squeal, but settled down with sobbing breaths that escaped her as she realized what I was about to do.

I pressed an open-mouthed kiss to her clit.

"Did I fuck your little cunt too hard?" I rasped.

She shuddered. Didn't answer.

I nipped the bud, making her yelp.

"Well? Did I?"

A moan escaped her. "N-No. You fucked me just right."

"Does your pussy want me again?" I asked before I slipped my tongue through her tender folds, moving down to the sensitive area I'd penetrated earlier. She wriggled on the bed, and I knew she was experiencing both discomfort and pleasure at the touch. Her breaths turned from small pants, to harsh ones as I reached up and began to rub her clit.

"O-Oh, God."

I pulled back and tapped her clit. When she jerked at the sting but released a throaty moan, I knew she liked the bite of pain. "Blasphemous girl," I chided. Not that I gave a fuck, but I liked punishing her.

So, fucking sue me.

She whimpered. "I-I'm sorry."

"Don't be sorry to me," I told her before I pounced once more, slurping up her clit, sucking down on it hard and fast until she was screaming, her body one big rictus of pleasure. Her legs came up to cup my head, but because her thighs were rounded and soft, it felt good instead of like being in a stranglehold.

I didn't mind. I loved her passion, and I rewarded her, letting her orgasm and find her pleasure, loving how it seemed to flood her. She didn't hold back, didn't try to contain her desire to make sure she looked beautiful. It ripped through her like the tide, and I fucking loved how unpracticed she was.

And her taste?

Fuck me, it was better than fucking whiskey.

Earthy and musky, to be sure, but like honey, too.

I growled, not having sated myself enough on her taste. I tongue fucked her, sucked her clit until she found her release two more times. I only stopped when she was begging for me to stop, begging to be released from the crest of ecstasy I'd taken her to.

And because she asked so sweetly, I gave it to her, but it didn't stop me from climbing back up, from pressing my lips to her ear, and whispering, "You're going to be begging me to stop every fucking night from now on."

She was too exhausted to do anything other than release a small whimper before her breathing evened out and she slept.

For once, I did, too.

I didn't stare up at the ceiling, twiddling my fucking thumbs as I thought about all the shit I hadn't managed to do today, and all the *fucking* shit I had to do tomorrow.

I cocked one leg over hers, and covered her like I was a heavy blanket, my face nuzzled into her throat. And for the first time in years, I slept the whole night through.

14

———

AOIFE

IT WAS the silence that woke me.

I wasn't used to it. I don't think any New Yorker was.

Well, I should correct that by saying any *average* New Yorker.

Not only was I on one of the best streets in Hell's Kitchen, I was about eighty stories up. When I looked out of the window, I couldn't see anything other than sky and buildings in the distance. The ground was way, way, way down, and peering out the window was enough to make me dizzy.

I wasn't sure I was surprised to find myself alone this morning.

Had I committed a faux pas by spending the night?

I wasn't sure. I just knew I'd had no alternative but to pass out last night. He'd given me so many orgasms that I'd had no choice but to sleep.

I mean, sure, I'd used my fingers, and a vibrator. Yeah, I'd thought that was better than a man could give me. But what Finn O'Grady could do with his body, his hands, and his tongue? Jesus Christ. No sex toy could begin to compare.

But oh, my God, I was sore.

Muscles that I'd never even known I possessed *ached.* This was more than just a bone-deep ache, too. It felt like, with each and every step I took, I was ninety years old.

My legs were sore, my thighs felt strained like I'd done a thousand squats. My stomach muscles were tight, and even my back had aches I'd never had before.

If nothing else, Finn O'Grady had given me the best workout ever.

Oh, and don't forget that he'd probably ruined me for any other man, too.

I should have loathed how he treated me last night. But what had started off rough and harsh had morphed into a bizarre tenderness once he'd realized I was totally new to this. He'd changed then, and I'd loved that even more. The sensitivity of his that came with a bite.

I knew I should scamper out of here, tug on my clothes and get out before he could find me, but I didn't have it in me to do so. I stood there, naked and unashamed for the first time in my life, and looked out at a view that had to have an eight-figure price tag.

It seemed surreal that I was standing up here, looking down at all the little folk below while I was covered in a lover's sweat and cum. My legs were stained with my release and his saliva. . . .

God help me, though, I loved it.

I *loved* it.

I felt so dirty. So deliciously, horrendously *dirty*. It was like I'd found my purpose. Like suddenly having good sex made everything make sense.

This feeling was why Jenny walked with a sensual grace after she'd been laid the night before.

This feeling was what made the world go around, and had men and women moving in an infinite, uniquely choreographed dance.

And, God, I wanted more.

I didn't like the reasons he'd brought me here, but what he'd done after?

I wasn't about to complain.

"Good. You're awake."

I stiffened at his brisk tone and turned around to see him eying me. I'd half-expected to see disgust or revulsion on his face, maybe even impatience at my still being there. But if anything, there was a possessive gleam that had my heart stammering in my chest. His ice-blue eyes were still flinty, but they glittered hotly as he took me in.

I remembered how he'd taken me last night. With each thrust of his hips, he'd declared I was his, and his stare this morning confirmed it.

"Did you lick your top lip?"

The question came out of nowhere. "I-I don't think so." His cum had dried on me last night, which was both gross and delightful. I wasn't sure why it was the latter and not just the former, but it made my insides turn squelchy and everything south, which had no business coming back to life, turning molten hot.

He hummed, then held out his hand. I stilled at the sight but took four hesitant steps toward him. When there were two left between us, he tutted, and I realized what that meant—I scurried forward, covering the distance. When he smiled at me, his impatience disappearing, it was like a cat purring its satisfaction.

With my hand in his, he led me to the bathroom. The elegance of the room looked even starker in the dull morning light, and he guided me to the shower, then switched on the faucet.

I stood there, just watching as he stripped. I realized then that he'd been working out because his chest gleamed with sweat, and he wore basketball shorts.

His cock was soft, and I was fascinated by the difference between last night and now, but as I watched, and he saw where my focus was aimed, it grew hard.

He grabbed my hand, making me jump, and curled it around his cock. Pumping it a few times together, his head tilted back as he released a guttural groan.

"How can you be this fucking potent?" he gritted out, surprising me by the admission.

I wouldn't deny that it made me feel like a siren, but equally, I wasn't actually doing anything, so it wasn't as if I could take complete credit.

Rather than say anything, I tugged at his cock, applying gentle pressure as I walked backward to move under the spray.

I wasn't sure if he wanted me to take charge at all, but fuck, this was the twenty-first century. If I wanted to feel him up while under the hot spray, then that was my prerogative. And boy, did I need that water. Not only did I stink of sex and cum and all kinds of nasty things, my body was aching like a bitch. I needed the heat to make me feel some semblance of human. Equally, though, I wanted to carry on touching him.

I liked the feel of him in my hands, loved the sounds he made as I touched him. I realized then that I'd never felt this empowered, this confident in who I was as I did at that moment.

I wore baggy shirts, loosely flowing camis, and dark jeans to hide my curves. I rarely showed that much skin, and I never, *ever* felt comfortable with no clothes on. That was when I was by myself, never mind with a man as handsome as Finn looking on.

But the way he made me feel?

It was like I was some kind of sex goddess, and I found that I loved that. Loved the way he made me feel about myself.

I didn't have to hide my curves; he loved them. He'd squeezed all my bits, grabbed a hold of them and used them to fuck me harder, better, faster, deeper.

Like that was what my body was made for.

To be fucked by him.

I shuddered at the thought as he reached behind me and grabbed a bottle from the silver shelf suspended from the ceiling. When he poured gel into his hands, I enjoyed the scent of the masculine fragrance and let him rub it into my hair.

Moaning at how good it felt, I pressed my forehead to his chest and let him tend to me. He massaged my scalp then rinsed me clean, and then, with some soap, he cleansed every other inch of me. Not leaving a single part of me dirty.

I loved it. Loved the attention. Wanted more of it, if I was being honest, and knew that was foolhardy because this man was here to use me. Just because I felt like I was floating on cloud nine didn't mean he was, too.

When he touched me between my legs, I released a sharp hiss. The sound was so raw that he jerked in surprise. I hadn't meant to make him jump like that, and my cheeks burned in response, but he tutted me.

"Don't be embarrassed. I fucked you hard last night, and you took me. Every inch. It will be better next time," he promised, and, God, there it was again.

Those two dangerous words.

Next time.

He'd said that a few times, and the promise inherent in them was enough to make my heart skip a beat.

I should be wanting out of this place, out of this man's life, his world. And yet, the things he made me feel? I was hungry for them. Greedy for them. Having never experienced them before, having never even imagined the power of what a man and a woman could share together, I wanted to explore it all with this unique creature who'd made me feel these wonderful things.

I didn't want to leave here even though I knew he was dangerous. Though, I knew his 'colleagues' were vile human beings.

Finn was, too, really.

Hadn't he manipulated me into being here?

Hadn't he used my secret meetings with my father for his own gain?

And yet, as he cleansed my pussy with a tenderness that almost made my eyes swim with tears, I had to wonder if I was dealing with Dr. Jekyll and Mr. Hyde here.

How could the same man be capable of two separate types of behavior?

When I was clean, he switched off the shower, grabbed a towel from the swanky heated radiator, and wrapped it around me before he grabbed a shorter one for my hair.

"Dry it and watch," he ordered me, surprising me into stillness until I figured out what he was doing.

The water came on, and this time, he cleaned himself. I watched him soap up all that hard muscle, watched the tendons in his arms flex as he washed his hair. I saw his throat move as he rinsed those silky black locks after shampooing it, and then, his hand went to his cock.

I released a moan as he began to jack off.

My pussy clenched, feeling so goddamn empty as I watched him find pleasure in his fist.

Fuck! That should be my hand. He should let *me* do that to him, even if I didn't really have a clue what to do to give him so much pleasure.

His eyes were glittering again as he stared at me from under dark brows, and I could tell my response excited him. His skin flushed red at his cheekbones, and his stomach muscles clenched as I realized his climax was approaching.

"Do you want my cum in your mouth?" he asked, his voice husky.

Shaken by the question, I was left wondering what the fuck was wrong with me because my answer was a hoarse, "Yes."

He smirked at me, and it was arrogant enough to make me want to hit him. Only, I didn't. When he told me to get on my knees, I didn't even give a damn about the cold tiles against my joints, didn't give a fuck that I was getting cold from not having dried off properly. All I could think about was having his cock in my mouth again.

"Open wide," he directed, and I did, I even stuck out my tongue slightly, and he tapped the crest of his shaft against it. My mouth watered at the taste of him. Last night, it had been kind of gross, but now I knew what it represented, and I wanted it.

I wanted every drop.

He laid his shaft there and gritted out, "Don't fucking move. Just watch me come. Swallow. Every. Fucking. Drop."

The way he ground out the words was almost like he was in pain. After last night, I knew what that variance of pain felt like, and I almost empathized with him. Then, his cock spurted, and his seed drenched my mouth. I quickly swallowed, not wanting to waste a drop by gagging on having too much liquid in my mouth.

With a grunt, he tugged at his shaft, milking himself dry.

I was trembling by the time he finished, and when he brushed his shaft around my lips like he was applying lipstick, I couldn't even find it in myself to care.

For the first time in my life, I was in lust. Head over heels with it. It couldn't have been at a worse time, couldn't have been with a man more wrong for me than Finn, and yet, my body had spoken.

For however long he wanted me, I was his.

15

——————

FINN

WITH A CUP of coffee in my hand, I leaned against the doorjamb of my bedroom.

As expected, the mice that were Aidan's clean-up crew had infiltrated my home and the evidence that had sullied my salon had disappeared while we'd slept.

The hall-long blood stain had been cleansed away, even the stains on my upholstered dining chair.

Even though the architect had gone, even though traces of his 'excretions' had, too, I'd still been pissed at the necessity.

I couldn't even say that it was the first time Aidan had pulled such a dick move before, just never in my goddamn home.

That was the trouble with my line of work, though. Nowhere was sacred.

As I took a deep sip from my mug, I kept my gaze focused on the woman currently dressing herself.

She didn't know I was there. Hadn't for the past ten minutes.

Her lack of environmental awareness concerned me, even if I *knew* that I'd been purposely clandestine with my movements. I was standing on the outer side of the bedroom door, not the inner, and I hadn't announced my presence.

With Aidan bouncing around like a demented basketball, the last thing I needed was Aoife being totally unaware of her surroundings.

Still, even as I groused, I didn't make a move to announce the fact I was there.

Why would I?

I'd loved watching her dress.

Normally, I liked watching a woman *undress*, but with Aoife? The tiny moves she made were almost as sensual as a strip tease.

I loved that she'd asked for a pair of my briefs to wear under her jeans. Loved it. Fuck. She wasn't coy. Hadn't made a joke about going bare. But my underwear rubbed against her cunt and would do so until I took her home. . . .

That got my cock way more excited than it should have been after last night.

I swear, I hadn't climaxed as hard and as often as that since I was a kid.

I wasn't exactly old, but you aged fast in this business. The stress levels weren't exactly easy to monitor, and when you were feeling overwhelmed, it wasn't like you could take a six-month sabbatical and go away to drown your sorrows on some Caribbean beach.

I'd never been on vacation.

Ever.

I guess if I'd asked Aidan, he'd have granted me some time, but in his defense, he never stopped working, either. None of us did.

It was that kind of fast-paced lifestyle.

While I was only thirty-seven, I still had thirty-seven years' worth of experience, and in those many years, I'd never had a night like I had last night.

Aoife was so earthy, so goddamn sensual that it seemed to flow from her to me.

Anything I'd wanted, it hadn't been too much. She hadn't been coy then, either. She'd thrown herself into everything we'd done with a passion I'd never felt before.

It made me wonder how many women who'd writhed under me had gotten off like she had. Had they faked it? The thought should be a bruise to my ego, but it wasn't. Not when Aoife had responded to me like a duck took to water.

Just watching her drag my briefs over the curve of her ass, seeing the fabric tauten around her butt and hips, pull tight around her thighs, had my eyes narrowing. I could see from her cheeks she was flushed. She tutted at how small the briefs were on her, and I didn't have to be a mind reader to know she wasn't happy about that.

Aoife wasn't a small woman.

And I adored her like that.

She was curvy and round, her body perfect for my tastes, my needs. She was, I guessed, thick. Solid. Every inch of her made for me.

When she twisted, bending down for her pants, I got a view of her slit, making my mouth water and my cock harden. *Again.* The folds of her sex were clearly visible through the briefs, and I clenched my teeth against the sight.

Jesus Christ, I could take her now.

Bend her over the bed and fuck her like there was no tomorrow, as though last night hadn't happened. As though my cock wasn't well-sated.

When she was dressed, I murmured, "Do you want breakfast?"

She released a low shriek and spun around to face me. Her cheeks, already pink, grew brighter, but she didn't chide me for sneaking up on her, even though from her furrowed brow and the fire in her eyes, I could see she wanted to.

My lips curved at the sight.

Fight me, sweetheart. Go on. Do it.

My words were internal, but they were encouraging. I wanted to see the true redhead temper, wanted to feel its burn. But she didn't give it to me.

I was semi-disappointed when she swallowed, gulping it down to murmur, "I-I should get back."

"No, you should eat breakfast first," I countered. I wasn't going to be able to see her for a few days. Not with the clusterfuck of yesterday to deal with—our architect wouldn't go to the cops, but Aidan had still shot him in the thigh, and Eoghan had to dig around in the wound to not only get the bullet out, but to make it look as though the guy had been slashed with a knife.

By that point, the poor bastard had been passed out dead cold. Still, I needed to make sure this wouldn't come back on us, and that the man was being taken care of—I needed him back on site as soon as possible.

Hey, less of the fucking judgment. He shouldn't have gotten into bed with us if he didn't want to risk dancing with the devil.

The man was paid well for his services, and I had no doubt I'd be authorizing a bonus as an apology from Aidan very shortly.

Some hands took and others gave.

It was the way of it.

With that to deal with, as well as the fact she was going to be sore for a few days, I knew I wouldn't be seeing her soon. Just being around her made me want to be inside her, and not only did I not need the break in focus, but she also needed some rest.

She wasn't a cheap slut that I didn't want to take care of, one whose state of being I didn't give a fuck about.

She was mine.

I cared for what belonged to me.

"I'm not hungry," she mumbled, dropping her gaze from mine.

"It's clean out there," I informed her briskly. If she was going to be around me, she'd have to get used to violence. It was an integral part of my world.

After swallowing again, she looked at me, and I knew she must have seen my inexorable stance. I wasn't about to let her weasel out of stepping deeper into my home than this bedroom. She'd have to get used to the place—I was ripping off the Band-Aid instead of letting her concerns fester.

I straightened from my position at the door and held out my free hand. When she eyed it like it was a cobra, irritation rattled through me, and I had to force myself to calm down. I wanted to be gentle with her.

As far as yesterday's plan was concerned, I'd gotten what I wanted. Her, in my bed, for a night. Usually that was enough, but now? It wasn't enough. It would never be enough.

I'd flung my weight about knowing it would pressure her to sleep with me, but if I wanted her to keep coming back, I couldn't be a bastard to her.

Trouble was, bastard was my usual state of being.

So, while I wanted to stride forward, grab her hand, and drag her down the hall, I didn't.

I composed myself, waiting a good forty seconds with her nibbling her bottom lip as she finally crossed the short distance between us.

When her fingers slipped into my hand, I squeezed them. Not tight enough to hurt, but tight enough for her to feel that I wasn't letting go.

She should get used to that feeling.

Tension strummed through her as we stepped out into the hall, but as we moved down the corridor and toward the salon, she released a soundless breath.

Relief was its principle source.

Rolling my eyes, I told her, "I'm many things, Aoife, but I'm not a liar. I won't, and will not, lie to you."

That had her head whipping to the side to gape at me—a move that I should have taken great offense over, but I didn't. Couldn't. In my line of work, whether it was the legit property development side of things or the shit I pulled for the Points, it could be said that we all needed the gift of the gab to get out of trouble.

Not me, though.

I didn't lie.

In the Five Points, lying merely had someone above you in the ranks coming at you with a knife to slice out your tongue.

Aidan hated liars.

"Lying is a serious offense in the Five Points," I told her gruffly, not sure why I was explaining but explaining nonetheless.

From the way her gaze was glued to the side of my face, I figured she was surprised, too.

"It is?"

"You know our reputation. Aidan O'Donnelly is a Catholic. Lying is a sin."

A shaky breath soughed from her lungs. "I'm not him, though. You don't have to tell me the truth."

I snorted at that. "You'd be surprised how much easier life is when you don't bullshit and you don't lie. I tell you true—I will not lie to you.

"Last night, Aidan's clean-up crew came and cleansed the place. It's spic and span again."

She didn't reply, but I could sense she was curious now—not that she answered its call. She remained silent as I guided her into the kitchen. A small gasp escaped her when we entered the room.

"My God, it's beautiful," she whispered, and I was reminded that she was the baker who had powered her small tea room from a run-of-the-mill cafe to something people spoke about on social media.

Did I feel guilty about taking away her business and the rep she'd worked so hard to grow?

Yesterday? No. I could say that you'd win some and you'd lose some. Today? Yeah. I felt bad.

Because of that, I wriggled my shoulders as she took in the expansive room.

I didn't cook. Ever. It just wasn't something I'd ever been encouraged to do. I'd been raised in a male dominant household, and even though my old man had been a cunt, his teachings had continued when I'd moved in with Aidan and his sons.

Magdalena cooked.

If Aidan entered her domain, her kitchen, she'd have whipped his butt with a towel and told him to get out of there. Even if he'd *wanted* to cook, which he wouldn't, ever, she'd never have allowed him to.

Because I didn't cook, the kitchen shouldn't have been important to me, but I had good memories of watching Lena cook, of even watching my bitch mother prepare evening meals while I did my homework.

It might sound like bullshit coming from a man like me, but the kitchen was the heart of every home. How appropriate was it that I was bringing someone into that very heart, someone who loved cooking.

"Seriously, this is absolutely stunning," she whispered, spinning around like some women might if I'd taken them to Harry Winston's or Tiffany's. I could almost see the drool longing to fall from the corners of her mouth.

The kitchen had a central island that was the size of a large dining table. Down the back side of it, there were red leather counter seats, and I released her hand to take my place there. She ran her hand down the length of the gleaming black marble, took in the central stove and sink that was in the island, then looked around the rest of the counters that were empty of gadgets. Cream cupboards lined the upper and lower walls on two sides, hiding some of the appliances from view. A large, humming fridge purred at one side, and she moved over to it, running a hand down to the handle like she'd touched my cock last night—reverently.

My lips twitched at that comparison, and I murmured, "If you don't mind cooking . . . you can make whatever you want for breakfast, or I can call in for some take out."

Her shoulders stiffened at that as she shot an outraged look at me. "I'll cook," was all she said, though, and once again, I was left amused by her stance.

Watching her maneuver around my kitchen made my chest pang with new and unusual feelings. There'd never been any woman in here. Not cooking anyway. One might have gone to the fridge for some water or beer, but they'd never cooked, and somehow, that felt right.

Like this space was hers.

My thoughts were enough to make me want to bash my head into the marble counter, but instead, I just accepted them. I was fucked over this woman, and I had no idea why.

Watching her move around this space was like watching a ballerina dance, and before I knew it, before my very eyes, she'd managed to find everything she needed—which was a miracle as the cupboards might as well have been empty for all I knew, not just of staples but of the appropriate kitchen tools—and had whipped up a stack of pancakes and served it with bacon.

I hadn't expected that.

Most women I dated ate salad around me, and like I said, they'd never cooked around me, either. Still, I wasn't about to fucking complain.

I'd half expected some miserly egg white omelet, especially when she'd started whisking a shit ton of egg whites, but instead, I was faced with the fluffiest motherfucking flapjacks I'd ever had.

As she cooked, I didn't say much. Just let her work and kept an eye on my emails and messages as I sat there. Normally, I was in the office by now. Fuck, sometimes I was in there at four in the morning.

Today?

No chance.

When she served up a large stack for myself and a small portion for her, I smiled at her in thanks. "I didn't expect this. Thank you."

Her cheeks bloomed with heat. "I-I thought after a workout, you might like something that will fill you all day. I-I guess I didn't have to use the bacon, but I use more eggs in my recipe, so the two sources of protein should—"

I reached for her chin and forced her to look at me. "I wasn't asking for a nutritional breakdown. Thank you. I can't wait to dive in."

She shot me a wary smile, and I cursed at a society that made a woman who was just fucking curvy question every bite she ate.

Jesus, what were we doing to the kids of today?

And even as the thought crossed my mind, I asked myself when I'd even started thinking gobshite like that.

Drenching my pancakes with syrup, I tucked in, and moaned after I got my first taste. "Fuck. These are good," I told her, half moaning the words, too. "Christ almighty."

Her lips curved. "Blasphemy."

"Worth any and all the repentance Father Doyle asks of me. Fuck, Aoife, fuck!" Seriously, this shit? It was fucking good. "Did you serve these at the tea room?"

Her mouth pinched as she shook her head and daintily forked up some of her own meal. "No. It wasn't that kind of place. I baked mostly cakes and made a lot of amuse bouches. Tiny little canapés, you know? I was getting a name for my scones, though. They're like the English sweet version of our biscuits. And my cookies and bread were popular, too."

My mouth watered. "Would you bake me some bread?"

The question startled her, and she reared back in surprise—shit, it more than surprised her. She almost fell off the counter seat. I grabbed her and steadied her, relieved she didn't flinch from my touch. I'd half expected her to, but she didn't.

Because it felt right, I didn't move my hand away. I pressed it to her lap and kept it there, letting my fingers dip into the seam of her thighs. I felt her press her legs together and wondered if I'd caused an ache to stir inside her also.

"You'd want me to?" she asked, sounding dumbstruck.

"Please?" There was a hoarseness to my voice that stunned me. The last time someone had properly baked anything for *me* was when I'd been back home.

Yeah, even though I hated my parents, I still considered the place where hell had been dished out to me, *home.*

Only fuck knew what a shrink would make of that.

"Now?" she questioned, her words a whisper.

"After breakfast?" I forked up some food, then after I'd swallowed, stated, "I have to leave soon. Business. But feel free to use the kitchen. It's yours to play with."

She gaped at me. "You're okay with me just hanging out here?"

"I'm more than okay with it if I get some fresh bread out of it." As she licked her lips and went to speak, I told her, "Samuel, my driver, will return here after he takes me to my office. I'll give him your number, and you can arrange with him when you'd like Sam to take you home. Okay?"

There were a million questions in her eyes, but she just nodded. "O-Okay."

She didn't eat much else, and I frowned down at her half full plate and my empty one. "Not hungry?" I inquired.

She shot me a tight smile. "Not really."

Narrowing my eyes at her, I murmured, "Was that a lie, Aoife?"

Her shoulders stiffened, and I wasn't sure if that was because she'd been caught out or if it was in umbrage. When I leaned over, cut off a piece of flapjack with my fork, speared it on the tines then pressed it to her mouth, she parted her lips and accepted the offering.

"Never underfeed yourself around me, Aoife," I ground out, not sure why I was so mad, just aware that I was.

She licked a drop of syrup that quivered along her bottom lip, and I almost groaned at the sight. "All right, Finn. I won't."

I fed her a few more bites, loving how she accepted them, how she didn't question this weird need I had to feed her.

"Honestly, I'm full," she told me after I'd given her several mouthfuls, and this time, I believed her.

"Good," I stated as I climbed to my feet. When she made to move, I asked, "Aoife? Who's the Senator to you?"

That her tension immediately reappeared at that question had irritation battering me, but I forced my temper back. I'd gentled her so far this morning, and I didn't intend on wrecking my advance.

"Does it matter?" she squeaked.

I clenched my jaw. *Did it matter?* The man wasn't fucking her. I'd had the proof of that around my cock last night. Whoever he was, though, he had to mean a lot to her for them to visit as often and as clandestinely as they did.

I had my suspicions, but I could wait to have them answered.

As I'd fed her, her cheeks had grown rosy with pleasure. Her eyelids had been drooping lazily. Now? After my question? She was tense again.

Though I'd raised the topic, I despised the fact another man had brought some walls up between us. Then I had to remind myself that Aoife had only known me for a few hours, and that what she did know of me wouldn't make anyone all that at ease with 'sharing.'

She'd learn, though. And soon.

I moved to her side and dipped my head, pressing a kiss to her mouth, I bit at her bottom lip, raking it with my teeth. I fucking loved how she whimpered at that move, her tension of seconds before bleeding out like it had never existed.

"Later on tonight, I'm going to think of you, baking in this kitchen, and I'm going to jerk off to it." I reached back and pressed my finger to her mouth. When she sucked it in, my cock leaped to attention, and I was hard pressed not to moan as I thrust my finger between her lips for a few seconds.

When I pulled out, she nipped at my fingertip, making me groan. Her eyes were sparkling for the first time that morning and I knew, point blank, that the way to get her more comfortable around me, the way to make her at ease with my sudden intrusion in her life, was to overwhelm her with sex.

Because I couldn't do that to her, not when she had to be sore as fuck, I had to take myself out of the equation.

Earlier on, I'd known that. I had business to take care of, I needed my focus, while she needed to heal. But now? The very prospect had me cursing.

My hands turned into fists as I gritted out, "Be good," and then, without a backward glance, I stormed out.

Fifteen hours later, after several meetings from hell with Aidan and my brothers, when I walked into my home, the sweet scent of freshly baked bread hit me.

I'd forgotten.

Not Aoife, never her, but my request. I'd forgotten that I'd asked her to make me some. Now, my house scented of the gift she'd left me, and it reminded me of how fucking empty the penthouse was.

I stalked toward the kitchen, uncaring that all I'd intended on doing was heading for the shower to jack off and clean up before diving into bed.

The sight of five loaves on the counter had my lips curving.

They were like what my mother had used to make. Farmhouse white, she'd called it. Big things like cartoon loaves. All doughy and pillowy, not sweet like the bread here.

It was uncanny how I knew what the bread would taste like before I even cut into it, slathered it with butter, and took a bite.

The taste of home hit me, and for once, it didn't turn my stomach. Before things had been *so* bad, my mom and I had been close. This reminded me of those times.

As I chomped on three slices, I reached for my cell. It was two AM, and Aidan had brought me back here after a meeting at his office. I'd seen no point in calling Samuel out from his warm bed, but now that I was here, I had questions.

Me: *Did Aoife get home safely?*

It didn't take Sam even thirty seconds to reply—it didn't matter that it was late.

Samuel: *Yes. She left at four—covered in flour she was, too. Gave me a loaf of bread of all things.*

Me: *Good. Enjoy the bread. I need you here at six tomorrow.*

Samuel: *Sure thing, boss.*

Putting the phone down, I smiled at the thought of her baking half a dozen loaves. As I looked at the army of bread, I had to concede that it wouldn't take me long to power through it.

In fact, I might be on the last loaf when I could finally bring her back here, and claim her as mine again.

16

———

AOIFE

I winced. "Me, either."

Jenny and I both stood outside what had been, until five days ago, my tea room.

Like rats that had left the sinking ship, the building was now vacated, and Acuig had builders swarming all over the place like fleas.

Even knowing Finn was at the head of Acuig—or Aidan O'Donnelly, I figured to be accurate—I hated what I was seeing.

It hurt knowing that the place Mom and I had built together would be no more.

"What made you do it, Eef?" she asked, shortening my name the way I'd allow only her to do. The nickname made me sound like some kind of Vape manufacturer, and only she could get away with it, considering I'd known her since I was ten years old, and she'd been at my side through most of the crappiest parts of my life.

This included.

"The money was too good to be true," I half-lied. I couldn't exactly tell her about my father, could I? Not even Jenny knew the Senator was my biological dad.

"That sucks. Are you going to open somewhere new?"

I pondered that a second, and shook my head. When disappointment flashed over her features, something I only saw thanks to her reflection in a car that trundled by, I murmured, "Not a tea room."

"Not a tea room?" She frowned. "Then, what else?"

"A bakery. Just a bakery."

"With a store front?"

"Of course. Where else could you sell stuff for me?"

She grinned at me. "Really?"

"Yeah. Really." I elbowed her gently. "I just don't know where."

"Has to be this neighborhood. Your rep has already soared, so let's face it, not being in this vicinity would just be stupid."

"True. But it limits us. It's not like there's a nice storefront around here that we don't know about."

She harrumphed. "We could think outside the box."

"We could?" I cocked a brow at her. "I'm all ears."

While she fell silent, I turned back to stare at the little cafe that had been the culmination of years of my mother's hopes and dreams. I felt so sad that it was coming to an end. Like a final chapter of a book I wasn't ready to put down, and yet, the tea room wasn't *my* dream.

I hated being nice to people.

Seriously.

I know it made me sound like a bitch, but I didn't want to be sociable, I wanted to bake. I wanted to try new pie recipes, make my name Insta-famous. I wanted to start the newest trends and have people coming from all over the States to find my treats.

That was my dream.

I refused to think that, in his own way, Finn had set me free. By paying above the market value, I had more than enough to buy the things I needed. And most of the equipment was paid off. Thanks to my father.

After that first initial meeting those many years ago, I'd had a call from the bank telling me that my student loans, as well as all the debt under my name, was cleared.

Yeah, talk about a big old birthday gift.

At first, I'd thought it was like a 'keep quiet' payment, but when he'd sent me a burner phone that was only for him to use, I'd realized it was to take the pressure off me.

I was lucky, I guess. Or maybe the fact that I hadn't demanded anything from him had made it easier for him to want to get to know me?

I didn't know, probably never would. Still, I was in a good position because of him and Finn. Especially when Dad had helped me after Mom's death. It meant that I could probably afford better premises than I even knew.

"What about that old hair salon on Seventh?"

I curled my nose. "The stench of old peroxide is stained into the floor."

She snorted then raised her hand and began to tick off on her fingers, "It's big. It has an outdoor space where we could put a few tables for people wanting to just sit down rather than run off on the go. It would probably be easy to customize the place to how you need it, and also, it's been empty for ages. The owner would probably snatch your fingers if he thought you were interested in renting that place."

I gnawed on my bottom lip. "That is very true."

"I think we should go get a coffee," she told me softly, and I realized I'd been staring at the building, while she'd been staring at me for only God knew how long.

"Yeah, sure," I replied, but my answer was lackluster.

She tipped her head to the side. "He screwed you, didn't he?"

"Screwed me?" I squeaked, my eyes flaring wide.

Jenny smirked. "Thought as much. Also thought you were walking a bit stiffly this morning." She let out a low moan that had my cheeks flushing crimson. "He looks like the type of guy who knows what to do with his body. Was he good? Was he big?" She groaned, like she was turning herself on with thoughts of *my* man.

That phrasing, even though it was inwardly spoken, had me freezing internally.

Finn wasn't 'my' anything.

I needed to come to terms with that very, very quickly.

"Eef," she whined. "Please. I need the details. I need to live vicariously through you."

I had to laugh at her melodramatics. "That's a change. Normally I'm living through you."

She pouted. "I know. Gah, you're lucky I love you like a sister, or I'd be jealous as hell. As it stands, I'm just relieved you got laid, and he popped your damn cherry. Now, just promise he did it well, so I won't go and knee him in the balls."

When her tone went from lusty to growly, I was touched that she cared enough for me to give a shit whether Finn had made it good for me or not.

Of course, we were like sisters, but Jenny was weird with men. That whole 'bros before hoes' thing? Well, in reverse, that wasn't how she lived her life.

I mean, I loved her, too, but she would dump me as soon as a guy in a bar waved at her from across the room.

I was used to it, even if, once upon a time, it had pissed me off.

"It was like . . ." I couldn't even describe what that first night with Finn had been like. The two subsequent nights after, I hadn't heard from him, and had been certain his promise of 'next time' had just been BS. Then, the third night, the car had appeared out of nowhere at my side on Canal Street, and he'd pushed open the door with a ground out, "Get the fuck inside."

I'd been surprised as hell, but something in me had leapt to obey.

I wasn't the obeying sort. That was why I loved owning my own business. Liked being the boss, and where my kitchen was concerned,

I ruled with an iron fist. But with Finn? It was like all that turned to dust.

I'd climbed in, and the minute the door had closed, he'd been on me like pastrami on rye. His mouth devouring me, his body pinning mine to the seat.

Even as I'd tried to get my breath, he'd bitten off against my mouth, "You're fucking addictive."

He hadn't sounded happy about it, but I'd definitely been content at his statement.

Later that night, he'd told me he'd had no choice but to avoid me for two days. If he hadn't, he'd have fucked me, and he knew I needed to heal.

It was like reverse chivalry, but I was learning I was far too easy where Finn was concerned.

I'd determined, though, that I needed to cut myself some slack.

Jenny went through more guys than I did panties, and she was used to the hustle. Used to the game. I wasn't. This was new to me. I was allowed to be overwhelmed, allowed to act like a fool for this, my first foray into what went down between men and women in the bedroom, and I'd also allowed myself to hurt and to rage when he eventually decided things were over.

It all sounded very wishy-washy, but I was on the bullet train to Finn-sville, and it was a direct stop.

There was no avoiding him when he could and would appear in my life at his whim, and more than anything, there was no avoiding what he could make me feel.

Many women might judge me as pathetic, might say Finn was using me for sex, but I'd challenge them to spend a night with a man like Finn O'Grady and not be affected. Truth was, I loved the way he bossed me around. I loved the way I wanted to obey because every-thing he asked of me was so damn dirty, it felt wrong to comply without being pressured into it. If he used me for sex, I was using him right back, and to me, that was Feminism 101.

Except, in my class, I came out with a shit-ton of orgasms, some that were close to nuclear, and I also came out of it with a body confidence that was better than six months of dieting.

I was suddenly hyperaware of my form. Of my strong legs, of my round breasts. Finn seemed to have taken the shutters off, and I was loving it.

"You know the sex you see in movies?" I finally said, managing to get some of my thoughts into words.

"Porn or regular?"

I pondered that. "A bit of both?"

She moaned again. "You lucky bitch!" she whined, and hell, I couldn't disagree.

Laughing as we headed into the nearest coffee shop that had, until five days ago, been my direct competition, we ordered coffee at the counter then headed for a small seating area.

As we plunked ourselves in the comfortable seats, I told her, "He's filthy, Jenny."

"Fuck," she whispered back. "How filthy?"

"Super filthy."

She snickered. "Only you could say that so piously."

"I went to Catholic school," I teased her.

"So did I!" she retorted, but we both laughed because Jenny had attended, but she'd spent most of the time not trying to learn or get her diploma, instead trying to get Father Bryan, the only priest on campus under thirty-five and who was surprisingly dishy, into her bed.

She'd spent years attempting to ruin the man's vows, and I was really glad she'd never managed it.

Jenny wore her sexuality like a suit of armor around her. It pissed me off sometimes, but she was my friend, and I could talk to her about anything.

Well, anything except my father. That was, for his sake, a no-go.

And though I was talking about Finn, there were some things I just couldn't discuss. Like how, that first morning, he'd fed me breakfast. How I'd felt his eyes on me as I'd moved around his kitchen. His request that I bake him bread, while anything but sexual, felt so intrinsically private, that I couldn't share that with anyone.

I'd used Fiona's recipe. It was imprinted in my brain anyway, and I guess I'd been mean trying to remind him of home. . . .

I wasn't sure if he'd been serious, first off. Asking your sexual partner to bake you some bread had to be one of the oddest requests around, right? Then, I hadn't been sure if I'd ever see him again. He'd been tender with me that morning, tender but strained. I'd felt certain I'd never see him again, even though he'd left me with the images of him jacking off that morning.

So, even though I'd complied with his request, I'd tried to make it bittersweet for him by reminding him of the mother he'd abandoned years before.

As I'd made the dough, kneading it by hand as Fiona had taught me, wasting hours at Finn's place while I let it rise then bake, I'd realized how much I'd missed baking. It was what had prompted me to think of this venture.

I wanted to bake. Nothing more, nothing less.

I didn't want to piss around with tiny canapés. I didn't want to deal with fiddly amuse bouches to tempt the tiny appetites of size-zero women.

I wanted, I'd realized as I knocked back the dough in Finn's ultra luxurious kitchen, to go back to my roots.

After I took a sip of coffee, I stated, "Fancy coming to the salon with me now?"

Jenny blinked at me. "Hell, yeah."

I nodded and downed the rest of my coffee, something in me settling as I felt like this was the right move to make. "If the management company can't fit me in then we can just case out the area."

Jenny snorted. "Honey, if they're not around like a fucking shot, they're morons. That place has been empty for years."

My lips curved at her statement. Jenny had many flaws but when it boiled down to it, she never packed her punches. Because I was accustomed to that, I figured it would keep me in good stead for however long Finn O'Grady graced my bed.

He might have my head in the clouds, but Jenny would ensure my feet stayed firmly on the ground.

17

FINN

I'D NEVER LIKED anyone watching me sleep, and had never appreciated the notion of watching anyone sleep, either.

It was fucking creepy in my mind, but Aoife was so goddamn peaceful that sometimes, I couldn't stop myself from waking up, and rather than heading to my personal gym, just watching her. The way her lashes fluttered in REM sleep, the way she slept on her side, her tits smushed together and quivering with each breath she took—it was like watching an angel. An angel with really big tits.

Yeah. I knew I sounded crazy. Knew that this *thing*, whatever the fuck it was, had taken on a life of its own, but even crazier, I was okay with that.

Was okay with this need that was unfurling inside of me for her.

It was pitch black outside—that happened when you woke up at three AM—and in the distance, the city lights sent tiny glittering specks along her creamy form. I wanted to touch her. I always wanted to touch her. Wanted to connect with her, and not always sexually, either.

My heartbeat seemed to slow when I was around her, and so far, we'd done nothing but fuck and eat together. I barely knew her, and I wanted that to change. I wanted to know everything, and not from some fucking file, but from her lips. I wanted everything, the full story, in her words.

This craving to know all of her came as a slight shock. I never usually gave a fuck about any of my other lays, but everything about Aoife was unusual.

She shuffled in her sleep, dragging me from my thoughts, and carefully, I crept out of bed, not wanting to disturb her. Only whack jobs like me got up at this time of the night, but I had a schedule to fulfill and these nutty hours were a part of it.

When I padded over to the bathroom, I had to shake my head at the clothes I'd put in there before bed last night. Yeah. I didn't want to disturb her so much that I'd begun anticipating the need to grab workout gear before I slept.

My throat tightened at whatever the fuck that meant as I pulled on a pair of basketball shorts and a shirt. I always dumped my sneakers in the gym, so I padded out, letting one long lingering glance drift over her resting form before I told myself to man the fuck up and get on with my day.

An hour on the treadmill loosened shit up, and with BBC World News on the box, I caught up with daily events around the world and monitored some of my personal investments. Switching gears helped. I had a lot of responsibilities, a lot of men to manage—some to even micromanage—and I didn't have time to be constantly thinking about Aoife like some pock-marked teenager who'd just figured out what his pecker was for.

By the time I finished running, I'd stripped out of my shirt and tossed it on the ground after wiping my torso down with it. Stepping over to the dumbbells, I started my free weight workout, and then, I jerked in surprise because in the mirror, as I watched my form for accuracy, I saw her there.

Watching me.

I hadn't felt her presence, and in my job, that was the first lesson

—environmental awareness was the difference between you getting shot in the head and walking away free and clear.

She was wrapped in a sheet, looking like a siren come to invade my thoughts after I'd only just cleared them.

I wanted to be mad at her, but shit, it wasn't her fault, was it?

"I didn't mean to disturb you."

Fuck, could that have sounded any grumpier?

Her cheeks flushed as she realized I'd caught her, and I had to grin. Turning around to mute the TV, I cocked my head at her when I faced her once more. "You okay?"

She licked her lips. "It's always surprising how . . ." Hesitation hit her, and she cleared her throat before blurting out, "big you are."

I couldn't stop myself from snorting. "Music to any man's ear."

"Oh, hush," she chided. "You know what I mean."

"I do. Exactly." I grinned and saw her eyes start to twinkle at my teasing. "Feel free to work out in here if you want, Aoife. I should have offered before."

"I don't really do gyms." She ducked her head. "I guess that shows, huh?"

I scowled at that. The last thing I'd intended was to make her conscious of herself. I'd just wanted her to know that *mi casa es su casa*. Striding over to her, I grabbed her chin and forced her to look at me. "Have I ever made you feel like I wanted to change how you look?"

"You've only known me ten days, Finn," she said wryly, but there was some color back in her cheeks.

"Well? In ten days, have I done anything other than worship your body?"

Her voice was small. "No."

"Well, then. This gym, use it, don't use it. Look out of the window if you want or pilfer the fridge for Gatorade, I don't give a fuck, Aoife. I was just trying to say, shittily, that you can use this place like your own."

A gasp escaped her. "I couldn't do that, Finn!"

"I'm giving you permission, Aoife." I cocked a brow at her. "And we both know how I appreciate it when you obey me."

She slapped her hand against my chest. "Shut up, you," she blurted out, and when her fingers connected with my chest, I was suddenly conscious of how sweaty I was.

"I need to shower." Before I could take a step back, she slid her hand over my chest, her fingers dipping and digging into my muscles. I watched her lick her lips, amused that she was turned on when I was drenched with perspiration.

"No, you don't," she half-purred, and my cock, sensing Aoife was goddamn close *and* horny like it had radar, began to stand at attention.

If she didn't think I was gross, then who was I to fucking complain?

I watched as she let the sheet drop, exposing every inch of her creamy skin to my ardent gaze. Against the navy walls, she looked like a bright light on a foggy day. Everything about her beckoned me, almost like she was a beacon, and I was lost.

I pressed myself into her and shoved her against the wall so that I could further enjoy the contrast between her and the navy. When I grabbed her hands and dragged them over her head, her tits brushed against my pecs as they shifted with the movement. With one fist, I kept her wrists cuffed together, and I ducked my head to press a kiss to her mouth.

As she moaned into my lips, I thrust my tongue against hers. She tasted of mouthwash, and it made me smirk to think she'd prepared for exactly this moment.

Even when I tried to be gentle with her, I couldn't. It just was outside my capabilities where she was concerned. I bit her bottom lip, tugging it back until it had to sting. Her moan of relief shuddered through me, and I pulled back to growl, "Spread your legs."

When she immediately obeyed, my dick began to throb, and I

slipped my free hand between her thighs. Finding her dripping wet, I pressed my forehead to hers and ground out, "What the fuck are you doing to me, Aoife?"

My lungs burned. Shit, they hadn't burned like this on my seven-mile run.

She whimpered in response, and I grated out, "Your pussy is molten, Aoife. Didn't I satisfy this greedy little thing enough last night?"

Her back arched, and I guess I had my answer. Grinning, so goddamn pleased with her I wanted to laugh, I pressed one last kiss to her lips before I dipped my head to catch one of her nipples between my teeth. I bit down. Hard. She loved it enough to squeak, and her hands struggled to escape my grasp, but there was no fucking way in hell she was going anywhere.

I laved the tip with my tongue, swirling around the areola until she whimpered, and her pelvis arched as she tried to fuck my hand, which was only covering her pussy, not actively touching it.

Nipping it again, I pressed my face between those gorgeous tits before I kissed my way to the other side. I loved these bad boys. I could get lost in the ripe generosity of her curves, and some days, I wanted nothing more than to do exactly that.

Slurping her nipple, I sucked as much of it as I could into my mouth, content when I released her to see my teeth marks around her skin and the bright-pink hue of her delicious flesh. Deciding to stop teasing her when she'd been such a good little girl, I slid a finger through her wet folds and felt her shiver as though it were my own.

"Oh, God, Finn. It feels so good." She swallowed, and I peered up at her, loving that her eyes were closed, that she was scowling at nothing, so focused on her own pleasure.

Using the heel of my wrist, I pressed it against her clit, so I could thrust two fingers into her. She was still so tight, so small, and I knew I made her sore, but she kept coming back for more. On the days where I tried to refrain, tried to hold back, she wouldn't let me.

Like this morning.

I hadn't intended on taking her until tonight, but here she was. Needing me. Exactly like I needed her.

Though she was wet, I scissored my fingers carefully, loving the snug fit. The tight clasp, and like that, it was too much. I pulled free, released her hands, and before she could complain, I hauled her up into my arms.

In seconds, we were in the bedroom. I carefully settled her on the bed, shucked out of my shorts, and grabbed a condom.

"I-I'm on the pill," she whispered, and my fingers froze around the foil wrapper.

I'd never trusted any bitch when she'd told me that, but Aoife?

I did, and that scared the shit out of me.

When I stared at her, my eyes burning with my need, her tone turned nervous as she whispered, "Irregular periods."

I gritted my teeth, clenched my jaw, and tensed the rest of my body.

I wanted in her so fucking bad that I couldn't think past getting inside her. But I was sweaty. Dirty, and I really didn't want to go for a shower now.

For a second, I realized how on edge I was. How close to losing control I felt. Then, I released a shuddery breath, and in a tone that brooked no argument, I bit off, "Next time."

Her eyes widened, but she nodded eagerly and held out her arms to me. Quickly sheathing my cock and regretting every shitty second of it, I turned to her, loving how she clung to me as I sank onto her.

"This pussy is mine, isn't it, Aoife?" I breathed against her mouth as I settled my cock between her spread lips, feeling the molten heat and wanting to sob that bare skin wasn't touching bare skin.

"It is," she whimpered. "All yours."

"Always mine?" I demanded.

"A-Always," she mewled.

That was music to my fucking ears, so I reared up, and slipped the tip of my cock into her. She clenched around me like she had the first time, and getting inside her was still a fucking back-breaking task, one I was willing to suffer through—the thought made me grin inwardly.

When I was finally inside her, she was panting, and her tits were jiggling all over the place. I eyed them, eyed her, then I grabbed her hands, bridged our fingers, and placed them on either side of her head. Pinning her down, keeping her in place.

As I looked her square in the eye, I began to pump into her. Slow, deep. Thrusting all the way inside before almost pulling all the way out.

Her eyes watered as we watched one another, and it was such an intense moment that I could understand why. Mine burned, too, and I realized I'd never felt this close to anyone, *anyone*, in my entire fucking life.

What was it with this woman?

Why did she get to me like this?

I'd noticed it from the start, and it had never been a problem. I knew that wouldn't be the case with anyone else, though. Anyone else, I'd have begrudged this closeness that had appeared like a genie floating from a lamp. But with Aoife? It was right.

It was good.

How it was supposed to be.

How long we stared at each other as I made love to her—*yeah*, I thought without a wince, *this is making love*—I couldn't say. Time could have slipped through our fingers, or it could have raced past us. All I knew was that I was here, in this moment, with her.

When she cried out her release, she broke eye contact. Her head whipped from side to side as though she couldn't contain all these feelings. I loved seeing her break, loved seeing her fall, and when her cunt clamped around me, intent on milking me dry, I let it. Knowing the next time I was inside her, I'd be feeling the real deal.

Each and every time was like a punch to the face. Not the best way to describe it, but it left me feeling punch drunk, and I slumped against her, loving how she curled her arms and legs around me, hugging me with her whole body.

My head settled against her chest, and I could hear the fast beat of her heart. It reassured me, and crazily enough, it sent me straight back to sleep.

18

———

AOIFE

SOMETHING CHANGED THAT MORNING.

After I told Finn we didn't have to use condoms, *he* changed. Not in a bad way. But in an 'I can't get inside you enough' way, and hell, I wasn't about to complain about *that*.

He'd still fuck me until I sobbed, but those moments were interspersed with passionate kisses, and he'd started holding my hand. I'd never thought that could mean so much, but it did.

He'd brought me here with a purpose. He'd wanted me, had wanted to use me, and yet, each time, each day that passed? It was like *he* changed. I felt it. You could call me crazy, but I wasn't. The way he looked at me, the way he touched me, this wasn't about business. This was real. I knew it, and no one would or could convince me otherwise.

When he claimed I was his, he wasn't messing around. He'd meant it, and God, how I wanted him to. I wanted to be his, and I wanted him to be mine.

My eyes drifted over to him. It was late, and he was still working —he worked more than anyone I knew, and I'd owned a tea room and had baked everything on the premises, so I knew what long hours felt like. We were in his office, not the kitchen, and I was sketching ideas of how I wanted the layout of the bakery to look. I was no artist, but I didn't need to be. I just wanted a rough working idea of where my equipment would go.

As my pencil scratched over the paper, Finn typed away like a demon on his computer.

I liked that he wanted me in here. After we'd eaten the meal I'd cooked for us, when he'd said he needed to work in his office, I'd offered to go to the salon—you know, the room where someone had been shot, gulp—but he'd dragged me in here with him.

Not that I was about to complain.

Finn was like a magnet, and I was a puny pile of iron filings that had no choice but to gravitate toward him.

Cutting him a look, I saw he was scowling at something in the distance. His office was set up so that his desk was on the back wall. He overlooked the seating area and had a view of the city.

In here, it was more modern. A silver desk with one of those expensive ergonomic chairs complemented a thick pile, emerald green rug. I was on one of two white leather L-shape sofas, with the Ls creating a kind of box. He had some framed lithographs on the wall, at least, I thought they were prints. With his wealth, maybe they were real.

But as I watched him, he looked so stark over there. So alone that I hated it.

From a drawer, he pulled out a letter opener and a pile of envelopes. The move was so old-fashioned that I almost smirked as he began to open his mail—at eleven PM at night—and I found that he fascinated me more than my prospective venture.

When he released a hissed-out breath and cursed, "Shit," I was on my feet and heading toward him.

"What is it? What's wrong?" I asked, already next to him.

He grunted. "Cut my finger. It's nothing."

Before he could even push his chair back, I grabbed his hand, studied the small cut, and felt relief swirl through me. I didn't even realize what I'd done until I'd done it. And by the time I had, we were both frozen, his finger in my mouth as I sucked at the blood welling from the cut.

It was such an intimate move that I couldn't quite believe I'd done it, but from the fire in his eyes? I knew he'd liked it.

My heart began to thud heavily in my chest, and every part of me quickened, ready to burn with him.

"Suck harder," he rasped, and I complied. As I always did when he used that tone.

I swirled my tongue around the tip, watching as he shuddered, and when he snarled, "Take off your pants," I did as bid when he pulled his finger free from my lips.

The second I was naked from the waist down, he bit out, "Bend over the desk."

And then, he showed me what magic he really could work in this office as he fucked me. With the view of Manhattan and stars in front of me, Finn took me to another place, another time, another universe where only he and I existed, and that, I realized, was becoming my most favorite place in the world.

19

———

FINN

A WEEK LATER

"DON'T you think it's about time you introduced me?"

Aidan Sr.'s question had me jerking in surprise. We were at St. Patrick's. Sunday mass had just finished, and I'd had to fight the urge to yawn through the service.

Only thoughts of what I'd done to Aoife last night had stopped me from dozing off, and yeah, I knew it was all kinds of wrong to have a hard-on in church, but fuck, that was what confession was for, right?

At least I wouldn't be telling the Father *where* I'd had my lustful thoughts–just that I'd had them.

It was beyond hypocritical in my mind to commit sins, uncaring that I did so, while knowing all would be forgiven when I told my confessor, and I uttered however many Hail Marys he deigned suitable for my punishment.

Still, those were the rules under Aidan Sr.'s leadership.

Fucked-up, but true.

At least once a week we had to go to confession, once a week we had to attend mass, and once a week we had to take the Holy Communion.

It was clever, actually. The Father never took confession on Sundays, so that meant we had to attend twice a week like good little Catholic boys.

Aidan always was too shrewd for his own good.

I was hovering outside the church's entrance, waiting on the O'Donnelly brothers and their parents to finally move ass. I was cold, and I wanted to get this Sunday over with because then I could call Aoife and spend the rest of the day between her thighs.

Yeah, I was getting to be like a broken record.

The last time I'd been *this* hard, *this* often, I'd been twelve and Aidan Jr. and I had taken turns in paying Mary Elizabeth Sanders one dollar bills to show us her bra.

Desperate times and all that. What teenage boys could get off on was weird as fuck, but I swear, every time she'd shown us her bra, it had been like finding nirvana.

I had to hide a grin at the memory, then I turned to Aidan Sr. and faced him down. "Introduce you to who?" My voice didn't hold a quaver of fear because Aidan was like a viper who had a rodent in its line of sight, ready for its dinner.

He could scent fear better than a bear in the woods, and I wasn't about to fall for any of his traps.

"Aidan tells me you didn't go to O'Shea's last night, and the others have dropped hints about you suddenly leading a very sheltered life." I didn't tense when he slung his arm around me. The leather coat he wore over his three thousand dollar suit creaked as he tucked me close. "I know my boys. Only pussy will have them staying in on a Saturday night."

My eyes flared at his use of the word 'pussy' so close to the church. Then, I realized he'd maneuvered me to the street *beside* St. Patrick's, and suddenly everything made sense.

The hypocrisy was enough to make me snort, but knowing Aidan didn't appreciate jokes that were against him, I kept my dark humor at his ridiculousness hidden.

"Who is she?" he asked, his eyes narrowed.

"Aoife Keegan," I told him, knowing he wouldn't know her identity. Things like stubborn owners who refused to sell out when Acuig came a-visiting, were only brought to his attention when I had to call in some of our thugs to show said stubborn owners the way ahead.

"That's a good, strong, Irish name."

"I know," I told him. "She's a good, strong, Irish girl."

"Which ways does she follow?"

That translated in Aidan's language to: does she go to church?

"She's not Protestant, is she?" he continued, asking the age-old question that concerned all Irish parents.

"She's Catholic," I confirmed.

That had him beaming brighter than if I'd told him I'd just deposited thirty million into his accounts. "You doing right by her?" he inquired, tilting his head to stare down into my eyes. "It's too much to ask that my lads don't dip their wicks everywhere they go, but are you treating her right?"

"She's the marrying kind," I informed him softly, and Aidan stilled at my side before he released a gentle laugh.

"One of my boys has finally been snared, hmm? Then I definitely need to meet her."

I tensed. "She's not ready for that."

Aidan sniffed. "She'll never be ready for it. She knows what you are, no?"

"Aye, she does, sir," I replied, and I realized I couldn't have sounded more Irish if I'd tried.

Sometimes, on Sundays, after service with the very Irish Father, and then with the lilting accents around the place, it was easy to pick up on that if you had a good ear.

I had a very good ear, which meant I sounded like I was being an ass.

Not great when Aidan was around.

"She knows to keep quiet?" he questioned.

That had outrage flooding me. "Of course. You think I'd—"

He laughed. "No, son. No. Just making sure. You ashamed of us?"

Was he purposely trying to piss me off?

Apparently, my expression said it all, and he beamed my way again as he pulled away to clap me on the back. "Good, good. Never be ashamed of your roots, boy."

"I'm not," I groused. "I just don't want to overwhelm her."

"If she's the marrying kind, then that's the only way this will work." He shrugged, and though it killed me to admit it, he was the only voice of experience I knew.

My father had been a cunt. Handy with his fists and other things. . . . I couldn't think back to that time.

Wouldn't.

When I did, the nightmares would start, and I was too fucking old for them now.

But my old man hadn't exactly taught me the ways of a good marriage, neither had my mother who'd just sat back while her bastard husband had done things to me that no fucker should ever do to a boy.

Be it his son or not.

Aidan wasn't the best father out there. He was deranged half the time, half-loopy the rest. His moods swung so hard from left to right, it was enough to give everyone in the vicinity whiplash, but the craziest thing of all?

He loved us.

He fucking loved us.

And I was included in that circle.

Aidan was the only one who knew what my father had done to me; was the only one I'd shared that part of my past with. He'd taken my shame and he'd done right by me. Not only had he taken me in, loved me as if I was one of his own flesh and blood, he'd taken the monster that was my sperm donor for a swim among the fishes.

Because of Aidan, I could hold my head up high. I ruled my part of Manhattan. I had millions at my command, and an investment portfolio that would make any entrepreneur envious.

Aidan had given me the world, and he and Magdalena were the only ones who'd given me an example to lead by.

"You'll be kind to her?" I asked, my tone hesitant.

He scowled at me. "You think I'll be mean to the first girl one of my boys brings to a roast? Not even Dec brought that Deirdre around," he grumbled.

I winced. "Not mean, just . . . you know, don't freak her out?" I was well aware I was pleading with him, and knew that could go either one of two ways.

It would stir his amusement or prick his temper.

"Like me to pretend to be a plumber or an electrician, would you?" he asked, and I was relieved to see the twinkle in his eye.

"Not exactly," I muttered. "Just don't mention the time you black-balled Jimmy the Fish, or the time you managed to knee cap two men who were tied together with one bullet."

He snickered. "Gotcha. I'll be on my best behavior. Go on with you. Get your lass and bring her to meet the family."

God, help me.

Or I really meant, God help Aoife.

20

———

AOIFE

I WAS SO SORE.

Seriously, my aches had aches and yet, I'd never had a bigger smile on my face. My body felt well used and loved.

Finn was. . . .

God, he was so rough with me. So dirty and hard, but then he could be so tender.

The dichotomy was enough to make me squirm as I stared up at the ceiling in my small two-bedroom apartment deep in the heart of the neighborhood I'd lived in since I was ten. When 'Dad' had died, and Fiona had decided to move in with us, we'd gone from the old building two streets away to this one.

It wasn't much better, but there'd been no black mold in the kitchen in winter, and there had been *some* room to swing a cat.

When Fiona had died, I'd moved into her room after years of sharing the other bedroom with Mom. Finally having privacy hadn't been worth Fiona's loss, though.

It was hard to reconcile the Fiona I knew with the Fiona that Finn had.

Why had he left her?

Why had he never come back to visit with her?

I knew she'd cried every day over him, over his loss—I'd heard her. Every morning after she prayed to St. Anthony—the saint of lost objects—trying to get him to find her son for her, I'd heard her weep.

Yet, Finn had evaded her for all those years. He hadn't even attended her funeral, and he had to have known. Right?

My thoughts troubled me, and though it was dumb, I shoved them aside. I hadn't meant to think on things that couldn't be changed, but I wondered so much about the boy who'd left this neighborhood all those years ago and who had been forged into the man who fucked me senseless at night.

Just thinking of what he did to me was enough to make me rock my hips.

I was alone, of course.

Finn never took me here. He collected me in his car—either with him, or just Samuel behind the wheel—and we went to his place.

I wasn't about to argue over spending time there. It was a delight. Comfortable and homey, even if I had seen a man tied and bound there as though it was as regular a sight as a vase in the corner or a dining nook.

Not even *that* thought was enough to ease the ache inside me.

I was naked under the sheets. After a lifetime of sleeping in PJs, I no longer liked the feel of them against my skin. On the nights when I wasn't with Finn—only three of the past twenty days—I'd taken to stripping before bed.

It felt deliciously naughty and with my breath hiccoughing from my mouth, I slid my hand between my legs to touch my clit. The soreness was still there. Finn fucked me hard, and he fucked me soft, but when he was done with me, I was like a limp rag. I loved it, but when would I build up some stamina?

Before I could grumble, I gently rubbed my clit. I never rubbed it like Finn did. Could never seem to get the same friction, but I tried.

In fact, I tried so hard, I began to sweat under the sheets.

Shoving them down, aware that my breasts were on display, I

swallowed thickly and tried to give myself a release that Finn pumped from me so easily.

By the time I was a panting wrecked mess on the sheets, I'd given up. My body ached, this time from need, and Finn had told me not to expect a call from him today. It was church and family time, and I guess I shouldn't have been surprised by that knowing what little I did of the O'Donnellys.

When a knock sounded at the door, I stilled.

It was probably Jenny, and I really didn't want to see her in this state. Ignoring the knock, I strained to hear if her heels clacked against the hall floor—yeah, the walls were *that* thin. Except they didn't. I heard bupkis. A louder knock came, and Finn growled out, "Aoife."

His voice sent molten shivers through me.

He was here, and I was a hot, needy mess.

Seriously, had God answered my prayers or what?

I jumped out of bed and dragging the top sheet free, I rolled it around myself and hurried out. He knocked again, this time sounding more impatient, but I unlocked it and giving him no time to take in my disheveled state, I grabbed his hand, dragged him inside, then shut the door and locked it behind him.

My hands were at his belt before I knew what I was doing.

I needed his cock. I needed his fingers. I needed the release he could give me.

I'd managed to pull his belt free, and I was scrabbling with his zipper when he grabbed my wrists and yanked them over head. With no support, the sheet fell to the ground and with those cool eyes of his, he traced my body from the top of my head to the tips of my toes.

"Didn't I work you over well enough last night?" he asked, and I could hear a mixture of amusement and surprise in his voice. "I thought you'd be too sore to fuck until Tuesday."

"I am," I rasped.

That had him tilting his head to the side, then as he stared at me, took me in properly—the heaving breasts, the flushed skin, the feverish eyes—his mouth flattened. "You touched yourself."

I licked my suddenly dry lips, and, feeling like a naughty girl, I dipped my chin. "Y-Yes, Finn. I'm s-sorry, Finn."

He growled at me. "Which one is your bedroom?"

I pointed to it and then shrieked as he picked me up as if I weighed nothing—trust me, I did—and carried me over to my room.

"Naughty girls don't get to come," he warned me, but I saw my bed, saw it and knew what he'd do to me in it.

Surely, when he was inside me, he'd forget this. Forget what I'd done.

I was panting, ravenous for him by the time he lowered me to the floor. When he ordered me to turn around and bend over, I complied. When he told me to put my arms above my head and rest them on the bed, I obeyed even though it made my thighs ache.

When his hands gripped my ass, and I heard his zipper, I felt like crying with relief. Then, his cock was there.

I was so wet.

So, so, so wet, it was almost painful.

He shoved inside me, heading deep, and it didn't even hurt I was so ready for him, for his cock.

"I give you pleasure," he ground out as he began to fuck me, and I didn't even care that he was hard or rough. I had an internal itch that only he could scratch, and each thrust of his dick bestowed that upon me like no other could.

When his cock hardened inside me in the way I knew was the warning he was about to come, my eyes flared wide with surprise.

"N-No," I wailed as he orgasmed, his cum pumping inside me, filling my core, stuffing me full of him. Since I'd admitted I was on the pill, he'd stopped using condoms, and I was glad. I loved the feel of him inside me, but bare? It was enough to make my eyes roll back with need. "I need more," I begged.

"I told you. I decide when you get pleasure." He slapped my ass. "Your pussy's getting too greedy. It's time we taught it a lesson."

When he pulled out of me with a squelch, I felt him grab the sheet, and then with the faint rustling sounds, I quickly turned my head and watched him wipe his cock on them before he tucked himself back behind the cage of his fly.

I licked my lips, knowing enough to maintain this stance until he told me what to do.

It never occurred to me that it was weird that I always did as I was told. Never occurred to me that lovers pleased one another with no expectations of obeisance.

Mostly, it never occurred to me because I loved this. Loved what we did. It turned me inside out and made me happy, and after months of grieving, this was exactly what I needed. Something physical. I didn't need to talk, I needed to do, and Finn was very, very good at doing.

"Lay on your back, legs spread," he commanded, and though my cheeks flushed, I was too used to his dictates to even hesitate.

It was amazing how any embarrassment could disappear in a few short weeks.

I rolled onto my back and spread my legs.

"Slide your fingers through my cum," he ordered, folding his arms across his chest as he watched me, his gaze focused on my pussy, a stern look on his handsome face. He was stark in an expensive suit with a shirt so white, it hurt my eyes to behold. He looked heavenly with just a dash of devilish to mar his pristine perfection.

Doing as he bid, I touched myself and felt, just from the brush of his eyes, something that had been missing when I was alone. I could come so easily, and the feel of his seed against my sloppy self was enough to make me want to weep with joy.

"Thrust your fingers inside," he told me, and again, I complied. "Feel me in you, Aoife. Feel all I have to give you."

I did. I truly did, and I moaned my gratitude.

"T-Thank you."

He laughed. "You won't be thanking me in a minute."

My eyes popped open wide after lazily drifting shut.

"Clean your fingers now, suck them dry. We're going out."

"Out?" I blinked at him.

We never went out.

Well, not unless 'out' was him finding me and taking me to his home.

"Yes. Out," he repeated gruffly, his cheeks staining with heat.

"Where are we going?"

"Never you mind. Just get dressed."

"Dressed?" I squeaked. "I need to shower."

"No. No shower. Serves you right for getting yourself turned on without me there."

I reared up at that. "Fuck you!"

"I want your fire, my beauty," he told me, a muscle twitching in his jaw, "but not right now. Get dressed."

"I'm not leaving all sweaty and stinking of you."

He shrugged. "Use some perfume to cover it. It's your own fault."

My bottom lip trembled, and I knew I was reacting like a spoiled child, but he couldn't expect me to leave the house smelling like him and of my arousal and of sex, could he?

I stank.

There was no kind way to put it.

"P-Please," I whispered, uncertain why I was begging but knowing that was the wisest course of action.

His eyes flared with white hot fire.

My discomfort, my plea, satisfied him.

God, I should have hated him then. Should have loathed him for this, but I didn't. Something inside me was panting like a bitch in heat at his dictates.

"Are you going to touch yourself again?"

"Not without your permission," I said immediately, my eyes widening as far as they could while I tried to look as innocent as possible.

"Good answer," he mumbled, rubbing his chin, his frown turning pensive as he stared at me. "You can shower." Just as joy leaped through me, he murmured, "Just don't wash your pussy. I want my cum leaking from you all day."

Though his words made me blush, everything inside me screamed that this was exactly what I wanted, too.

My eyes closed in delight at the command, and though I rocked my hips to try to satisfy the ache deep inside, I didn't mess around. Finn was never very patient, and the last thing I wanted was him taking away my shower.

As I climbed out of bed, I felt his eyes on me. Mostly on my tits and ass. As he was standing near the door, I had to pass him, and when I did, he grabbed my arms and dragged me to him.

Before I could even gulp in a breath, he was there. His mouth on mine. He fucked his tongue into me, thrusting it hard and fast against my own. I was left panting and shaken against him, clinging to him for support as he robbed me of air, as he claimed my lips for his own.

When my fingers bit into his leather coat—something I knew he only wore to church because, and I quote, 'it was fucking freezing in St. Patrick's even when it was high summer'—he released a growl.

Pulling back, he stared deep into my eyes as he shoved a hand between us and slipped his fingers between my legs.

"Do you want to come?" he grated out, his voice a harsh rasp that made my nerves sizzle.

"O-Oh, God, y-yes," I half-sobbed, my body flaring to life once more at his touch.

He dipped his head and gave me his customary kiss—a harsh bite of my bottom lip that had me rocking onto tiptoes and pushing myself harder against him.

I knew this wasn't in his plan, but I was just glad he'd changed his mind. Until I realized what he was doing.

He pressed two fingers to my clit. Left them there, just covering it, then he whispered, "Get yourself off."

A whimper escaped me, but I didn't argue, didn't complain. I just pushed my forehead to his chest and rocked my hips, trying to grind down against the minimal pressure he exerted against my hungry nub.

The gasps that escaped me sounded tortured, and that was because they were. I was in agony, absolute agony. My stomach muscles burned, but there was no way I was moving away from him without coming. And yet, after God only knew how long, he moved his fingers away with a tut.

"Time's up."

I wanted to scream. I could feel it burst inside me, the rage and the indignation curling in my veins as my hunger, a hunger that only this man could appease, roared to life.

I loved the way he bossed me around in the bedroom—I truly did. It turned me on something fierce, so why I countermanded that, I'd never know. I leaned up, bit his lip as hard as he did mine, and spat, "Fuck. You."

His eyes flared at that. Deep in their ice-blue depth I saw warring emotions. Wrath, which made my own anger pale in comparison, but satisfaction, too. The latter made no sense, but when he pushed me back and I landed on the bed. I wasn't surprised when he pulled his cock from his pants again.

He was hard.

Thick.

Like he hadn't just climaxed moments before.

When he shoved it inside me, I released a keening shout of relief.

"Thank you," I cried out, and repeated the two words like a litany.

"Your pleasure is mine," he ground out, bracketing my head with his forearms as he pumped into me. "I own it, and I own you, Aoife." He fucked me so hard the bed rocked, and I didn't even care if my neighbors knew what was happening. Didn't care if they could hear. I just needed this man inside me, needed to come so badly I felt like I'd go insane.

When I just kept on saying 'thank you,' his pistoning hips

stopped. Before I could sob, he grated, "Say it, Aoife, say it. Tell me you're mine."

"I'm yours!" I yelled.

"This cunt belongs to me, doesn't it?"

"It does, it does."

"Your tits are mine, aren't they?"

"Only yours!" I wailed.

"I possess every inch of you, don't I?"

I heard the shake in his voice, recognized it even in my panicked state of hunger.

"Y-Yes," I told him, aware he needed the words, hoping that the sweetness of mine would induce him to let me come. That didn't mean the words were empty, though.

As crazy as it was, I knew I did belong to this infuriating man.

At least, my body did.

"Marry me, Aoife."

Those three words had my heart stuttering in my chest. His hips ceased their swift pace, and he began to rock into me gently, coaxingly.

For a second, I stared blindly at him. "M-Marry you?"

We'd known each other just over four weeks now, and when I said 'known,' I meant in the Biblical sense.

This man was so beyond closed off anywhere outside the bedroom that I knew nothing about him. Nothing at all.

Yet. . . .

I knew he loved watching me cook.

And when we weren't in the bedroom, we were in the kitchen. He'd worked from there, getting a kick out of watching me as I prepared our meals.

He could kiss me as though I were the most precious person in his life, and then he could fuck me as though he hated me, as though the need I inspired in him was something he couldn't handle.

I knew he spoke in his sleep, harsh words that had me waking up, wondering what tormented his dreams. Because, I knew, deep down, it wasn't in relation to his work. Finn was too pragmatic to let that worry him.

He'd told me that the guy I'd seen being tortured that first night shouldn't have messed around with Aidan.

That was how he saw it.

If you did what you said, if you kept your word, you were sound.

That was the Five Points' code, and though it was beyond messed up, it was so simple that I understood his nightmares had a different source.

I knew he liked his coffee black but his tea milky and sweet. Coffee was for mornings, but on a night, when he was tired and didn't want whiskey, I'd make tea and we'd sit in the kitchen at the counter, him eating some of the dessert I'd made earlier as he told me things about his day and I talked about my bakery, my goals.

I knew he touched me like I was a queen, and that he enjoyed feeding me, loved bathing me, and after he'd fucked me raw after a long night, he'd tend to me as though I were his princess and he my prince.

No, I didn't know this man. But I knew enough. I knew that I needed him as much as he needed me. This fire we created together, I knew it was rare. That was evident, because every time, Finn seemed stunned by the inferno we created together.

Maybe a relationship couldn't be forged on sex, but this wasn't just sex. This was everything.

He was a man who lived in a world of violence, a world of extremes, one I'd never understand but one that I'd been raised to accept, and I knew, point blank, he'd never hurt me. Ever. Not physically, anyway, and as long as I never lied to him, I knew that he'd hold me up like I was a delicate doll.

His to bend, not to break.

It was insane.

I knew that.

It was ill-advised, unwise, every synonym of stupid in the thesaurus, and yet, there was no whisper of a doubt in my mind, no hesitation in my voice, no question of what my answer would be as I told him, "Yes."

His nostrils flared and relief made his ice-blue eyes warm for a fraction of a second. Then, his cocky side came out. I watched it happen, reveled in it. Burned for him.

He'd stopped thrusting, had stayed thick and hot inside me as I'd deliberated my answer.

Now?

He fucked me.

Hard.

Until I was screaming, until I was sobbing, until I was begging for more and pleading for less. He took me to the edge of ecstasy but didn't let me fall over. He kept me there. Always there. With him, waiting, hovering, then, I felt it.

Deep inside, the second splash of his cum.

And like that, I was a goner.

Hell, who was I kidding?

I'd been a goner since the first day he'd walked into my tea room.

21
————

FINN

WATCHING Aoife at the large dining table with my family had something settling inside me.

It was like I was finally calm, something inside me was able to rest.

It was crazy to feel like that.

At any moment, one of the dipshits could say something to hurt, offend, or terrify the crap out of her. It didn't matter that no business was to be discussed while we ate the roast beef with thick gravy which Magdalena served us on Sundays. Such talk earned us all a slap around the head with her towel, but it didn't mean it never fell from our lips.

Magdalena liked her, though. I saw that. She kept looking between me and Aoife, a sparkle in her eyes whenever our gazes clashed.

I hadn't told them I'd proposed. Even if Aidan Sr. expected it, I didn't say a word because I wanted to keep it to myself for a while.

Not a secret, just mine to have and mine to hold. Exactly like the woman herself.

I'd kept my hand planted on her lap all throughout dinner. My fingers tightening about her thigh when she laughed, the tips caressing her knee as she talked to one of my brothers.

They liked her.

I couldn't blame them.

I did, too.

It was early to propose. We barely knew each other, but I knew enough to know I'd want her. Until I took my last breath, I'd need and want and crave this woman, and there was nothing and no one that would take her from me.

A wedding ring wouldn't cement any of that, but it would stop anyone in the parish from fucking with her. It would keep her safe, keep her inviolate.

The women were never involved in business, but that didn't mean it didn't overlap from time to time.

Magdalena knew the extent of Aidan's work but she knew none of the details, nor was she interested. He kept her safe, he provided for her and her sons, and she kept house for him and had a little business on the side that Aidan deemed 'women's work,' and thus, acceptable. That was how it worked.

Aoife wasn't like that. Though deep down, she was a traditional little thing, she wanted her own business, and I respected that. I didn't want, nor did I expect, her to change because I knew, having her hanging around the house, bored out of her brains, wouldn't be good for either of us.

For me, because I'd never want to get out of the penthouse. Thinking of her there, in what would become *our* space, would be enough to have me working from home every day of the goddamn week.

And for her, she *was* independent and she had goals and dreams of her own. Ones that I wanted for her, too.

Plus, that cooking of hers? Jesus, I wanted to hoard it to myself, but I was already working out three times longer than before to keep up with the fact I wanted to faceplant in her food. If she stayed at home, cooking only for me? I'd end up four hundred pounds.

So, no, we wouldn't be like Aidan and Magdalena. We'd be like Finn and Aoife, and that made me happy. As happy as seeing how seamlessly she fell in around the table.

Sure, she'd been nervous at first. I thought she was going to start choking when Aidan Sr. greeted her with two ebullient kisses to the cheek, then as my brothers had greeted her with polite tips of the chin, knowing there'd been the promise of slaughter in my eyes if they approached her like Aidan had, I'd seen the state of play settle. . .

They knew.

Knew she was mine, and I wasn't about to let her fucking go.

After Magdalena had bustled out of the kitchen, hugging Aoife then cooing at how pleased she was to finally meet her—finally, ha. I, myself, had only met Aoife four damn weeks ago—she'd taken Aoife into her sacred place, the kitchen, and that was that.

Any nerves she'd shown on the drive over—not many because I knew she was tired after what I'd put her through—had disappeared in the face of helping Magdalena. If Aoife got a hard-on for the penthouse kitchen, I knew she'd have loved Magdalena's. I'd wanted to see her reaction to the room, but Aidan had dragged me over to his office with Aidan Jr. and Eoghan before the 'no business over lunch' rule was truly enforced.

The Colombians had figured out we were behind the killing of the Mexican cartel leader. Eoghan had earned his penthouse on that hit. He'd shot the Mexican then made it look as though the Colombians were to blame. It had taken them three years to figure it out, but it seemed like they were baying for blood.

There'd been a drive-by shooting at a Points-protected establishment, and some of the girls who stripped at one of our joints had been badly beaten.

Much as I felt for them, it was small stuff, but that was how a war started—with small stuff.

Unease made the delicious roast beef settle heavily in my stomach. I hadn't cared before. I'd had no reason to. But now, I had Aoife to protect, and I'd protect her with my life.

There was no way I was living in a world without her in it, which made me as dangerous as any of those motherfucking Colombians.

"You don't!" Aoife's amused but outraged squeak had Declan snickering, as she knocked me from my thoughts of how to contain the threat to our territory.

"I do."

I wasn't sure what he'd done or hadn't done, but I focused my attention on him—Declan wasn't exactly a happy-go-lucky kind of guy. Hadn't been since he'd lost his childhood sweetheart twelve years ago. Trust Aoife to get him smiling again.

"What is it?" I inquired, my hand tightening on her knee as I asked to be included in the joke.

Aoife, wine glass in hand, tilted it at Declan. "He likes chain store donuts."

Because her outrage had seemed more appropriate to something a little more worrisome than donuts, I had to laugh. Then, to Declan, I told him, "Wait until you try some of Aoife's. She cooks like a dream."

My fiancée's cheeks bloomed at the compliment, and the happy sparkle in her eyes made my heart swell in my chest.

"Finn tells me you're going to open a bakery?" Magdalena prompted, apparently deciding the two of us had made gooey eyes at one another for long enough.

I hadn't told her that, and I frowned at her then a smug Aidan. Narrowing my eyes at the man who was like my father, I realized I'd been had.

He'd asked me about the woman in my life, knowing full well who she was.

He gave a carefree shrug, but the humor in his grin had me shaking my head.

"Yes," Aoife replied, her excitement for her new venture evident. "I can't wait. I've visited the store three times now, and I'm certain it's the right place."

"Where is it?"

"The old salon on Seventh," I told Magdalena, answering for Aoife because I wanted her to know that I listened.

Aoife didn't talk about her new venture all that much, not unless I asked her questions, and I made sure to—I wanted to know everything about this enchanting creature. I wasn't sure if it was because she didn't think I'd be interested, or if she was hesitant to discuss it because she didn't understand what we were to one another.

It was one of the reasons I had asked her to marry me. I wanted the prevaricating out of the way. I wanted the doubt in her eyes to disappear. I wanted to know *everything* about her. Nothing was too small, no fact too irrelevant. I wanted her to feel secure around me because, more than anything, I hadn't forgotten about the Senator.

I hadn't forgotten that on Tuesday, she'd be heading to meet with him at that goddamn hotel on the Upper East Side and before then, I wanted to know why.

I'd leave her with her secrets before we married, but after? No way. I wanted total disclosure even if that meant offering the same to her.

There was some shit that was safe from her. There was no reason for her to ask about my past, still, anything else she could ask and within reason, if it wasn't about the Points, I'd tell her the truth.

She shot a look at me when I spoke on her behalf, and I knew I was right—she was shocked that I'd listened. Surprised I'd taken enough interest in her, thus far, to remember that.

The woman was lacking in serious confidence, but I had thirty years to rectify that so I wasn't worried.

"On the corner?" Aidan Jr. asked, frowning.

"Yes." I shot my brother a warning look.

"That isn't one of ours," Aidan Sr. stated.

Aoife's eyes flared with concern, and I squeezed her leg again. "Aoife isn't a part of the business."

Magdalena snorted. "No, but she will be now, won't she?"

When her cheeks burned pink, I gaped at Aoife. She'd known

Magdalena less than a few minutes before she'd been bustled into the kitchen with her, and she'd told her we were engaged?

"I asked, child, I asked," Lena told me, waving her hand as I shot her, then Aoife, disbelieving glances.

"I didn't think it was a secret," Aoife mumbled, ducking her head. Whenever she did that, it made me want to tip her head back, so I could bite her bottom lip. If we were anywhere but here, I would have done that, too.

"It isn't. I just didn't think the first person you'd tell would be Magdalena!" I wasn't lying, either.

"Oh crap. Jenny," she moaned. "She'll be mad."

Magdalena hooted. "It can be our little secret, Aoife. She needn't know she wasn't the first in on it." Lena tapped her nose confidently.

Aoife's smile was shaky but it was a smile nonetheless. "T-Thank you."

"The way my boy was looking at you? I'd figured it out without you uttering a peep."

I groaned at that. "Do we have to talk like this around the table?"

"Prefer we talk about it later during the football?" Lena retorted sweetly, and I rolled my eyes.

"Yes. These eejits wouldn't be listening in like old gossiping hens."

When my brothers snickered, I knew they knew I was right. They were listening in on all of this shit, and they were going to give me crap later.

I could handle it, and when they fell ass over tit over some broad, I'd make them pay, dole it out twice as hard.

That was brotherly love for you.

Aidan Sr., however, wasn't to be swayed. "Finn, that isn't one of ours."

I huffed out a breath. "I know it isn't, but it's the best spot for what Aoife wants."

"Well, buy it for her then," Conor said easily, slouching against the comfortable, padded leather seat by hooking his arm over the back.

"Good thinking, my boy," Aidan stated, beaming at him proudly.

"I-I don't need you to buy it, though," Aoife told me, her voice small, and I quickly squeezed her thigh.

"No. You don't need us to buy it, but buy it we will," Aidan Sr. told her, his grin wide and happy again, like Conor had just solved the problem that was world peace. "Think of it as our wedding present to you."

When she gasped, I squeezed her leg harder until I felt her wince. I'd prefer her to wince at that, though, than to outright refuse Aidan's offer. He was happy as a pig in shit now, but if she rejected the gift?

Fuck knows how the meal would pan out.

I tilted my head to buss her on the cheek, and as I moved away, I whispered, "Let me deal with this."

Her nod was slight, so minute I knew no one else would have spotted it, and that she read the nuances in here so well came as a great relief to me.

I'd told her, on the way over here, that Aidan was volatile. Not that I needed to hammer that home. The man had a serious reputation, after all. But she'd understood, and had apparently surmised the way of it.

Conor, though he'd looked relaxed, had made the prompt to stop his father from going off the rails.

I tipped my head at him in thanks as I sat back in my seat. His lips curved to the side as he accepted my gratitude. He was a chilled bastard, but that was one of the reasons I loved working with him.

"Conor, you buy it for us," Aidan ordered him. "Finn has other things to worry about now. Like the wedding." He rubbed his hands together. "I want to be there when you tell Father Doyle."

I groaned. "Seriously?" Jesus, I'd never felt like a teenager more than I did now.

Was this why men dreaded bringing their partner to meet their parents?

Having never done it before, having never even contemplated doing it before, I couldn't say.

Aidan grinned. "Seriously."

"You'll need at least three or four weeks, Finn," Lena informed me.

I frowned. "What? I'm not waiting that long."

Aoife squeaked. "A month isn't a long time."

"It is for me." Aidan would be pissed if I moved her into my penthouse without us being wed, and I wanted her in my goddamn bed every night. I shot him a look. "After what we talked about earlier, don't you think it's wise we get married as soon as possible?"

"And they say romance is dead," Lena muttered, rolling her eyes and making Aoife laugh.

Aidan tapped his chin. "It's the banns, son. It takes three weeks for them to be called out."

"They're not a requirement now, Dad," Conor informed him.

"Maybe not to regular people, but since when were we regular?" Aidan drummed his fingers against the table. "You're right though, son," he aimed at me, confirming with his concession what I already knew—that the threat against us was very real. "Father Doyle won't be happy about it, but I think the roof has a leak that needs fixing." He shot Eoghan a look. "Arrange for that, would you, Eoghan?"

His youngest son dipped his head at the request, and Aoife gasped at him as she obviously figured out that the roof wouldn't have a leak until Eoghan arranged for one to exist.

Aidan didn't seem to hear it, thank God, and mumbled, "I'm not happy about it. You two living in sin, but I'll accept it considering the circumstances." He rubbed his chin. "When can you move her in?"

I shrugged. "Tonight."

"Tonight?" Aoife cried. "I need more time than that! I have all my things to pack up."

Lena snorted. "You're wealthy now, Aoife. You pay other people to pack your things for you."

"I-I . . ." Her words drifted off, and I turned to look at her, an apology in my eyes if not falling from my lips. She saw it, though, saw my restraint, and while her mouth worked noiselessly with how her life was being organized around her, she seemed to take my lead.

Thank God for smart women.

She rested her hand atop mine, and I moved it, so we could clasp fingers. It was probably the first time we'd done that outside of the bedroom, and it felt good. Very good.

Gently squeezing mine, I felt her accept my apology.

One of the reasons I hadn't been mad she'd kept me waiting for an answer to my proposal was that I knew she had to process exactly who I was and what I did.

Not that it would have stopped me.

She'd be my wife before the year was over, and that was the truth. But I hadn't wanted her to feel forced. She had to accept the man I was, the men I knew, and if not embrace it, at least accept it.

Any other woman might not have. But I knew Aoife had been raised to fear and respect the Five Points. Anyone outside our territory, which extended quite far—through Hell's Kitchen and onto its neighboring areas—wouldn't understand. But Aoife had accepted the Points a long time ago. Whether she realized it or not.

To her, the violence that was inherent in this world was something she was accustomed to because she'd been raised with warnings about our Family.

Some little farm girl from Idaho wouldn't get it. But someone born and bred here in one of our neighborhoods? She knew to fear where she trod.

The rest of the meal wasn't as carefree as before, but there were laughs to be had and we all groaned when Lena brought out her famous crumble. She didn't make it every week, it depended on how busy she was on the Saturday before, but when it made an appearance, the huge casserole dish always emptied even if we were stuffed full.

The twelve-seater table was covered with white linen, silver cutlery, china dishes that were patterned with ancient detailing—Aidan had bought Lena the china service as an anniversary present from Sothebys two years ago—as well as the detritus from a good meal.

I'd brought Aoife to meet my family, and though we hadn't passed unscathed, in the grand scheme of things, we'd sailed through troubled waters quite easily together.

It was, I thought, a portent of things to come. No matter what happened, from this moment on, Aoife and I would work through it together.

I'd have no distance between us. No space.

I needed her. Like my lungs needed air, I needed her, and I knew, whether she wanted to admit it to herself or not, she felt the exact same way.

22

AOIFE

I BLEW out a breath the minute my butt hit the backseat. Settling in for the short ride from the O'Donnelly's home to Finn's building, I watched as Finn hugged Aidan for the final time before making his way to the yard where Samuel was waiting to shut the door behind him.

It was an unusual sight.

Finn didn't normally wait on Samuel to open or close the car door for him, but at Aidan O'Donnelly's home? Sam had done so upon arrival and departure.

I could understand after having met the man.

My first meeting with the crime lord had been without the other man's knowledge. I'd seen Aidan waving a gun, pacing back and forth as he worked off his anger at the architect he'd been torturing in Finn's salon.

Seeing him with his family? With his wife?

It was an experience–that was for sure.

It told me their business persona was not how they were when at home.

I wasn't sure whether to take comfort from that or not.

When Finn climbed in beside me, Sam shut the door, and called out a goodnight to Aidan and Lena who were hugging one another against the night chill as they watched us drive off their land. His scent filled the small cabin, and as was often the way now, I thought of sex and long nights with him.

"Well, that was unusual," I told him, deciding it was time to stop watching my tongue.

I wasn't a shrew, but the man had asked me to marry him. He needed to know the real me, so he could call it off before we wed. We were Catholic. There was no such thing as divorce, and in light of Aidan's zealous ways, divorce was undoubtedly as perilous as any mortal sin.

Before he tied himself to me, he needed to know that I wasn't always meek. I took direction from him, just as I had at the table, but I had a voice.

"Unusual isn't the word," he mumbled, running a hand over his face. Leaning back against the seat, he turned his head to the side to stare at me. "You did well in there."

"I had a good time until things got weird."

He winced. "Things often get weird with Aidan. You need to get used to it. It's just how he is."

And it went without saying that I'd be dealing with him until either he died or I did.

Hopefully, considering my age, it would be him shuffling off this mortal plane first.

"I know," I told him, well aware that was the truth. "I'm not afraid of that side of your life, Finn." Then, I immediately pulled a face. "Okay, that's a lie." He laughed. "Well, not an outright lie. Just, I mean, I'm not afraid to own up to what you do. If that makes sense."

"You couldn't hide from it considering how we met."

How little he knew. I'd met him years before, and he couldn't remember me, but why would he? When he'd left, he'd been around fourteen, and I'd been two, for God's sake. Why would he remember a toddler?

Still, I remembered him. Mostly because Fiona had kept him alive.

There was a starkness to his tone, though, and I knew it was founded in guilt. I knew the reason I met with the Senator, my father, was a nagging sore that ate at him.

"Are we really going to get married?" I asked, my voice soft.

He frowned at me. "Of course we are. Aoife, don't be backing out on me now—"

Before he could rant, I rolled my eyes at him. "I wasn't backing out. I was asking if *you* were going to. You haven't necessarily seen the best side of me, Finn. What you've seen is a side that I don't even know myself. I-I'm like a different person around you."

"I know," he told me, and the pride and satisfaction in his voice had me snickering and hitting him on the leg. When his thigh tensed where my hand lay, I liked the tiny response so I kept it there.

"But I'm a pain in the ass, Finn. When I don't sleep, I get really grouchy. Not like a regular grouch, but I snarl and shit. I'm like a gremlin. Seriously."

He laughed at that. "Impossible. You're too sexy to be a gremlin."

I wrinkled my nose at that. "Only to you," I told him honestly.

Lifting his free hand, he cupped my chin. "I'm the only one who matters, aren't I?"

A smile curved my lips. "I guess you are." Well, that made me feel like I was going to glow. He was right. To the one man who mattered, I was as sexy as a pin-up model. Because even with low self-esteem, there was no way I could mistake how hard he got around me. And how often.

"I work too much, I get really engrossed with what I'm doing, and I might even forget to pay some bills because I just forget about that stuff."

He chuckled, and the sound was so light, it made me feel like I was floating. I'd never heard Finn chuckle before. Sure, he'd laughed, and, of course, he'd smiled and grinned. But that sound was so carefree and light-hearted that I thought I might melt.

"You don't have to worry about the bills anymore. Lena was right. You're going to be a wealthy woman when we're wed. I work too much, so if you're working, too, it won't piss you off when I'm called away or if I'm not home every night at seven on the dot. And you're focused. As someone who has been at the center of that focus, I'm not about to complain."

My cheeks heated, but I didn't think he could see that in the dying light.

"What I'm trying to say, Aoife, is I don't care if you're a pain in the ass before you've had an IV of coffee. I don't care if you'll butt heads with me over random shit. I don't care if you're stubborn. All that matters to me is you're happy and safe. With the latter taking precedence from time to time."

Considering what he did for a living, that made sense.

I bit my bottom lip, and when he reached over to tug it free, he murmured, "That's mine to bite, not yours."

I shivered at the raspy note, loving how he could make me feel with just a simple touch and a few words.

"S-Sorry," I half-whimpered, and I knew my tone, if not the apology, satisfied him because he fidgeted in his seat, sinking slightly lower—to ease the bulge of an erection, maybe?

Ugh. My mouth watered at the thought. I didn't even care that Samuel was less than two feet away!

This man, and what he did to me, was addictive. It was like he took me out of my own skin and made me someone else, someone who was free to live and love and to be.

"Are you scared about what I do?"

I thought about that for a second, and though it was a dash of cold water on my libido, I shook my head. "If my mom was still alive, then maybe."

He frowned. I saw it through the headlights that flashed in the window. "What? Why?"

"Because she'd have tried to talk me out of this, even though she always told me to never say no to a Five Points man."

He cringed at that. "I'm glad you were never in that position."

"Me, too," I told him softly. "But she'd have tried to convince me, and I don't want convincing."

That had him clearing his throat. "Why not?" He cut me a look then. "I understand to a point. I'm not the kind of guy you'd take home to a Catholic mother."

I snorted. "It depends. Don't forget, most Catholic mothers don't care so long as you go to church."

"True. That's Lena's fixation."

My lips curled—mothers were the same the world over, but Irish Catholics? They were a different breed.

"So, I wouldn't want her to convince me because she'd tell me you're A, B, and C. But I see D, E, and F." I shrugged. "We'd never agree, and she'd probably piss me off in her attempts to change my mind.

"I'm not an idiot, Finn. This thing, it *is* crazy. It's so fast, it makes a whirlwind look slow. I know that. I do. But no one has ever made me feel the way you do. I'm not about to pass that up."

He laughed softly. "Good to know."

Maybe he was relieved that I hadn't used words of love. But I wasn't like that. I wasn't going to gush over him—*well, not outside of the bedroom,* I thought with an inner giggle. I wasn't going to expect declarations of love from him, either.

This wasn't about love.

It went deeper than that.

And mothers the world over would roll their eyes at me, but I knew it to be true.

Finn's soul spoke to mine.

That went deeper than love.

When I looked into his eyes, I saw a man who was capable of violence. One who would do things most would shy away from. I didn't mistake him for a good man—our first meeting proved that. But

I considered him a decent man. He had standards and morals, but they didn't fit the current status quo.

He'd never beat me.

He rarely even *swore* around me outside of the bedroom. If he was on the phone and he started cursing, he'd head into another room, for God's sake, and apologize after he returned.

He'd look after me. Keep me safe. Protect me.

I'd considered all that when he'd proposed.

Yes, he was a mobster.

He covered it up behind expensive suits and a penthouse that would make any millionaire cry with envy. But deep down, I saw the boy Fiona had told me about all those years ago. I didn't remember him well. How could I? I was two. But I remembered her love for him. I remembered how she'd marveled over how smart he was. How deeply she'd mourned him.

Finn was one of the most complicated men I'd ever met, and me? I was a sucker for a puzzle.

"Next Tuesday..." His words petered off.

I patted his lap. "I'm telling you this as your fiancée, Finn. I know full well how this could wreck Alan's career, and I also know that if you told Aidan, he'd probably use it to cripple him. Or try to, at any rate. Alan is a very stubborn man. It's where I got it from I think because," I said on an exhalation, "he's my father."

Whatever he'd expected me to say, I doubt it had been that. He rolled my fingers in his and asked, "Your mother raised you alone?"

"No. Not until I was twelve. My stepfather died, but he wasn't much of a loss if I'm being honest." It was a cruel thing to say about a man, but it was the truth. "He drank too much, wasn't interested in me or Mom, and while he worked, Mom paid for everything. His money went to the pubs and the bookies."

He squeezed my hand. "I understand more than you'd think about feckless fathers."

It would have been a good time to segue into my knowledge of his past, but I doubted Finn would want to know about my connection with his mother.

Maybe one day, I'd feel comfortable opening up to him about Fiona. But as it stood, it wasn't a *lie*. It might have been considered faintly duplicitous but, to be honest, my knowledge of his history was the one reason I was so comfortable with this whirlwind relationship.

For that, he should have been grateful.

"I'll have someone pack your things tomorrow and bring them to the penthouse."

His words were out of the blue, especially when I'd expected more questions about Alan. Still, I wasn't about to complain. I didn't exactly want to pass up the chance of help, and truthfully, I liked waking up in his bed.

In four weeks, I'd grown to like having him at my side. I rarely woke up without one of his fingers inside me, and even when he wasn't awake before me, I enjoyed the way he curled into me.

Because, for all he was a big, burly brute of a man, Finn was a cuddler in his sleep.

My lips curved at that, and he grumbled, "You're not going to argue?"

"Argue? About what?" I blinked at him.

"Moving in with me?"

"I agreed to marry you, Finn. I didn't expect you to move in with me, or for us to live separately," I joked. "Plus, you're mad if you don't think I want some help. I have a lot to clear up, but I want to be involved. Some of the stuff can go in storage," I explained before he could argue. "Then there are personal things from my family that I need to figure out where to put."

"Do you have any pieces of furniture you want to take with you?"

At that, I laughed. I had to give him credit for maintaining a very straight face. "You think I'm going to mess up your pad with my crappy stuff? Don't worry, Finn, most of it can stay for the next tenant."

He chuckled. "Good to know."

Still, I knew he'd have let me bring something with me even if it destroyed the aesthetics of his space.

His penthouse was like something from a magazine, except it wasn't cold and clinical. It was warm and comfortable. I could easily see myself in there.

"What's the issue with the banns?" I asked him softly. "Why do I have to move in with you now?"

He grimaced and turned his head away from me to look out at traffic. "Business."

I pursed my lips, knowing that would be all he'd tell me. I figured that was an important part of being a mobster's wife. Not that I wanted to know all the details. . . .

Squeezing his fingers, I stated, "You can tell me it's business, and I'll take it under advisement if you expect me to modify my behavior. But if I'm in danger, then I want to know. Keeping me in the dark about a threat isn't the same as telling me the 'who, why, and when.'"

He pondered that. "No, you're right. In this instance, it's a nasty threat. If you had the tea room still, I'd assign a few men to you, but until you get the bakery up and running, your schedule is random, so there's no need to worry."

My eyes flared wide in surprise at that. "Men? Like bodyguards?"

"A man protects his treasure," he rasped, lifting my hand to his mouth and just about flooring me with his words.

Whatever I'd expected him to say, it wasn't that, but God, it made everything inside me melt. Not with lust, although there was a bit of that. But with hope. Hope for more. Hope for what we could build together.

Because I'd seen the danger in my neighborhoods, I didn't argue with his statement about my needing guards. Certain parts of the city would never be safe, and certain streets in this area would always be rife with danger. I wasn't Aoife Keegan anymore. Owner of a teashop, tenant of a very crappy apartment, with my one secret being a genetic connection with a very important man.

No, I was going to be Aoife O'Grady, and that came with ties.

"Understood. I'll be careful," I told him.

"That's all any of us can ever be," he replied, his tone pensive, and to be honest, that surprised the hell out of me.

Finn was never pensive. He was so sure of himself, it would be annoying if I didn't want to ride him like he was a bucking bronco.

After that, we didn't say much, but I was happy to go to his place and to realize that now, it was *our* place.

23

FINN

WATCHING Aoife in the kitchen was almost as hot as watching her writhe underneath me.

Yeah, fucked up, but true.

She was so graceful in there that I got a kick out of watching her work, and there was the added bonus of the meals she created.

It was probably chauvinistic of me to get so turned on by the fact she loved cooking and baking, because it was so ultra-feminine. But it was what it was.

It wasn't like I had a say in how hot I found it that she loved the whole domestic Goddess shit, and it wasn't like I was about to tie her to the stove or hand her a mop and bucket—we had a team of house-keepers that would do anything and everything to maintain the penthouse. And, if she didn't want to, she didn't have to cook. I'd eaten before her, and we'd eat without her being in charge of the kitchen.

I knew, though, that she'd get pissy if I even made the suggestion. Something about cooking relaxed her, and watching her in here was like watching a dancer in motion.

A part of me knew she liked feeding me, too. Maybe it was an Irish thing. Who the fuck knew?

As she stirred a pot that had her cheeks flushing from the heat, I watched her a second before I averted my attention to my laptop.

Her old building was due for demolition in three weeks' time, and my project managers were quarrelling on instant messenger. They didn't need my input, but I kept an eye on things—I always did.

My phone rang and spying Declan's name, I quirked a brow. Of all the brothers, he called me the least. Not because we weren't close, but Declan wasn't close to anyone. He was quiet, kept his head down, and did his job. I loved him, but he could be a boring bastard.

"Dec, what's up?" Not only was it weird that he'd called me, but it was late for him, too.

"There's been another robbery."

Well, fuck.

I hissed between my teeth. "Where?"

"The strip joint on Fourth."

We had six in this area, and while they weren't in my official purview, this current issue was a Family problem. That meant all our necks were on the line if we didn't try to fix it up.

"Has Eoghan pinpointed where their base is?"

"No. The bastards have managed to keep things tight. But you know why. They'll be working with the Mexicans. We're approaching gang warfare, Finn."

My brother's tone was grim and for a reason. I ran a hand through my hair as I leaned over the counter and pressed my elbow to it. Ducking my head, I countered with, "We need help from the Russians."

Aoife released a deep breath, and I knew she was listening. It didn't make me get up and move, though. I didn't want her involved in the business, but I needed her to know how in danger she was before she married me.

Our vows would be to the death.

There was no out with a Catholic marriage, and there was no out from a Points man.

I'd never let her go. I couldn't. But I needed her to be aware.

Aware helped her be, as she'd told me the other day on the ride back from Aidan's place, prepared for every eventuality.

Declan cursed. "Those pricks can't be trusted."

"And the Latinos can?" I ground out. "At least they run shit like we do."

"No fucker runs things like we do."

"Is your Da there?"

"Yeah. 'Course. He had me call you. He's fucking foaming. Pricks sliced this chick up good."

"They killed someone?" Rage buzzed inside my brain.

"Yeah. One of the girls. Made a real mess of her. It's a message."

"It's a fucking catalyst." Rubbing my temple, I grated out, "You need me there?"

"No. But Da wanted me to tell you there's a meeting tomorrow at four AM."

"Got it." I didn't wince at the timing. Aidan worked all hours, and we'd grown accustomed to that a long time ago. "The house or his office?"

"House. He's too pissed to go in. I suggested we stay at the house."

What that meant was 'Aidan couldn't be around anyone that wasn't family without wanting to throttle them.'

Aidan had trust issues. Quite naturally, I thought, but those trust issues reared their head when there was a threat. This was a level ten on our Richter scale of disasters, and that meant Aidan would go off half-cocked on anyone he thought might be working against us.

We routinely flushed out rats. Be they DEA, NYPD, FBI, or even other spies from other gangs, but at times like these, there could be a witch hunt brewing, and spreading our focus would do none of us any good. Keeping Aidan at home would work to our advantage in that.

Aidan was capable of intense hyper-focus. We just needed to make sure that was aimed at the outside threats first and foremost.

"I'll be there."

"See ya, bro."

We cut the line, and I stared down at my lap for a second, not wanting to lift my head just yet. When I heard soft steps, I peered over at Aoife and asked, "You hear any of that?"

She wrinkled her nose. "Was I supposed to?"

I tilted my head to the side. "Good question. To me, you can say yes. If Aidan or my brothers ever ask you that, you say no. You play dumb. Got me? You're safe with them, but not with Aidan Sr. He's a live wire."

She grimaced. "You think I hadn't figured that out?"

"You're too smart for your own good." I scraped my hand over my head. "If they ever ask you a direct question, don't lie. If you think you can, prevaricate." The no-lie rule wasn't just for the men but for their women, too. "Aidan isn't a total sexist prick, but he has outdated ideas. If you act like you can't add two plus two, he'll skim over you and look at me to answer any questions."

"That sucks."

"That's life in the Five Points." I blew out a breath. "Look, about tomorrow morning—"

She waved a hand. "I don't need a ring."

"You fucking do," I growled at her. "I want everyone to know you're mine, Aoife." More than anything, I wanted her father to see the ring when she visited him in the afternoon.

Her lips curved. "Want a tattoo on my forehead? Property of Finn?"

"Finn O'Grady," I corrected. "Let's make sure they know not to fuck with you."

She smirked, and her smart-assery lightened my heart some. I hadn't expected this resilience from her. She wasn't panicking, and she had overheard some heavy shit.

After clearing her throat, she asked, "Who died?"

"One of our girls."

A grimace marred her face. Most women in the life never liked to think about the prostitution racket that was part of the Family's side business. It wasn't something I liked either, truth be told.

Having been abused myself, I hated to think of anyone in that position, but Aidan ran a tight ship. We protected the girls, paid them well. We had a ring of girls to suit any and all pay ranges, and fuck, if any of the Johns, be they millionaires or misers, hurt one of our own? They paid the price. Dearly.

I knew whoever had been foolish enough to hurt this particular whore would probably have their balls cut off before they died.

Having seen Aidan do it before, I was under no illusion he'd do it again. And worse. Especially if there was a tie to the Colombians as Declan suggested.

Rubbing my chin, I predicted, "There's going to be a war."

Her sharp inhalation stung me. "R-Really? I remember the last one."

I jerked my chin. "In '09?"

"Yeah. Mom was terrified when I left the building, even to go to school."

"Smart woman," I admitted. "The Haitians were small fry by comparison, though. These are Colombians . . ." I ran a hand through my hair. "I want you to have your bakery, Aoife."

She frowned. "I know you do, Finn."

"I'm just not sure if this is the best time for it."

That had her tilting her head to the side. "I can see that."

"Would you hold off for now?"

She stared at me, her eyes drifting over my face as she took me in. I didn't know what she saw, but her bright-green eyes grew soft as she rounded the counter and cupped my chin. "Thank you for being honest with me and not laying down the law."

My lips curved. "Don't thank me yet."

A snicker escaped her. "You mean, you'll lay down the law if I don't agree?"

My stomach felt like it was loaded with stones. "I can't lose you," I rasped, and both of us were taken aback by the intensity in my voice.

She licked her lips, then leaned forward and pressed a kiss to my mouth. "I'm not going anywhere."

I bit her bottom lip, reminding her she belonged to me. "Good."

Pressing my forehead to hers, I closed my eyes and felt her soft breath against my mouth. "Can we hold off on the bakery?"

"We can. Not forever, though?"

I liked that she tried to reason with me, and I wasn't an unreasonable man. "Not forever," I confirmed. "The last thing I want is you cooped up in here, Aoife. I just want you safe, and I can't lie to you, it isn't safe at the moment."

"I understand, Finn, truly I do."

A relieved breath escaped me. "I'm glad."

"I need to visit my dad tomorrow, Finn."

Her words had me tensing. "I know." After clearing my throat, I stated, "Samuel will take you, and I'll have someone ride with you, too."

I knew she didn't like the sound of that, but I didn't, either. There were a lot of changes heading Aoife's way, and I was scared they'd frighten her off.

I could be an obnoxious bastard, but even I knew someone could only withstand so much.

Aoife had lost her business, been coerced into a sexual relationship with me. Then I'd proposed, and now there was a gang war heading our way that necessitated her traveling with security for a while. . . .

If that wasn't a culture shock, even for someone who knew how the gang worked, then I didn't know what was.

"All right," she told me, and I pressed a kiss to her mouth in thanks.

I wasn't stupid. Aoife wasn't biddable. She was in bed, but not anywhere else. I'd learned that at the O'Donnelly's dining table. She hadn't quivered or quaked under Aidan's scrutiny, and she'd held her own with my brothers.

For any woman to do that?

She had balls of steel. I just hoped she wouldn't run scared from all the changes that were heading our way.

24

AOIFE

THE HOTEL RECEPTIONIST smiled at me. I'd been coming here for so long now that everyone knew me, and I was under no doubt that they assumed the same as Finn had—that I was screwing the Senator.

It was an expensive place, though. Class and discretion were its promise. Boutique in size, it catered to diplomats and politicians in the city, and I knew its motto was secrecy.

God only knew what went down in these walls, but even the housekeepers knew not to talk. Now that I thought about it, I wondered if a Family ran this place.

Such discretion?

Money couldn't buy it, only threats could. And whose expertise ran in threats? The mob.

Still, if they were in charge, I could imagine cameras recording shit, and blackmail threats in the mail.

My lips curved at my vivid imaginings as my boots crushed the thick carpet when I strode across the foyer toward the banks of elevators.

Alan, Dad, had the same room each time, and I never had to ask to go up. It was a standing arrangement.

William had followed me inside, but he was staying in the lobby. As I headed into an elevator and turned around, I nodded at him when he took a seat on one of the sofas, pulling a paper from his leather coat.

He was in his fifties, had a scar that ran down the left side of his throat, and looked like the archetypal mobster if I was being honest. Discreet he was not, but I figured that was the point of security.

What use was there in having a heavy following you around if no one knew you were protected?

I'd seen the gun in his holster when he'd opened the car door for me this morning. His jacket had pulled open, and the weapon had glinted in the light. I was under no illusion that the man knew how to use it, too.

A part of me wondered why I wasn't freaking out.

The last time I'd met my dad, I was single, and had a growing reputation in the city. I'd also been desperately lonely, lost after my mother's death, and floundering.

Now?

Everything had changed. Everything. Me included.

Finn brought something to my life that I'd never realized I'd been missing. There was a fire in my belly now. Sure, his world scared the shit out of me. The news of a war coming to town? I was fucking petrified that either he or I would get caught in the cross fire—it was why I'd agreed to postpone my plans for the bakery.

Though Finn brought danger to my world, he also brought life.

It was like I'd seen everything in sepia before him, and suddenly, everything sparkled with vibrant colors.

The height of insanity?

Maybe.

But I was happy.

Really happy, and God, it made me wonder when the last time I'd felt that way was.

As the elevator purred to a halt, I stepped out into the corridor and walked toward the room my father had hired for us.

I opened it and stepped inside, knowing it would be unlocked in preparation for me. The room, as always, was empty. He arrived after I did. We'd tried to keep things hush-hush, but apparently, hadn't done that great a job of it if Finn had managed to figure out what we were doing.

Should I tell Dad that we'd been caught? If I did, it would make him doubt Finn, and I really didn't need his approval or disapproval. He was my father, I knew, but we had more of a friendship than a father-daughter relationship. He'd been a stranger for too long for me to allow him to have a heavy hand over my life, but I didn't want to argue. I saw him little enough as it was, and I didn't want to waste time on something that was going to happen whether he liked it or not.

The next time he saw me, I could be Aoife O'Grady, and that was that.

The suite was comfortable and elegant. The bedroom was separate from the living room where we always sat. A large window overlooked a small gated garden, and there were two sofas opposite each other with two ornate armchairs, the kind that had golden scrollwork as a frame with horsehair cushions, flanking them.

On the coffee table, there was a tray of tea and a selection of sandwiches and cakes.

I took a seat in my usual place, the sofa that overlooked the park, and grabbed my phone to wait for him.

Dad only ever made me wait ten minutes tops, so I didn't have much time to kill.

I had two messages. One from Finn and the other from Jenny. The sight of the latter's name had me grimacing because I realized I hadn't exactly been communicative of late. Finn had steamrolled his way into my life, and I'd been absorbed in him. That wasn't fair to Jenny, though. I'd been a shitty friend.

Well, not totally shitty.

I knew she'd be a pain in the ass when I shared what was happening between Finn and me and, truth be told, I was putting the confrontation off.

Jenny could be a bitch sometimes, and I had no doubt that she'd be bitchy when I revealed my new status as an engaged woman.

Sometimes, my neighborhood was ridiculously old-fashioned. The Irish ways, though many of us hadn't even visited the old country, still ran true like we were back in the eighteen hundreds.

It was nuts, but I knew Jenny would be jealous as hell about my news.

Finn: *You get there safe?*

Me: *Yep. Just arrived.*

Finn: *Billy treat you okay?*

That had me cocking a brow.

Me: *How should he have treated me?*

Finn: *With all the deference owed to a woman who belongs to me.*

I snorted at that.

Me: *Belong to you now, do I?*

Finn: *You know it, and you fucking love it.*

Because I could imagine his smirk, I squirmed a little in my seat. He said incendiary things that should have had me blowing my top, but they just made me melt. It was all kinds of weird, but the way he talked got me so hot, I wanted to burrow into his arms and never let go.

Me: *Maybe.*

Bigheaded jerk.

Finn: *Only maybe...? I'll have to remind you of that tonight.*

I shuddered.

Me: *Please?*

Finn: *My pleasure.*

I could imagine his purr as he murmured that.

Crossing my legs to assuage the sudden ache that had sprung up out of nowhere, I began to type out another message: *You make me ache,* but then I deleted it. He knew that already, and the words weren't what I wanted to say, anyway.

I wanted to tell him that I needed him, but I didn't want to freak him out even though a part of me recognized he needed me to need him.

He craved it.

Finn was a control freak.

When I'd hidden in his closet that first day, I'd been too scared to notice, but he had everything organized by use and then color. The man had more clothes than I did. He had drawers with rolled up ties that reminded me of the opening sequence of *Fifty Shades of Grey,* then he had another drawer with socks, and another one with cuff-links and watches.

His wardrobe was any woman's wet dream. But the man in the clothes from the wardrobe was a sinner's paradise.

The penthouse was organized, too. The fridge done in a way I'd had to figure out at first. Nobody stored onions next to Nutella . . . they either went in a cool, dry cupboard or in the chiller section at the bottom of the fridge, right?

Nope.

Not Finn.

Apples went side by side with BBQ sauce, and a jar of pickles was followed by those microwaveable pots of brown rice—who put rice in the fridge?

Finn did.

Why?

Because everything was in alphabetical order.

I mean, his cupboards were full of food, too, and they were in the same order, but there were just random things stored side by side. As though only he understood the way of it, and ironically enough, I knew he didn't cook for himself. Didn't even go grocery shopping for himself, for Christ's sake. Had he asked a housekeeper to arrange that stuff for him? He had to have.

His office?

His desk was neat as a pin.

No papers anywhere.

Not because he was worried about me reading anything, but because he dealt with everything as it came, even if he'd been doing something else. The man was a machine. I'd seen him work while I cooked, and had come to see how he shifted gears when he received a call before going back to his original task.

The man fascinated me.

Was it any wonder I was in his thrall?

I bit my lip, wanting to say that to him, tell him how I was feeling, but I wasn't sure if it was wise. Sure, we'd be getting married ridiculously soon, but I wasn't ready to tell him anything earth-shattering.

I guess, deep down, I wanted him to know what he meant to me, but the only way I could do that was by sounding sappy. I knew he appreciated the way I worked.

It seemed like I constantly surprised him. Whenever he asked me anything, or stated it as an order like with the postponement of the bakery, he was always hesitant, almost like he knew I'd argue. I liked that he was wary, though. I'd never raised my voice at him, hadn't had to so far, but he knew I'd fight if necessary.

It pleased me that he knew that without us having had a fight yet. It told me that I'd comported myself well around him. That he knew, just because I'd roll over at his command when I was in his bed, didn't mean I'd do the same in life.

He was a Points man. He'd gotten me into his bed the first time because I'd had no other choice but to do as he wanted, not if I hadn't wanted to ruin my father's career, and yet, somehow, he'd seen beneath that veneer to the real me.

I didn't reply to him in the end. Instead, I texted Jenny.

Me: *Hey you. Fancy a coffee later on?*

Jenny: *Hey!! OMG, you've been ghosting me. Bitch!*

I had to laugh.

Me: *Nope. Just really busy. It's been crazy on this end.*

She put the frowning emoji, mostly because she knew that I was never busy unless I was in the kitchen at the tea room. Which, ya know, didn't exist anymore.

Me: *I'll explain another time. Coffee?*

Jenny: *No can do, girl. Had to get some shifts at Al's. Just to tide me over until you get the bakery up and running.*

That had me wincing. Shit. I felt so bad considering the tea room had closed down with no notice, and though I'd paid her and my other two staff members a few weeks' wages to help them out, it was nothing in comparison to a steady income.

Getting rid of them had sucked, and I'd done so with the promise that I'd be setting up a new business ASAP.

Which, cue sigh, wasn't going to happen with someone gunning for the Five Points.

Me: *You tell me when and we'll meet up, okay?*

Jenny: *Great stuff. Gotta go. You caught me on a break. Love you. xoxo*

Me: *Love you, too. xoxo.*

Putting my phone down, because one of my contacts had made me feel guilty and the other had made me horny, I decided it was safer just to stare at the walls until my dad came.

There was a boring picture of a horse standing outside a stable, and I studied it like I hadn't seen it before until there was a knock at the door, then it opened.

Turning back to see my father stride in, I got to my feet with a smile. His arms were open as soon as he closed the door and turned back to face me, and I rushed at him, loving the way he hugged me.

No, we didn't have a regular daddy-daughter relationship, but in our way, we were close.

He embraced me tightly then pressed a kiss to the top of my head. "New perfume?"

My eyes widened at that, and I pulled back to look up at him. "Huh?"

"You smell different."

I had his eyes, but that was it. His face was patrician and mine was anything but. He was tall and lean like the All American he'd been as a kid. He'd met Mom during summer break when he'd been home from West Point. A one-night stand had far reaching consequences that he'd never really known about until his campaign manager had found me. A big, black secret that marred his reputation.

"I do?" I cleared my throat and pulled away from him, returning to my seat on the sofa. As he followed, taking the opposite side, I told him, "I guess it's because I used my boyfriend's soap this morning."

He stiffened, his eyes widening in surprise at my announcement. "You have a boyfriend? Since when?"

I decided it was best to lie. "Quite a while." I smiled at him. "It only just got serious. Nothing worth mentioning until now."

He grimaced. "I don't want to know what it was before you 'got serious.'"

Smirking at him, I joked, "Be grateful you only have one daughter."

"I am," he teased. "Sons are far easier to corral than girls."

"I'll bet." I pursed my lips in amusement then, as was our way, I served us both tea, and we settled back to talk. Considering the way we'd started off, I decided to take a deep dive into troubling waters. "I'm getting married to him, Dad."

Alan half-choked on his tea. "What?"

"You heard me," I jibed. I stared down at the murky brown liquid in my cup—I took it with just a dash of milk to take the bitterness away, but it certainly didn't look palatable. "He asked where I went every Tuesday."

That had him stiffening. "What did you tell him?"

"That I had a standing appointment with my father." I looked him square in the eye. "Nothing more, nothing less."

It wasn't really a lie.

Finn knew what was happening here from his own intel, not from anything I'd shared with him.

Alan grimaced. "I'm sorry, Aoife."

"It's okay, Dad. It is what it is."

He leaned forward and rested his elbows on his knees, tipping the cup in his hands as he stared down at his feet. "I hate that you have to lie for me."

"It's worth it." I licked my lips. "I-I know you won't be able to meet him, and I also know you won't be able to come to the wedding. It's okay, Dad."

He gritted his teeth. "It's anything but okay, Aoife. Dammit to hell."

"You have goals." I didn't say it to piss him off or to hurt him. If anything, I told him to reaffirm the fact I was okay with it. "The White House needs you, Dad. I'm not about to get in the way of that."

His jaw flexed. "What kind of father am I where I can't even walk you down the aisle?"

I shrugged. "It's only going to be a small affair."

"You're Catholic," he countered. "Catholics don't do small. Is the groom Catholic, too?"

There was a hoarseness to his tone that told me my words were hitting home—his daughter was going to get married, and he couldn't have anything to do with it. To be honest, I was touched. I hadn't been sure what his reaction would be, and it warmed me that he was disappointed he couldn't be there.

"He's more devout than I am," I told him honestly. "But we're getting married too quickly for it to be too big of a deal."

He frowned. "Are you pregnant?"

I snorted. "Nope."

"Then what's the rush?"

"The time's right." I shrugged. "I want to be with him, Dad. I moved in with him this week, and–"

"You moved in with him?" Unsure why that was what had him shouting, I watched as he ran a hand through his hair. "I don't even know his name, Aoife."

"Finn, Dad. His name's Finn." As far as I was aware, a quick Google of his name would reap only legitimate results.

Until he'd announced his affiliation, I hadn't heard of Finn O'Grady for years. Not since Fiona had died.

Considering the neighborhood's size, it was a wonder the news hadn't spread, but then, if the Five Points didn't want someone to know something, they would be ruthless in keeping it quiet. . . .

I just wondered what the hell had happened to make Finn disappear, and what would prompt Aidan to help him cover it up.

Still, that was a worry for another time.

"Finn. God, he's Irish, too?"

"That surprises you with my circle?" I grinned at him. "Everyone's Irish in my neighborhood."

He grunted. "True. What does he do?"

"Flips properties."

"There's money to be had in that. Does he expect you to quit your work?"

I cleared my throat. "No, but you remember I told you about that company that was looking to knock down my building? They came in with a better deal for me a few weeks ago. I accepted."

I hadn't told him any of this the last time we met. My head had been in the clouds and I hadn't wanted to focus on what Finn had done to me—professionally and personally—which meant this was the first time he was hearing any of this.

"You did?" His eyes widened. "Christ, is it only three weeks since we last met?"

"Yep. Things are happening quickly, I guess. I sold up and am going to put in an offer on another building a few streets away. It's bigger, and I'm not going to do the teashop side of things. Just focus on baking."

He nodded. "That makes sense. You never liked that part of the business anyway. Your heart was in the kitchen."

I smiled, touched that he knew that. "Yeah. So, it was a wrench to sign it away, but I knew it was a good move."

"When are you opening the bakery? Do you need any extra capital?"

There was the Dad in him. Always generous.

I shook my head. "Thanks, Dad, but no. You've done enough for me. The investment in the tea room means I can start the bakery up without needing a loan."

Though he frowned, he just grumbled, "Good. I don't want you to be in debt, and . . ." He swallowed. "I can't be there, and I hate it, but I want to pay for the wedding."

I sighed. "That isn't necessary. Like I said, it's only going to be a small affair."

"A meal, then? Afterward. The wedding brunch?"

Because I could see how much it meant to him, I leaned forward and grabbed his hand. "Okay, Dad. Thank you. That means a lot."

He squeezed my fingers. "I wish I could do more."

"Honestly, it's fine."

"Stop saying that," he grumbled. "It makes me think you don't want me there."

Snorting at his sulky tone, I told him, "If you stick your bottom lip out, don't think I'll cave in if you pout."

That had him grinning. "My temper never works on you, does it? I can have all my staff flustered and flared with a single bark, but not you."

I shrugged. "You never shout at me, nor have you given me a reason to get flustered."

"That's not the truth," he stated, and I knew we were both thinking back to that time when we'd first met. When he'd grated out his terms in the back of his limo, and had expected me to comply.

I'd told him to fuck off and never darken my door again.

He hadn't listened.

I sighed. "No point in thinking about that. We're here now."

"I want to meet him," he said, his gaze catching mine.

"How would we arrange that?"

Alan reached up and tugged at his bottom lip. "I don't know. But we'll figure it out. I can't let my daughter marry a man I'll never meet. Christ, Aoife, just the thought kills me."

Because I understood, I murmured, "Finn probably goes to charity events—he's doing well for himself, Dad." I cleared my throat. "We could maybe arrange to go to one you're attending?"

"Do you trust him with who I am to you?"

It said a lot about my faith in the man, especially considering how we'd met, that I felt no compunction in telling my father, the Senator, the presidential hopeful, "Absolutely."

25

———

FINN

AFTER THE *SHESTYORKA*, the Bratva equivalent of a runner, patted me, Aidan, Jr., and Eoghan down, the guy guided us along the dimly lit hall of the warehouse.

I wasn't exactly happy to be here, and I sure as hell didn't like being unarmed right in the middle of Bratva territory, but we needed help if we were going to stop a war, and the Pakhan, the head of the Bratva in this area, owed us a favor.

The Bratva had a different way of working than most Irish Families; there was a lot of 'eye for an eye' shit that the Irish didn't go for so much. But with the Five Points, things were different. Aidan Sr. made the Old Testament look softcore, and that meant our core values were aligned with the Russian brotherhood.

That didn't mean I liked them, or even wanted to deal with them. But neither did I want a war.

War was good for no one.

It stopped free trade because the locals stopped going out, and it got the police involved if too many people were killed. No one wanted the pigs sniffing around us.

The Bratva included.

The warehouse was grim, old, and dank when we made it into an office which wasn't much better. The walls were painted white, but the paint was peeling, and the desk looked like it belonged in another era—I noticed a few marks where it had been kicked a few times—and there were several bullet holes in the paintwork that caught my attention.

On either side of the door, there were two men I recognized, with several more unfamiliar faces in the room. Antoni Vasov, the Pakhan, and his two spies. His bookkeeper, the Sovietnik Denis Abramovicz, and the head of his security, the Obschak Basil Lukov. That they were here boded well. They knew what our purpose was, and their presence meant shit could get real sooner rather than later.

Though the office was a dump, the suits the three men wore cost over ten grand. The Bratva were wealthy fuckers, but their money came from less legitimate revenue streams. We had our vices, drugs and girls, but they were dirty. Hardcore. They trafficked girls, something I loathed, and shipped guns from the Motherland to America.

Vasov didn't stand when we all strode in, and I knew Aidan Sr. would take that as an insult. Aidan Jr. elbowed him, though, and Sr. took the hint and seated himself in the only chair in front of the desk.

"Thank you for meeting with me, Antoni," Aidan started, his tone cool but polite.

Vasov dipped his chin. "I know why you're here," he replied, his accent thick with his homeland. "I'm not sure I can help."

That had me inwardly groaning. Fuck. I'd thought they weren't going to bullshit. Because Aidan's temper ran on a short fuse, I stated, "Cut the crap, Vasov. One good turn deserves another, and it's time to pay up."

Vasov cut me a look. "Your errand boy talks for you now, Aidan?"

Rather than being pissed, Aidan laughed. "More like my Sovietnik, Antoni." He grinned good-naturedly. "I'm certain Abramovicz would try to cut out my tongue if I'd slurred his name that way, so maybe you should be grateful that Finn isn't armed."

Vasov sneered, but he ducked his head in apology—that was

about as much of a sorry as I was going to get. I wasn't pissed, though. Rank meant shit to me. The money was what mattered, and I had millions under my control.

"Last year, when we learned our little rat had DEA ties and we saved that shipment of coke from being transported straight into the government's hands, I estimate we saved you a loss of over two hundred million."

Abramovicz barked something at Vasov, who narrowed his eyes. "I remember," was all the Pakhan said, though.

"Well, my little problem will cost far less to resolve," Aidan replied, his tone bizarrely cheerful—only Aidan could find something funny within these walls.

"You pissed the Colombians off. Word is, you made it look like they'd killed Suarez."

"I neither confirm nor deny that," Aidan retorted, "but they're making moves on my patch and none of us want to come to the attention of the cops, do we? Only the Colombians are stupid enough to try to bring shit to my territory and think there won't be consequences, but I understand they're pissed and want to bitch at me. They've done that now. I've had enough."

"And what do you want me to do about it?"

"We know you have their ear. They're your main supplier of coke, after all. You have a mutually beneficial relationship."

"Why would I risk my supply for you?" Vasov retorted, sitting forward so he could rest his elbows on the table.

"Because you owe us," I retorted easily, and before he could sneer that it was in the past, I smoothly continued, "Plus, a little piggy may have told me something interesting about your movements in the Baltics."

Vasov's eyes flared. "What the fuck are you talking about?"

The Sovietnik and Obschak began hurling Russian at Vasov, and from the way we could see the whites of the Pakhan's eyes, I knew my tip off was good.

"I think you know, Antoni," I told him softly. "I think it's time you stopped bullshitting us and we figure out how we're going to make peace in these troubled times."

"You know nothing about the Baltics."

"I know you've been supplying the Ukraine with guns. I don't think your President would appreciate that. Do you, Aidan?"

"No, Finn, I really fucking don't."

"And let me see, funneling weapons to them is an international war crime and wouldn't you know it, I have someone in the press who likes me and who's willing to break the news on this scandal on my behalf."

"You wouldn't dare," Vasov barked.

"I really fucking would."

Aidan sat straighter in his seat. "Now that we have your attention, gentleman, let's get down to the details. The Colombians are becoming meddlesome. I want you to talk to them, make them see sense, and if they don't, I want you to threaten to cut ties with them."

Vasov's jaw twitched. "That's ridiculous—"

"Is it? Fancy being tried at the Hague, do you? Or how about landing in a Siberian gulag? I'm sure the cells there are real comfortable," I sneered.

His Sovietnik ground out, "We are due to meet in four weeks' time. They are erratic. They have no base that we have found. We will not be able to speak with them until they communicate with us. It has been that way for five years."

Aidan grunted. "That's a damn shame." He sighed. "Well, the wait can't be helped, but are we agreed that you'll be helping us out, Antoni?"

Though it obviously pained him to say it, the Pakhan gritted out, "*Da.*"

It was the first step in a dance, but we'd made the first move, the first parry. That was how you did business with the Russians.

You made them your bitch.

26

AOIFE

"IT'S TOO BIG, FINN."

He clucked his tongue. "Don't complain, Aoife. We both know you like it big."

Despite myself, I had to giggle. My cheeks burned though because the assistant was watching us and I knew she'd heard what Finn had said. "Finn," I hissed. "You're incorrigible."

He pressed a kiss to my lips. "I try."

Rolling my eyes at him, I gnawed on my cheek as I stared down at the princess cut emerald that Finn swore was an exact match to my eyes. It was huge. So big I was terrified I'd lose it. "I don't need it to be so big, Finn."

"No? Well, I need everyone to know you're mine."

I huffed a breath. "I thought we'd already established I was getting a tattoo on my forehead with your name on it?"

A snicker escaped him. "Well, that's a far cheaper option, but I decided against it. I love your creamy skin the way it is."

That had my lips curving in a deep smile. "Okay, then. If you insist."

"Oh, I do," he teased, his eyes flaring wide as I reached up to kiss him in thanks. When I pulled back, we were both panting a little, and his tone was gruff when he turned to the assistant. "We'll take it." He handed her a debit card, she dealt with the transaction, and ten minutes later, we walked out with a three million dollar ring on my finger.

The price tag made me want to choke, but every time I'd tried to look at something that cost less, Finn had growled and dragged another expensive one down my finger. I mean I'd figured fifty grand was a hell of a lot to spend on an engagement ring, but every day I was reminded that the wealth Finn commanded was beyond insane.

Speaking of insane, when we stepped out of the jewelers, Aidan Sr. was standing there with Conor and Magdalena at his side.

"Aidan? What's wrong?"

I heard the concern in his voice, and though I didn't have to wonder why, I knew he was under more pressure than I'd imagined if he figured Aidan would bring Lena out when he, too, was on edge.

"Nothing," the older man said, beaming a grin our way. Conor rolled his eyes, and I realized how alike the two of them looked. Finn, though he was definitely *not* family by blood, bore a striking resemblance, too—with their Black Irish locks, silky skin, and stark blue eyes, they were all handsome brutes.

Magdalena and I, by comparison, were everything they weren't. The men were tall and lean, their bodies a weapon. Under their coats, guns bulged—even Conor who, I knew from what little Finn had mentioned, worked mostly behind a computer—and though they all wore expensive clothes, they still managed to look more dangerous than stylish.

Lena wore a simple white sheath dress that skimmed over her generous curves. Her hair was tied back in a loose chignon, and she had kitten heels that took her from five feet nothing to five-five nothing. She clutched a purse in one hand and Aidan's arm with the other.

I, on the other hand, was not dressed appropriately for the occasion. My ring cost three million straight. My entire outfit cost three million and twenty bucks. Yup. My dress was Primark, a gauzy, floaty thing that I'd paired with ballet pumps and a denim jacket.

My wardrobe needed an overhaul if I wasn't always going to feel like the poor relation.

"I wanted to go out for coffee with Aoife," Lena declared, "and my husband and son decided I needed an escort." She tutted. "You can come with us, but you're not sitting at the same table."

Her words were a decree, too. She meant it.

I had to hide my smile as Aidan shot her a mulish glower at which Conor, again, rolled his eyes.

Finn blinked at her statement. "That can be arranged."

"Oh, I know it can," she told him sweetly, and then she waved a hand my way. "Come on, Aoife. Leave the men to talk."

Shooting Finn a grin when he grunted with displeasure at her dictate, I moved toward her. She detached herself from Aidan's side, ignoring his grumble—I mean were all the men in the extended O'Donnelly clan this possessive?—and together, we walked down to the end of the street where there was a small coffee shop.

The men stuck close to us as we took a seat, but they did take their own table a few feet away. From this angle, they could hear us, and we could hear them. That was why when Conor stated, "I swear, you two are so pussy-whipped," Lena called out, "Better to have a pussy than no pussy at all."

Conor glowered at her. "I have girlfriends."

"Imaginary ones," Lena retorted sweetly. "Let's face it, sweet boy, you can't get laid by a computer."

Conor ground his teeth but apparently, decided not to engage in open battle across a coffee shop. I smirked at Lena who beamed a self-satisfied grin at me.

"There, now they'll know to keep their voices low and won't be interested in what we have to say."

I tilted my head at her. "You manage them very well, don't you?"

She busied herself by picking up the menu. "I wouldn't say so."

"I would." I snorted when she looked at me from under her lashes, amusement brimming in her wide hazel eyes.

"It takes practice," she admitted, tapping her nose with her finger. "They're all stubborn, but eventually, you can wrangle most things out of them. Just know what you want, don't waver, and aim for it like you're a heat-seeking missile."

Her comment made me wonder if she knew Finn had asked me to reconsider opening the bakery. "I didn't waver, Lena."

"Whatever do you mean, child?" she questioned, but I hadn't been mistaken.

"You know what I'm talking about. Finn told me there's too much danger to have a storefront at the moment. I heeded his caution."

Lena's head tilted to the side in surprise. "He told you that?" She frowned as she looked at her husband. "What else did he say?"

"Not a lot," I stated, uneasy now. Hadn't Aidan told her of the threat the Colombians posed?

She tutted. "He tells me nothing."

"There isn't much to know," I replied honestly. It wasn't like Finn had spilled the beans to me. What I knew was incidental mostly. "But the bakery is only on hiatus. Just until things calm down."

Though she nodded, she narrowed her eyes at me. "Aoife's an unusual name, isn't it?"

"I suppose," I replied, surprised where she'd taken the conversation.

"For these parts, I mean. And with Keegan, it's even rarer." She pursed her lips and cut me a look that said 'this isn't over' when the waitress came to take our order.

"Hardly rare," was all I said.

"Did you know Finn ran away from home?"

My heart stuttered in my chest. "He never mentioned it."

"No, he never does. But did you know, Aoife?"

"Why would I?" I rasped. "If he didn't tell me, I mean."

She clucked her tongue when the waitress reappeared, depositing our coffee in front of us. While Lena dosed her latte with sugar, I felt my heart sink to my stomach as she eventually commented, "Finn came to us a very troubled young man. I didn't know his parents, but I know his father was one of our runners."

My eyes flared wide at that. "He was?"

"You say that like you knew of him?" Lena cocked a brow at me, and once again, my stomach felt loaded down with stones.

"I'm just surprised."

She pursed her lips. "Well, I half believe he's purposely shoved most of his memories of that time away. Stored them in a box in his head. He's stubborn enough to do it," she mumbled.

"He has nightmares," I admitted, not sure why I made the admission except that Lena was obviously in mother hen mode. How could I blame her for protecting Finn? For looking out for him?

"He does?" In her eyes, I saw her sorrow, and she sighed heavily.

Her love for Finn obviously ran true, and I was glad he'd had her in his life. He'd left a mother behind who'd adored him, but for whatever reason, that hadn't been enough to keep him home. "I'd hoped he'd have grown out of them now."

"They don't happen often," I told her, my voice a rasp. "But he's scared in them."

"I imagine. What his father did to him..." Her nostrils flared. "He won't speak of that time with you, Aoife, but I will. Not to unman him, because I know how these boys are. All pride and ego. I only found out from Aidan because I was worried about his night terrors, but if you're out to hurt him, I'll hurt you first. The boy's been hurt enough—"

"Hurt him?" I squeaked. "The reason we met, Lena, is because he was trying to extort me into bed with him. In this relationship, Finn's the one who you should be warning."

"Extort you into bed?" she sputtered, then she fiddled with her earring as a sheepish look etched itself onto her features. "Well, at least I know you didn't machinate your way into his life."

I snorted. "No, Lena, I did not."

"Still, why haven't you told him who you are?"

"Who am I?" I whispered, suddenly grateful that the café was noisy. Finn couldn't hear this conversation, and I didn't want him to.

"Your mother and his were best friends, weren't they?" She snorted. "Not that she was much of a mother to him."

"What do you mean?" I cried, then, aware of how loud my voice was, I bit out, "Fiona loved him. She mourned him until the day she died."

"You love a child, you protect him. Fiona never did that."

Stung, I leaned forward and ground out, "What did you know about her? Nothing, that's what. You just stole her son from her! She thought he was dead."

"That was how Finn wanted it," Lena retorted with a sniff.

"He was a boy! You should never have allowed him to make that decision." My heart ached for Fiona who'd been so goddamn heartbroken. Every day praying, every day her hopes dashed. "My mom used to say she died early because of Finn."

"She died early because she was ashamed. That woman should have made her knees bleed as she tried to atone for her sins."

I scowled at her. "What the hell are you talking about?"

"You were a child," Lena conceded, "I know that. You wouldn't have been aware of the inferences."

My throat thickened as I recalled something that always put me on edge. "I know her husband beat her. I remember seeing her with bruises and asking my mom why that was."

"Her husband," Lena retorted. "The bastard. And you think he left Finn alone, do you? Just focused his fists on his wife?"

A lump formed in my throat. "Oh."

"Yes. *Oh.* And I can tell you, that bastard did more than just hit Finn." She firmed her chin. "He ran from home, was on the streets. Only the fact that he was friends with my boys saved him. They encouraged him to come home with them, and when I saw the poor wee man, my heart bled for him."

"He abused him?" I whispered, my eyes welling with tears.

"Aye. He did. And she didn't stop it, Aoife." Lena took a deep sip of her coffee. "Are you here for some kind of revenge?"

"Revenge?" I shrieked. "Lena, he dragged me into this world. I was quite happy with my tea room, safe and single and bored. So damn bored," I admitted. "But he most definitely brought me into his sphere, not the other way around."

She pursed her lips, and I felt her judging me. With each sweep of her gaze upon my face, it was like she was scanning my words and my expression for the truth. I'd admit to sagging with relief when she informed me, "I liked you when you came to dinner the other day, and it will be a pleasure to have you around my place more often.

"Finn's needed someone like you for a while. You're very calming, and he runs himself ragged. I saw how he responded to you, how you eased him, and that's all I've ever wanted for him. But I had to make sure that you weren't out to hurt him."

I swallowed thickly. "Lena, I would never do—" Because I was at a loss for words, I blew out a shaky breath. "Look, I haven't raised the topic with him because I didn't know what to say. The minute he walked into my tea room and introduced himself, I knew who he was, and I couldn't believe it because Fiona grieved for him, Lena. She was heartsick."

"I won't feel sorry for her," Lena retorted. "I can't. It's not in me. It didn't happen just once, Aoife, and I can't tell you how hard I worked to drag that fact out of Aidan, and how long it took for him to get Finn to talk. What she allowed to happen . . . a mother would be heartsick."

My hand came up to cup my throat. "I-I don't know what to say. I just know that I . . . well, there isn't anything to talk about with Finn. That's why I haven't mentioned it. Fiona died a long time ago, and she's in the past. I knew her, and I knew Finn when I was two. The little insight I have into him comes from her, and that doesn't tell me much about the man himself."

"Will you make my boy happy?"

The quiet question had tears pricking my eyes again. "To the best of my ability. But I'm not perfect. I make mistakes, too. And I'm certain Finn will piss me off and we'll fight. I promise that I won't hurt him, not intentionally."

A smile crested Lena's lips. "That's a good, strong answer."

"It is?" I asked, totally confused.

"It is." She rubbed her hands together. "He doesn't need a woman who'll quiver when he says boo."

Well, I quivered when he said dirty things, but *boo* certainly didn't get me hot.

"Well, that's okay then because I'm not afraid of him. The Five Points? I'm afraid of them."

"That's wise of you, dearie," Lena muttered. "I'm not a fan of them myself, but that's not our place to question." She tilted her head to the side as she studied me, and in the crowded coffee shop, I suddenly felt hot. It was autumn, not exactly warm, but the way the place was set up, with plush sofas and armchairs, all in warm colors, and under Lena's spotlight, I felt overheated to the point I could feel sweat gather at the bottom of my spine.

"What is it?" I croaked, aware I was more cautious around her than I was Finn.

"There'll be women," she stated, her tone sad. "They'll come onto him. He won't be able to help himself."

My mouth gaped at her. "There'd better not be."

"I wish I could agree, but I can't. Just . . . be aware and then you won't be hurt."

I heard her resigned tone, and for a second, I couldn't reconcile the possessive way Aidan held Lena, with the notion that he'd cheated on her.

I couldn't imagine Finn cheating on me. Not because I was stupid, but because what we had together was so explosive, it surprised even him. Which told me I was the best he'd ever had. And yeah, that made me preen, I wasn't about to lie.

Still, marriage was for a long time, and we'd only been together a short while. Life got in the way, and things happened that no one could foresee. Though I appreciated her warning, I took it with a grain of salt. I wasn't about to condemn him before he even left the starting gate.

She patted my hand, maybe sensing my rejection of her words, and asked, "Aidan tells me you're seeing the priest tomorrow."

"Yeah. It's been a while since I've been to church."

When she rolled her eyes, I hid a laugh. "I'm not as ardent as Aidan, so I won't judge. It's enough for me that you're Catholic, but not for Aidan. The Church is... Well, we all need a crutch, and his is our Lord and Savior. Doyle will make you pay for not having gone to confession. Just be warned when he doles out the Hail Marys like they're going out of fashion."

And there was the voice of someone who'd been on the receiving end of such treatment.

I wanted to like Lena. Back at her place, this Sunday, I had. She'd invited me to her kitchen, and together, we'd cooked. Though she'd put me on edge with this discussion, could I blame her? She wanted the best for a man she considered to be her sixth son. Wouldn't I do the same to protect my child? Yeah, I damn well would.

Still, I needed to know. "Will you say anything to him about my knowing his mom?"

She smiled at me. "No. You passed my test, so that's the end of it as far as I'm concerned."

I'd never know what Fiona had or hadn't done. I'd never know how much she'd known about Finn's suffering. A part of me couldn't reconcile this knowledge with the woman I knew, but Lena wasn't bullshitting me. And I'd heard Finn's nightmares for myself. I'd thought they were centered around the crap he'd had to do as a Pointer, but now that I knew this? It was an insight into the man I was going to marry.

Having loved Fiona, it hurt me to think she'd been aware of what her husband had done to Finn and hadn't stopped him, but there was nothing I could do to change what was done to him in the past.

I couldn't take his pain away, nor could I make things better.

But, I *was* Finn's future, and I fully intended on making a brighter path for us both, one that would enable him to let go of the past and hopefully drag him from the shadows and toward the light.

27

———

FINN

FATHER DOYLE STARED at me over his glasses. "This is very fast, Finn, my child. Do you have something to confess?"

I scowled at him. "Aoife is not pregnant." I glared at her when she choked back a giggle. "Tell him, Aoife."

Her lips curved. "I'm not pregnant."

Sighing, I mumbled, "You could have said that with more conviction."

She snickered, and Father Doyle glared at her disapprovingly. "You think it's a laughing matter to be with child?"

"No, Father, but Finn's reaction was too amusing not to laugh."

Father Doyle narrowed his eyes. "Your parents are dead?"

She stiffened, and because I knew her secret, I knew why. "Yes."

"Shame, shame, for two good Catholic souls to be taken from their daughter while she's so young. They were, I presume, Catholic?" That was what he really wanted to know.

"Indeed, Father. Both of them. My parish is over on Hawk Avenue."

Doyle stiffened. "You're a part of Father James' flock?"

"Yes."

"When was your last confession? We stick with the old ways here, Aoife. I know Father James is very slack on that front."

She cleared her throat. "A while ago?"

Doyle tsked. "We'll have to remedy that."

I shot her a sympathetic look, and she grimaced at me, then tightened her fingers about mine.

The priest's office was dour, cold, and very, very brown. Except for the avocado green desk chair he sat in, one that he'd used since he'd first accepted me into his flock after I'd run from home. Everything was the same. Old and worn.

The walls were clad with wooden panels which made the room even grimmer, and a set of three windows looked out onto a street.

It was like stepping into the seventies when you came in here, and outside was the promise of the return to the modern world.

"I'm sure, Father. I'll be attending on Sunday if that's okay?"

"More than okay, my child," Doyle said, beaming at her.

I'd told Aoife that Sunday service was an important part of life for all of us. Even Conor, who'd broken his parents' heart by coming out as an atheist.

When that had happened, I honestly thought Aidan would have preferred him to come out as gay. And Aidan was one of the biggest homophobes I'd ever encountered. He was of the 'Adam and Eve, not Adam and Steve' belief. But then, he was old-school. So old-school he belonged in this office with the rest of the time warp.

When I'd told her of the duty we'd now be performing as a couple, she'd moaned, "No sleeping in?"

I'd grinned. "Nope."

Doyle grumbled under his breath. "Still, this expediency is very strange, Finn. You're certain you're not with child, Aoife."

"Very certain, Father."

"To bypass the calling of the banns, you know how traditional we are, Finn."

"I do, Father, but as I'm sure you can understand, I want Aoife protected."

The old coot pursed his lips—Father Doyle wasn't as old as the church, but he was *as* decrepit. He steepled his fingers as he narrowly avoided the fact he knew exactly what I, and the rest of the O'Donnellys, did for a living.

"Your father's been in touch with me," he murmured. "I thought I was going to see him today."

"Business called," I retorted shortly, knowing that even though I'd have loathed Aidan being here, witnessing this as he'd promised last Sunday, I'd have preferred that to his reason for canceling on us.

Some Colombian shitheads had hit another one of our protected businesses—a jewelry store.

Aidan asked for a protection fee from most stores in the area, but unlike most Families, he actually gave a damn. Whatever was taken on his watch, he refunded.

That meant every crime the Colombians committed on our territory was a hit to our wallet.

I was almost certain that they wouldn't be doing this if they'd known that particular salient fact.

Doyle drummed his fingers against the table. "Wouldn't you like a big white wedding, Aoife?" he badgered, making me roll my eyes at his attempt to lengthen our engagement.

"No, Father. It wouldn't be right, anyway. Not with my mother. . . . I should still be in black, after all."

I had to hide a laugh at that—Aoife, as she was wont to do—had a habit of reading a situation and reading it well.

To anyone else, the idea of wearing black for a year after a loved one's death was beyond ridiculous. To Doyle? Well, let's put it this way, when Aidan's mother had died ten years ago, if we hadn't attended church with a black band around our arms, Doyle would have sent us home.

In his own way, this man had more power in this parish than anyone else. He had the Rottweiler that was Aidan Sr. at his beck and call, after all.

That was why it was important Aoife impress him. It sure as fuck wasn't for my benefit.

Doyle sighed at Aoife. "I see no justifiable reason for doing without the banns, *but* in these circumstances, I will wave it."

"Much appreciated, Father," I replied, smiling at him and feeling a huge chunk of relief.

It was ridiculous, considering my business, how much time I wasted in this church, and yet it was as integral to my work as it was sitting in my office.

Nuts.

Aoife squeezed my hand as Doyle told us some of the available dates for the event, and together, we worked out when we'd be getting hitched.

I'd never imagined I'd actively want to tie myself up with a ball and chain, but Jesus, Aoife was so beyond different. I didn't feel hemmed in, didn't feel like she was overtaking my life. Hell, I wanted more of her. Wanted her with me all the goddamn time. It was an ache, a constant goddamn ache that I should be ashamed to admit to.

But with Aoife?

Everything made sense.

My inner monster, the fucker that could shoot someone with no compunction, end a life or tear someone a new asshole, was at peace. I slept better. I wasn't drinking as much because, God, help me, I didn't need to with her in my life.

I wanted her tied to me in so many ways she'd never be able to be rid of me.

Where Aoife was concerned, not getting her bound to me ASAP would be the height of idiocy, and Finn O'Grady was many, many things, but an idiot he was not.

28

———

AOIFE

I frowned at Jenny. "Don't talk to me like that, Jenny."

She raised her arms and encompassed the building we were standing in. "You're going to put off your dreams for him."

"No, I'm not." I clucked my tongue at her. "This place doesn't exactly have potential tenants lining up to take over the lease, and it's only for a short time."

She sniffed. "You said you'd never let any man stop you from doing what you want."

"And Finn isn't—"

"Bullshit, you've been dating him like four weeks and now you're getting married? And he's asking you not to get started on the bakery? What the fuck is that about, Aoife?"

I resented that she thought I was too much of a dumb bitch to see the bigger picture. Finn was *not* manipulating me. I knew that like I knew Jenny was spitting fire at me now because she was jealous.

And it was for a stupid reason, too.

I knew Jenny thought Finn was hot, but more than that, it was to do with the fact that I'd be getting married first.

Being someone's wife had never been on my to-do list. It really hadn't been an issue for me if I were to never marry at all. Definitely an anti-Catholic sentiment, but I wasn't exactly devout. Mom would have liked me to settle down, so I could have kids, but, shock, horror, I didn't need kids to make me feel like I'd lived my life.

Not that I'd have told her that.

She'd probably have thought she'd raised me wrong. Either that or would have asked me if I was, gasp, a lesbian.

Jenny, though, was just jealous because she was the kind of girl who'd been dreaming of her wedding day since she was four and had learned that men and women got married.

It didn't help that Finn was gorgeous, loaded, and seemingly head over heels for me when he'd seen Jenny at the same time.

It sounded so petty in my head, but that was the gist of it. Jenny wasn't happy for me, and she was showing that now.

I was pissed at her stupidity, to be honest. Pissed that she was letting the fact I was going to be married first get between us. Who did that?

Christ, I'd only said yes to Finn because of who he was. Not just his status as a Five Points man, but because, internally, he was a possessive man. I knew he wouldn't have stopped asking me until I said yes, and even if he thought he was mature enough to let me walk away—like he'd done three nights ago by letting me in on the fact there was a war brewing—he never would.

I was his.

Had been since he'd figured out I was a virgin.

Was I enamored with the fact he'd put his stamp on me because he'd taken my hymen? Nope. But I *was* touched by the respect he gave me because of it. That kind of chivalry didn't exist that much anymore. Having a cherry to pop was more of a hindrance than anything else, but not to Finn. He'd put me up on a pedestal because of that, and I was charmed by it.

So, rather than be happy for me, Jenny was just being a Bridezilla. Without the fiancé.

"Finn isn't going to put a halt to my dreams, Jenny. I will make this bakery, but there's shit you don't know."

"Shit like what?" she sneered.

Jenny wasn't a stupid woman, even if she was being really fucking stupid now. She knew what my next words signified, "Finn's a Points' man."

Her mouth dropped open, and her arms, still raised to encompass the building, dropped to her side. "He's one of them?"

I dipped my chin brusquely. Maybe this wasn't wise to talk about, but I wasn't about to have a fall out over this.

Jenny and I had been friends for too long to let a man get between us, and it wasn't like she wouldn't figure shit out quickly. If there were bodies suddenly piling up in morgues around here, the gossip mills would already be churning.

Because she'd lost her position with me, she'd picked up a waitressing job at a diner around the corner to tide her over—soon enough, news would pass around the tables there, and everyone would know a war had come to our streets.

"Fuck, Aoife," she rasped, her eyes wide, pupils dilated. "Aren't you scared?"

My lips curved. "No." The question amused me because I knew she'd dated several Points men in the past.

"But he's dangerous."

I shrugged. "Not to me. And he isn't a danger to my dreams, either. Something's happening, Jenny," I warned her, and she winced.

"Don't tell me. I don't want to know."

"I wasn't going to tell you," I retorted. "I don't have that much to share. Finn just told me to hold off on getting this place. That's all I know."

Her mouth firmed into a perfect O. "Is this to do with that stripper that died a few nights ago?"

"Do you really want to know?"

She swallowed. "Is shit about to go down?"

I nodded, not about to lie to her. "There's no need to worry about this place, either," I informed her. "I'm getting the deeds as a marriage gift."

"What?" she squeaked. "He's buying you this place?"

I'd prefer her to think it was Finn than know the gift was actually from Aidan O'Donnelly. I didn't want her to know how close to the inner circle Finn was.

None of us knew how the Five Points worked. They were secretive, and though we knew who was aligned with them, we didn't know the inner circles. Only members did.

Aidan O'Donnelly was the face of it, and only then because everyone was fucking scared of him and what he was capable of.

He was like a human bulldog with rabies. Everyone knew to avoid his bite. Just not the people who were messing with his business, it would be seem.

I didn't even have it in me to feel sorry for them. They'd killed an innocent woman to get back at the Points. They deserved whatever evil was coming their way.

"What are we doing here then if you're not getting this place ready?" Jenny asked, and I was glad my revelation had jerked her out of her sulk. She peered over her shoulder at the two men standing outside the store front. "Is that who the other guy is? I figured he was with the real estate guy."

My lips twitched. "You thought Billy was in real estate? He's my guard." I had to laugh at that, and though she pouted at my amusement, she started snickering, too.

With his scar and the bulge at his shoulder, Billy looked more like he was prepped for a bank robbery than a tour around a vacant property. But, he was my guard. He was here to keep me safe not to look pretty.

"Okay, so my eyes were definitely not focusing right when I came to that conclusion."

"Ya think?" I joked. Then, I sobered and murmured, "I wanted to see all of it again before Finn bought the place for me. Now I have, now that I'm certain I want it, I feel comfortable letting Finn get involved."

She gnawed on her bottom lip. "Am I ever going to meet this Finn?"

"You already have," I teased.

"Once," she pshawed. "That's not enough. I need to vet him, make sure he's good enough for my BFF."

"He's busy, Jen. But you'll see him at the wedding."

She grunted. "That sucks."

"Such is life," I told her with no apology.

Maybe I was being a bit mean, but I didn't appreciate how she'd acted earlier. I wasn't a little girl, and she wasn't my mom.

"I can't believe you're getting married, Aoife," she murmured, her gaze glued to her feet.

"Me, either."

She peered at me under her thick lashes. "You sure you're not making a mistake?"

I shrugged. "Who knows? I just know I'm happy, and after everything with Mom. . . ." I released a shuddery breath when I thought back to not just *how* she'd died, but the fact she wasn't here anymore. "It's good to be happy again, Jen."

She strode forward and wrapped me in a hug. "Okay, then I'll stop being a bitch and be happy for you, too."

"Thanks," I whispered, pressing a kiss to her cheek. "That means a lot."

29

FINN

"YOU'RE NOT INVITING any family to the wedding?"

I frowned at Aoife. "I don't have any family save for the O'Donnellys, and they're trouble enough, trust me."

Her chin jerked up as she pondered that, then she shrugged. "Okay."

"Your dad can't come, can he?"

She shook her head. "No. But . . . he does want to meet you."

I cocked a brow at that. She'd never mentioned her dad or their meeting, and because I knew there was no secret there, I hadn't pried. It wasn't in my nature to want to know where she was, who she was seeing, what she was doing, twenty-four seven.

I was possessive and cautious about her safety. I wasn't an overbearing asshole.

If she didn't want to tell me something, I could handle it.

"He does?" I reached for the coffee cake she'd plated up for me a moment ago—I swear, I could live in this kitchen for the rest of my life. Trouble was, they'd have to roll me out of here. "I figured he'd want to keep things on the down-low."

"He does, but I told him I trusted you with his identity."

She'd never had a choice in the matter . . .

For that reason, I asked, "Do you?"

Her back was to me because she was at the stove, but she turned her head to look at me. "Of course. I figure you'd have told Aidan before now, and he'd have contacted Alan and made his demands if that had been your intention all along."

True.

Did that mean she did trust me? Had faith in me?

Fuck. That mattered so much to me.

"What's his deal then?"

She licked her lips. "He said that he'd tell me his schedule. He wants to meet at a party. You know? Keep things quiet and easy."

I thought about that, figured it made sense. "I'm not exactly the kind of guy who attends charity galas, but to meet him, we can go. Before or after the wedding?"

"When schedules allow, I guess."

"You told him when we were getting hitched?"

"I texted him and he called me back immediately. He about bust a gut," she said on a laugh, then she shrugged. "Tough."

Billy had told me that Jenny and she had argued while they were visiting the bakery yesterday. Aoife hadn't mentioned that, either.

"What did Jenny say about the date?"

Another shrug. "That it was too fast, but I told her you make me happy."

"That true?" I was like a broken record, but I wanted to, no, *needed* to know.

Her smile was warm. "Oh yes, that's true."

My throat felt thick as I smiled back at her. Then I forked up some cake, and she went back to humming as she stirred the pot that contained our dinner.

For a second, things seemed to slow down. My heartbeat seemed to settle into a quieter rhythm, and I realized that I, too, was happy.

Bone deep content.

A breath shuddered from me at the realization, and I had to ask myself how long it had been since I'd felt like this.

Conor could accuse me of being pussy-whipped all he wanted, but I'd take it for this feeling.

Shit, it was better than that weed I'd smoked as a kid.

I licked at a crumb that had fallen on my bottom lip, then reached for my cup and swilled down some coffee.

The feeling of contentment swirled inside me to the point where I didn't actually know what to do with myself. It felt so alien to be happy.

Of course, it couldn't last. I didn't even have to think that before the buzzer to the penthouse sounded.

I frowned because I rarely had guests, and the minute the buzzer sounded, I heard the bell that meant the elevator to the penthouse had been activated. Seconds after that, my cell rang.

Each wave of activity came within a second of the other, and I grabbed my cell, aware Aoife was watching me.

Spying Eoghan's caller ID, I picked it up and demanded, "Tell me you're the fuckers barging into my penthouse?"

"Yeah. We've a man down."

My nostrils flared. "Since when was this the fucking ER?"

"Don't be a dick. He was shot. It was clean. Went straight through. I just need to sew him up, and I need somewhere clean to do it."

I gritted my teeth, hating that, just as my thoughts had been settled, just as peace had stirred within me, chaos was crossing my threshold.

Though it would always have irked me to be disturbed, what pissed me off was the fact Aoife was going to see this.

She wouldn't stay in the kitchen if I asked her to. And maybe that should have pissed me off even more, but it didn't.

She wasn't a dog. She couldn't be leashed in her own goddamn home.

"Fine," I bit off, and climbing off the counter seat, I padded out of the kitchen down to the doorway. I was fully aware that Aoife was watching me, that she crossed the kitchen to follow me to the hall.

She didn't move closer, though, just stayed there. Witnessing the sorry shit that came with being a Five Points' man. Even one as high up in the ranks as I was.

That was the Family for you.

No matter how high you soared, they'd always bring you down a peg or two, and keep your feet fixed firmly on the ground.

When I saw the injured man, I grimaced. "You should have said it was Donny."

Eoghan snorted. "Would that have had you greeting us with hot tea and cake?"

I flipped him the bird. "Don't be a cunt."

"But I play the part so well," he mocked.

Donny sent me a ragged smile—his teeth were coated in blood. "Sorry about this, Finn. I might stain your carpet."

While Eoghan chuckled, I shook my head. "It's been a while since you were last here, Donny. I had the carpet taken out. You fuckers kept leaking on it."

I liked Donny. He was good people. Truth was, I'd been intent on having him as Aoife's guard, but I knew he'd been assigned to the whole shit-storm that was brewing with the Colombians.

We had an unusual hierarchy.

Everyone answered to Aidan.

Then, each of his sons, and myself, spearheaded a certain aspect of the business.

We had men under us, men who answered to us, the joeys, the runners, and our captains, for example.

We weren't as organized as the Russians with their military style hierarchy, but it made sense to us. It worked.

Donny was assigned to a captain on Aidan Jr.'s side of the business.

We were due to play poker soon, and I'd been hoping to win

Donny by whooping Aidan's ass. Just not soon enough to save him from being shot.

I backed up, letting Eoghan guide Donny in.

"What the fuck are you two doing together anyway?" I inquired as I led them both to one of the guest bedrooms. I knew Aoife was watching, but she kept quiet, so I wasn't concerned.

This bedroom was one I'd made sure was ready for events such as this. The furniture was simple, easy to sterilize, and I had all the necessary shit required for on-the-go injuries. The upper ranks all had rooms in their home like this one—thankfully, they weren't used that often.

"I was checking out something in Eoghan's turf."

"And I was bothered enough that when Donny asked for clearance, I tagged along. Good thing, too," Eoghan grunted. "It's a clean shot, but you'd still have bled out. Fucker hit his head when he went down."

"You could be concussed!"

I winced when I heard those four words and turned around to see Aoife was standing in the doorway, her hands on her hips.

"Aoife," I warned, but she scowled at me.

"He could be concussed, Finn," she repeated. "You need to get your head checked at the hospital."

Eoghan, being Eoghan, grinned at her. "You're a fiery wee thing tonight, Aoife."

She narrowed her eyes at him. "Be careful you don't get burned, then," she retorted, making me and Eoghan snort.

I'd admit, I'd never seen this side of her before, and I was definitely intrigued. This was the third time she'd met Eoghan, but it was the first time she'd been this feisty in front of any of my brothers.

She stormed into the room and moved toward the trestle table where Eoghan had propped Donny up. It was like the kind you found at the doctor's office.

Uneasily, she stared at the blood gushing through Donny's shirt, and mumbled, "Where are the stitches?"

I gaped at her. "You're not going to—"

"I'm a trained chef, Finn. I've sewn more flesh together than either of you have."

That had me wrinkling my nose at her. "You have?" And she was a trained chef?

How the fuck had I not known that?

Well, I guess I'd been gorging on her food all this time, but still . . . shit. She was trained? I'd known she'd gone to college, though.

"Yes. I went to culinary school. I could probably cut up a body better than either of you, too." She blew out a breath that had her bright-red bangs flopping on her forehead. "Why did that come out sounding proud?" she mumbled, more to herself than us.

"Well, that just gave me a hard-on," Eoghan admitted, and I elbowed him in the side.

"Sick fuck," I told him, then elbowed him harder when he grinned at me.

Aoife glowered at us both. "Well?"

I moved toward her when Eoghan grabbed a fresh towel and shoved it against Donny's wound to stop the blood flow. Still surprised I'd mistaken college for culinary school, I told her, "Darlin', Eoghan was a field med for the Rangers. He can handle this."

She blinked up at me. "Really?"

"Truly," I told her, bending down to kiss her on the nose. I was, I'd admit, touched that she'd care for one of our men this way. And from the respect in Eoghan's eyes, he was, too.

"O-Okay," she told me quietly. Then, to Eoghan, she asked, "Do you need any help?"

"I've got this, Aoife. You go on now. You don't need to be seeing the likes of this," he told her softly.

She licked her lips and looked at Donny. Patting his knee, she asked, "Would you like some cake?"

I snickered. "Cake's the last thing he'd like, Aoife, baby. Could you grab some whisky?"

Donny grunted. "Please? A big bottle."

Though she was a little wide-eyed, she scurried off to do as I'd asked. When I turned to follow her, then tilted back to look at Eoghan and Donny, I saw they were looking at me like I'd grown two heads.

"Never thought you'd marry, Finn," Donny mumbled, tipping his head back against the wall as Eoghan motioned at me to press the towel against the wound.

Fuck, I hated getting blood on my hands—it was a bastard to get out from under your nails—but I moved forward and did as asked, letting Eoghan bustle around to collect the various shit he'd need to cleanse and stitch up the wound.

"Me, either," I admitted.

"Can see why, though," he stated.

"She's good people," Eoghan added. "Anyone can see that."

I dipped my chin in agreement, and felt, literally fucking felt, when Aoife was back. Her feet slipped soundlessly against the floor, but I knew she was there without even having to turn my head.

"Are you sure you should be drinking this?" she asked when she handed the open bottle to Donny.

"Trust me," he rasped. "I'm positive." He grabbed the bottle and drank a good five fingers. Though he coughed as it went down, he admitted, "That feels fucki—" He cleared his throat. "That feels better," he corrected without my even having to glower at him for almost cursing in front of her. "Thank you."

She gnawed on her bottom lip. "You really should see a doctor after you've been sewn up."

That she cared enough to pressure Donny had me grinning at her. "His head's too hard for a concussion. Not even a kick to the head by a jackass could knock some sense into Donny."

He laughed at my joke, and though Aoife still looked worried, she ceased pleating her hands together and took a step back.

"If you need me, just call."

"Will do, honey," I told her softly, seeing her gaze was glued to my bloodied hands, I watched her bite her lip again before scurrying out of the room.

None of us said anything while Eoghan cut off Donny's shirt and cleaned up the wound. He was a good field med, the perfect man to be with if you got hit out on the streets, and he kept up-to-date with his certification as well. Not that this was legal, but fuck—what did legal matter inside these walls?

I had a bedroom dedicated to basic medical care.

Did it seem like I gave a fuck about the letter of the law?

Donny had consumed half the bottle by the time Eoghan started sewing him up. He'd numbed the area with some purloined local anesthetic, but having been shot myself, I knew that it didn't do shit.

It wasn't like we could walk into the ER without questions being asked, so this was just a part of the job.

My calf ached where I'd been shot over nine years ago. It hadn't been as clean cut as this wound, though. Eoghan had to dig around in the goddamn hole like he was looking for gold. I swear, I'd cried like a baby while he'd gone hunting. Donny was too hammered to cry, though.

His eyes were closed, and it seemed like he was dozing—either that, or he'd passed out.

"Who was it?" I asked, sensing he was too out of it to listen in.

Eoghan shot me a look. "He said he'd had word of where the next hit was going to be. Because Aidan's a dumbass, he didn't listen, so Donny went looking on his own. But he had the wherewithal to ask me first, and because I have a brain, I went with him. Even if it was a false lead, any information is for our benefit. There were four of them. Tagging some shops over on Sixth and Regis."

"Spraying their markers?"

"Yeah. They were just kids. It wasn't anything major, we figured. But we didn't know they were armed." He wrinkled his nose. "We asked them to move on."

"Polite as ever," I mocked, knowing Eoghan would have gone in there, guns cocked.

"Of course," he replied, eyes glittering. "One of the little cunts fired before we knew what he was doing."

"You get him back?"

If his eyes had glittered before, that was nothing to now. "What do you think?"

"Where is he?"

"I brought Paulie with me; had him take the fucker to Dad's."

I grimaced at that. "Not a good day for that little bastard."

Eoghan's teeth gleamed white. "Nope."

Within twenty minutes, Donny was as cleaned up as could be expected. I'd moved away and grabbed him a shirt to cover up, and after we managed to get that over his head, Eoghan had to help him off the bed while I steadied them both, because Donny was wasted. He was even whistling one of the hymns we had to sing at church— *All Things Bright and Beautiful.*

As if anything was like that in our world.

Well, I thought, *there was something bright and beautiful in mine now.* But it only hit me when I saw Aoife fretting in the hall as I helped them to the elevator.

"You need me to get him in the car with you?"

Eoghan shook his head. "Nah. Thanks, though. Sorry to wreck your evening, Aoife," he called out, arching his throat, so he could see over my shoulder.

"No worries," she replied, but her voice was shaky.

Eoghan heard it and shot me a wince. "Sorry, brother."

"Had to happen at some point," I mumbled under my breath, though I wished he'd gone across the way to Conor's place before he'd come to me.

He sighed but nodded. "True that."

As the doors closed, separating us, I sucked down a breath and turned on my heel to face the music.

I didn't expect Aoife to hurl herself at me, tears in her eyes as she clutched me in her arms.

"Hey, hey, what is it?" I asked, hugging her back and trying to figure out what the fuck was wrong. For her to hug me when I was covered in blood? Jesus.

"That could have been you!"

Her words were muffled against my stained shirt, and I closed my eyes, pressing my lips to her temple to kiss her there.

"Would you care?"

She stiffened in my arms, then pulled back to stare at me with confusion. But I didn't back down. I needed to know.

I'd dragged her into this life kicking and screaming, and though I thought that had changed, though I knew she hadn't agreed to become my wife because I'd coerced her, I still needed to know she gave a damn. If she didn't. . .I couldn't say I'd let her go, but, I'd rethink the situation.

This wasn't a regular courtship.

We hadn't started with candlelight and a supper at a fancy restaurant. I'd bribed her, then fucked my way into her life.

I fully deserved for her to hate me, but the idea of this woman loathing me brought me to my knees.

"Would I care if you were hurt?" Her scowl scorched me. "Finn, of course, I'd care. What would make you think otherwise?"

My tongue felt thick in my mouth as I shook my head. I slipped my hand back up to cup her chin and gently tilted it forward so that she wasn't looking at me like I was some kind of freak. I couldn't speak, didn't have words.

I wanted to believe her. Wanted to think she'd care if I was hurt, but only time would tell.

How long we stood there like that, I wasn't sure, but she made no move to step away. I was the one who whispered, "Come on, let's get ready for bed."

She nodded, and together we walked to the bedroom, where she changed as I got cleaned up.

It was the first night I didn't send us both into a frenzy as I fucked us both to another kind of ecstasy. Instead, she lay curled in my arms as we drifted off to sleep, and again, Conor could call me whipped as many times as he wanted, but it felt good. Not as good as an eye-crossing orgasm, but good in a different way.

Like I'd finally found my way home.

Even as the thought crossed my mind, for the first time in my life I prayed without Aidan Sr. forcing me to. As I silently whispered the words to a God I wasn't sure I believed in, I prayed she felt the same way.

30

———

AOIFE

TWO WEEKS LATER

"IN TWO HOURS' time, you're going to be Mrs. Finn O'Grady."

A laugh escaped me as Finn slid his tongue down my throat. My nerve endings sizzled in response, and I arched my neck, rocking my hips up in delight as he slowly thrust into me until he was all the way home.

"You're going to be Mr. Aoife Keegan more like."

His snicker was a delight for my ears, but I loved, even more, the feel of his mouth curving into a smile against my skin.

"Touché," he said, and then he peered at me. "You're going to change your name, aren't you?"

"How antiquated of you to ask," I teased, lifting up to press my mouth to his. "I'll carry your name with pride," I told him, loving how his shoulders straightened at my words, his own pride so evident that it was like it glowed from his pores.

Almost as though he was rewarding me for the statement, he began to move faster. Not too fast. This wasn't fucking. He was making love to me. It wasn't the first time he'd moved slow and gentle, but it felt like it mattered more considering what was going to happen soon.

Aidan and Lena had tried to insist that I spend the night before the service with them, but Finn had told them to butt out of our business and even when Aidan's eyes had flashed with fury, I'd tried to settle the storm by saying I only felt safe with Finn.

Aidan had flushed guiltily at my words, and that was that.

There were ways and means of getting around these men, and I was slowly learning them—with Lena's aid.

She told me that if I wanted anything in this life, to think smart. Not to whine or complain, but to do. And, whenever possible, remind them that the restrictions on my life were their fault.

For some crazy reason, the O'Donnelly men weren't as antiquated as I'd just accused Finn of being. They were as modern as any guy was nowadays. They knew women had hopes and dreams and aspirations, and they didn't shoot that down—it was why Lena had a dress shop over by Regis Park. The men understood that their women's lives couldn't revolve around them.

Even if they wished that were the case.

Plus, I'd started to see that Aidan thought of Lena's work as a means of keeping her out of mischief, and Finn seemed to share that train of thought.

I wasn't about to complain.

Releasing a moan when Finn hit that special spot inside me, I gripped his ass and dug my fingers into him, my nails clutching at his firm butt so hard, I knew I'd leave bruises there. I loved that, though. I wanted my marks on him.

When my release powered through me, I screamed. It was so intense, so goddamn wonderful, that I'd thought I was about to lose my mind. Finn's hoarse yell was enough to make my nerve endings spark and sizzle, as though they were embers that were ready to combust again.

As we both climbed down from the highest of peaks, Finn's panting breath in my ear, he managed to mumble, "Don't take the pill today."

I stiffened. "Huh?"

Sheepishly, he propped himself up on his elbow to stare down at me. "I don't want you on the pill."

That had me frowning, but I only replied when I wasn't panting from my orgasm. "Finn, no way are we ready for a baby."

"I know."

His logic made no sense to me, but I knew it would to him. Damn man.

"Then why would you risk it?"

"Because it could take years for you to get pregnant."

I knew that was true. The pill messed with your cycle, but fuck, it was still really easy to fall pregnant while taking it.

Gnawing on my bottom lip, I whispered, "I'm not ready to risk it."

He pressed his forehead to mine, and his proximity had me closing my eyes.

"Please, Aoife. I'm thirty-seven. It never mattered before, but . . ."

When his words trailed off, I stiffened underneath him. "Is something happening with the business?"

That was about as much as I'd ask, as deep as I'd delve.

His laugh was short, but he shook his head. "Not more so than usual."

That made me relax. Him wanting to be a father before he hit forty made sense to me. But it scared me to think he wanted to knock me up just in case he got taken out by the Colombians that were causing the Five Points trouble.

"Let me think about it?" I asked, surprised by the way he'd thrown this at me. Finn could be an asshole, and no mistake, but it was the first time he'd asked something so major of me.

If I was being honest, to me, this was even bigger than him proposing, and we were Catholic, for Christ's sake. Marriage to us was until death. No take backs.

But . . . a child?

A little boy with Finn's dark hair and Fiona's blue eyes.

A little girl with my red curls. . . .

I gulped at the very prospect.

He released a sigh and pressed a kiss to my lips. "Okay."

I could tell I'd disappointed him. I curved my arms around his waist and tugged him close. "Do you know how my Mom died?"

He stiffened in my embrace. "No."

"She died in an accident. A car careened into her, thirty miles over the speed limit. She was on life support for a week, and then, I had to make the decision to . . ." I couldn't even say 'switch off the machines' without my eyes welling with tears.

"I understand," he appeased, bussing my temple.

"When she died, I was alone. All alone in the world, Finn." I closed my eyes because those damn tears wanted to fall. "I don't want our baby to be alone."

"He wouldn't be. He'd have us."

"You could get hurt, Finn. I could. I-I mean, it's not like you're a regular businessman, is it? We have men with gunshot wounds coming to our door, and over dinner, you get calls about prostitutes being raped. . . ."

A kiss was pressed to my forehead. "That doesn't mean our child will ever be alone. Lena would love them until the dawn of a new age."

I thought about that, then said, "That's a funny way of phrasing it."

"Lena's a funny woman all round."

I had to snicker at that. Then I pinched his side. "Don't be mean."

"Hell, I'm not. She's the first to admit it."

Because I knew he was right, I laughed. "You think she would?"

"I know it. And you don't have to worry about me. I don't work out on the streets. Not like Aidan Sr., Jr., and Eoghan."

That had me gnawing on my bottom lip. "We could still be hurt, though."

"Yeah, we could, but your mom wasn't involved in Five Points' business, Aoife, and she got hurt. That's life, baby. Sometimes, we get dealt a shit hand."

I knew he was right. Knew I was being irrational, but I also knew I was being *rational*. All of this was so fast, and throwing a baby into the mix was just nuts. But I knew it meant a lot to him, could see it in his soulful blue eyes.

It was then I realized how they'd changed.

I'd always thought of them as ice cold, so starkly blue that they were frigid. But now? As he looked at me, I saw the difference.

There was a light to them. A warmth that curled around my heart like an embrace.

"Okay," I breathed, overwhelmed by the difference in the way he looked at me.

Those beautiful baby blues flared in surprise at my words. He frowned. "Huh?"

"I won't take the pill today." It was madness, but hell, he was right. It could take years for my cycle to regulate—I hoped.

"You promise?"

I promised him. And three hours later, I promised him more things.

To love him in sickness and in health.

To be true to him through the good times and the bad.

And to hold him for richer or for poorer.

As I made those vows, and as he made them to me, something settled inside me.

I was in St. Patrick's; the huge church was frigid even though it was temperate outside, and there were only a handful of people standing in the pews.

I had no family here, no one except for Jenny and the other waitresses from the tea room, and yet, with each vow I spoke, I was enveloped into a new line.

I became a part of the O'Gradys and the O'Donnellys, and it filled me with a warmth I hadn't realized I'd been missing since my mom's death.

I missed her. Terribly. I wished she were here, even if she'd have bitched at me about marrying Finn. I'd have given my left tit for her to have walked me down the aisle instead of Aidan Sr. To have had her with me as I went out and bought a simple white suit, not a dress, for the ceremony.

Lena had tried for us, though.

I hadn't thought about flowers. Hadn't thought about little bags of birdseed. But she had.

As I'd walked with Aidan toward Finn, Lena had given him a bouquet for me to hold. And on the way out, with Finn at my side, a newly inked marriage certificate back in the chapel, I saw the floral touches that Lena had arranged.

When we made it outside, the O'Donnellys swarmed us from the back, and they pelted us with a shower of birdseed. Finn and I laughed, ducking our heads as the grains collected in our hair, and I knew that smile of his would forever be imprinted on my memory banks. His sheer, unadulterated joy at that moment made him look ten years younger and a hundred times more handsome in his navy-blue suit.

As he turned around to chide Conor for tipping his bag of seeds down the back of Finn's collar, I saw it.

The truck was big.

Out of place in this neighborhood.

It wasn't the most affluent of places, but this van was beat up enough that it caught my eye. And then, the door to the side slid open as it started down the road.

I saw the two men hanging to the sides before I saw the guns.

Frowning, I reached for Finn, grabbed his arm to warn him, but before I could, they fired.

After the crowing laughter from the brothers, the joyous tears from Lena, the staccato bursts of gun shots interspersed with screams, sounded all the more obscene.

And just as my happiness turned to dread, my pure white suit which Finn had insisted upon because of my virginal status before he'd deflowered me—as he called it—bloomed red. Where before, there'd been joy, now there was only pain.

And blackness.

PART 2

SCREW ME

31
___

FINN

I THOUGHT I'd known rage.

Truly, I did.

I'd been abused by my father, and had known my mother was aware of it.

I'd run from home.

I'd killed.

I'd sought a fortune and I'd made it.

But catching my new bride on the church steps as a bullet tore through her body showed me that the rage I'd experienced in my life, was nothing compared to *this*.

It surged inside me like a tidal wave. Forging more fury as it destroyed the limits of my control.

On the streets, you learned to live fast. It was either that or die young. I'd never intended on dying young, and my bride, who was twelve years younger than me, wouldn't either.

Not if I had a say in it.

There was a shocking scarlet stain on her white wedding suit, and suddenly, I regretted her not wearing the white meringue dress, having all the bridesmaids and the big wedding party. She'd deserved that. Not this small affair.

She deserved the fucking world.

My throat clenched and I refused to believe the world wasn't still hers for the taking. I'd give her that and more if she just. Fucking. Lived.

A part of me wanted to breakdown. To cry. But I couldn't.

My instincts were too strong. I wasn't like my brother, Eoghan. I wasn't a sniper, but he'd helped train us. Had helped forge our skills so that the O'Donnelly sons and myself weren't dumbshits when it came time to hold a weapon.

Clutching Aoife with one arm, I pulled the gun from the holster on my other shoulder. It seemed like fate that I didn't even have to shuffle her in my hold to grab the gun. It slid seamlessly into my dry palm as I quickly took in the scene around me.

At my back, there was chaos.

I could hear moans of pain and low curses, as well as someone on the line with the emergency services.

But I blocked it out.

Blocked everything out as my gaze switched to hyper focus on the scene ahead.

The gunmen hanging out of the van were barely twenty, and had they been older, they'd have fucking figured out that drive-bys were supposed to be fast. In and out before anyone could lay chase.

Either they were slow, wanting to watch some of the pandemonium they had stirred, or the world had slowed down *for me* so everything took incrementally more time than usual.

I saw the door to the truck the Colombians were using was still open as it drove past. I saw the grinning clown faces, loaded with those ugly fucking tats as they celebrated their 'win,' but more than that, I saw a target.

As Eoghan had taught me, I took aim. I held my breath to steady my heartbeat, then I released it on a slow exhalation as I squeezed the trigger.

It seemed to take forever for the bullet to find its way home. Proof of how time had slowed down for me. I watched its trajectory. My focus pure, like I could will it to hit the exact spot I required.

Was I surprised when the back of the driver's head exploded?

Yes and no.

My aim had been true, sure, and Aidan O'Donnelly's boys were all naturally good shots, but to stop the driver? God was on my side. Maybe He was pissed at the bloodshed on the steps to His home, maybe justice—Old Testament style—was exactly what the Colombians deserved.

Whatever the reason—God's hand, my skill, sheer fucking luck—it worked.

The truck jerked, and because this was a residential street, it crashed straight into the low wall separating someone's front yard from the sidewalk.

The momentum was enough to have the gunmen, who weren't strapped in, soaring through the air ten feet and landing face first.

They might have survived if my brothers hadn't been there. But I was no longer interested. My focus switched to Aoife even as I heard several gunshots and more screams. Then, in the background, the wonderful wail of an ambulance.

I looked down at her. My woman. My wife. And knew she was it for me. I'd never been so fucking certain of anything in my life.

My eyes took her in. From the wine-colored hair that made her skin look so milky, to the glorious freckles I knew covered her everywhere. The white suit should have drained her, washed her out, but instead it augmented the different notes in her hair. And in the sun? It seemed to shine like burgundy.

I wanted to fuck her under the sun, I realized. Wanted to see all that hair curtain me as she rode me on a beach somewhere. Bora Bora, Rio, Barcelona... I didn't give a fuck. Just knew it had to happen at some point in our lives together.

The stain blossoming through her wedding suit was almost as dark as her hair. The sight of it sickened me, and I wasn't a man who was caught short by the sight of blood. But this was my woman, and before I could even feel fear at her life potentially draining from her, I couldn't stop myself.

I dipped my chin, kissed her mouth, then bit her bottom lip.

Hard.

She moaned.

And this time, my throat *did* clutch.

I found it hard to breathe for endless fucking seconds as she whimpered, "Finn?"

My eyes watered and I burrowed my face in her hair and clutched her harder to me. "You stay with me, Aoife. The ambulance is coming. Don't you fucking leave me."

I felt the curve of her lips against my cheek. "Won't leave you."

"You'd better goddamn promise me that," I rasped, unashamed when the tears fell and dampened her skin.

She made a gurgling sound that had my heart stopping, then she breathed, "Love you, Finn," and she fell silent.

For a second, that silence roared in my head.

It was...

Was this what insanity felt like?

I'd always ridden a thin line. My past warring with my present. What had happened *to* me, battling with all the shit I'd done.

But this?

I'd never felt so lost, so on edge, so out of control.

I almost decked the guy who pulled her from me. Figuring it was another Colombian, I lifted the gun and stared down its sights before I even blinked back the tears marring my vision.

A startled yelp and a crash had me jerking back to attention. The EMT's hands were raised, his kit plunked on the church steps, and I lowered my weapon, muttering, "Sorry."

I received a well-deserved glower for my pains, but the man took one glance at Aoife and said, "We need to get her on the ground, sir."

The next ten minutes were the most confusing of my life.

I crouched next to my bride, unsure if she lived or died from how hard the men worked on her. Did they think I'd shoot them if they failed? Every now and then they eyed my gun, and though I wouldn't hurt them, I wasn't trying to 'encourage' them to succeed either.

But there was no way in fuck I was sheathing this weapon when we were in the middle of an active threat.

Sure, it was unlikely another round of Colombians would come roaring around the corner, but I wasn't about to take any chances.

The EMTs had ripped her jacket and shirt, exposing a silky bra I should have enjoyed removing later. Instead, some fucking EMTs were ogling my bride's tits and I couldn't even punch them for it. Not when I saw her breathe. It was the first time I realized she *wasn't* dead, and I had to press a hand to the cold stone steps to prop me upright.

She lived.

There was blood everywhere and I wasn't sure how they saw anything, but after another few minutes, I helped them move her onto a stretcher.

As they rolled her down to the ambulance, I recognised that I wasn't hearing anything. I turned around, saw Aidan Jr. had been shot and was being worked over by another EMT, Lena was sobbing, Conor was clutching his arm, and I didn't hear any of it.

I didn't hear the sirens.

The whispers of the audience we'd gathered even though the fuckwits, after a drive-by, should have stayed inside.

I didn't hear the wheels of the gurney on the stones as Aoife was taken to the ambulance.

I heard nothing.

I should stay. I knew that.

In the ultimate of ironies, because this life was like that, I hadn't been shot. Looked like Aidan Sr. hadn't either.

The good really do die young, I thought.

We needed to get to work. Needed to handle this threat, but I wasn't capable of anything.

For the first time in my life, I wasn't. Capable. Of. Anything.

I was an intelligent man.

My fortune, and that of the Five Points, had soared thanks to that intelligence. Thanks to my reasoning, and my business savvy. I knew where to apply pressure on our allies, how to twist the arm of our enemies. I was needed here to rectify this wrong, but Aoife needed me more.

"Sir?"

Someone grabbed my arm and shook me. I was too dazed to react this time. Too dazed to smack the shit out of anyone who touched me.

They were the first words I heard, though.

"...coming with us? Need to leave. Urgently."

I realized I was holding up the ambulance. Not that they usually waited for shell-shocked grooms, and in her state, I knew they wouldn't ordinarily allow people to travel with them.

But I wasn't just anyone.

I was a Five Points man, and Aoife was my bride.

Shit worked differently for us.

I jumped on board the ambulance, knowing that if I got in the way I could endanger Aoife's life, I resented my six-foot-four frame more than ever as I tried to make myself as small as possible. Not easy.

There was a short counter beside Aoife's gurney, and next to that, a kind of seat. I folded my form into that tiny ass enclosure, sitting sideways so I wouldn't be a burden in the limited space.

Seconds after I settled myself, the ambulance took off and my heart rate went along for the ride too.

____

32

AOIFE

THE BEEPS.

It was the beeps that woke me. Fuck, they were so irritating. What was it anyway?

They reminded me of Chinese water torture, except with sound and, ya know, no water.

I wrinkled my nose as I tried to lift my hand to shove the pillow over my face, but when I tried to do that simple thing, my entire body ached.

"She's waking up!"

The roar disturbed me. Jolted me in surprise and that sent agony shivering through me. It was then I realized how much I hurt. Jesus. It was everywhere. In my head, in my chest, even my toes ached.

It was like when you worked out for the first time in months. A forty-minute TABATA workout didn't just kick your butt during the session, but after? Talk about moving like a ninety-year-old. This was that kind of pain I was talking about, but it went deeper because I felt so weak. So frail.

My brow puckered with irritation from the way I was hurting

with no comprehension as to *why*, and I decided I needed to open my eyes. But for some reason, that wasn't easy.

How could eyelids *hurt*?

What the fuck was going on with me?

Another yell roared from someone close to me, and I felt my hand being picked up and my fingers being squeezed. A scent blossomed in my nose, but I didn't know it. Or at least, I didn't recognize it over the thousand other scents in this space. Then, I felt the soft brush of something against my temple, and as the scent and touch worked together, I realized who it was.

Finn.

I moaned his name and I heard him grit out, "Open your eyes for me, beautiful, my *cailín*."

God, I wanted to obey. I really did. But opening my eyes wasn't as easy as it sounded.

"They're coming, Finn," someone told him, and there was a lilt of Irish to the tone that comforted me. In fact, Finn had it too, which was funny because I knew he hadn't been raised in the Old Country. His mom had been though, just like mine. We both had sayings and particular phrases that came from them—even if Finn had run from his mother while I'd clung to mine.

"Please, Aoife, let me see those beautiful eyes."

Finn? Being charming? In front of someone else?

Christ, was I dying?

That thought, not his request, had me tearing my eyelids open. I wasn't ready to die, dammit. I had so much sex to make up for. And not just any sex, but sex with *this* crazy, beautiful man. A man who made Jamie Dornan look like a six out of ten. *Yeah, that hot.*

I heard a groan escape him, one so filled with relief that I frowned in confusion.

"Finn?" I repeated, my eyes foggy as I stared up at him. I couldn't seem to say anything else, my tongue incapable of forming other words. He was my anchor in that moment. My everything.

"Aoife," he breathed, then he squeezed my hand and whispered, "Let the doctors take care of you. Be a good girl."

More confusion filled me, but he squeezed my hand just as a team of people surged in from a door to his right.

Not people.

Doctors.

Finn backed up to let them move around me, but I wanted him close. I needed him at my side—I was scared and hurting, dammit. I needed him, where was he going?

"Her pulse is spiking."

"Finn," I moaned.

I heard him as he gritted out, "Aoife, baby, I'm here. I'm over here."

"And he shouldn't be," someone mumbled under their breath as they touched me, moving me and prodding me here and there. Places where it stung, places that sent shards of agony slicing through me.

"He's a Points man. You don't argue with them," another person muttered.

"They're all thugs."

Didn't they know I could hear what they were saying? About my husband?

Because, yeah, I remembered that.

I remembered saying 'I do,' and hearing him say it in return. I remembered walking down the aisle and seeing the white peonies and baby's breath that Lena, Finn's adopted mother, had strewn along the pews in heavy garlands. I even remembered the feel of those silky flowers brushing against my hands as Aidan Sr., Lena's husband, passed me my bouquet.

We'd been in St. Patrick's and now, we were here.

Trouble was, I just wasn't sure what had happened between walking down the aisle and this moment.

I dozed off, which might have seemed impossible considering how the rude medical team were attending to me, but I was tired.

Bone deep tired.

I awoke to the sounds of Finn's luscious voice rasping, "You've done everything you can?"

"Of course!"

The affronted tone had my lips twitching. Finn did that to people. He was a bit of an asshole, but I loved him anyway. Yeah, I did. I loved him in spite of his being a dick. Which made me either too stupid to live, or just someone who let hope run their lives, not realism.

"You'd better have," someone else growled, "I made it a point to find out where your family lives."

"Oh God! I-I promise. She doesn't even need it," came the panicked squeak. "It's just her spleen. She might have some digestive issues as a worst-case scenario but otherwise, many people live comfortably without them."

"Like tonsils?" Finn asked, his tone doubtful.

"Yes," the other person seemed to clutch at Finn's question. "Exactly like tonsils."

"What else?"

Finn's demand had the woman—my doctor?—audibly gulping. "She was incredibly fortunate that the bullet didn't hit her stomach or damage her pancreas. We performed open surgery and as a result, she will have scarring. As it stands, she has some faint damage to her ribs that will take a few weeks to heal."

"Why has she been out of it for so long?" That wasn't Finn. I didn't know who it was, but he sounded like he took my lack of consciousness as a personal affront.

"For several reasons. Her lung collapsed and then we had to deal with two nasty infections at the incision site."

"But she'll be okay now?"

She sucked down a sharp breath at the man's question—I didn't know who he was just that he wasn't Finn—and seemed to brace herself. "While you can live without your spleen, it does put her at risk for infections. Before she leaves, we'll vaccinate her against several viruses and bacteria. There are annual vaccinations she will have to have now to ensure she's protected. The spleen helps filter blood but it's a vital part of the immune system."

"What's the worst that can happen?" Finn asked, and his voice was dulled, like he was trying to contain his emotions and succeeding.

The doctor hesitated. "We don't need to think about those things just yet. She'll be in the hospital for a few more weeks so we can keep an eye on her. Usually, after a splenectomy—the removal of the spleen—we send patients home after a week, and they're to return if certain symptoms develop, but because of the other issues, we'll need to monitor her."

"I want to know," Finn growled, this time sounding like he was rapidly losing patience.

Finn was like that, I thought fondly. Impatient and cautious, wanting to know all the risks before he stepped into any fight.

"Some patients can develop a certain kind of infection called OPSI. It can occur years after surgery," the other woman explained, her voice soaring to a high pitch that had me wondering what my husband was doing to her to make her sound like that. "It has a high fatality rate."

Finn released a muttered expletive and I heard his shoes tap against the floor as he began to pace.

"It should be me, Aidan," he ground out. "I should be the one dealing with this shit."

Oh, it was Aidan Sr. The head of the Five Points, and a man who was like a father to Finn.

It made sense why the doctor was scared. *I* was scared of Aidan, and I knew he liked me.

The man made the term 'loose cannon' seem like a friendly warning. I was half certain Aidan was a lunatic so it was no wonder the doctor was pissing herself.

"That's a worst-case scenario, sir," the doctor informed him, sympathy coating her words. "We have plenty to be grateful for." She swallowed. Audibly. "I was her surgeon and I saw the bullet's trajectory. If there was ever a good way of coming out of a gunshot wound to the abdomen, your wife found it. Clean entry and exit. No fractures to the ribs, just slight fissures on the lower ribcage. No nicks to any organs—just the spleen. God was certainly on her side."

"He works for the righteous," came Aidan's voice, and I opened my eyes at that.

Of all the things anyone could say, that was the most stupid of them all.

"It was good luck, Aidan," I rasped. Or, at least, I tried to—because no one in this room was righteous, certainly not Aidan O'Donnelly! My tongue was thick though, and the words didn't seem to form normally.

"Aoife!" Finn cried and my blurry eyes managed to focus as I looked at him and saw he had, of all things, a beard.

A beard?

Jesus.

How long had I been out?

He ran to my side and grabbed my hand. Pressing it to his lips, he whispered, "Baby, what do you need?"

"Water," I half-whimpered, wishing it hadn't hurt so much for him to bestow that kiss to my knuckles.

The doctor bustled to my side and she pressed an ice chip to my mouth. "You're fine, Aoife," she said soothingly—but her eyes were cold. I remembered what somebody had said the last time I'd been awake and wondered if it had been her.

They didn't like me because my husband was a Five Points man.

Well, tough shit.

The older woman, somewhere in her fifties, studied me then Finn as he squeezed my fingers again. Though a frown flickered over her brow, I saw that her eyes weren't cold, actually. Just scared.

I couldn't blame her.

Not when Aidan O'Donnelly was in the room, and with a rep as large and notorious as the state itself.

Hell, maybe they were scared of him in other parts of the States too, but never having left New York, I wouldn't know. Considering I'd seen the man in action, I wouldn't put it past him.

When the ice had melted and my tongue felt less like a swollen hamster lolling around in my mouth, I whispered, "Stop scaring the doctors, Aidan."

A snort brayed from behind the doctor and Aidan strolled up, looking a lot smarter than Finn. He peered at me. "Scaring people is what I do best, Aoife. Figured you'd know that, being a Hell's Kitchen girl."

The other woman whimpered, and I shot her a look. "His bark's worse than his bite," I tried to offer, but it wasn't working. Her skin was whiter than mine—which was saying something. I made milk look colorful.

"We'll be in shortly to run some tests," she mumbled, dipping her chin before scurrying out of the room.

I got the feeling that in normal situations, my husband and his adoptive father would be the ones ushered out, while a team came to tend to me. Of course, things never worked any normal kind of way with the Five Points in attendance. Certainly not when those men were the head and one of his right hand men.

My gaze returned to Finn's haggard face, and I saw his eyes were wet as he stared down at me. He'd bowed down slightly so my triceps could rest on the sheets, but he could support my forearm and use the position to press my hand to his stubbly cheek.

That he was being so affectionate in front of Aidan surprised me. PDAs weren't exactly good for the reputation of a man in Finn's position—it spoke of how scared he'd been for me.

By the sounds of it, I'd come off lucky. Well, as lucky as a bride can be when she gets shot on the church steps just moments after signing the wedding certificate, that is.

My lips curved at that, because yeah, I remembered what happened now. At my rueful smile, Finn gaped at me. *What?* Did he expect me to sob? Maybe I should have. Maybe I should have broken down and screamed at him, demanded he leave the room, leave me alone, but God, I really didn't want to, and I figured the chick who'd just been shot could get her own way for a while.

"Was anyone else hurt?"

Finn's features turned stoic. "Aidan, Lena, and I were the only ones who weren't shot. All the brothers got hit."

"Badly?"

He shook his head. "Aidan Jr. took the worst one—it fractured his patella." My eyes widened at the repercussions of that injury. That would require months of rehab and some PT too. "Brennan and Eoghan were grazed. Conor was also, to the bicep of all places because it was such a large target or so he says—" Aidan snorted at that. "Brennan was mostly hurt when Aidan fell into him. Broke his wrist."

I was inordinately grateful our wedding party had been so small. There'd been a few other guests, but the brothers had swarmed around us at the entrance, leaving the others stuck inside and safe.

"Jenny?" I asked after my best friend.

Finn's fingers danced over my skin. "She's fine. She was inside."

Thank God for that.

Fumbling with the paper cup the doctor had rested close to my hand that contained mostly melted ice chips, Finn saw my struggle, dipped into it and placed a small piece in my mouth. He frowned at the cup, reached for it and mumbled, "I'll get some more."

Because I couldn't tell him I'd prefer him to stay rather than Aidan, he headed out, apparently grateful to have a purpose.

Blowing out a breath, I caught Aidan's eye. He was studying me like a scientist might peruse a new species of frog.

"What is it?" I asked huskily.

"You angry?"

The question made me frown, but I answered honestly, "I'm too tired to feel anything but thirsty."

He pursed his lips after contemplating that for a few seconds. "I can understand that. Don't blame Finn."

Did I?

I didn't think I did, even if that wasn't a rational response.

Finn wasn't directly at fault, but equally, the Five Points were at war with a Colombian cartel for a reason. They'd obviously done something to make the Colombians get itchy trigger fingers.

Still, I didn't want to be angry with Finn. He was my husband for a reason. I'd only known him a short time, but he was rapidly becoming the person around which my baseline was set.

If he was okay, then I was okay.

Pathetic but true.

Was that what happened when you loved someone? Or was it just because I was a doormat, waiting for a Points man to trudge on me?

"The boy worships you. Any man with eyes can see that," Aidan stated gruffly. "He'd take your place in a heartbeat."

"Maybe, but he can't actually do that, can he?" I replied, my tone soft. "I love him, Aidan. I don't want him to beg for forgiveness on bended knee."

"What do you want then?"

I shrugged, then grimaced as the simple gesture sent shockwaves of pain through me. "I don't know," I answered hoarsely. "Nothing just now. I'd be happy if this pain just went away for a while."

Closing my eyes because I was tired again, I heard him sigh. He stepped away, not totally out of the room because his footsteps grew nearer not distant. Then, I heard Finn's strident pace, and the room got warmer the minute he crossed the threshold.

"She's sleeping again," Aidan told him with a grunt.

"Fuck. I wanted to talk to her some more."

"She needs the rest."

"I know." Finn swallowed. "I-I just needed to see her awake."

Aidan released a heavy sigh. "I'm sorry, son."

When Finn whispered, "Me too, Aidan," those were the last words I heard before I tumbled into a deep sleep.

33

———

FINN

"GO HOME. Get some rest. You're not doing her any good here."

I scowled at Eoghan as he stepped into Aoife's private room. "What do you want?" I asked gruffly, not needing his advice and not appreciating it either.

"Came to check up on you. See if you guys needed anything."

I released a breath and though it made me feel like a kid, I rolled on my side on the too-small trestle bed Aidan had arranged to be placed in here.

It was marginally more comfortable than the armchair I'd been using for the first two days, but because it was the only thing that could fit in here without causing any obstruction, it still wasn't like my bed at home.

Not that I deserved to be comfortable.

"You sulking?" Eoghan asked.

With my back to him—and he and the rest of my family were the only people I could turn my back on—I scowled at the wall. "No."

"Why aren't you answering Mom's calls, then?"

"Don't have anything to say."

"You know she'd come if Dad was letting her out of the compound, right?"

My nose wrinkled. "He put her on lockdown?"

"Yeah. The rest of the women too."

We had a compound over in Queens. It was a small hotel that, in a pinch, we could shove our men's wives and kids in if shit hit the fan.

An out-and-out attack on the Five Points' council?

Yeah. There'd been a veritable explosion of shit. Golgothan sized.

"Bet she's loving that," I said dryly. It wasn't the first time, nor would it be the last, that Lena had been holed up in Queens. I wished Aoife was there now instead of here. Fuck, I'd give my left nut for her not to be drifting in and out of consciousness the way she was.

"Yeah, she's bitching. As usual."

The bed dipped at my side and Eoghan rested against me like I was an armchair.

"Dick," I groused at him.

"Eoghan, actually. Didn't know you lost your memory during the drive-by."

"Ha-Ha," I retorted. "Fuck off, would you? I'm just trying to get some sleep."

"Don't know how you can on this thing. Looks like you're going to fall off, and bro, hate to tell you this, but you stink." Eoghan grunted. "Can't you move her to a room with space for a bed and a private bath so you can shower off some of that stench?"

"They're moving her tomorrow."

We had been in the ICU for a while, but I had a feeling Aidan had put pressure on the right people to keep us close to the 'facilities.' It sucked that we were taking up an urgent care space, but I couldn't find it in myself to give a damn.

This hospital got a huge chunk of its running costs from donors. What Aidan donated to this place, thanks to me, was enough to run this floor for a year. I figured we deserved some of the gold treatment, and Aoife deserved platinum.

She'd been my wife for five minutes before the impossible had happened…

Sometimes I wondered if she slept to avoid me. If she pretended just so she didn't have to face me.

Was she scared?

Of the Points? Of our future?

Of me?

I couldn't blame her.

I was scared, but I couldn't let her go. More selfishness but she was… even sleeping half the time, she was my fucking life. I'd killed for her, and I'd do it again and again. I just wished that I'd been the one to spot the truck. If I had, maybe I'd have stopped the drive-by from happening before it had a chance to begin.

"It's not your fault, Finn," Eoghan whispered.

"Isn't it? I shouldn't have married her, shouldn't have brought her into this life but I can't live without her, *dearthàir*."

He sighed at my Gaelic use of the word 'brother.' Something we only used to mess with each other or in times like these. Times where we were at a loss and needed one of our kin to keep us from drowning.

"You don't have to live without her. Dad told me himself that the bullet couldn't have had a finer path."

"He's sure it's God's will," I stated wryly, amused despite myself. "He'll be saying she needs to be up for sainthood next."

"Wouldn't put it past him," Eoghan agreed. "What is it? Two miracles before the Church will consider it?"

I snorted. "One miracle is enough for me."

"Seriously though, she's okay, right?"

"She's going to be on antibiotics for the rest of her fucking life, and she's going to need vaccinations every year too," I ground out.

"Aidan might have a limp for the rest of his life, and Brennan's wrist?"

"What about it?"

"It's the one Dad kept on breaking when he was fucking around with that Bratva chick."

I rolled over onto my back. "Shit."

"Yeah."

"Lena find out?"

"Not yet."

"Think she will?"

"Probably. Dad's freaking out."

"I wondered why he hadn't been hovering around this place for a few days."

"I think he'd prefer for the Colombians to kill him rather than Mom."

I snickered at that—I couldn't help it.

"That's not funny, Eoghan," Aoife rasped in that new way of hers. It was like the intubating tubes had damaged something on the way down. I'd gut the bastard who'd hurt her if I knew *who* to gut.

"Isn't it?" Eoghan replied rhetorically, getting to his feet to walk toward her. "Hey, little sister, you faring well?"

That he called her that, and so soon, didn't surprise me. Aoife had bled for the Five Points. She was one of us now.

I rolled up into a sitting position and quickly scrubbed a hand over my face. I knew I looked like shit, but it suited my mood, and Aoife was too out of it most of the time to really care.

"I'm just tired," she whispered. Her head rolled on the pillow, her hair spilling over it like wine from a glass, and I realized she was looking for me.

My heart leapt because, when she saw me, she released a shaky breath—relief had the frown on her brow unfurling. I strode over to her and grabbed her hand, then ducked down and pressed a kiss to her knuckles. The IV infusion was there, and I wanted to punch the dude who'd stained her skin with a shit ton of bruises—they never seemed to be able to find a line. I'd watched them stick her so many times, I'd wanted to throttle them.

Her knuckles scratched my jaw and, not wanting to disconnect from her, I kicked out with my foot and hooked the armchair behind me. Sitting back in it, I pressed my face into her hand.

"You aren't shaving."

Eoghan snorted. "Your powers of observation are coming in leaps and bounds, Aoife. All this sleep is serving you well."

She huffed at him, then studied me again. "Have you showered?"

"Can't you smell him? Christ. We need the doctor back in here if you can't."

"Why aren't you taking care of yourself?"

I choked a little. Wanting nothing more at that moment than to climb into bed beside her. Fuck the shower. Fuck the goddamn world. "I'll go clean up when I know you won't wake up without me being here."

She was silent a second, then she murmured, "Oh."

Eoghan shot us both a look, and I could tell he didn't understand.

Why would he?

Though I kept expecting her to wake up with loathing in her eyes, the minute she was awake, she wanted to see me. I'd watched her pulse speed up on the monitor then had seen it start to slow the second she found me with her gaze. My voice wasn't enough. Sight was the only thing that calmed her.

I wasn't about to complain. Not when she should be asking for a lawyer to demand an annulment.

Christ, would any judge in the land refuse her?

Nausea swirled inside me at the thought, and I pressed another kiss to her fingers.

Eoghan grunted. "That means we have to put up with his stench a while longer, hmm?" Then, he snickered. "Dear God, Aoife, get better soon, yeah?"

Her lips curved—I didn't have to look up to hear it in her voice. "For your sensibilities, I will, Eoghan."

"That's an Irish woman for you. So accommodating."

She hooted softly. "Which Irish women do you know?"

"Well, they're always accommodating to me," he purred, and I raised my head to spear him with a glower.

"You're not flirting with my wife, are you, *dearthàir?*"

He grinned at me unashamedly. "She's too beautiful not to."

When Aoife giggled, I didn't snap at him, just rolled my eyes. It was good to hear her laugh, and for some reason, she found my brothers amusing.

Yeah. *Funny*-haha, not funny-strange, either. The latter being substantially truer.

I'd seen her talk to them several times on her own at Sunday lunch at their folks' home, and had monitored how she'd settled in. I still wasn't sure how that was possible, just knew she'd relaxed around them. Had started to build a rapport with five of the most dangerous men in Hell's Kitchen, Manhattan.

Aoife had been raised in Five Points' territory though, so I knew she'd been taught by her mother to always placate our men. Her relaxing around them didn't gel with that, which made me think she genuinely liked them.

I mean, it wasn't too crazy a concept. *I* liked them, but I'd been raised with them. I knew them before they'd become the generals in the Irish Mob. Fuck, before I'd become one myself.

"Are you hungry?" I asked her, praying she'd say yes.

Her nose wrinkled. "No."

She'd lost weight in the nine days we'd been here, and I fucking hated that. I loved her as she was, and I didn't want her to change—especially when it was involuntary.

"Eat something? For me, baby?"

Every time they brought her something to eat, I ended up coercing her to down the pudding, if nothing else.

"I'm really not hungry, Finn," she told me softly, her green eyes like dewy grass in the morning. They had the power to ensnare me, as well as torture me with guilt. I never saw any hatred or bitterness in those gem-like orbs, even if I deserved to have both sentiments aimed my way.

"Would you like me to bring you some of Mom's cooking?" Eoghan asked. "I've eaten hospital food. It makes shit look tasty."

"Ew," she complained, but I saw the twinkle in her eye and knew he'd amused her. Again.

What the hell?

Eoghan was making her laugh while I was making her wrinkle her nose?

Grunting, I watched as my brother patted her arm. "You like Mom's food."

"I do."

"And she's bored, Aoife," he told her earnestly. "I'll bet she'll make you three square meals a day if you asked her to." He grimaced. "She hates that she can't visit."

"What's lockdown?"

"When someone is locked down?" Eoghan snarked, and Aoife stunned me when she lifted her arm, and scratched her nose with her middle finger.

"Someone got served a bird," Brennan hooted, and I turned my head to see my brother walking in, a basket of fruit in his hands.

I almost shook my head at the sight of the gift. Considering the Points were a general down because I was in here with Aoife, it was amazing how often my brothers could find the time to visit.

If we were on lockdown, it wasn't just because of the drive-by. We'd retaliated. I didn't know how, didn't want to know either, but I knew the protocol we had in place.

I'd drafted it my fucking self.

"Hey Brennan," Aoife said, her tone sleepy again.

Goddammit.

She was sleeping so much it frightened the shit out of me. When I asked the doctors though, they just said she needed the rest and that everyone had different reactions to the anesthetic.

I was about to lose my fucking mind, though.

Every time she dropped off, it scared the shit out of me.

"Can I have some grapes, please?"

My head shot up at that. "You want something solid?"

Her eyes were closed again but she nodded. "Please."

"So polite," Brennan teased as he ripped into the cellophane. "Whatever did you do to deserve her, Finn?"

"I don't know," I whispered, and I heard the guilt in my voice. Knew my brothers did too.

Aoife didn't though. Eyes still closed, she smiled. "He kisses like a dream."

Brennan and Eoghan started snickering. "He does, huh?"

"Oh yeah," she murmured. "What's your favorite food?"

Brennan, amused, shot me a look that had my lips twitching. "Mom's meatloaf."

Eoghan piped up, "Her apple crumble."

"Think of meatloaf for your main, and apple crumble for dessert, then multiply that by ten and that doesn't even compare to how well he kisses."

It was probably the longest thing she'd said in days, and it was about my kisses?

Well, fuck.

I needed to keep on kissing her to keep her hooked, by the sound of it.

Because I *did* stink, I kept myself downwind and pressed my lips to her knuckles again. "Baby?"

She hummed and opened her eyes so I could see the smile in them too. "You okay with my brothers while I get a shower?"

Her head tilted to the side. "You going to shave?"

I was about to nod, when I saw something on her face. "Want me to keep it?"

She bit her bottom lip and grinned at me as she nodded, and I had to laugh.

It was slow going, and she might be sleeping more than a koala bear, but my Aoife was coming back to me.

Thank God for that.

34

AOIFE

"IT'S ITCHY."

"Tough."

"I'm horny."

"Me too."

"I don't want to stay in bed."

"I wish I could."

Finn had an answer for every statement, and it usually had me wanting to throw the remote at him.

As he pressed the tray to my lap, I stared at the delicious plate of food mulishly. "Please, Finn."

"You're not supposed to be sitting up for long."

I'd developed anemia and that, alongside a potassium deficiency, was making me tired as hell.

"I won't be sitting up. I'll be lying down. Please. I hate being in bed without you." I knew I was whining, but from my recuperation in the hospital to moving home, Finn had turned into a Drill Sergeant.

He monitored what I ate, handed me my meds, and generally acted like a pain in the ass.

He also watched me shower. Helped me. Not to cop a feel but to make sure I didn't fall over.

Sigh.

He grunted at my words as he took a seat next to me on the bed. "Eat," he commanded, and because he could be a pushy pain in the ass if I didn't, and because if I tried to eat, he might concede, I picked up the spoon and ate some soup.

I didn't want it, but I ate it anyway.

I hated soup. I mean, it tasted good, but it was wet and thick and just, ugh, no.

Running a hand through his hair, he admitted, "I like you in the study with me, Aoife, but…"

"But?" I asked, my tone so eager I wanted to roll my eyes. At my-damn-self!

I sounded like a puppy dog desperate for a belly rub.

Although, that didn't sound like such a bad idea at the moment.

A bit further down would be perfect, though.

"You don't want to overhear the conversations I'm having."

I wasn't certain how he was pulling it off, but Finn hadn't left my side since I'd been shot. Even when he'd showered, he'd used one somewhere in the hospital and had come back dressed in scrubs.

McDreamy had nothing on my guy.

When I'd seen him, I'd told him that if the Mob became too much of a hassle, he should go into acting. His brothers had hooted, and he'd smirked at me, but under his eyes, those sharp cheekbones of his had been dusky with embarrassment.

"You think I don't know you're plotting the demise of a bunch of Colombians?" I tried to sound laissez-faire and knew I didn't pull it off when he shot me a look.

"Think of it as chess. It's easier."

That had me scowling. "They're just like us."

"They're nothing like us," he spat, and his sudden burst of temper had me jolting in bed. Of course, because I was on a stupid soft-foods diet, the damn soup sloshed everywhere.

When it spilled onto my lap, I yelped and Finn, eyes wide, grabbed the tray and nearly threw it on the floor as he tugged the comforter away.

The near panic on his face had me tugging my sleep shirt away from my thighs with one hand, and then grabbing his hand with the other. "Finn, I'm okay!" I half-yelled at him as he started trying to strip off my shirt.

I mean, I wanted to be naked with him but only if it involved him being naked too.

I knew I wasn't up to anything like we'd done before, but God, just his fingers between my legs would scratch this itch he'd made in my body.

I thought, oddly enough, it was my way of bounding back from the whole charade. Dead, I was not. Alive and kicking, that was me. Well, not kicking. Not yet. But alive, definitely, and I had the sexiest man in the universe tending to me. I just had to make him see me as less than a patient and more as his wife and lover.

"You're scalded," he swore as he stared down at my pale thighs.

"They're just pink from the heat. It's nothing. Trust me, I've had enough burns to know." That didn't improve his scowl, and I snickered at him. "I'm a baker, Finn. A trained chef to boot. If you don't think I know what a true burn is, you're nuts." I shook my head when he growled under his breath. "You're such a bear."

"And you're remarkably at..." He stilled, swallowed, and seemed to settle on, "...ease."

"Is that a complaint?" I frowned at him, wondering what he meant by 'at ease.'

Was I supposed to be uncomfortable in my sick bed?

Shit, the site where I'd been operated on was itchy. It wasn't gross anymore and didn't 'leak' when Finn cleaned it—because yeah, he'd taken that upon himself, too—but it was like when you broke your foot and had a cast on for eight weeks. By the end of the two months, you were sticking God knew what down the cast to scratch your ankle.

I was tired *all the time*, felt weak and quivery when I exerted myself by using the damn bathroom, and my once enormous appetite for all things edible had diminished considerably. Even if Finn wasn't intent on feeding me a hundred varieties of soup, each one that made a swamp look tasty, I didn't even want to eat cake.

Yes.

I didn't want to eat cake.

Let that sink in for a second.

If any of that seemed like I was *at ease*, then I wasn't certain what was going through Finn's mind.

"Are you sure you don't need a new sleep shirt?"

I blinked at him. "Later will suffice." I really didn't have the energy to get changed. "Tell me what you meant."

He climbed off the bed, and just as I feared he was going to leave, he started to pace. Back and forth at the foot of the bed, so fast and so often I sank back to observe him in surprise.

I wouldn't have been shocked to see sparks crackle around him as he worked through whatever he was dealing with, and boy, was he dealing with something.

"Why don't you hate me?"

Well, that was easy. "Because I love you."

His nostrils flared, and though I knew, *point blank*, he loved when I said that, he always responded like a deer in headlights. He also never replied.

I'd decided not to take offense at that.

Fiona, his mom, had loved him. Dearly. But I knew Finn didn't believe that, and considering what Lena, his adoptive mother, had told me about his father? And that Fiona had known of the abuse? I couldn't blame him for being confused about love, even though the O'Donnellys had most definitely cocooned him in the love of their family.

"Love isn't a 'get out of jail free' card, Aoife."

He sounded so impatient, and I had to snicker at him. "That's a shame," I told him wryly. "I'm sure a lot of your boys on Rikers Island wished it was."

"This isn't a joke," he exploded again, and once more, he began to pace.

Jesus. It was a wonder he didn't start running.

I'd known he wasn't handling my being shot well—yes, I was aware of the irony in that sentence—but this was the closest to combusting I'd seen him.

Trouble was, I didn't know what to do to make things better for him.

I understood he felt guilty, and because I wasn't being mean to him or hating on him, he wasn't sure how to deal with me.

Weren't men strange?

Would he have preferred for me to stop talking to him?

Then, I realized something I should have figured out before.

Finn, whether he was devout or not, was a Catholic.

Catholics practically got off on penance. It was what we did best.

"Finn?" I asked quietly. "Have you gone to confession?"

That had him braking to a halt. "Huh?"

It was the first time I'd seen him speechless, but it was a week for firsts. I hadn't seen him so close to losing control, either.

"I asked if you'd gone to confession. Since the shooting, I mean." How I kept my tone so calm, I wasn't sure.

From something Brennan had said while my eyes were closed and the guys had thought I was sleeping—I hadn't been pretending, had just been drifting—I knew Finn had shot and killed one of the Colombians. I also knew that the shooters had, somehow, been tossed out of the moving truck and the brothers had shot them too.

That was a lot for anyone to deal with.

A Catholic?

Someone used to purging their soul after every sin?

It was a doozy.

"I only go because of Aidan. And I'm not going anywhere. You need me here."

"I do," I admitted. "But I need *my* Finn. You seem to want me to punish you, Finn. I'm not going to do that."

He grew still at that, and with his back to me, he stared out the wall of windows that overlooked the city of Manhattan, and tension crawled down his spine. "Why not?" he asked quietly.

"Because what happened wasn't..." Blowing out a breath, I covered my face with my hands and rubbed my eyes. I was too tired for this, but Finn was suffering more than I was.

And that was saying something.

Mom had always told me that men could be big babies sometimes. I just hadn't believed it.

I couldn't say it wasn't an accident. Because it wasn't, was it? The drive-by had been Cause and Effect 101. Still, I didn't think Finn needed a lesson on causality.

It wasn't his fault, though. Not directly.

Did I hate him for putting me in a hospital bed? No. Did I wish it hadn't happened? Of course. I wasn't a fucking idiot. But it was complicated. Just because I didn't hate him, didn't mean I was happy with what had gone down. I was in a lot of pain—unnecessarily so. But my sulking with him wasn't going to do anything.

It wasn't like I could even use this against him as leverage. Everyone knew how it worked. You were a Five Pointer until the day you died—unless you'd served them well and they let you retire. *If you were lucky enough to live that long,* I tacked on ruefully.

So, my holding a grudge and saying, 'It's me or the Five Points,' wasn't going to get us anywhere, was it?

Had I expected to be shot on my wedding day?

Nope.

Did I expect him to feel guilty about it?

To be honest, yeah, but that didn't mean I wanted him to be miserable. I just wanted it to make him think about his actions. That wasn't so much to ask, was it?

"Finn, go to church."

He turned around to scowl at me. "I'm not—"

"Just do it, would you? For me?"

His jaw worked but as he stared at me, his conscience warring behind his eyes, before he turned on his heel, and stalked out of the room.

The minute he left, it was like all the air was sucked out with him. Fuck, I hated it when he was in the other room, never mind not *here* somewhere. And if that made me a pussy, well, you try being shot, having your spleen removed, and then...

Well, walk a day in my shoes before you fucking judged.

The last thing I wanted was for him to be anywhere but with me, but if confessing his damn sins put him in a better mood, then I was game for anything.

35

———

FINN

ONE OF THE reasons I was so mad?

I knew Aoife was right.

I hadn't confessed, and I had a lot weighing me down.

Irony being, of course, that I hadn't really thought I believed in this bullshit. But, in a crisis, it looked like I did.

Samuel was silent on the drive over to St Patrick's. Normally he liked to chat. Tell me about his missus and the herb garden he tended on his rooftop, of all things. I didn't mind. It was like white noise after a while, and because I'd trained myself to, I picked up on what he said even if I was focused on something else.

Every man appreciated being listened to. It was the personal touch. It created camaraderie and loyalty—Samuel, though he knew of the consequences, would never betray me anyway because I cared.

I knew when his wife, Miranda's birthday was, knew his daughter Ciara was studying at Columbia University and that Aidan was helping him pay for most of it. Not just because he was a nice guy, but because Ciara was pre-law and was as deep in with the Five Points as her brothers were, and fully intended on serving with us after graduation. I knew his sons were all under Brennan's watch, and

I knew which ones were heading for promotion and which would stay as runners.

The personal touch.

So for him to be quiet was a testament to his reading of my mood.

It was just before three, and the streets were marginally less crazy than usual. As always, Samuel provided a smooth ride as he drove me and my turbulent thoughts to church.

I swore my frame of mind was almost a physical entity beside me, and it was wearing on me.

The guilt.

Fuck.

It was ripping me to shreds.

My chest felt constrained, all the damn time. When I looked at Aoife, when I glanced over to the sofa she'd taken to sitting on in my study—where she currently wasn't and where she most definitely should be. Because of me.

When I was heating up soup my housekeeper made for her, I felt so bad because Aoife loved cooking and couldn't cook at the minute. Because of me.

When I climbed into bed at night and I couldn't pull her into my arms because she was so fucking delicate right now. Because of me.

The journey blurred at some point as I thought about what I was going to say, what I *needed* to say to clear my brain, and when Samuel parked the car, I jolted to awareness and saw that we'd arrived.

"Thanks," I told him gruffly and climbed out to face the building where my worst nightmare had played out.

The front facade of the ancient building was pockmarked now. Bullets had sprayed into the stonework, and I knew Aidan was funding the work that was needed to restore the mess.

As I walked down the cobbled path, the gravestones on either side of me were a reminder that I might have been here this week, burying Aoife.

The pain that caused me could only be matched by the fucked-up guilt I'd endured as a kid.

It was a weird time for those memories to surface, but it was like 'let's hate on Finn' week, and all the shit I'd done was just piling on top of me.

Scrubbing a hand through my hair, I stepped under the stone arch into the building proper.

Most churches were closed this time of day, but Aidan funded this one so that his men could drop in for confessional any time their schedules would allow.

A man who'd confessed had a clean soul and could meet his Maker earnestly, was his philosophy, one I'd thought to be bullshit until now.

I gnawed on my bottom lip as I wondered if I was about to turn into some religious zealot. Then, I realized I blasphemed too much to ever be that, and there was no way in fuck I wasn't going to do dirty and despicable things to Aoife the minute she was back on her feet... things that were definitely not approved of in the Bible.

So, yeah. I needed to purge this shit from my soul and move on.

It wasn't like we could talk to a goddamn counselor about the shit we did and saw. Father Doyle was that to us, and Aoife was right, I needed to confess my sins.

Because it was a busy confessional, there was a bell on the door. You rang it and it sounded in Doyle's seventies chic office. If he hadn't appeared in ten minutes, you assumed the drunken old coot had passed out, and went and sought his ass out.

The man wasn't as pious as he liked to preach, but Aidan said that no man was a saint and seemed to think it made him a more honest priest because he wasn't perfect. My brothers and I usually rolled our eyes at that—Aidan could spew a lot of crap.

I rubbed my chin as I took a seat inside the confessional.

It was cold in here, and I realized I'd forgotten my coat—my first penance because the Arctic was warmer than St Patrick's on some days.

Soon, I'd be on my knees, but I wasn't waiting on Doyle's rheumatic pace to kneel. When he arrived, I'd take up the stance.

It didn't take long.

I heard the slip-slip of his soft shoes against the stone flagons and when the confessional door opened, I flowed down to the floor, finding the movement strangely cathartic.

The window in the booth opened, and Doyle recounted the usual prayer. After he'd finished, I bowed my head and whispered, "Bless me, Father, for I have sinned. It's been fourteen days since my last confession, and I accuse myself of the following sins..."

My voice petered out there, and I had to shudder to concentrate.

See, my trouble was that I didn't feel like I'd sinned.

I'd killed a man.

I didn't repent it.

I'd do it again.

And again.

Anything to save Aoife. To keep her safe in the future. So, what did I feel guilty about? The fact that she'd been hurt when I deserved the bullet? That I hadn't kept her from danger? They weren't sins. Not in the eyes of the Church. Just in my heart.

When I fell silent, uncertain of what to say, Doyle queried, "Finn, my boy?"

It came as no surprise that he knew it was me. Going two weeks without confession broke one of the Five Points' cardinal rules.

"Yes, Father?"

"You killed a man, didn't you?"

My throat closed up. "I did."

Not that it was on record. Still, that wasn't how the soul worked, was it?

"And do you repent?"

"No." I released a shaky breath as I realized how fucking good that felt to admit.

"It's a mortal sin that you've committed, child," Doyle stated, but I heard no judgment in his words. I didn't even want to know how often he heard this type of confession on a weekly basis.

"They almost killed my wife."

"Indeed, they did, and they had no Last Rites to cleanse their soul. The Devil has them now. They are his to punish."

It was very Old Testament, but I found that pleased me.

"I've had lecherous thoughts." Okay, so it was a cop out, but I had to start somewhere.

Doyle snickered. "That doesn't surprise me."

What surprised *me* was how chilled he was being. Usually he sounded like he'd been snorting sour Altoids. Was it because of the situation? He'd never usually been so kind.

"I-I want my wife."

"No shame in that, son. In fact, that's where your lustful thoughts should be centered. I think God would be pleased you made the right choice."

Releasing a shaky breath, I switched tactics. "I want to hurt the people who hurt her."

"They're already in the Devil's care, Finn. There is no worse hurt that can be bestowed upon them."

"Their leaders still live," I rasped.

Doyle fell silent. "Why are you here, child?"

"Aoife told me to come."

"Well, I didn't expect that."

"No?" My lips curved as I found myself amused by the notion that I'd surprised Doyle. I'd been doing that a lot lately.

What with turning up with a fiancée, asking him to do without the traditional declaring of the banns before the wedding ceremony... Now this. It was a time of change for the old coot.

"No. I know she's not a believer. Not like her mother was."

"How do you know that?"

"I spoke with her priest, of course." He tutted. "I don't invite just anyone into my flock."

I rolled my eyes at that—he invited who Aidan commanded. "Aoife is... She's being very understanding, Father."

He hummed. "She thinks you need to atone?"

"No. I think she believes I need to confess, to get things off my chest."

"And you disagree?"

"I'm here, aren't I?"

"True." He sighed. "Finn, child, you're not new to this process. I can't grant you the appropriate penance, if that's what you need, unless you have something you wish to make reparation for, over the harm you've caused."

I licked my lips as I bowed my head. "I will do anything to protect my wife, Father. I wish that hadn't induced me to act in the way I did."

"It's a start, I suppose," Doyle grumbled. "If you were anyone else, I'd ask if you were scared to confess, but I know you too well."

Was I too scared?

I didn't think so.

I was angry, and the anger was welling up inside me.

"I'm not scared," I admitted, my voice hoarse. "Not about confessing. I'm scared she'll leave me. That she'll hate me. You and I both know there's no way out of the Points, and I wouldn't want to leave," I finished on a rush—I knew no other life, didn't want another life.

"Has she asked you to?" Doyle didn't sound shocked, so I wondered if Aoife should have. If that was considered normal from a wife in this situation.

"No."

Another hum. "She's an unusual one. How's she doing?"

"Could be better. The infection at the wound site has cleared up, but she's still sore. Will be for a while."

"And are you treating her well?"

I scowled at that. "Of course."

A low chuckle sounded then. "I didn't mean 'are you beating her,' Finn. I'm under no illusion that you're probably cosseting her—anyone with eyes can see how you look at the lass." He heaved a sigh. "Never thought I'd see the day when Finn O'Grady came to me to talk about banns and the like." I could well imagine him rubbing his chin in contemplation. "But there are more ways to treat a patient than with just due diligence. If you're wearing your guilt on your sleeve because she isn't making your life miserable over what's happened, then that will wear on both of you."

That had me blinking and I covered my eyes with my left hand, digging into the sockets to relieve the ache that was gathering there. "I don't understand why she isn't mad at me. She's teasing me. Making my brothers laugh. She's been so good, Father. I don't deserve her."

"Then, all I can say to you, my son, is to be the man she deserves."

The words resonated with me. I wanted to be that man, but I didn't know how to be what she needed.

Where it counted, little could change.

I didn't work for a high-power law firm in the city, and it wasn't like I could go on a sabbatical so we could take a break where she could recuperate. It wasn't like I could quit my job, nor did I want to. The Five Points was the Irish Mob. My responsibilities were waiting on my total attention, but I was allaying my duties by working from home.

Even as I cared for her, tended to her, I had a duty to the Family.

"How do I be the man she deserves?" I asked, wanting that for her so fucking much, my chest ached with it.

"Do you love her, Finn?"

Silence reigned for a handful of seconds until I choked out, "Yes."

"Have you told her that?"

"No."

"Why not?" Doyle asked on an impatient huff. "The woman took a bullet for you, Finn! You could at least have told her you loved her."

My jaw clenched. "To say it now, to say it when she's going through all this because of me is like..." I blew out a sharp breath. "I won't tell her I love her like it's a magic cure-all."

"What do you mean?"

"If I'd told her before, she'd have believed me. Now, she might just think I'm saying it because I feel bad."

Doyle snorted. "Only a man could say something so ignorant. She doesn't care why, she just wants your love. She's sore, she's hurting, and she's on the road to recovery... she wants your love, Finn," he repeated. "Love her. Give her what she needs within reason and be the man she needs you to be."

Could I do that? He made it sound so easy, but life was never that simple, was it?

"Apologize to her. For the shooting. For the fact she's injured," Doyle carried on when I stayed silent, processing his words. "Apologize for being stubborn, for being an ass. Make reparation to the one person who bore the brunt of you and the Points' sins." He paused. "That and three Hail Marys *and* three Our Fathers as well as the Act of Contrition is what I ask of you today."

I hadn't expected him to go so easy on me. Especially when I wasn't here to atone for the one sin that mattered the most.

Did he understand?

"Thank you, Father," I said softly.

"There will be a time when you're ready to seek penance for the other matter, but as they say, if the mountain won't go to Mohammed, then Mohammed must go to the mountain."

As I rasped out the Act of Contrition, Father Doyle finished with, "Go in peace, Finn, and say a prayer for me."

36
———

AOIFE

I MAY or may not have fallen when I went to use the bathroom.

FML.

There was going to be a bruise where my side collided with the dresser and Finn was going to be wicked pissed.

Not with me.

With himself.

I knew it like I knew I was really glad the dresser was there, because if it hadn't been, then I'd have gone down.

And only God knew if I'd have managed to get myself up again, so I guessed I should be thankful for small mercies.

He'd see it when he changed the dressing on my stomach. Cursing my luck, I lay in bed and stared up at the ceiling. I felt like I'd been doing this for a lifetime, when really, I'd only been stuck in bed for just under two weeks.

I was a jumble of so many mixed emotions and I was getting kind of pissed that Finn was the one blowing up when I was laying here grouchy, horny, itchy, and fidgety. And shit, I was bored. So bored. I loved reading, and when I'd had the tea room, I'd wished I had more time for it, but now that it was all I could do?

It didn't help that I loved romance books, and those books were steamy, which made me even hornier, and it was all kinds of wrong that I could be in pain and need sex at the same time.

Hoping to God that Finn's visit to the confessional would improve his demeanor before I had to rip him a new one, and wishing that he'd hurry the hell up because I missed him like nuts and he'd been gone for just over forty minutes—I know, I know, pathetic—I carried on staring up at the ceiling.

It provided no answers.

Well, I learned that the housekeepers cleaned the corners of the ceiling—there were zero cobwebs. Something I'd never done in my own apartment. How did they even reach those areas? I'd seen them. They appeared like little mice at around ten AM and when I said they were little, they'd need more than a stepladder to reach the high vaulted ceilings that were a feature all over the penthouse.

The private elevator pinged, breaking into my exciting thoughts on whether the maids were actually witches who used spells on those pesky, hard-to-reach areas, and the second I heard it, excitement whizzed through my veins as I realized Finn was home.

When his shoes clacked against the tiles, I waited with bated breath for him to come in, to visit with me, but he didn't. His shoes, attached to those sexy rugby-player legs, passed by our bedroom.

What the fuck?

He wasn't going to talk to me?

Even as bewildered hurt swirled inside me, I wanted to cry out for him, wanted to ask him to come in, but something stopped me. Tears pricked my eyes as I questioned what on earth I'd done to deserve the silent treatment, but then I realized *why* I hadn't called out.

The gait wasn't right.

Finn walked smoothly. Like he did everything else. Damn his sexy hide. He walked like he was fucking waltzing, without the mincing—although I'd pay to see him dressed up in a tux. His smooth steps, shod in expensive leather, weren't the same as the clod hopping sound of leather boots. I'd never seen him in boots. If he didn't wear Oxfords, he wore loafers, with even his sneakers looking like they cost a few hundred bucks.

Finn wouldn't be seen dead in a pair of cheap, squeaky boots.

Which meant that someone was in the apartment.

Someone that shouldn't be here.

My heart began to pound, and nausea swirled in my belly. No one should be able to access this place except for Finn, myself, and the housekeeping staff—who'd already been in this morning.

Was it Aidan Sr.?

He'd already proven he could get in here without Finn's say so, but I wasn't scared of Aidan anymore. Right?

He didn't make me feel warm and cozy inside, but I wasn't scared. Not outright.

I would never be able to say why I did it, but something had me getting out of bed. The pain that spliced my nerve endings in two had me staggering to a halt to suck in air. If I moved slowly, there wasn't much pain, but I had to shift my ass, and that wasn't easy at the moment.

I cursed each second that delayed me, but rolling out was no longer as simple as it had been a few short weeks ago—how had my life changed so radically in under a month? Just smoothing back the sheets, so it looked like it was made, was hard going, but I managed and padded over to the closet as fast as I could.

Having hidden in here my first day in this apartment, I knew how cramped it was, and there was no way I could smoosh myself into a ball like I had before.

I could hide behind the clothes, though. There was wiggle room and I had lost a good fifteen pounds—amazing what no appetite could do to a woman. Shame it sucked hairy monkey balls because I missed cake almost as much as I missed Finn's cock.

Yeah, it was that bad.

Opening the wardrobe door, I slipped inside just in time to hear the bedroom door click. When Finn didn't call out my name, I knew I'd been right to hide.

Fear washed through my veins, though.

If someone was looking for me, would they think to look here?

They'd know I was sick, right? Would know I couldn't have gone far.

Then, I heard it.

A low curse, then someone started talking even though I only heard the sound of one person's footsteps in the room. Had they picked up their cell? I strained to hear what was being said, but it was foreign. I could speak some Spanish, but it wasn't any kind of Romance language I knew. It sounded Russian.

Fear made me feel light-headed. I hadn't stood up this long in days, and my heart was pounding, making my temples pulse with a cruel kind of pain.

I clung to the rail with my right hand. Stretching had me seeing stars, but I needed the support and could only hope it wouldn't come crashing down if I put too much weight on it. I tried to control my breathing, but it came out in gusts that sounded extremely loud to my ears. I felt hot in the small space and I wanted nothing more than to get out, to get some fresh air.

After what felt like a lifetime, the Russian faded, as did the sound of the stranger's footsteps. Whoever had come up here hadn't been very thorough.

Had they been looking for me? Or for Finn?

I sent up a quick prayer of thanks that I'd sent him out to confess. God, talk about perfect timing.

The only problem was, I didn't dare move. How would I know the apartment was clear? How would I know it was safe, and that the Russian wasn't waiting for Finn to arrive? And *if* he was waiting on Finn's return, I had no means of warning my husband, because, dammit to hell, I'd left my cell phone charging on the nightstand.

Oh, God. I was one of those women. One of those stupid damn women in the horror movies who went outside when everyone behind the screen was yelling at her foolish ass to stay *inside* the house.

Fuck.

Fright crashed into my very fragile sense of self. I was shaking like a leaf from both the exertion and terror, and in the end, I had to slump against the side of the wardrobe, my head pressing into the maple, to stop myself from passing out.

I didn't know how long it was, hours or minutes later, but I heard Finn's panicked voice as he called my name.

"Finn!"

God, was that me?

So weak? So quivery?

I wasn't sure he could hear me, but how would I find the strength to speak up?

I clenched my eyes shut, gathered all my strength in preparation for yelling out his name, but I didn't have to.

The door opened. The clothes were shoved aside, and there they were.

The O'Donnelly brothers and Finn. All armed. All looking a mixture of piss-your-pants scary and concerned for me.

When Finn's worried gaze snared mine, my knees buckled like that was all I'd been waiting for. He swore and dove to catch me. I had no doubt he would, just hated that I looked so damn weak—especially in front of his brothers. They were men who respected strength, something I'd seen the first time I'd met them that initial Sunday lunch I'd had with the family.

Flopping into Finn's arms wasn't exactly a show of strength, and I felt sick about it, but I nuzzled into Finn's arms the second he hauled me into him. Needing his support, needing to cling to him. Just knowing he was here made me feel safe, when life had already proven to me that there was no such thing as safety anymore.

God, what had I gotten myself into?

"Fuck, Aoife, fuck," he whispered, kissing my head, kissing the side of my face. Anywhere he could reach, he kissed, and I sensed his panic in each caress.

"What's going on?" I whispered back, frightened by how quiet my voice was.

Shit, was I on the brink of passing out?

The combination of the heat from the closet, the fact I'd been standing for only God knew how long, and the gut-wrenching fear were plaguing my besieged system.

But I had to be strong.

Had to be.

Finn didn't need a wimp for a wife. It was bad enough I'd hid in a fucking wardrobe again, but I'd had no choice, had I? It wasn't like I had a gun in my bedside table. Crap, it wasn't like I could even fire one.

Putting shooting lessons on the top of my to-do list when I got back on my feet, I let Finn carry me to the bed. Declan had already dragged the covers back, and Finn lay me amid the sheets and covered me.

I shot the brothers a look and saw they were staring back at me grimly. The only one who wasn't here was Aidan, and considering he was still in the hospital, that made sense.

"How did you know someone was here?"

"Someone hacked the code box on the elevator. I got a notification on my phone." Finn took a careful seat at my side as he leaned over to drag open the nightstand drawer.

The good stuff, like lube and condoms, had been shoved in the middle one, and pain meds had been stored at the top.

I really had not envisaged starting married life out with pain meds in the top drawer of my nightstand.

"He was Russian," I told Finn, catching each man's eye. Before they could ask how I knew—no, I wasn't a mind reader, but the way they gaped at me was irritating—I continued, "H-He came in here and was looking for me. He spoke with someone on his phone. I didn't understand any of it."

Finn shoved an empty tumbler behind him, waiting for someone to get the hint. Declan did and clomped over to the bathroom. As Finn doled out meds like a pharmacist, I took them in my hand and popped them when Declan gave me the glass.

I thought I'd been in pain before, but it was nothing compared to the come down that let me feel all the myriad aches that encompassed my body. They were suddenly there, suddenly so acute I wanted to cry out, but I firmed my mouth and gritted my teeth to withhold the moans of discomfort that longed to break free. Fuck, when were the meds going to kick in?

"We need to take her to the compound."

"No!" I barked, surprising myself with how strident my tone was after I'd just been inwardly whining over how weak my voice sounded. "I'm not leaving Finn."

I grabbed his hand and he tightened his fingers around mine. He looked carefully into my eyes and murmured, "I'm going to do some things you won't like, Aoife."

"I don't care," I told him instantly.

His nostrils flared. "I care. I'm going to be the husband you deserve."

Panic fluttered through me, but it was oddly muted. What did being the husband I deserved entail? So long as he didn't leave me frickin' alone again, he could do whatever the hell he wanted.

I squeezed down hard on his hand and said as much. "Finn, do not put me in lockdown unless you're going to be there too."

He dipped his chin. "I never intended to do anything less."

From the surprised looks on his brothers' faces—Conor looked particularly awestruck by Finn's statement—I gathered that was unusual.

Typical men.

Shove a bunch of women together while they go off and play war. *Bastards.*

"You promise?" There was a quiver to my voice, but it wasn't from weakness, it was from fatigue. It was from the rage I'd feel if he lied to me.

"I promise."

I sank back, flopping like a whoopee cushion someone had sat on, then regretted it when my left side twinged like a busted guitar string. "Good."

"I'll pack your things."

"How long will we be away for?"

He shrugged then leaned over to kiss my temple. I grabbed the front of his shirt so he couldn't pull away.

"How long, Finn?"

"As long as it takes, Aoife," he rasped, then dropped me another kiss—this one to the tip of my nose.

I tried not to be charmed by that and called myself a sucker when I fell into those bright blue pools that were his damn eyes.

My body needed more than a kiss on the nose and a pat on the hand, but what it needed, it wasn't ready for.

Someone had just tried to—

I wasn't even sure what their intention had been. Just knew that they hadn't dropped a bouquet of flowers at the bottom of the bed with a 'Get Well Soon' card.

For whatever reason, we seemed to have two enemies now. A war on two fronts—the Colombians and the Russians vs. us.

I tried not to feel sick at the thought, and then just embraced the nausea because no amount of lying to myself was going to make this situation any better.

37

FINN

I KEPT ON SURPRISING MYSELF.

My control seemed to grow exponentially as each hour passed, even when I felt sure it would fold in on itself, crumble, leaving me a raging lunatic, it didn't. Its limits increased until I knew even Aidan Sr. was impressed.

Not that he could judge.

The fucker had zero control, and if Lena had been the one who was targeted today, then I knew he'd be on a rampage. Exactly how I wanted to be.

I didn't just need to cut some motherfuckers, I craved it. Craved it like no good Catholic ever should, but screw that shit. If they thought they could get to me through Aoife, they could think again while I hung them up from their wrists like a dead cow on a hook. The slaughterhouse was there for a reason, just waiting for me to figure out what the hell was going on.

"The Russians are either working on their own, or have united with the Colombians," Conor stated something we all knew but didn't want to say.

"That's not like Vasov," Aidan Sr. grouched, rubbing his chin.

"He said it himself. The Colombians are his biggest suppliers," I murmured, my voice hushed as I traced the lines of the mahogany table around which the council was seated.

Only Aidan Jr. wasn't here, and he wouldn't be for at least another eight weeks thanks to the new steel pins in his leg.

All the other O'Donnelly brothers, myself included, were here though, as well as the three men Aidan considered advisors, but I thought Tony, Mark, and Paul spoke bullshit. Aidan only kept them around because they'd come up together from school. They were dipshits, but they knew to keep their mouth shut unless Aidan asked them anything, so I could handle having their dumbasses around.

"Aoife's certain he's Russian?"

"She said he was. Why would she lie?" I countered, frowning at him and the question he'd posed. "She was fucking shitting herself, Aidan."

"You should have seen her, Da," Eoghan rasped. "Shaking like a leaf, looked like a kitten could push her over."

Aidan slammed his hand against the table. "No one should be able to get into our homes. What the fuck went wrong?"

Conor scrubbed a hand over his face. "They hacked our systems."

"And I thought you were our resident boy genius?" he sneered, making fury flash in Conor's eyes.

"I developed that code myself. It's good. But someone beat it. I need to develop something else. *Evidently*," he bit off. "I'll be putting in extra safe guards too."

"It's because of Conor that we knew to get back there ASAP," I told Aidan, who was on his feet now, pacing back and forth like a pissed off lion in a cage. "When the guy broke into the system, I got an alert on my phone."

"We all did," Brennan added.

Aidan sniffed, but didn't apologize.

"I think retina scans might be the next step," Conor inserted on a heavy sigh. "It's hardcore to get into your fucking home, but with the threat level this high?"

"Do it," I insisted. "I have a wife to protect."

"She's in lockdown now, son. She's safe," Aidan tried to comfort, but it wasn't much help.

"She should be at home. She's sick. She doesn't need to be in an unfamiliar environment."

"Lena will look after her the best she can."

I wanted to snap that it wasn't good enough, but I didn't. Aidan was trying to help even if he was only succeeding in pissing me off even more.

I ran a hand through my hair as I slouched over the table. "Why target her? Why me?"

"You're the money man," Declan pointed out softly.

Aidan whistled. "I said it to Vasov myself. You're my Sovietnik."

Sovietnik in the Bratva brotherhood was a leadership role—the Pakhan's accountant. And at our meeting, when we'd asked the Brighton Beach brotherhood for their help in containing the situation with the Colombians, they'd agreed after I'd pulled the favor card.

I rubbed my chin. "It still doesn't make sense to target me."

"Not to kill, but to pressure?" Aidan tilted his head to the side. "You're a husband now. You have a weakness. You know what they're like."

"You think they want to kidnap Aoife?"

"I think when she hid in that closet, she did a smart thing."

"Why didn't he check the wardrobe?" Brennan asked, his tone worried. "Isn't that Kidnapping 101?"

Because I wanted to beat something up, I reached around and massaged the back of my neck.

I didn't want to be here. I wanted to be with Aoife.

She needed me.

For the first time in my life, someone needed me with no ulterior motive in mind, and instead of being with her, I was discussing the events that had led to her getting shot and now, almost kidnapped.

"Think outside the box," Conor urged after a second. Leaning forward, he added, "The Russians owed us, guys. Big time."

"For doing them a favor. That's no leverage in the here and now," Aidan said with a sigh. "No honor among those cunts."

"What did Vasov say when you called him?"

Aidan frowned at me, the bridge of his nose scored with wrinkles at my question. "Why would I call him?"

I stared at him, dumbfounded. "You haven't called to ask if he was involved?"

"He's going to lie about it."

"Maybe. But maybe not." Seriously, did I have to do everything around here? "Aidan, please, call him. Let him gloat or let him deny it—we need to know the lay of the land."

His lips firmed. "Look, Finn, I know you're upset—"

"You're goddamn right I'm upset. My wife's been shot and might have been kidnapped today!" I roared, uncaring Aidan Sr. was a lunatic and that he might cut off a finger if I back talked him much more.

The older man narrowed his eyes at me. "Watch your tongue, Finn."

It was a warning I should heed, but rage made me reckless. "No, Aidan, you watch your fucking tongue. I've been married for a month and my woman has spent every day of our marriage in her sickbed. How would you feel if it was Lena? If she'd been shot, if she was under threat?"

The darkness that came into Aidan's eyes was a familiar warning, but he nodded brusquely. "I'd be mad."

Ha. Understatement of the fucking year.

"Exactly," was all I said though. "So, before we go to war with the Colombians *and* the goddamn Russians, let's find out what the hell they have to say first, yeah?" I felt like tugging my hair out, but that was how it went with Aidan Sr. sometimes. The bastard could be stubborn as fuck.

I knew he didn't like it, and he'd shout me down later on for talking to him like that in front of the whole council, but he could. I'd let him break my fucking nose so long as I could climb into bed with my wife at some point in the next eight hours knowing which way was up.

Shooting the shit about theories would get us nowhere. We needed facts, and we couldn't get that unless someone was made to answer for their behavior.

Aidan dug into his pocket and pulled out his cellphone. Scrolling through his contacts, he hit call and turned it to speaker before he dropped the expensive gadget onto the table.

"I thought you might ring me tonight." There was a note of gloating to Vasov's voice that rubbed me raw. It irked the shit out of me, but the words confused me.

I knew Aoife was safe. I'd put her to bed myself in one of the rooms at the compound. No way anyone had broken in there. Not without getting laid out with a bunch of Tommy guns—as Aidan liked to call them; said his grandpa had used one in the Irish Civil War.

Yet Vasov spoke as though whatever he'd done had gone according to plan when Aoife was tucked up in bed, safe and relatively sound.

"We want to know what the fuck is going on, that's what," Aidan snarled, his usual diplomatic self.

"I think we can call our favor canceled out, no?"

Favor canceled out?

"Now, why the fuck would you think that?" Aidan shot me a perplexed glower.

"Because my Boyevik took out that Colombian cunt."

What. The. Fuck?

What Colombian cunt?

Aidan grated out, "I don't have a clue what you're talking about, Vasov."

"You don't—" Vasov spat out something in Russian, and in the background a volley was batted back his way. Then, Aidan's phone dinged and Vasov stated, "Look at the pictures I sent."

"Two minutes."

Aidan picked up his cell, then in less than five seconds, had sent them to our secure group chat. As one unit, we scanned the photos and I frowned down at what I was looking at.

The Colombian was unmistakable. His face was slathered with Roman numeral tattoos, well, the parts that weren't covered in blood were.

What the hell was going on here? Who was the bastard?

"I see them. I see the dead Colombian," Aidan confirmed when his sons and advisors shrugged with their lack of understanding. "Why you sending me snuff pics?"

Vasov grunted. "The boy was sneaking into your Sovietnik's building. According to my Boyevik, he hacked his way into the private elevator where my soldiers took him out. When my man went to check all was well in your apartment, he found no one there.

"I see no reason why the Colombians would try to infiltrate an empty apartment unless there's something stored there... I think it's time you upgraded your security, Irish."

Aidan shot me a startled look. "You weren't there to kidnap my Sovietnik's wife?"

An explosion of Russian burst down the line. "What bullshit is this?" Vasov spat, rage coating his every word.

"Until you sent me the fucking picture, Vasov, I had no idea a Colombian had been anywhere near my boy's place. This is the first I've heard of all this."

There was a sound, like a click, and another man began speaking —Basil Lukov, the Obschak, the leader behind the Pakhan's security. "Since our meeting, we've been maintaining an eye on your council."

"Why would you be doing something so foolish as that?" Aidan demanded, his tone cool.

"Because the Colombians are crazy," came Basil's answer, and he sounded candid. "In fact, that's an understatement. They're insane and they don't give a fuck who they hurt in the process.

"We've been gradually weaning our supplies from them to the Mexicans. They're far less volatile. Keeping an eye on major players can be lucrative for us. In this instance, we consider your marker with us canceled."

Aidan snorted. "Much as I love my boy and his woman, Lukov, there ain't no way in hell their lives are worth the two hundred million dollars we saved you when we gave you that pig all those months ago.

"You consider spying on my major people to be something good? How the fuck do I know you didn't take some random Latino, slice him up, and tattoo his face?"

There was a hushed sound. "You do not."

"Exactly. You still owe my people and me. And rather than considering it a favor for a favor, maybe we should be working together against the Colombians if you're wanting to cut ties with them permanently."

"I'm listening," Vasov stated.

"I'm friendly with the Mexicans."

"Hardly. You killed their cartel leader."

"On their instruction," I inserted coolly.

Silence fell as they processed that. "The new leader paid you?"

"Ten million. My friends can be your friends, Comrade."

"I need to discuss this with my people. I will call tomorrow."

"Can't fucking wait," Aidan snapped and slammed the phone down before he rubbed a hand over his face.

"Seriously?" I blurted out. "*Seriously?* They were spying on us, caught a goddamn assassin trying to break into my place, so killed him, then broke into my fucking home anyway, and expected us to thank them?" But dammit, they *had* saved Aoife, hadn't they? I wasn't even sure which part of my statement was the most fucked in the head.

My heart felt like it was going to pump its way out of my chest. My blood pressure was soaring so hard I could hear it whooshing in my ears.

"It's good she's on lockdown," Brennan said calmly, and I glowered at him.

"That has nothing to do with this."

"Yes. It does. She's safe, and that's what matters," Declan insisted, nodding at Brennan. "Plus, we know there's a weakness in our security that's twofold. If the Bratva can follow our top people around without us knowing it, and a Cartel foot soldier can hack their way into our penthouses? Jesus, what fucking use are we? Useless cunts, that's what."

The words resonated. I saw that. Aidan ground his teeth at his son's candor, but he ducked his chin as he processed the bare, hard facts. "We've grown lazy. We're not as hierarchal as the Bratva. We've been making money hand over fist and instead of shoring our defenses, we've taken a step back from our roots." He ran a hand over his head. "If the Russians cut a deal with us tomorrow, and we act as middleman for the Mexicans, first thing we do is recruiting and training."

"It shouldn't be hard to double our numbers," Conor stated, tone confident. "Lots of kids have been trying to get recruited. We've just been limiting who we take on."

"They think it's like Sons of goddamn Anarchy, Conor. What use are they to us?" Brennan snapped.

"We have to train them, dick," Conor snapped back. "Not saying even ten percent of them will be worth shit, but we have room to be selective."

As the two bickered, I realized I needed some air, but I wasn't going to get any.

Aidan's main office was close to the Hudson and from atop the roof, you could even see the dingy water if you tried. In here, he could be as paranoid as he wanted to be.

There were no windows in case an enemy tried to assassinate one of the council, and back in the early years when safe rooms had become a 'thing,' he'd had this space converted into one. Making it half safe room/half nuclear bunker.

The only trouble was, whenever I was in here, I felt like we were running out of air. We were safe but closed in like a can of goddamn sardines.

I pressed my elbows to the mahogany table and leaned over the desk, trying to ignore my straining lungs, my madly beating heart.

"What's the intention here?" I rasped. "We train new guys up for what reason? To run the Colombians out totally? Or because there's safety in numbers?"

Aidan shrugged. "Don't see why not. Lukov's right. They're crazy motherfuckers."

"Most of the Latino gangs are," Brennan tacked on dryly. "They're all snorting their own shit. Crazy cokeheads."

I nodded because that was partly true. "At least the Bratva are disciplined."

Aidan shot me a look. "You believe Lukov?"

"I don't see why he'd be lying."

"Explains why Aoife's hiding place held. If he'd really wanted to find her, he'd have looked in the goddamn wardrobe," Declan said, his tone rueful, and though I understood his humor, we were talking about my fucking wife here.

I wanted to snarl at him, but he was right, and there was no need for me to take out my piss-poor mood on my brother.

Aidan sighed. "Son, go to her."

"There's shit to be done here, Aidan."

"Not until Vasov calls in the morning," he corrected. "Conor, you'll secure Finn's place, right?"

"Sure as shit," he mumbled. "I fucked up. I'm sorry, guys. I thought my code was untouchable. That's what you get for being an arrogant shithead. If some piece of crap cartel foot soldier can break through it..." He gritted his teeth. "Once this meeting is finished, I'll be over there to figure out how he did it."

I wasn't about to pile guilt on his shoulders, but I wasn't going to disagree either.

"You need to check out all our places," Aidan stated. "Update it all, if you need fucking finger and retina scanners, then we have the money thanks to our boy, Finn."

"And me, too," Conor grumbled, and for the first time that evening, I did want to laugh.

"Yeah, he helps," I joked, and Conor flipped me the bird but grinned good-naturedly. We were a team, and we both knew it.

"Eoghan, I want you on these Bratva packs that are following us around." He grunted. "It goes against the grain to have security with us. But we don't have eyes in the back of our goddamn head, and this proves it. Pick some of your men and get them moving in with you."

My eyes widened at that. "You want us to have live-in bodyguards?"

"Until the threat's over, yeah. Those Colombians are whack jobs. Only Jesus himself knows what they were going to do today.

"I mean, what they did at the church was crazy enough. To outright declare war on us when we outnumber them three to one?" He shook his head. "Fucking mental, that's all I can say."

"More like they have a death wish," Brennan stated. "They never could get their numbers up around here. In LA, they're close to King."

"Yeah, well, this is fucking NYC, not that piece of shit hellhole," Aidan ground out—he was the kind of guy who'd live and die in the city. He'd never vacationed outside of the state, not even to go to the Old Country. Lena had gone though, mostly with Brennan, to visit family.

I got to my feet before Aidan could get on his high horse about how much of a dump LA was. The man had never been there, so how the fuck he could judge, I had no idea. I wasn't in the mood to listen, not when he'd said I could go home.

"I'm going back to the compound."

"Never thought I'd see the day you'd be sleeping there," Eoghan said with a smirk. "You going there too, Da?"

"What kind of foolish question is that, boy? I go where your mother is. And if you feckers weren't idiots, you'd get yourself settled down too," Aidan retorted, sniffing his displeasure at his sons' intent to remain bachelors forever.

They all rolled their eyes, but I was the one who smirked.

They could have their one-night stands and the whores crawling all over them because of who they were. They thought they knew what sex was?

Until I'd fucked Aoife, I hadn't realized what good sex even goddamn was. They'd learn one day, and when they fell, I'd be there to laugh as they hit the ground running.

Still, my current need to be with her had nothing to do with sex. I needed to look at her, have her in my line of sight so I could see she was safe. Her safety was my only priority.

38

—————

AOIFE

I WOKE up to the feel of Finn's hand between my legs.

My breath caught in my throat because it felt like it had been a lifetime since I'd last experienced his touch, and then, it caught again because would he stop if he realized what he was doing?

I thought he was sleeping. Thought it was an involuntary move, but then, I felt it. A slight click and the vibrations hit me.

A squeak escaped my lips but it soon morphed into a groan, and I pressed my face into the pillow to control it—only God knew what the other women in the compound could hear. I hated this place. Had been here a night and a day, and I already wanted to go home.

The bullet vibrator was tucked dead against my clit, and the sensations were marvelous. I couldn't move, not with the way he was pressed against my back—with my butt in the curve of his body, I couldn't even move my legs restlessly. He had his arm clamped over my lower torso, and that hand was the one holding the vibrator in place.

"It's not my cock, sweetheart," he rasped in my ear, making me wonder if an orgasm was his gift to me, to make being here better. He hadn't touched me like this before at the penthouse, so there had to be some reason for his abrupt about-face. "I wish it was. I'd love nothing more than to slide right inside you, but I can't and this will give you some relief."

Relief?

Ugh.

I had to be the freak who missed sex when she was recuperating, didn't I?

I knew he was always surprised when I said I was horny, but fuck, read what I read and you'd be horny too! You could be dead from the waist down and some of those erotic romances on Amazon would bring you back to life.

It may have been the time to read other stuff, but I didn't want to. I was currently in a reverse harem phase, and there was no way, no how, I was about to stop reading this trilogy I was devouring.

"Does it feel good, baby?" he asked, and I felt his cock—the thing I actually wanted, not this cold metal—prod me in the ass.

There was a wet kiss as his cock nudged the curve of my butt and I half-wept for the want of it. The vibrator *was* helping but it wasn't him. It was a good idea, I guessed, even as I wondered when he'd bought the damn thing.

Our trouble was I couldn't move. Had to stay still, and like this, I didn't have to move.

More than anything, it was wonderful to feel Finn so close. Because he was scared of hurting me, he stayed on the opposite side of the bed now. Which, in itself, was a concession. He'd been relieved when I'd vetoed the notion of him sleeping in the spare room, but I was upset that he'd raised the topic period.

No way, no how, was I not sleeping with him.

It was bad enough not being in our penthouse, so there was no way in hell he'd be sleeping elsewhere when he was at the compound.

"I can't wait to fuck this little cunt," he growled in my ear, and suddenly, my focus was on him. Not on the buzz, not on the necessities of staying at a compound, not on sleeping arrangements.

No.

It was on his cock, his words, his body pressed so tightly to me.

A breath gasped from my lips.

"The minute the doctor clears you, I'm going to slide so fucking deep inside you, you're not going to know where I end and you begin. When you're ready to climax, I'll stop, tease you some more, because you're such a filthy little thing that you'll want that anyway." My moan had meant to be a disagreement, but it sounded more like an assent. "I'm going to get off, come inside you, and when my cum pours from your cunt, I'm going to make you use that as lube to touch your clit."

My throat felt thick and the vibrations were suddenly hitting the right spot.

"I'm going to watch you get off, watch all that creamy skin turn pink." He grunted under his breath. "Who does this pussy belong to, Aoife?"

"Y-You," I rasped.

"Damn straight," he whispered, then he tugged on my earlobe, and slipping it between his lips, he sucked fiercely on skin I hadn't known was sensitive, then bit down.

Hard.

A yelp escaped me, one that soon morphed into a low moan as the pain, mixed with his words, worked their magic on me. His hand tightened on my belly, keeping me still, keeping me in place, and that little touch, that physical manifestation of him caring for me, was just the icing on the cake.

I came, and it felt *good.* Better than good. It felt like that crazy need I'd been feeling of late was finally being appeased, meaning I could breathe easier, and relax more.

When my breathing reverted to normal, he pressed a kiss to my throat and slowly began to pull away. I wanted to cry out, beg him to stay, but he wouldn't. I knew that. His concern for me was more than the concern he showed for himself.

I loved him for it, even if it made me want to strangle him sometimes.

Not even in sleep would Finn O'Grady hurt me. It just seemed like he hadn't received that particular memo.

I couldn't roll over to glower at him. I had to stay on my good side, which meant I was turned away from him. My legs moved restlessly, and as they did, I felt the hot juices between my lips and knew he must have felt them against his thigh earlier.

God, this man's control.

He'd not only bought a vibrator to assuage my need, but when his cock was so close to my pussy, not once had he made a move to come inside me.

"We can't do that often, Aoife," he murmured in a soft voice.

"Why not?" I pouted.

"Because you'll pay for it in the morning. It feels good now, and I wanted to take the edge off, but I know what it's like to be shot. The pain comes in waves." He blows out a breath. "I hope I did the right thing."

"Thank you, Finn," I whispered, and even though I was still riled up because he'd provided the appetizer but no entrée or dessert, I actually *was* tired.

Not because he'd woken me up, but because he'd given me some relief.

Then, hours later, when I woke up, I cursed because he was right.

Dammit.

My abdomen felt like I'd been kicked there, and I realized that even though we'd been as still as possible, my muscles must have clenched down as I orgasmed and that was as much of a workout as they were capable of.

"I knew I should have left you alone," he ground out, and I realized he was hovering by the dresser, wearing pants, his bottom half fully shod, but his top half was bare, and he had shaving foam covering half his face—what a delicious sight. For a second, I was able to forget the pain. That was how beautiful this man was.

"No. I needed you." And I had. It wasn't much of a reconnection, but it was something, and where he was concerned, something was better than nothing.

He clucked under his tongue even as he was reaching for my meds. As he passed them to me, watched me drink them down, his tone was bitter as he stated, "I'll throw the bullet away."

"No!"

"Yes," he ground out, and before my eyes, the bullet appeared from nowhere, and he threw it to the ground and stomped on it with his heel.

The sudden flurry of violence, first thing, stunned me. I gaped at him, gaped at the busted vibrator on the floor, then felt my anger stir inside me.

"What did you do that for?" I snarled.

"Because I want you to have a dose of pain with your pleasure, Aoife," he grated, "but not the kind of pain that requires you dose up on codeine the next morning."

My nostrils flared. "I needed to come."

"No. You need to get better."

"I know my body better than you do."

"Apparently not, because you should have told me to stop last night." He ran a shaky hand through his hair. "Fuck, Aoife, I—"

My ears pricked up, waiting for him to finish the sentence. But he shook his head and turned away from me, gripping the sides of the dresser as he sought control.

I gaped at him, wishing he'd finished speaking, wishing... My phone buzzed, breaking into my reverie. I'd been so sure he was about to tell me he loved me.

I reached over, grimacing when the slight movement caused pain. He cursed under his breath and I realized he was watching me in the mirror over the dresser.

A few strides brought him to me, and he grabbed my phone. I guess it was an invasion of privacy for him to look, but I didn't have anything to hide from him so I didn't really care.

"Jenny," he stated as he passed me the cell and retreated once more.

I watched him grab a belt and tuck it through the loops on his pants, waiting for him to speak, even as I wondered why he was half-dressed when his face was still loaded with shaving foam.

Finn had an edge about him. Sometimes, I just knew when he was calming himself down, but in this instance, I just wasn't sure what had riled him up in the first place.

I eyed the text from my best bud, determined to answer it after Finn had left, and when I looked up again, I saw he was staring at me.

"When was the last time you heard from your dad?"

"Ten days ago."

His nostrils flared and he tipped up his chin in understanding.

Hurt settled inside me, as I knew what the gesture meant. Was I surprised I hadn't heard from my dad? Yeah. I was. I just hoped it was because he was busy. Finn, on the other hand, was far too cynical to let that reason excuse the Senator's behavior.

When he'd buckled his belt, he returned to my side and asked, "Want me to help you to the bathroom?"

And have him be reminded of how hard it was for me to still get out of bed? No way.

I shook my head as he crouched down beside me—even that, he did for me. He couldn't sit on the bedside, not without hurting me.

Reaching over, he tucked a lock of hair behind my ear. "I'm sorry about last night, Aoife."

Glowering at him, I grumbled, "Don't be. It felt good. Yes, it aches now, but it was worth it."

His nostrils flared again, his disagreement apparent.

"What are you doing today?"

"Trying to find us our peace."

I tilted my head to the side as I took in the beautiful features that were half-covered with white foam, and I realized I must have moaned in my sleep before I woke up. He must have been in the middle of shaving when he heard me and came to see if I was okay.

"You know how you're going to do that?" I asked quietly, touched by his concern for me.

He winced. "Might involve one of the brothers getting married."

A snicker escaped me, and his lips twitched at my laugh. "I shouldn't laugh," I said apologetically. "But they're all so unashamedly single."

"That's why this is actually the answer to Aidan's prayers," Finn said on a sigh. His knees tipped forward so he was kneeling on the floor beside the bed. I closed my eyes as his mouth hovered over mine for a second, and I could scent minty fresh breath and foam.

He pecked me on the lips, nothing like what I wanted or needed, and I giggled as he got foam on my nose and chin.

"There, now you can shave if you need to," he teased.

I squinted up at him. "Are you saying I need to shave my moustache?"

It was his turn to snicker. "I wouldn't dare."

"Finn?"

He reached for my hand and kissed my knuckles. "Yes, baby."

"I'm sorry if I'm whining."

A scowl creased his brow. "Fuck, Aoife, you're not. Jesus, I'm lucky you're talking to me." He rubbed his eyes. "I've—" He shook his head. "I don't deserve you."

"Bull."

A smile had his lips curving. "Bull, huh?"

"Yeah. Bull." I grabbed his hand and squeezed his fingers. "Will you—" I licked my lips. "Will you look after yourself out there?"

"I will," he said, and even though I wanted him to promise, I knew he couldn't.

My throat felt thick as I asked, "Who was the Russian, Finn? What was he doing?"

"You know you're not—"

I jerked his hand. "He came into *our* home, Finn. Who. Was. He?"

He sighed. "He was on our side. He stopped one of the Colombians from infiltrating the apartment and was making sure he hadn't missed another one."

Well, shit. That didn't exactly make me feel better.

A shudder washed through me, and with it, came the dull throb of pain.

He saw it, of course, and pressed his lips to my knuckles once more. "I will do whatever it takes to keep you safe, Aoife."

I looked at him, studied the face of the man I loved, and wondered if I was crazy or just plain stupid.

"You can't promise me that, Finn," I rasped out, finding it impossible to keep my tone level.

"No, but I can promise that I'll kill to keep you safe."

He meant it too.

Was that supposed to make me happy?

I wasn't sure. I wasn't even sure if it worked. Did I feel better for him threatening to kill any dude out there who threatened me?

Because I was literally without words, I just watched him as he kissed my knuckles again before getting to his feet. He retreated to the bathroom, I knew, to escape this conversation, and I studied him as he reached for his razor.

Feeling my eyes grow heavy, I began to relax now that the pain meds were starting to work. Just as he started to shave, the rasp of the razor a pleasant sound that reminded me of an ASMR video I liked watching on YouTube, I heard them.

And just as my heart began to pound, my stomach twisting with nausea, I knew Finn had heard them too as he raced out of the bathroom.

Gun shots.

A lot of them.

39

FINN

THE SECOND I heard the gunshots outside, I grabbed the gun from the dresser where I'd dumped it earlier, toed into some shoes, and took off at a run.

About to cross the threshold, I growled at Aoife, "Can you make it to the safe room?"

She flinched at my question. "The safe room?"

I tried not to lose my patience, tried to keep my cool, but it was hard when there were shots being fired outside and every instinct was telling me to get out there.

"Yes. Remember, baby?"

I saw the daze in her eyes and wondered if the gunshots had spooked her or if it was the meds going to work. I felt like a shit for hoping it was the latter, but I couldn't blame her if the shots had freaked her out. I was used to the noise, well accustomed to it after years of dealing with this kind of violence, but after our wedding, the sound of rapid firing took me back to what happened *after* we'd wed.

It was a ridiculous time for the thought to occur to me but, at some point, we were going to get married again. There was no way in fuck that my wife's sole memory of tying her life with mine was going to be that one.

I strode forward, knowing she was back there, remembering that moment. I felt the distance between us, even though she was barely feet away, tucked up in bed. It wasn't a physical separation, more like a hazy one that was forged from her being plunged to another time, another place.

The shots had slowed down, but I needed to know what the hell was going on outside.

Someone had obviously tried to breach the compound, and I needed to know if they'd succeeded.

As the most senior member of the Five Points here at the compound, men would be looking to me for answers, and yet, she was my priority.

There was no way I could leave her to make her way to the safe room. She could barely walk a few paces to the bathroom without clinging to furniture on the way—and even then, watching her was agonizing because I wanted to help her. Her stubborn ass refused, though.

But no amount of obstinacy would get her to the basement. She just didn't have the strength to go so far on her own.

I needed to be in two places at once, and then, like that, I realized something. If, like most of the men, I had left my wife here to be safe, I wouldn't be here. *I wasn't supposed to be here.* The guards would have had to do what they were trained to do in these situations.

I had to have faith in Eoghan's strategies, and he rarely, if ever, let us down. The man had a brain for that shit. If he hadn't had a future with the Five Points after the army, he'd definitely have been suited for the security industry.

Realizing she was staring at the gun in my hand, I dumped it back in the dresser and reached for my cell instead.

There'd been no more shots for another minute, minimum, so I called the head guard, Liam. When he picked up, I knew he didn't

want to be bothered with my ass but he had no choice. I was his superior and I wanted answers.

"What happened out there?" It was harder than I realized to keep
my tone level, and the only reason I did was because I moved toward
the bed and took a seat at her side. When she practically threw
herself into my arms, I marveled at how she trusted me. Trusted *me*,
when I was the one who'd brought her into this danger.

My stomach felt like it was twisted in knots as I pressed my face
into her hair.

"Three fuckers thought they could get over the east wall."

"Details. Who?"

"Colombians."

"Did they infiltrate?"

Liam clucked his tongue. "Didn't you hear the shots?" The
gunfire had been ours. Thank fuck. "They're already on their way to
the slaughterhouse."

I grunted at the news—Aidan, rightly so, had to be furious to have
them sent there. They'd rue the day they stepped a hundred feet near
our compound. Well, they'd rue until they never met the next day.

Aidan would not be kind. Not when Lena was at the compound.

"Good. So it's safe?"

"Always was. They didn't have a chance. Idiots." He grumbled
under his breath. "What the hell were they thinking? Surely they
knew we'd have this place secured?"

"Just trying their luck?" I threw back at him, wanting to speak
more freely but not wanting to frighten Aoife with hard talk. "I'll be
down later. I'm with Aoife."

Liam clucked his tongue—the man had one wife here in lockdown, as well as four daughters. "She doing okay?"

"Could be better. Speak later." I cut off the call and curved both
arms around her. As I stroked her hair, I gently hugged her, wishing I
could show her the ferocity of my feelings for her, but her body
couldn't take it.

Where she'd always been so strong, so robust—something I'd

adored about her—now she was frail, and I'd done that to her. By association, sure, but that didn't take my guilt away. Nor should it. I'd regret the pain and suffering she'd endured for the rest of my life.

Pressing a kiss to her crown, I murmured, "Aoife?"

I felt her tears, felt them crest over her cheeks and fall freely, wetting my shirt. I rocked her as gently as I could, then I whispered, "I will do whatever it takes to keep you safe. Remember that, sweetheart."

I wasn't sure if it was the right thing to say, mentioning more violence could go one of two ways, but her breathing seemed to calm so I took that as a good sign.

She pulled back to look at me, and I was surprised when she giggled. "What is it?" I asked, wondering if she was hysterical.

Her hand came up to touch my cheek, and when she pulled away, I saw the foam on her fingers. Then, of course, I saw it in her hair.

"Aw, shit," I mumbled, reaching up to touch her locks. How had I not seen that? I grabbed some of the bedsheet and used it to get rid of the rest of the shaving foam still covering my face.

Lips curving, she rubbed along the smooth side of my jaw. "So handsome, even with foam everywhere," she mumbled, her eyes dark pools that spoke of a combination of things.

I knew she wanted me. Just as I wanted her. Broken and battered, the want never dissipated. She felt the same, even though she was in pain, and somehow, through that, she still needed to reconnect with me.

We'd only developed our relationship to a certain extent, and a level of intimacy was being denied to us by not being able to come together in the way we'd had until now.

In those green pools, I saw that need warring with her fear of the past. It was natural, when scared, to want to feel alive after the fright had passed—another avenue that was being denied to her.

It killed me, but I decided to accept this was a natural progression in our relationship. We'd grow closer through a different kind of intimacy. It wasn't what we wanted, but we were Catholic. That was par for the course.

She released an impatient sigh and her hand dropped back to the sheets. "I froze up."

"You did." I grabbed her hand again and squeezed. "Only natural."

Her gulp had me reaching for the tumbler of water on the nightstand. She accepted it and took a deep sip. "Freezing wasn't useful."

I couldn't withhold my snort. "Fear isn't useful, it's still perfectly natural."

"You wanted to go and see what was happening out there, didn't you?"

"Yeah. I did."

"But you couldn't. Because of me."

It didn't take a mind reader to see where this was going, and I didn't like it. "Hey, what's this?" I chided. "You don't think you're the only thing that matters to me?"

"There are so many people here," she whispered, and I sighed because I knew she'd been overwhelmed by that the other day when we'd arrived.

I'd shown her around, even though she hated the wheelchair the clinic insisted on, and made her see the place, learn the amenities.

For a compound that was essentially a pretty prison, it was comfortable. Aidan's father had it custom-built back in the seventies when shit had got real with the Italians.

Gang war had been rife then, and Aidan had kept up this place after the trouble we'd had with the Guatemalans in the nineties. It seemed like every few decades, shit rolled around, and we had to use the compound.

It was definitely a luxury, one that sapped our resources, but what were the resources for if we didn't divert them to the most precious people in our lives?

There were several living rooms and games rooms for the kids, then TV rooms where the women could get together. The kitchen was industrial-sized and fully equipped, and the dining room was fit for families of all ages and sizes. In the basement, there was a safe room, the one I'd wanted her to go to while I checked on what was happening outside.

"Aoife, you're the only one that matters to me," I told her firmly.

When she smiled, it surprised me. "Liar. Lena's here too."

I grunted because she had me there. "I forgot," I admitted, and her eyes sparkled.

"Good to know I take up all your thoughts in a crisis," she teased, and it warmed me to see her coming back to herself.

Aoife wasn't the kind of person who let herself be down for long. It made her a delight to be around, if I was honest.

She didn't have lightning moods, flashing from one to another in less than a heartbeat. It took a lot to make her irate—I knew, because she'd never been that way around me despite all the crap we'd gone through.

"Always," I admitted easily, and the ease in which I spoke seemed to resonate with her. Her shoulders, still a little high after the shock of moments before, relaxed, and her cheeks bloomed with warmth as she absorbed what I said.

"I'm sorry I froze up."

"If anyone's entitled to freeze up, it's you." If my tone was matter-of-fact then so be it, because I meant it. "Hell, it's a wonder you didn't turn hysterical. I wouldn't have blamed you if you did.

"I'm just..." I blew out a breath. "I'm sorry you had to hear that so soon after, you know."

She swallowed. "I guess that's why I'm here. You guys aren't being too over-protective."

"Exactly." There was relief in my tone. I knew she didn't want to be here, knew she wanted to recuperate at home, but this was proof she was exactly where she needed to be. "I only want you to be safe."

"And you? What about you? Are you going to be safe?" she queried, and shadows darkened her bright emerald green eyes.

"When I'm not here, I'm going to be in my office," I told her, and I wasn't even lying. "That's where I'll be waging my war, Aoife."

"Will your brothers be safe?" She gnawed on her bottom lip. "I-I know Lena's all crazy because of what Jr. is going through."

That had me sighing. "Conor's safety is pretty much assured, too. He's like me. Our work is different than the others."

"It's still dangerous though."

I thought back to the meetings with the Russians we'd had and would be having in the future. "Yeah. It's still dangerous, but less so."

"Have you seen Aidan?"

"Not since they let you leave the hospital. I'm going today actually."

"You are?"

There was a fear in her voice that had me lifting her hand and pressing a kiss to her knuckle. "I am. It's okay, baby."

"Why is it safe for you to be out on the streets but not us?"

"Because the bastards who hit us knew to aim for our jugular—our women, our kids, our families, they're our weakness. If it had been just men on that church step, I have no doubts they wouldn't have carried on with the shooting."

Her brow furrowed. "Really?"

I shrugged. "Yeah. Men can be replaced, Aoife. It might cause a power struggle, but with a mob like ours?" I shook my head. "We're not some two-bit operation. We function like a private damn army. Everyone has a role. But with you and Lena there? It changed shit up."

"D-Didn't they realize they'd be raining a whole lot of hell down on themselves?"

I grinned at her—satisfied that she knew we'd be the victors in the end. Hell wouldn't rain down on us, but on *them*. "They got too big for their *cojones*."

She didn't smile back. "Are they going to die?"

"For what they did to you and Aidan? Yes." I made the admission with no guilt. "Aidan Sr. will see to that."

"Won't that just create a vicious cycle?"

"It's the way of the world, baby." If regret laced my words, then that was also the way of it. "There's no point in thinking like that."

"Violence begets more violence," she whispered, worriedly, and I saw more shadows develop in her eyes as her worry took form.

"Sometimes it's the only way to stop it in its tracks. Guys like that? They only respond to a show of strength." I got to my feet. "Now, let's get you settled. You need to sleep."

She released a sigh, and I could see she wanted to argue but knew I was right. "You won't be here when I wake up, will you?"

"No, angel. I'll be here tonight though." I had promised her I'd be here every night this week. It was a promise I wouldn't be able to maintain for longer than a week, though. I had some moves to pull, some strategies to work out, and I'd need to be on location for that.

Helping her settle down, I bent over and kissed her gently. "Sleep well, baby."

She hummed. "Take care, Finn. For me?"

"Always."

I retreated to the bathroom, moving quietly around in there as I readied myself for the day.

I'd intended to see Aidan Jr. later, but after what had just happened, I wanted to see him first then get to the office so I could work straight through before heading back here.

Within twenty minutes, I was dressed and ready for a report from Liam. But there wasn't much to report.

"Think they were just trying to scope the place out," he commented.

"They must have been expendable then."

"You know what those gangs are like. They always are."

He wasn't wrong. Our foot soldiers mattered to us. To the Russians, the Latinos... it wasn't the same. Family didn't count as much with them as it did with us. I liked to think it made us a better breed of mobster—*if such a thing existed,* I thought dryly.

"Did they get over the wall?" I asked.

Liam glowered at me. "What kind of security do you think I'm running here? You think three eejits can climb on my wall like it's a jungle gym and I won't know about it?"

I rubbed my chin to hide my smile. "I was only asking if you needed more back up, Liam. Calm down."

He huffed. "I'd ask Aidan if we did."

"Well, don't be scared to ask him. We can get private security in if needs be."

Surprise flashed in his eyes. "You'd outsource?"

Not to one of the regular security companies, probably a group of mercs that Eoghan knew, but it was something I'd be more than willing to do if it meant keeping Aoife and the rest of the women out of danger.

I nodded, saying nothing more. I couldn't act without Aidan Sr.'s approval, but if I was ever going to be a rebel, it would be because he refused. Not that he ever cut costs when it came down to our women's security.

Even on our wedding day, we'd had a few men on the church grounds. It hadn't been enough to stop the bastards, but drive-bys were perfect opportunities to create havoc and cause terror.

Samuel was outside in the car waiting for me when I left Liam. With his wife in lockdown too, I knew he'd be staying here when I did, so I had even less time to wait than usual.

"Where to, boss? The office?"

"No. To Aidan Jr.'s clinic."

He nodded and as he drove, and I caught up with the barrage of emails and calls that had flooded my phone while I'd been getting ready.

News had hit about the attempted infiltration, and I knew Aidan was wicked pissed. I spoke with him, and arranged for a meeting later on today even though I couldn't tell him anymore than what Liam had told me.

By the time I made it to the hospital, I was relieved to take a break. I'd dealt with more shit on the forty-minute drive than I'd intended to deal with this morning.

"Bro," Aidan called out when he saw me enter his private room.

I knew Lena was chomping at the bit not being able to see her son as much as she wanted, and her guilt was evident with all the crap in here.

Because he was a big kid, there was a huge ass plasma screen and a games console that would make any teenage boy hard. There were things here that told me Aidan Sr. had slipped the hospital some-thing-something to put up with all the crap she'd hauled in to make him comfortable.

"Hey Aid, how you feeling?"

"Hurts like a motherfucker." Just like with Aoife, pain and worry shadowed his bright blue eyes. "Hot nurses, though."

"Good view. Shame you can't do anything about it, huh?"

He grimaced. "Don't remind me." Then, he grinned as he tapped his nose. "Working on it, though. Don't count me out just yet."

We both knew he was bullshitting. He looked like he was stuck in one of those kids' climbing nets. From all the pulleys and wheels that kept his leg in traction, there was no way in fuck he was ready for anyone to be bouncing on top of him.

Although, a BJ was definitely possible, I calculated.

I gave him the gift I'd ordered online yesterday. It had shown up this morning—just in time.

"Know you like killing shit when you're sick," I told him as he crowed about the game. "Although I still think you're too old to be playing that crap."

He was a few months older than me, and I'd outgrown games in my early twenties. Aidan was hooked, though.

"You give with one hand and take away with the other," he said mournfully, even as I saw the gleam of pleasure in his eyes as he looked at the gift. "Before you go, put it in for me?"

"Thought you'd want one of the nurses to do it for you. Or do you really just want a chance to study my ass?"

He smirked. "Not this morning. I call her Big Bertha. She makes Mom look like a pixie. She's a fucking battleax."

"Makes you piss yourself?" I teased. "Lena's frightening as fuck when something's upset her."

He snickered. "Yeah, I'm shaking in my *boot*," he retorted, eying the special cast he wore on his foot. When he'd been shot, he'd gone over on his ankle. Two hundred pounds of muscle meant he'd fractured that too.

I took a seat beside him and rested my elbows on my knees as we chatted.

"Get the message about the compound?" I asked about twenty minutes later after we'd shot the shit and caught up.

"Yeah. Fuckers," he admitted, scrubbing a hand over his face. "Girls all okay?"

I nodded. "Didn't even get over the wall. Still, they're cunts for trying."

"True that," he replied. "What's their game, Finn?"

"Fuck knows. I get that they're pissed about us putting the shade on them with the cartel, but the Mexicans and Colombians are always fucking bickering. If it wouldn't be about this, it would be about trade." I shrugged. "It seems unusually excessive."

"Makes me wonder if they're trying to take over our territory and are using this as an excuse."

"Well, they'd be fucking stupid if they thought that was a possibility," I retorted, my tone dry. "We outnumber them eight to one. How the fuck would they keep things running?"

He shrugged. "They have bigger balls than dicks."

"Chodes," I choked out, laughing at the image.

"Yeah." He grinned at me, and it was good to see, so good it made me fucking sentimental.

"Great to see you, bro. Sorry I've not been around much." Since Aoife had left the hospital, I hadn't visited in over a week.

"Don't be stupid. You're at the end of the phone if I need you, right?"

"Course," I told him with a scowl.

"Well then, nothing to feel guilty about. Not when Aoife has to be a bit fucked up over what went down. She doing okay?"

"Yeah. Could be better."

"I like her, Finn. I'm glad you married her."

His remark surprised the hell out of me. "I figured you wouldn't approve."

"I only disapproved of the fact you wouldn't let me organize a damn bachelor party. Fucking party pooper."

"That's me," I told him with a grin. "I fucking hate that shit. You know that."

"Still, it's not for you, it's for me! And you didn't even need a goddamn best man. I'm hurt, bro."

"Don't worry about it. After that fuck up, well, let's just say we'll be renewing our vows at some point."

His eyes sparkled. "You gonna go the whole hog?"

After he'd almost fucking died when his femoral artery had been severed? Sure as shit I was.

"You can do the whole shebang, but no goddamn strippers."

He pouted. Honest to God, pouted. Fuck me. The man was thirty-seven.

I pointed at his lower lip. "That shit might work with the nurses, but it doesn't with me."

His smirk said it all. "Okay, no strippers," he conceded. "Pussy-whipped already. I mourn you."

"You don't have to mourn me when the pussy that's whipping me is twenty-four carat gold."

Aidan puffed out his lips. "Well, I didn't think any less would snare you. In fact, never thought *anyone* would snare you. You've always been shy around women."

I gaped at him. "Shy? You were with me when we fucked those three chicks in Denver, right?"

He grinned. "Don't mean timid. Meant shy as in 'not even a

shotgun up my ass will get me to the church' and Aoife didn't look like she was carrying a Voodoo doll and making you say *I do*."

Despite myself, I had to chuckle. "Okay, you're right. But she's different, man. Can't tell you how, she just is."

He rolled his eyes. "Don't get sappy on me. Last thing I need is you working with Mom to get me to settle down." Then, even though he'd just been joking, his mouth firmed. "Knowing the bitches around our way, they won't want a dude with a fucked-up leg."

"You're the heir to the Five Points, Aidan. They'd want you if you looked like Mutley." I tapped my chin. "Or do I mean Dick Dastardly?"

His nostrils flared. "Fuck. That's the best compliment I've had from you in five years. Minimum."

I waved my hand in a bow. "I try, I try."

His tone turned somber again. "They're saying I might have to use a cane, Finn."

"Just for a while, Aidan. Don't worry."

"No. Forever. The pins didn't take well. Might have to go in for another surgery."

"Shit. I'm sorry, bro."

He blew a breath. "I always did have the luck of the angels. Must have been my time to get burned."

"Those fuckers... we'll make them pay, Aidan. Don't you worry."

My best bud, my brother from another goddamn mother, and one of my closest confidants, smirked at me. "I didn't doubt it, Finn. You're a mean motherfucker when you want to be."

Seemed like the two of us were both shit with compliments.

40

———

AOIFE

THREE WEEKS LATER

I WOKE up to find Finn watching me.

Because I was surprised to see him, I blinked a few times before rubbing my eyes. When he didn't disappear, I whispered, "Hey."

He reached over and trailed a finger along the curve of my jaw. "Hey."

I hadn't seen him for a day or two. He slept here most nights, but he was in and out of bed while I carried on sleeping.

"You look exhausted."

And he did. His skin was pale, not the usual glorious creamy gold that spoke of his Black Irish heritage. He had shadows under his eyes, and from the divots in his cheeks, I wasn't the only one who'd lost weight.

"I *am* tired," he admitted, closing his eyes as he rested his head against the pillow.

Just watching him for a handful of seconds had a sense of peace settling deep inside me, and knowing he was resting, I let myself sleep too.

I'd never felt this way before. Like my happiness, while not exactly dependent on someone else, had a kind of checks and balance system. It mattered to me if he was stressed or discontent. It affected me if he lost weight or didn't sleep.

Having never been in a long-term relationship before, it was strange to have my life so affected by someone else.

Sure, my mom and I had been close and had lived together. But we were two separate people. Of course I cared if she lost weight or was stressed, but when Finn climbed into bed with me, slept with me —I laid next to him, sensed his emotions, and they affected *me*.

I thought, to a point, that was what surprised me the most.

Call me dumb or a noob, I just wasn't used to my moods correlating with someone else's, and Finn? I didn't want to say he was moody, but he was often pensive. And with no sex to ease his tension, I felt like I was floundering with no means of connecting.

For hours he'd lay behind me in silence, one hand on my leg, his thumb moving back and forth as he gently caressed me. Not to entice or excite, just to touch me.

With no sex on the table, I guess I should have been scared, but I didn't really believe he'd cheat on me. Lena, Aidan's wife, had warned me he would, and maybe I was stupid, but I felt like Finn wouldn't. Still, he wasn't getting his rocks off with me, and a man like him, with a high sex drive? Celibacy didn't seem as though it was high on his checklist.

Days had passed, morphing into weeks. The situation never seemed to improve, the only thing that did? My health.

I had a hole in my abdomen that had to 'fuse' back together. I'd lost my spleen. I needed to take prophylactic antibiotics for the rest of my life, would have health issues forever, and I realized this was one of the true costs of a life in the mafia—people got hurt. They bled. It was a world forged on loss and greed and all the sins that Aidan's Church preached were enough to send you to hell.

Weird then, that he was one of the most devout men I'd ever met —and I was Irish. Being religious was like loving Guinness and celebrating St Patrick's Day—they all went hand in hand.

As I thought back to that morning when I'd blinked awake and found Finn had disappeared on me again, Lena murmured, "Your head's in the clouds."

Her words broke into my thoughts. I wasn't down, I had to admit. I was like Finn—pensive. It was like getting married, being shot, and not being able to have access to one another had put us in a philosophical state of mind.

"Not exactly," I countered, grimacing as I turned to face her at the stove.

The compound, as Finn called it, wasn't as rough around the edges as it seemed. It was actually like a large hotel with eleven floors. There were no rooms, but small apartments, and the higher up the building you went, the higher the rank your man had. Because, yup, it was like that here.

I hadn't met many women I liked except for Lena, and she wasn't exactly someone I could relax around. She was the nearest thing I had to a mother-in-law and I felt that although she approved of me, she was monitoring me too. For Aidan and for Finn. It wasn't the most pleasant of sensations, and I really missed my best friend Jenny as well as my dad. Neither of whom I'd seen in weeks.

My last visit with Jenny had been in the hospital before I'd been moved here—it was too dangerous for her to come to the compound, or so Finn had said when I'd asked about the possibility. With my dad? It had been longer. A week before my wedding.

We texted, but it wasn't the same as seeing him, and we were always cautious anyway with things that could be tracked and traced.

Senator Alan Davidson was on his way to the White House, and I wasn't going to do anything to stop that. I was already a dirty secret in his past, and now I had links to the Irish Mob. The last thing he needed was for his ties with me to go public. I intended on keeping our relationship private. Our meetings meant a lot to me.

"Aoife!"

Lena's bark of my name had me jerking in my seat. "Hmm?"

"You're daydreaming! I need those carrots soon."

I stared down at the carrots and carried on with the task she'd given me. I still wanted to sleep a lot, but Lena dragged me out of bed and had me moving around, even when it meant pushing myself a tad too far for comfort. My PT didn't disapprove though. In fact, she said I was improving in leaps and bounds, which made sense considering Lena had probably been around a lot of people who'd been shot up at some point in their life.

As I peeled the veggies, I wondered what my dad would have to say to me the next time we met. After the shooting, which had hit the press, as well as my injuries, he now knew who my husband was. Knew *what* he was too.

A part of me wondered if he'd cut ties with me because of his career, and I really hoped that all my years of faith in him weren't about to disintegrate. It was one of the reasons that, though it sucked, I wouldn't be seeing him for a while. I could remain with my head in the sand about the situation until things were normal enough for me to meet with him again.

Lena huffed. "Would you spit it out?"

"Spit what out?" I asked, frowning at her.

"You're sighing about something, girl."

I shrugged. "Just thinking."

"Stop it. Start doing." She waggled her knife at me, and Mary-Ellen, one of the men's wives who Lena actually liked, giggled.

There weren't many women that Lena approved of. Those she did were allowed into the kitchen where she cooked. Every day. For over one hundred people. She didn't have much help, but she did it. Without complaint.

I could see why Aidan was so enamored with her.

She was a general's wife. What a man in his position needed at his side. In essence, I knew I'd have to take after her at some point.

"You *are* dithering today," Mary-Ellen murmured quietly, making me grimace.

Her husband wasn't high up in the ranks, but he had standing. Far as I could tell, it worked like this:

Each brother ran a certain aspect of the Points' trade.

I knew Finn worked on property, and Conor did something with computers. I thought Declan dealt drugs and Brennan, I'd come to believe, handled loans. But as for Eoghan, I could only guess. Guns, girls, and/or gambling? The three Gs? With Aidan being the heir, I figured he had a hand in every pot.

Each brother, in turn, had around forty men under him. At the bottom, they had the 'joeys,' as Aidan called them. Above them were the runners, and then, there were the captains. Just like in any job, each position came with certain perks.

Mary-Ellen's husband was a captain, and she was, as my mother would have said, straight off the boat from the Old Country. She was already pregnant and was expecting twins. Every time I looked at her, she seemed to get bigger. Her cheeks were bright red like apples freshly picked from the tree, and there was a constant twinkle in her eye that invited anyone to smile.

In comparison to my best friend, she was staid, but I liked her. Jenny swore like a trooper and would fuck anything that wasn't pinned down. But Mary-Ellen was surprisingly restful, and with my current health, I realized I needed that. I liked her, and we were becoming good friends with how much time we spent together in this gilded cage.

"Aoife?" She reached over and gently patted my hand. "Are you feeling okay?"

"I miss Finn," I told her quietly, not wanting Lena to hear.

The older woman grew defensive whenever I said anything like that, would splutter about the men being at war. I figured she missed Aidan just as much as I missed my husband, but rather than moan about it, she got on with shit.

It was easier said than done, though, when you were tied to a seat all the time.

Okay, not literally tied, but I couldn't exactly bustle around the kitchen like Lena was.

"I know you do." Mary-Ellen's smile was sad. "At least he comes and visits though."

Not every night like he had at the start, but he tried. I'd grant him that. "You still haven't seen Stephen?" I tried not to gape at that, absolutely staggered by the idea that the men felt okay with dumping their wives and kids here without visiting for weeks on end.

It was disgustingly medieval, I thought, my disapproval ranking up a notch at the way things were ran.

Aidan wanted to think the Five Points were based on good Catholic values? I called BS. Marriage and family were the basic tenet of any religion, and at the moment, the Five Points were in danger of forgetting that.

I wasn't and never would be overly religious, but as Finn's wife, there were certain things I had to do, which I'd never have done in my past life. Things like going to church on Sunday and confession as well.

The only good thing about lockdown was that both of those requirements were put on hiatus.

"Stephen calls every night," Mary-Ellen told me cheerfully as she chopped up potatoes into small chunks.

Refraining from snarkily stating that he damn well should, I slumped into the kitchen seat. My wound was itching—a good sign, Lena said. When it itched, it meant it was healing, apparently. I thought it meant it was infected, but when she or Mary-Ellen cleaned the wound, there were no signs of infection so that was something.

"Do you have phone sex?" I whispered, one eye on Lena who was making clanking noises while she stirred the ingredients she'd prepared for tonight's dinner.

There were five other women who helped with the meals, and they'd already done their chores. Mary-Ellen and I were the slow pokes.

Her cheeks heated. "I wouldn't know where to start."

I sometimes wondered if Stephen had kidnapped Mary-Ellen from a convent. I mean, I thought I'd been bad. A twenty-five-year-old virgin? I'd fooled around though. I knew what phone sex was and was game.

Asking if she thought Stephen was getting his rocks off elsewhere would have been cruel, and I hated the idea of it enough to murmur, "Just tell him what you're feeling."

She bit her bottom lip. "Do you with Finn?"

"I wish." I heaved a sigh. "He's scared I'll hurt myself." Then I shot her a grin. "Death by masturbation. What would Father Doyle say?"

Her eyes flared wide and I knew she feared for her immortal soul. "We shouldn't."

I shrugged. "Why shouldn't we?"

"It's wrong, isn't it?" She worriedly eyed Lena and then the potatoes.

"The joy of the marriage bed," I crowed. "Nothing is wrong if you both want it."

"What do you even talk about?"

"What you wish he was doing to you?" I made it a question because I'd never done it before myself, and I was making the suggestion for her.

Maybe I was leaping ahead, but Stephen, after barely seeing his pregnant wife for weeks, was unlikely to be keeping it in his pants.

A lot of the women seemed to accept the fact their husbands strayed, and others bitched about it in the common rooms. Enough that I knew Lena had been right when, all those weeks ago, she'd said the Pointers were rarely faithful to their spouses.

She'd said it to warn me, but I knew, deep down, Finn wouldn't cheat on me. Maybe if I stopped putting out just to be a bitch he might, he was a man after all, and they were led around by their cocks, and I knew Jenny had several guys cheat on her—and she was not only hot as fuck, but had the flexibility of a pole dancer. If a guy would cheat on her, I sure as hell wasn't safe.

But Finn felt guilty I was wounded, and he was in the middle of a war that hadn't started because of me, but to him, it had. He'd taken it as a personal affront and wanted to 'avenge' me.

I almost shook my head at the thought.

It sounded like something from a comic book, except gunshot wounds really fucking sucked. I was like a modern day Helen of Troy, but I just hoped in this version, my Achilles didn't suffer an arrow to his heel.

So, unlike Finn, Stephen didn't have the same goals. He was just a soldier being steered this way and that, who suddenly had an empty bed...

Perhaps it was mean of me to judge him without even having met the guy, but Mary-Ellen was so sweet. I really hated the idea of her being cheated on, especially for her lack of knowing how to please a man.

The way she pinkened whenever I brought up sex made me wonder if those twins had been conceived through divine intervention.

I cleared my throat, trying to think of a way to prompt her to spice up their nightly phone call. It was a long shot, but it could work if he loved her.

"You know the things he does to you in bed?" She nodded, but kept her eyes on the potatoes. "Do you like them?" This time, her nod was a little more eager than before. Aha! So no divine intervention had been necessary. I grinned at her. "Talk about that. Pretend you have to say the things instead of just doing them."

"Isn't that hard, though?" Her blush was almost as potent as mine—made sense considering we were both redheads.

"Very hard, I imagine." I shrugged. "Everything gets easier with practice though, doesn't it?"

Her eyes caught mine, and this time we both grinned at each other. "I might try that tonight. I miss him."

"You mean you're horny."

More pink appeared in her cheeks. "Maybe."

"Definitely." I laughed. "I am too, and I've been shot. You're only pregnant. Doesn't that mean your hormones are all over the place?"

"They were at first," she said with a shrug. "I-I didn't want him at all. But now?" When she blew out a breath, it made her bangs flutter a few centimeters off her forehead.

Nodding my understanding, I murmured, "Totally get where you're coming from."

"For God's sake, do I need to peel the damn things myself?" Lena spluttered. "Doreen, Linda, Jane, Maisy, and Laura finished ages ago. What on earth's taking so long?"

I scowled at her. "We have several pounds of vegetables to peel. They didn't have much to do."

Lena doled out her chores like Father Doyle would penance. Except I wasn't being punished—peeling was all I could really do. I wasn't able to stand for long periods of time still, not without feeling shaky. Being perpetually weak was wearing on my nerves. I was used to being strong, not so goddamn fragile.

Lena glowered at me but went back to stirring a shit ton of onions in a bucket load of butter. Colcannon was on the agenda today, mashed potatoes mixed with sautéed onions, cabbage, and bacon, and that was enough to put me in a shiny mood.

Mary-Ellen whispered, "You're the only one who can talk back to her."

I shrugged. "She's like my mother-in-law."

"All the more reason not to." Mary-Ellen shuddered. "Aren't you scared of her?"

"Nope." Before, maybe, but now?

Being shot changed things.

I'd taken a bullet because of the Five Points. Someone had infiltrated my home, and they hadn't done it to come and tuck me in and give me a box of chocolates. Not once had I complained about any of that. I wasn't scared of Lena. I was scared of our enemies. Actually being hurt by one of them put shit into perspective.

"Why not?"

"She won't make you bleed. Will just lash you with that tongue. I can survive that." My mom had a barbed tongue too. Not purposely cruel, but just one of those mothers who knew what was what and wouldn't let you get away with shit.

Lena reminded me of her in some ways. It was probably why I liked her. Even if she was a pain in the ass that managed her kitchen like it was a Nazi stronghold.

"Didn't you see Louisa being shot down by Lena?" As soon as she asked the question, Mary-Ellen smacked her hand to her mouth. "God, Aoife, I'm so sorry."

I stared at her, bewildered. "For what? She didn't bitch at me—"

"Shot down," Mary-Ellen repeated, then wafted the potato peeler at me. "I'm so sorry."

Snorting, I told her, "Takes more than that to offend me." I wasn't putting a brave face, I was just... I guess my perspective was different than before.

Almost dying did that to a person.

You could be sensitive about it, or you could just get the fuck on with it. I was of the latter school of thought. Another reason I think Lena liked me. Her disrespect was evident for weak women.

Of course, I kept my weak moments to myself. When I was lonely and wondering what the hell I'd done by tying myself to a man whose business necessitated a hotel as a safe house, I'd cry myself to sleep. But mostly, it was out of self-pity and Lena wasn't the only one who abhorred that.

I had plenty to count my blessings over, and I needed to focus on that.

"Why did she shoot Louisa down?" I inquired, curious.

"She was crying. Said she missed Conrad."

Mary-Ellen, though newly married, had been with Stephen a while so she knew everyone here. I, on the other hand, barely knew half the names, and it was hard to make friends when Lena watched over me like a hawk.

"So? She's allowed to miss him, isn't she?"

Mary-Ellen winced. "Louisa's impetuous."

As well as young. She looked about fifteen, but as much illegal shit as the Five Points handled, illegal marriages weren't one of them. She had to be eighteen, just acted like an eight year old.

I clucked my tongue. "What did she do?"

"Said she was going to run away."

"Bet Lena liked that." I snorted, just imagining what Lena's response would be.

"She slapped her, told her to get on with it, and that if she was missing him so much, that meant she was bored, and she gave Louisa a ton of chores."

Lena would have made a great Mother Superior.

I had to hide my smile because I couldn't easily imagine Lena in a habit, even if she had the strictness down pat.

"What are you two gossiping about?" the woman in question asked, as she took a seat beside me.

My brows quirked at the sight of the coffee jug and three empty mugs in her hands. When she served us, then took a deep sip of her own, I eyed her cautiously.

"What's wrong?"

She scowled at me. "Nothing's wrong. Well, apart from the fact you two are so bloody slow I'm going to have to help you out."

I snorted. "You're all heart."

"What were you talking about, anyway?"

Because I wanted to see her reaction, I told her, "Phone sex."

Naturally, she wasn't surprised. Even if Mary-Ellen looked like she wanted the floor to open and swallow her whole, Lena's mouth quirked in a wicked smile.

"The only way to get through lockdown."

Laughing, I toasted my coffee with her. "I wish I was so lucky. Damn bullet."

She studied me over her mug. "Have the doctors mentioned when you can have sex again?"

"Why?"

She shrugged. "I'm sure Finn's ready for a family of his own."

Considering on the morning of the wedding he'd asked me to stop taking the pill, she was right on the money.

"I'm sure he is. I'm the one who isn't ready." I cocked a brow at her when she scowled. "I've just had emergency surgery, Lena. I'm not ready to give birth any time soon."

She dipped her chin. "You want children though?"

"Would it matter if I didn't?" For some reason, her concern irked me.

I knew she considered herself Finn's mother, but what right did she have to ask me if I wanted kids or not? That was between my husband and me, and I sure as hell wasn't about to get knocked up after having gone through what I had these past couple of weeks.

My recovery wasn't even over yet, we were in a hotel with very little access to our men or their 'soldiers,' and she was trying to pick out the paint for my nursery walls?

I think not.

"It's between you and Finn, I'm sure," was all she said.

Narrowing my eyes at her, I nodded, agreeing with her—it *was* between Finn and me. Nobody else.

When I caught Mary-Ellen's eye, I had to hide a smile.

She looked in awe of me, and I realized that most people would have cowered or immediately replied to Lena's invasive questions.

Well, not me.

Maybe before the shooting, but not after.

Lena wasn't *my* mother. Nor was she my damn boss. I'd keep the peace, but I wasn't about to roll over and play dead for her. Fuck, I wasn't about to do that for anyone.

Not even Finn.

Before the shooting, I could probably have been considered marshmallow fluff-soft, but after? No way. I'd learned a lesson about life in the mafia and I knew I was going to have to toughen up if I was going to be the wife Finn needed.

I saw how Aidan, in his own way, depended on Lena. I wanted to be that for Finn. I didn't want to be a drag, didn't want to weigh him down with crap that just wasn't important. But to be that, that meant not taking any shit from anyone. Including the man I loved.

41

FINN

"FINN!"

The sound of my name being called had me cringing. Standing outside the office building, I turned and saw Eoghan waving at me.

Fuck.

"What?" I snapped, then cringed when he reared back in surprise at my tone.

"Finn?" he questioned.

I blew out a breath. "Yeah."

"What's up?"

"Nothing." I waved at the office front. "I'm just about to head to an appointment."

Eoghan narrowed his eyes as he looked at the building behind me, then a grin showed on his face that told me he knew exactly what this place was.

Shit, I was never going to hear the end of this now.

"Didn't realize a sex toy store was considered business," he teased, his eyes fucking sparkling with amusement.

"Yeah? If you knew what this place is, that means you've been too. Your cock not up to the job?"

Eoghan was a cock-sure shit, so he just sniggered at me. "I can handle my dick. Don't you worry."

"Wasn't worried," I rasped. "Just... fuck off, would you?"

"No. This is funny shit."

"You're not going in with me," I stated bluntly.

"Aren't I?" He rubbed his chin. "I don't know, I think I should. You didn't bring your guard with you."

I grunted. "Your guard isn't with you either."

He tapped his nose. "I'm good at evading him. Never send in a trainee to guard the general."

"You wish you were a fucking general."

He slapped his chest, the place right over his heart. "That fucking hurts."

"I'm sure it does. Not enough, though," I grumbled. "Look, you know why I'm here, you can tell all the guys if you want, but I need to go in."

"Aoife horny?" he asked, and I saw the concern in his eyes.

Concern.

For my woman's horniness.

My life was starting to belong in one of the Pink Panther movies.

"Been a long time," I bit off.

"Yeah. I'm surprised. Thought you'd have fucked that Tanya bitch by now."

My eyes widened. "What the fuck?"

He shrugged. "You liked her before."

Wanting to strangle him as he talked about my sex life on the side of the goddamn street like we were two girlfriends, I ground out, "I'm married."

Eoghan pursed his lips. "So? Or are you gonna be like Dad?"

"What's that supposed to mean?"

"I didn't mean insane," he said dryly. "I meant possessive. Faithful."

"That such a hard concept to believe?"

Despite myself, I was fucking furious at the inference I might cheat on Aoife. It wasn't the first time I'd had looks cast my way when my brothers happened to mention a slut they'd been screwing, but the only pussy I wanted was on lockdown.

In more ways than one.

Tugging at my tie, feeling way too hot under the collar to be dealing with this shit, I watched Eoghan watch me. "What?" I snapped.

"I'm just surprised."

"Which part of my getting married have you forgotten?"

"Aoife can't put out," he stated, like I didn't already know that. My cock was going to turn blue, never mind my balls.

"Yeah. Trust me. I received that memo."

"So... why haven't you gone with Tanya?"

"Because I'm married."

He smirked at me. "Still can't say the words, huh?"

"Fuck. You."

A snicker sounded from his lips, making me want to throat punch the bastard, but that wasn't going to happen. No one got the drop on Eoghan.

"See, that was so easy for you to say."

"Fuck off, Eoghan. I don't have time for this."

I pushed the buzzer to be let in and thanked God when the door opened. Before I could slam it in his face, Eoghan's shoe wedged itself in the doorway, and even though I shut it on his foot and he swore under his breath, he followed me in.

It took a lot to embarrass me.

Looking at false cocks wouldn't have usually, but with Eoghan engaged with my brothers in a group chat about the various models, yeah, I started to feel faintly *ticked* off.

I knew it was because it was for Aoife.

They'd never let me hear the end of this shit, but I didn't want news getting back to her. Not only because she'd think I was joking about our sex life with my brothers, but because she'd turn bright pink if they teased her on this.

"If you say a fucking word to Aoife about this," I grated with my purchase in hand, "I will put a bullet between your ears. I don't even care if Aidan Sr. will go ape shit on my ass."

Eoghan grinned down at the bag. "Thick for her pleasure, huh?"

I elbowed him in the side. "Eoghan. This isn't a fucking joke."

His smile was still there, but in his eyes, I saw understanding. "We won't say anything. To her. To you is another matter entirely."

I knew how a bull felt when a matador was taunting it.

"How's she doing, anyway? Aside from being horny, I mean," he jibed.

"She's better."

"Good. I'm glad to hear it." He hummed under his breath as I hailed a cab, and the fucker got in with me when one pulled up. Before I could speak, he gave the cab his father's office address. "Dad wants to talk."

"That why you were following me around like a bulldog?"

"No. I happened to see you and just got the text from him."

I released a sharp breath. I needed to find some patience because Aidan Sr. always drained mine, and Eoghan had already worked his shitty magic on me.

"Isn't she mad at you?"

"Who?" I inquired, turning my head away from him.

"Aoife."

"About what?"

He shrugged. "The compound. The shooting. *Everything?*"

"No. She isn't."

A whistle sounded from between his teeth. "Huh."

"What's that supposed to mean?"

"It means I'm surprised. I thought she'd be making you pay for it."

"Well, she isn't."

"That why you haven't called Tanya?"

For fuck's sake. "I'm. Married. Which part of this aren't you understanding, Eoghan?"

"The entirety of that statement, Finn. I mean, I knew she was different, otherwise you'd never have put a ring on her, but after all these weeks of her being a no fly zone? I don't know. You're surprising me, man."

"I didn't realize you had such little faith in my willpower," I retorted dryly. I knew what he wanted me to admit, I just wasn't sure why, and because his motives weren't clear, I was going to evade him with all my might.

"Oh, I don't doubt you're a strong-willed motherfucker. I'm just curious."

"Yeah? Well, you know what curiosity did, don't you? It killed the fucking cat."

Though he laughed, he carried on studying me for the remainder of the twenty-minute ride. When we alighted from the cab and headed into Aidan's office building, I could feel the tension in my shoulders ratchet up a notch.

What did Aidan want to talk about? He'd been leaving me alone to get on with my duties, and I liked it that way just fine.

"Ah, Finn, my boy," he murmured, slapping me on the back when I made it into his office.

He bumped knuckles with Eoghan, and I had to hide a laugh at the sight. Eoghan and he had an unusual relationship. He was a lot less intense where his youngest was concerned.

"What's wrong, Aidan?" I asked, wanting to get this shit over with. The vibrator didn't weigh much, but having it in Aidan's office made it feel like I was carrying a bronze statue around. I'd had two things on my to-do list this week. Buy Aoife a gun, and buy her a vibrator.

Today, when he wanted to speak with me, just had to be the day when I got her a fucking dildo, didn't it?

"I wanted to talk to you about this shit with the Colombians."

I blew out a breath. "I thought we'd already been over this."

He winced. "We have, but you're talking a lot of money here."

Pursing my lips at him as I settled back in the leather armchair opposite his desk, I dropped the bag to my left, and tried to figure out a way to explain shit to him that would make him agree to the plan Conor and I had concocted.

"Look, it's not going to cost us much. Not when we hack into the Colombians' accounts."

"If we can," Eoghan interrupted.

"You don't have much faith in your brother if you think he can't," I said dryly. "That security shit was a one-time thing."

"If it can happen once, maybe it can happen twice," Aidan intoned, his words grim.

I shook my head. "No. You said it yourself, we've all grown lax where security is concerned." Pressing my fingertips together, I murmured, "Look. Once we get that money, we're okay. I have to front the money now because the Mexicans are insistent and it's going to take Conor some time to get shit together."

"Why, though?" Eoghan questioned.

"The Mexicans don't trust the Russians," I stated bluntly. "Look, the twenty-five million I'm finding has to go into escrow. We won't be able to touch it until the initial period of agreement is over. By that point, Conor will have gotten it back for us."

"So, the Mexicans are agreeing to ship to the Russians. That's in writing?"

"Yeah, of course," I told him. "The Mexican side of shit is dealt with. The minute the money is in the account, they'll start transporting it here. With the Russians' coke shipments secured, they're a go also."

Aidan rubbed his chin. "And the other?"

I cut a look at Eoghan, well aware he didn't know what Aidan meant by that, so I simply nodded—Vasov was willing to tie our Family to his in more ways than just business.

Clearing my throat, I changed the subject by saying, "He's agreed to get the leader to us." I tilted my head to the side and asked, "I thought you gave me a green light on this, Aidan? What's wrong?"

"Man's allowed to question shit."

"Not when I've already started moving the fucking money," I

growled. "I've loosened up five million, Aidan. If you want to change shit, it's a bit late for that."

Aidan waved a hand, then slouched back in his desk chair. "How's Aoife?"

What was it with the O'Donnellys today and my wife? "She's getting better."

"Glad to hear it."

"Can I go now?" I requested. "I was on my way to her."

Eoghan snorted. "I bet you were."

Aidan frowned at his son who just grinned. "What's going on?"

"Nothing," I insisted.

"Just taking the mick, Da."

Rolling his eyes, Aidan grumbled, "My son, the joker."

I got to my feet, antsy to get this vibrator well away from Aidan. God only knew what he'd say if he found out. I'd probably get a lecture from him about how good Catholics didn't use sex toys.

That was the last thing I needed.

"Look, if you don't need me?"

Aidan flicked his fingers in a dismissal, and just when I was a few feet away from the door, he said, "Lena says Aoife doesn't want a family."

Closing my eyes, begging for patience, I turned back and murmured, "That's nobody's business but hers or mine." But even as I said it, I was well aware *this* was the reason Aidan had brought me here.

Shit. What had Aoife said?

"Not normal for a Catholic woman not to want a family," Aidan retorted.

"She's just been shot up, Da," Eoghan inserted, and I shot him a grateful look. "In the abdomen. She couldn't have kids yet if she wanted to."

"She's depressed?" Aidan asked, and fuck him, I heard the relief in his voice.

Depression would have Aoife's unique view of children make some semblance of sense.

Did I lie? Christ. I never lied. But in this instance, it would clear things up sooner...

In the end, I decided I preferred my tongue where it was. "No. She's fine. She's just very sore." I cleared my throat. "Look, we talked about it before we were married. She wants them. The shooting changed shit. You can understand that, right? She's questioning a lot of things at the moment."

"Tell her we'd keep your kids safe."

I had to admit, the ferocity in his voice warmed me. "I know, Aidan. I'm sure she does too."

He grunted. "Well, as long as you know you can change her mind..."

I snorted. "Would you have me annul the marriage because she won't give me kids?"

I wanted a family. But only with Aoife. If she wasn't willing to give me kids, and I couldn't talk her into it, then I didn't have the gift of the gab and didn't deserve a fucking family of my own.

"No, of course not," he grumbled. "Just wanted you to know the lay of the land."

I refrained, barely, from rolling my eyes. "Look, I'll see you later."

He nodded. "Tell Lena I won't be coming to the compound tonight."

"Will do," I agreed, making a move to leave before he could ask me to stay.

I wanted out of there. Stat. And not just because of the dildo.

42

———

AOIFE

"WHATCHA DOING?"

"Not a lot." I sighed as I stared up at the ceiling, having plopped my phone on my tits and put the call on speaker. "I'm bored shitless."

"I wish I *could* be bored. I'm working so goddamn much, I don't know whether I'm coming or going."

I snorted. "You can't have hooked up in a while then."

"Bitch!" Jenny retorted, and I laughed.

"You're only pissed because you know I'm right. Jesus, I know way too much about your sex life, Jen."

"That's because I had a sex life to talk about. Now, Mrs. O'Grady, you do too. Spill the beans."

"Not much sex to be had when you make a skeleton look like it has the fidgets."

She clucked her tongue. "I know, honey. I meant before."

"Oh." My cheeks burned. "Yeah. I told you. He's awesome in bed."

"You can't just tell me the details once, Aoife."

"Why not?" I whined.

"Because I need to live vicariously through you. I seriously have no energy at the moment. When I climb into bed, all I want to do is sleep."

"Shit, you must be tired."

She blew a raspberry. "You know it."

"He's just... you know, dirty."

A snicker sounded down the line. "And here's me thinking you'd be all prim and proper in bed."

"Hey, just because I was a virgin didn't mean I was innocent." Innocence was Mary-Ellen, and I'd never been like her. I don't think Jenny would have hung around with me if I was.

"That's true. I've seen your kindle. I know what you read."

That had me grinning. "I read an awesome one yesterday. This chick had five guys."

"Five?" Jenny sputtered.

"Yeah. It was hot as fuck. They were all geniuses and they lived together in this house in London." I clucked my tongue. "The sex was dynamite."

"I'll bet. I can't imagine Finn sharing you with four other guys."

A smile curved my lips. "Nope. I doubt he would."

"Don't sound like the cat that got the cream, would you? Jesus. You're going to make me jealous."

"You already are," I stated. "Don't make out you weren't pissed at me for getting married first."

"Yeah, I was, and then I almost died at the wedding so that might have put me off being a bride for life."

I winced. "I'm so glad you weren't hurt, sweetie, and I'm really sorry I put you through that."

She pshawed. "You think I thought you did it on purpose? I'm just fucking devastated you got shot, Eef. And I hate that I can't visit. This lockdown shit sucks."

"Don't worry, hon. I know how busy you are so this makes it easier on you. We're way out in Queens, so that's too far even if you could visit."

"I can't believe they have a safe house."

"Believe it," I said with a grunt. "I hate it here."

"You do? Why?"

"I just want to be at home, and all the kids make a shit ton of noise even though I'm up on the top level so I shouldn't be able to hear anything at all."

"You're just grouchy because you can't get laid."

I snickered. "That and the hole in my abdomen aches like a bitch."

"Bet the ache down below is worse," she retorted in a singsong tone that had me rolling my eyes. Before I countered it though, she blurted out, "Man, I forgot to text you last night. You'll never guess what happened in school."

Jen was studying to be an accountant at night school, and I felt guilty not only about her losing the tea room job because I'd always worked out ways for her to have shorter days on her school nights, but also because now she was working flat out to cover her bills.

"What? Did that hot guy—what's his name, Chris?—sit next to you again?" She might have been twenty-five too, but when it came to guys, Jen could be like a teenager.

"Yeah, and he asked me out, but you should have seen his shoes yesterday, Aoife. They were gross."

That had me laughing. Jen had a thing about white teeth and clean shoes. Anything else was pretty much a green light when she was horny.

"Go on, what was it?"

"The teacher was new. Only called me goddamn Fionnabhair."

I winced. "Seriously?"

"Yeah. I wanted to crawl under the desk. Not only couldn't he say it, he made a joke about it. The shithouse. I mean, you know I hate my name, Aoife, but Christ. The dude totally deserved a slap."

"I'm surprised you didn't give him some attitude after class."

She hissed. "I did. Bastard."

Jennifer was the modern-day version of Fionnabhair, and she'd been calling herself that ever since Dougie MacIntyre had taken to calling her, 'Flea in a bed' in elementary school. To an American ear, there was a slight resemblance between the two. Not that I'd ever told Jenny that.

"Good. Hope you gave him a tongue lashing."

"Well, no. He'd better be giving me one though. I made time for him in my busy schedule next Saturday."

"You're going to date him?" I squawked. "What was all that crap about being too tired for sex?"

"I made an exception. He has McDreamy hair, Aoife. I wasn't about to pass that up."

I chuckled. "You're crazy."

"Crazy good," she purred. "Anyway, I'd better get going, sugar. I have so much crap to do before my shift. If I don't call you in a few days, call me, yeah?"

My lips curved in a warm smile. "Thanks, Jen. You take care and get some rest when you can."

"Will do, Mom." She snorted then cut the call.

The last thing I wanted was to lay in bed for the rest of the day, but because I had no say in the matter, I reached for the headphones Finn bought me as a gift after I'd complained about how loud the kids were here, and picked up my kindle.

If I couldn't get any of the shit done for my bakery, and if all I could do was lie here in this damn bed, then that's what I'd do.

Quintessence here I come.

43

FINN

A BREATHY SIGH escaped Aoife and it had me jolting at my desk.

I was in my office. Where I spent nearly ninety percent of my goddamn time as I worked to help broker a deal among the Russians, the Mexicans, and us.

The Mexicans didn't trust the Russians, and the Russians would only move if we guaranteed the Mexican deal. Which left me having to scrape together the remainder of the twenty-five million dollars to cover the Russian's first shipment of coke from the Mexicans.

I wasn't concerned that the Mexicans would screw us over. We were friendly with them, and their new leader owed us a favor or ten, but the Russians wanted us to put our money in, and because we needed their men, we had no choice but to comply.

Pulling together that kind of money wasn't exactly easy, but that was the way of gang wars now. They were fought in boardrooms more than on the streets. The latter kind of fighting was a show of brute force that was no long necessary, even if it did have an efficacy that couldn't be denied.

I was dog tired, grouchy, and I missed my woman.

Speaking on the phone wasn't enough, I realized. I wanted to be inside her, wanted to slide so deep into her we wouldn't know where the other ended. Only then would I feel some semblance of peace.

I'd been using the bedroom attached to this office to sleep in, because there was no way in hell I was using the penthouse when she wasn't there. Her scent was everywhere, lingering in the air like a ghost. Just the thought had unease slipping through me and I focused on our phone call.

"Aoife, what's wrong?"

Another breathy sigh.

I tilted my head to the side. "Aoife," I barked. Was she touching herself?

Goddammit, I'd made a monster.

Wanting to face plant into the desk because I seriously didn't have the strength to deal with her making those sounds without wanting to bust through my zipper, instead I palmed my dick through my pants, squeezing slightly to reduce the ache.

"The doctor said no." Goddamn her.

"I need you, Finn," she whispered, and my heart began to pound. Deep, quaking thuds in my chest that left me shaken.

I grabbed my phone and slipped it off speaker as I pressed it to my ear. Spinning around in my desk seat so I was turned away from the door—no one would come in without knocking first, but I appreciated the idea of privacy—I gave in to temptation, "Aoife, I need you too."

That little gasp? It about broke me.

Clenching my eyes closed, wishing I could resist her, I bit off, "Are you in bed?"

"Y-Yes," she whimpered. "I want your cock, Finn. My fingers aren't good enough."

My nostrils flared. "Did I say you could touch yourself?"

"No, but you're mean."

I couldn't stop the chuckle that escaped me. "You like me mean, baby."

Hearing her sulky grumble had my lips curving even wider.

"Don't you?" I prodded, wanting her to confirm what I already knew to be true.

"Yes," she mumbled.

"And how would someone who's mean, punish you for not doing as you're told?"

"Make me stop touching my clit," she said on a pant, and I had no choice but to shove my cell between my shoulder and throat to prop it up as I opened my fly and freed my cock. The second I fisted it, I released a deep groan.

Fuck, it'd been too long since she'd touched me. Too fucking long. I needed her small fist around my shaft, and that glove of a cunt sucking me in like it was demanding I return home.

Because, yeah, call me a pansy but Aoife was fucking home, and she was fifteen miles away. That was fourteen miles and just over seventeen hundred and fifty nine yards too far.

Jesus, her sitting on my sofa across the other side of the room was too much distance between us. I wanted us skin to skin, and only that would do.

The minute she heard my groan, her breathing increased. "O-Oh God, Finn, I wish I could suck you down, I wish I could feel you inside my pussy."

Dirty words coming from my angel's mouth?

So wrong, but so right.

"Tell me more, angel," I half-purred, needing to hear my sweet Irish girl be filthy for me.

"I'm so wet, Finn. So wet. I want your mouth on me. I need it. I need your tongue sucking on my clit, I need you to tap my pussy when I get too greedy. I-I want you to slap my ass if I'm—"

My eyes flared at that. "I want my hands all over your ass, Aoife. I want to slide my cock inside that tiny little hole and make it mine."

"I-It is yours, Finn. All yours. Are you jacking off, baby?"

"Of course, I am," I ground out, closing my eyes as I leaned back and began to use my pre-cum as lube. "I wish you were doing it for me."

"Come home," she breathed. "I will."

"I can't," I whispered, regret lacing my words. "Tomorrow. I'll be there tomorrow." I hoped I wasn't promising her something I couldn't keep, but I'd try my damn hardest even though I knew we couldn't do any of the things we were talking about. Her body wasn't healed enough for that.

"I dream about you," she whispered. "A filthy dream. I'm in the kitchen, making dinner, and you come in, you grab me and kiss me. Fucking my mouth like you're about to fuck my pussy. You make me melt, make me forget everything I'm doing. Then, you slap my ass. You tell me I was a bad girl, and you bend me over the counter and pull my pants down." She gulped, and I heard a thwap-thwap sound, could fucking *hear* how wet she was. Jesus. "Then you grab my hands and drag them behind my back, and you keep my pants high on my thighs so I couldn't move. So all I can do is be fucked by you. Then, you slip your cock out and push inside me."

"And I'd fuck my beautiful angel," I grated out. "I'd fuck you so hard that you'd feel me inside you all day, and my cum would be buried in you while you cooked, because I'd make sure you didn't shower, that you stank of me, and us, and what we did all day."

Her breath hiccoughed. "Will you let me come?" she pleaded, the words high-pitched.

"Do you want to?" I asked, narrowing my eyes at the view ahead of me. The Hudson didn't deserve my scowl, but my wife did.

"P-Please."

"Beg me, Aoife," I ground out.

She whimpered. "Please, Finn. Please."

I licked my lips, loving hearing my name on her tongue like that. "Not enough. I don't think you deserve to," I said, my tone purposely cruel.

Her fingers didn't stop, I could hear the slick slide in the background thanks to the mic, and the prospect of fucking my fist when I could be fucking that tight little snatch about blew my brains.

She's injured, she's healing, I told myself, repeating the words until they were a litany.

She needs rest.

Rest.

Rest, goddammit!

I ground out, "Stop touching yourself, Aoife."

At my bark, she mewled but there was silence.

"Lick your fingers. Tell me what you taste like."

She hummed and I heard a slurping sound as she sucked the digits clean. "Salty, I guess. A little sweet. Clean."

"Wrong," I informed her. "You taste like mine."

"Y-Yes. Oh, Finn. *Yes.* I'm yours."

"Come for me, angel," I guided her, letting her have this, knowing she needed it and that she'd sleep after, and I needed her to fucking sleep, so she'd heal.

Her high-pitched cry had me closing my eyes, clenching them tight as I grabbed my cock and fucked my fist to the sounds of her climaxing.

It seemed to go on for ages, like the dirtiest soundtrack I'd ever heard. The best porn background ever, because this was personalized and between the whimpers and the moans and the tiny mewls, came my name.

"Finn," she cried out, and she wailed, and she groaned.

My name was a litany on her tongue, and my cock spurted to the final breathy sound she uttered, one of relaxation and repletion. One of satisfaction, even though I knew her fingers couldn't do the job I could for her.

When I came, I grunted long and low, catching as much cum as I could in my fist. It wasn't ideal, and I made a fucking mess, but I felt better. My heart pumped like the piston it was, but it felt lighter somehow.

I should have called her earlier. She always did this to me. Made me feel brighter because she was my reminder of why I was here in this goddamn office instead of with her.

Brokering this deal was a priority. I had to ally the Mexicans with the Russians so the Russians would have our back. Once that happened, we'd have their fire power and their men, so the Colombians would run sniveling away like the cowards they were.

I had three million to come up with. Not bad, considering for the last three weeks I'd been liquidating assets that wouldn't hit our finances long-term.

I was close, so close, and when the deal went down, we'd be home free.

A contented sigh escaped her. "I feel better."

I snickered, not having expected her to say that. Any other woman might have told me she missed me or loved me. She might have asked me to come home, been coy or manipulative. Not Aoife. Never her.

Because of that, it made me want her all the more. Because she didn't drag me down with feelings, I wanted them from her. I wanted the words again. I wanted her to tell me she loved me without her almost having to die. I wanted her to say them and mean them with no fear or pain clouding those beautiful eyes of hers.

But I'd bide my time. I'd put us into this situation. I needed to get us out of it.

I released a quiet breath. "I feel better too." And I did. My need was like a toothache, and I'd just taken a shit ton of Ibuprofen to get rid of it.

She hummed. "I'm glad."

"The PT came today, right?" It seemed incredible that we were approaching the tenth week since the shooting. Soon, we'd be in the clear.

And I meant that.

We.

I'd felt every single one of her restrictions. I hadn't suffered pain, but I'd felt it for her, had watched her struggle. Had hated myself for being the one to have put her through this.

Guilt drove me, shame made me persevere.

Nine weeks to broker peace wasn't, in the scheme of things, a long time to wait, but we were going long-term here.

The Colombians, after the shit show of the drive-by, then that crap at the compound, had gone quiet like the punkass numbskulls they were. They'd realized what they'd done. Realized the shit they'd brought down on their heads, and they'd retreated. But they knew we were coming for them, and they'd be trying to prepare.

What they wouldn't expect is for us to double our numbers with the Bratva. And those sons of bitches were ice cold. They were on par with Aidan on the insanity front. They'd slice you up like a mother-fucker for looking at them the wrong goddamn way.

A few more weeks, Aoife would be better, and we should be able to go home.

I clung to that like a lifeline. How much I needed her astonished me.

"Yeah, she came today." The PT clinic had sent a man at first—I'd sorted that out fucking quickly. No dick was going anywhere near my woman. Fuck that shit.

"What did she say?"

She huffed. "You and Lena, I swear, like mother hens."

My lips curved as I stared down at my fist where my cum was still sticky in my palm. I imagined making her lick it clean, then stopped thinking that because I'd get hard again and after I finished speaking with her, I had plans to be on the phone with Conor for a few hours. I reached for my pocket square and cleaned up the mess as quickly as I could.

"That's because you're surprisingly naughty where your training is concerned." I had reports from the clinic sent to me, and though she was getting stronger, I knew she still found the exercises hard.

Another huff. "I'm trying."

"That's all I can ask," I murmured, meaning it, but knowing that would induce her to work harder as well.

"I'll try harder."

I smiled, satisfied that I'd read her right. "Good girl." Air gusted from my lungs as I made an admission that I knew would please her. "I miss you, Aoife."

She was quiet a second, and I knew she was, indeed, surprised. "I miss you too, Finn."

"I miss not waking up beside you. I miss your food—God," I groaned, "I miss your bread. I want you in my kitchen all the time. Fuck the bakery, just bake for me."

Her giggle made my heart soar. "You want all the bread, huh?"

I laughed. "Yeah. All of it."

"Well, no can do. The minute I'm back on my feet and out of this stupid hotel, I'm getting that bakery ready."

I could hear the determination in her voice and was pleased by it. This entire situation might have caused her to be depressed. I hadn't abandoned her, but I certainly hadn't been as supportive as I wanted to be. She was around women she didn't know, had no access to her best friend or her father, and yet, she remained surprisingly cheerful.

Aoife was resilient in ways that made me appreciate her all the more.

She didn't whine or complain, was one tough cookie and it made me realize that, for the first time in my life, I had someone at my back. I'd always had my brothers, Aidan, and Lena, but this was different. Aoife was uniquely mine.

"Aoife?"

She hummed. "Yes."

"Thank you."

"For what?" she asked, sounding surprised. "I haven't done anything."

"For being you. For... knowing I'm doing this for us. Thank you for that."

"I know you'd be here if you could, Finn," she said after a few moments. "I'm not going to say that there aren't some nights I want to bash your head in with a pillow, because there have been more than one of those—" I laughed as I conjured up a mental image of that. "—but I knew what I was getting into when I said, 'I do' and I don't regret it. You make me happy, Finn. I'm not one hundred percent at the minute, I won't lie, but our day is coming, isn't it?"

Her honesty made my throat clutch, and it was really damn hard to get out, "It sure is, my angel. We'll be home soon, and I'll be wearing us both out again in bed."

A sigh of delight slipped from her lips. "You promise?"

I smirked. "I can more than promise it, Aoife. It's a damn guarantee."

Putting the phone down ten minutes later sucked. It sucked hard. I wanted nothing more than to be in my office at home so I could just walk down the hall and get into bed with her.

But I couldn't.

I had shit to do.

Slipping in my AirPods for extra privacy, I called Conor. When he grunted out a greeting, I asked, "How are we doing?"

"We're close."

"How close?" I demanded.

"Very fucking close," he snarled. "Just wait a minute. I have two more lines of code to write."

I rolled my eyes at his statement and heard the way his fingers were flying over his keyboard. "Why answer the fucking phone if you couldn't talk?"

He grunted, and his fingers seemed to speed up all the more. Then, he gave one last tap and I could hear his damn grin as he stated, "Done."

"Seriously?"

"Yeah."

I snickered. "They're going to be confused as fuck, aren't they?"

"Sure are. Dumbfucks." I heard him rub his hands together. "Now those assets are frozen, they're going to have serious issues getting any product out of the country."

"For how long?" I inquired.

"I'd say an extra two months."

Rubbing my forehead, I murmured, "Is the boy dead now?"

"Yeah. Da finished him off."

After nine weeks of torture, that was probably a blessing. See, my brothers hadn't killed the gunmen who'd gone flying from the truck. No, they'd just hustled them to one of our warehouses in the chaos.

Death was a blessing. Especially considering Aidan Sr.'s rage. Aidan Jr. was going to have to walk with a cane for the rest of his goddamn life because of those cunts, and then, what with Aoife and the rest of the shit the Colombian bastards had pulled? They'd been the whipping boys for each and every temper tantrum Aidan had experienced these past couple of months.

"Well, we got as much information out of them as possible."

It was amazing how much foot soldiers picked up on and were willing to share when a crazy motherfucker was their tormentor.

We'd managed to rat out at least five of their most recent hauls to the DEA, meaning their stock was perilously low, and now, after having learned the dumb bastards had most of their capital in a cryptocurrency they'd developed themselves, Conor had spent the past week hacking into it.

Aidan was going to go back to calling him boy genius again.

"We're crawling out of this intact," he stated down the line, his own satisfaction evident.

"Yeah." I ran a hand through my hair. "Not long now until this shit is over, and those dogs are going to wish they'd never pissed in our path."

I took comfort from that and together, we did what we did best, made money and laundered a fuck ton more.

44

AOIFE

SIX DAYS LATER

THE BED JOSTLED and I stiffened as discomfort washed through me because I'd stupidly settled on my back. Then, I smelled him, and I released a deep sigh.

The tension that had prevented me from sleeping deeply dissipated as I turned on my side and pressed myself against him.

I was stiff and sore, but for the sixth night in a row, after a few weeks of sporadic appearances, Finn had returned to our room at the compound. Phone sex had worked for me, but either Mary-Ellen hadn't tried it out on Stephen, or he'd not been interested as he hadn't visited her.

Bastard.

We were silent as we arranged ourselves amid the sheets. He slipped one knee between mine while curling his foot beneath my ankle, and I threaded one of my hands around his arm.

The air that soughed from my lungs earlier matched his as he settled down. A peculiar kind of relief warmed me. Knowing where he was, knowing he was safe, it was enough.

"You okay?" I whispered.

I'd barely seen him since he'd brought me here, and to be honest,

I was getting a bit cabin feverish. This need to be with him wasn't dissipating. I hadn't needed him this much before, but I hadn't been shot outside a church before, had I?

I just... With Finn, I felt safe. Which, again, was stupid because my injuries had occurred while standing right beside my new husband.

Anxiety didn't have to be rational. To be honest, I thought I was dealing with this pretty goddamn well. Jenny agreed too. She knew what was happening, knew I was on lockdown, and I knew she wanted to cheer me up, but I'd gone from being free to do whatever the hell I wanted, to literally being caged on a compound.

It might not have been so damn bad if I'd been able to move around with more ease.

Every day I rested, I grew stronger, but I was bored shitless and going to lose my mind if my body didn't start healing faster.

The doctors said light activity for twelve weeks.

The prospect of ten days to go was hellish.

"Just tired."

Finn's abrupt answer startled me, I'd forgotten I'd asked the question and he'd taken so long to reply.

I could feel his hard-on pushing into my side and there was an answering ache in my core.

Fuck, I wanted him.

Before I'd been shot, I loved when he'd slip into bed while I slept, and he'd wake me up with his mouth or fingers somewhere on my body.

To say I sucked up courage for what I was about to do was an understatement.

Finn wanted me, I knew that. He was so hard, so close, so hot, that my body couldn't fail to respond to the physiological changes in his. But he was also stubborn and mule-headed enough to refuse because the doctor had yet to sign off on any sexual activity.

This man was better than a chastity belt.

So, taking a huge risk, I reached between us and palmed his dick. He groaned and went to move back.

"Aoife, no."

This man's willpower would be the death of me.

I squeezed his shaft. "Finn, yes," I countered, sliding my hand under the waistband of his briefs.

When bare skin met bare skin, he released a groan so pained it sent an answering ache deep inside me.

His hand snapped out to grab my wrist, but with my thumb, I caressed the tip. Sliding my finger through the drop of pre-cum that had spurted there. For endless seconds, I waited, wondering what he'd do, then after my lungs felt like they were burning from holding my breath, he hesitated, and finally rolled onto his back and covered his face with his forearm.

Was that green for go?

Unsure of what to do, I waited an additional moment, then he rocked his hips slightly, and I smiled, knowing I had my answer.

I didn't take it for granted.

Time was of the essence. I needed to keep him on the precipice, otherwise he'd revert to his he-man, know-it-all attitude, and I'd be left feeling so empty I wouldn't be able to sleep all night.

Slipping my other hand under his briefs, I pulled him free. When the tip of his cock grazed the fabric, he released a groan, and I moaned at how hard and fucking sensitive he was.

God, I had to have him in my mouth. It was a biting urgency in my blood.

"Finn, help me. I want to taste you."

His second groan was heartfelt. "N-No, Aoife."

"I need to, baby. I want your cock in my mouth and your cum streaming down my throat."

When he grunted, I felt his cock pound out his heart rate in my hand.

"Please, Finn, I need you," I crooned, dipping down to press an open-mouthed kiss to his pecs. He shuddered when I moved my tongue around the area, palpating the skin softly.

That this man could react so strongly to me fired my blood like nothing else could. I'd missed this, missed *him* so fucking much.

I knew this side of him. Knew how to read him. Knew how it affected the man outside of the bedroom, and without this aspect of our relationship, I felt like I was walking blind. The intimacy was gone, and I hated that. It was like missing a limb. I'd lived pretty much my whole life without sex, but after a few months with Finn in my world, I never wanted to be without it, without *him*, again.

"Are you sure you're ready for it?" he asked, his voice almost soundless as he breathed the words.

"I need you," I purred, hoping against hope that I didn't sound stupid and, instead, sounded sultry and sexy. "I'm so empty, baby."

He was still for a second, then he murmured, "Stay where you are."

Resting on my good side was the only real way I could get comfortable, but I faced outward and not toward the center of the bed. To accommodate him, I had to be maneuvered across the mattress.

By the time he'd helped me move so I was centered on the bed and farther down, I was feeling a lot less sexed up. Pain had made my brow sweat because I was on my back with pressure directly on the wound, but I knew Finn. I knew what he tasted like, what he felt like, and I needed that.

This intimacy was important to my mental health, but more than that, he was a craving in my blood. An addiction that hadn't been fed in over two months.

He was breathing heavily when he rounded the bed, not from exertion but from excitement.

It never ceased to astonish me that I could do that to this man. This gorgeous creature who would make any woman drool. Whose body was made for sinning, but whose face was that of an angel.

My mouth watered as the automatic spotlight from the yard bled through the blinds for a second, illuminating his chiseled jaw before flashing over his pecs and delineated abs. I saw his cock too, and realized he'd pulled off his briefs.

Fuck, I wanted to be naked too. Wanted to feel his skin against mine but I couldn't.

Not yet.

I shuddered as he approached me, and he tilted up so his hips were slightly angled for me to suck him without exerting myself.

His scent floored me. Pure man. Mine. Musk. Soap. They hit me in waves of longing that had me wishing I could take him into my body, but not yet. Not yet.

Soon, though. Soon.

I licked my lips, gathered spit in my mouth, then slipped him inside, dragging my tongue down each crevice and curve. He moaned, his body stiffening, and I tasted pre-cum.

So delicious. How had I not appreciated the sticky saltiness before?

"Fuck, Aoife, fuck," he ground out, and one hand gently cupped my head and the other grabbed a hold of the sheet.

I knew he wanted to grab my head. Wanted to fuck my mouth. We were rough together, and he didn't treat me like I was fragile. But now? I was like glass in his hands and though I loved him for it, I longed for the time when he could do what he wanted—what *I* wanted—to me.

Slurping him down like he was my favorite soft serve, I tormented him by grabbing his balls and rubbing them in my palm. Each time I felt his cock twitch like he was going to cum, I twisted them gently and tugged down. Every time I did it, he swore, and his fingertips dug into my skull just a little bit harder as the rocking of his hips grew jerkier with need.

"Fuck, baby, please. Please, Aoife," he demanded, his tone robbing the words of his pleas. I loved that about him. Always so fucking arrogant, this man. My man.

I took him as deep as I could in this position and swallowed around him as I gently released his balls from my grip.

"Oh fuck," he spat, sounding anything but pleasured as his cock jerked in my mouth and he pelted me with his seed.

The first time he'd done this to me, I remembered being disgusted by his taste. Now? I swallowed every drop without hesitation.

His panting breaths sounded thready in the quiet room and I slowly released his shaft from my mouth. Gripping him again, I sucked at the tip, cleaning him off and dipping my tongue to make sure I got every last drop of his cum.

He shivered and bit off, "Fuck, Aoife, no. Enough."

I smiled, content I'd pleasured him, and rested my head on his lower belly.

Was I tired? Yeah. I was. Sore? That too. But I was even more achy between my thighs.

What I wouldn't do for my vibrator right about now. Why had I tossed them out when I'd hauled my stuff from my apartment to Finn's, no, *our* penthouse?

His hands drifted through my hair, stroking the strands and rubbing them between his fingers. "Are you feeling—"

I cut him off, "I'm feeling like the cat who got the cream."

He snorted at my gentle laugh. "Well, I don't know about the cat part, but you sure got the cream."

"Lapped it all up like a good little girl, too, didn't I?" The dark hid my knowing smile—I knew how those words would affect him.

"How's that greedy pussy of mine?" he rasped, and I closed my eyes, wondering if I was glowing with happiness at his question.

"It needs you. *I* need you. Deep inside me." There was no spare flesh on his stomach, but I managed to nip him.

"Soon, Aoife. Soon." He shuddered. "Don't lie. How does your abdomen feel?"

I thought about it. The ache came from being in an awkward position more than anything, because I hadn't had to move all that much to suck him off. Initially, the change in pressure had made me uncomfortable, but I wasn't lying when I said, "Fine."

"Fuck," he whispered, surprising me. Then, he swallowed. "If we prop you up on the pillows..." Those eight words had fire racing through my veins. I heard my heart in my ears and I almost missed what he said, "...would you try to keep as still as you can?"

"I promise to try."

That was about as good as I could do.

I rubbed my thighs together and closed my eyes as the ache gathered there, and spread through my body like a warm glow. I felt like I was lit up inside, and at the prospect of his touch? It was a wonder I wasn't floating.

"I'm a fucking moron for doing this," he mumbled under his breath, but I noticed his cock was hard once more as he stacked pillows up at the head of the bed, then helped me prop myself against them so I didn't have any pressure on my wound.

I was aching again, a slight sweat on my brow from all the jostling around, but my cunt was slick and wet and ready for whatever he was going to do to me.

He climbed off the bed, then surprising me further, I heard the nightstand drawer open. For a second, I thought he was grabbing a condom, then I remembered we didn't use those anymore. But was I even ready to have sex? Mentally, fuck, yes. Physically, no. It would hurt in the morning.

It wasn't that I was frightened if I said no, he wouldn't listen. I was frightened that if I said no, he'd listen too damn well, and I'd spend the rest of the night rocking the chick equivalent of a hard-on.

Finn would never be cruel. But cruel to be kind? Yeah. I could see him in that role if it meant saving me from myself.

Before I could say anything though, before I could even fret, I saw his shadow at the base of the bed and heard him murmur, "Spread your legs as wide as you can for me, sweetness."

An internal shudder had me rocking my hips up and doing as bid.

When I'd widened them as much as I could, I felt him crawl onto the bed and settle between my legs.

I shuddered when I felt his warm breath blow against the spread lips of my cunt, and then he lapped at my clit and I made a keening sound as my hips jerked back.

"Aoife."

My name was a warning. My eyes flared wide at the sound of it. "F-Finn?"

"If you move a fucking inch, I will stop so fast it will give you whiplash. Do you understand?"

I believed him.

Clenching my eyes shut, I nodded quickly, then realized he couldn't see me. "Y-Yes."

He nipped at my inner thigh, then murmured, "I got you something."

He had?

His fingers slipped higher until he'd caressed the entirety of my slit. He tutted under his breath. "So wet, you greedy little thing."

"Only for you," I rasped, and a guttural sound escaped him.

I knew I'd floored him with those three words. His hand curved into my thigh and his fingertips dug into the soft flesh there as he fought himself for control.

That I'd ruptured it with three words made my heart soar.

I had power over this man, and what woman in love didn't want that? Not to use or abuse, just to know that I was important to him.

I wished like hell I could see him, see his eyes, and know, truly, what he was thinking, but that was like asking for the moon.

A semi-warm object touched my thigh. I almost jolted, then remembered what he'd said. It was a texture I knew, and my mouth curved at the prospect of Finn buying me a sex toy.

"Do you know how much it kills me to fill you with something that isn't attached to me?" he growled, sounding utterly in pain.

"Then don't," I whispered. "I just want you."

He pressed his face into my thigh. "Aoife, you're fucking killing me here. Fuck!" His body jostled the bed slightly and I realized he'd readjusted himself because his cock had been pressing into the mattress.

"Please, just..." He swallowed. "Don't talk, yeah? I'm too old to come again this soon."

My lips curved and I bit at my bottom lip.

He tapped my thigh to grab my attention. "Understand?"

"I wasn't supposed to talk," I said with a pout, and he laughed slightly before I felt the toy move along my slit, rubbing down the length of it, getting soaked with all my juices.

"Fuck, you're so wet," he groaned as he pushed the toy in.

My eyes flared because it was thicker than anything I'd used before and faintly wider than even Finn. I was stuffed full.

"We can't ease that itch deep inside you, but maybe filling you up will help," he rasped, a second before he turned on the toy, releasing the faint buzz that shot down my nerve endings.

A keening cry escaped me, and my hands dug into the sheets, tearing them free from the mattress as I strained to remain still.

I wanted to fuck the air, rock my hips, get myself off, but I knew Finn would pull away from me entirely, taking the vibrator away and leave me desperate for him all night long.

My lungs felt frozen with panic as I clenched my eyes, trying not to move, desperately pleading with any saint who'd listen to make me stay still.

Then, Finn blew my brains by moving his mouth to my clit.

Oh. Sweet. Jesus.

I was full, vibrating, and he was sucking down on my clit better than a goddamn plunger.

Holy crap, how did he even do that? How was it possible?

I wasn't sure if I could withstand not rocking my hips. The desire to alleviate this ache swelled inside me to the point where I could explode, just not in the way I needed.

I was stuffed full, but it was cold. It wasn't Finn. He wasn't on top of me, his body touching mine, my legs clasping his hips as he rocked atop me.

He was there, getting me off, but I wanted his cock in my pussy, not this cold machine.

"Finn?" I asked on a high wail.

"So juicy, Aoife," he moaned, and then he surprised me. He began to nudge the toy deeper into me, before pulling it out an inch.

It wasn't enough.

It wasn't him.

But it helped.

Oh fuck.

I felt it surging through me like a tidal wave. Like a geyser that had no way to go but up. It rattled through my bones, making it so impossibly difficult not to move.

As the loud, wailed moan escaped me, I felt Finn's smile around my clit. Then as I lay there panting, trying to get my breath back, he pressed a kiss to it, switched off the vibrator, and moved his face, wiping his chin on my thigh, leaving trails of my arousal there as his stubble made my sensitive skin tingle.

He climbed off the bed, then turned on the light. My eyes ached at the sudden illumination, but before I could even adjust, his fingers were back on me. I felt them slide through the sopping mess of my cunt, before he grabbed his cock and used my juices as lube.

My mouth felt dry as I watched him jack off. The movements hard and fast, jerky and abrupt.

"Unbutton your sleepshirt, Aoife," he commanded, breathlessly.

I moaned but complied, keeping my legs spread as I parted the two sides of the shirt. When he came, he aimed first for my pussy, and then the last few drops he managed to spray over my tits.

My heart was thumping in my chest again at the sight of his seed against my bright red sex and without pause, I reached down and rubbed his cum into me.

His nostrils flared in response. When I tried to retrieve the toy, to pull it free of my body, he slapped the back of my hand.

"Leave it in."

My eyes widened. "But why?"

"So you can appreciate my cock when I fuck you soon."

For some reason, that hit me hard. I closed my eyes as my body responded like I'd been jolted with an electric shock.

My tits wobbled with each shaky breath as he ducked down and kissed me. He thrust his tongue deep into my mouth, sliding mine against his in a rough pattern that had me shaking as he stole the air from my lungs. Then, as was his way, he retreated by nipping my bottom lip. This time, he bit down hard, and God, it hurt, but equally, it had been so long since he'd not just nipped but bitten.

I moaned, hoping I'd feel the slight sting tomorrow, praying it wouldn't have disappeared.

He switched off the light, rounded the bed, then climbed in beside me. He spent a few minutes helping me get comfortable, before he curled onto his side, curving into me.

I fell asleep to the feel of one hand cupping my breast while his thumb smoothed his seed into my skin, and the too-thick toy still inside of me, reminding me of things I couldn't have yet, but desperately wanted.

45

FINN

I AWOKE to the sheer wonder of seeing my wife asleep with her legs parted and her tits bared to my gaze.

I'd hated how she'd been hidden from my sight recently. I'd hated the distance between us in bed. I'd hated not being able to feel her against me, to touch and taste every part of her.

My morning wood was alive and kicking, but I was strangely sated. I reached down to pet her pretty pussy and glowered at the warm plastic still inside her.

I'd done that to punish both of us.

She hadn't been ready for this, and my impatience could cause a setback. I'd known seeing the dildo in the morning light would piss me off and remind me to be careful with her. For her, I'd done it to teach her the lesson that nothing felt as right as my cock inside her.

Tempted to let her sleep, I moved my fingers away, but the second I did, she mumbled, "Don't stop."

I grinned and turned my face into my bicep as I snickered.

"Why you laughin'?" she grumbled, one eye popping open. "Felt good."

"Too good," I chided her sadly.

"Soon," she whispered, staring at me sleepily.

"Soon," I promised, giving her the word that was like our pass-code, our vow to one another.

"Will you take it out now?"

I grinned at her again. "Didn't like it?"

"It's not you."

Well, if that wasn't good for a man's ego, what was?

Sitting up, I moved closer to her so I could press a kiss to her mouth. She flinched when I licked my tongue over her bottom lip and I shot her a knowing smile when she pinkened adorably.

"I missed you," she whispered when I stared deeply into her eyes.

Pressing my forehead against hers, I sighed. "I'm sorry I've been so..."

"Bullheaded?"

"That." My lips curved. "I came here as often as I could though, didn't I?"

"Just really late and you were like a bear with a sore paw."

I whistled. "Two animal comparisons in less than thirty seconds. Someone's feeling spunky."

A laugh escaped her. "I am, actually."

"Not too sore?" My tone sobered as I asked the question.

"No. Bit achy, but nothing terrible." She bit her lip. "The doctor came yesterday, by the way. Said it's healing so well because I was healthy before, you know? PT's helping and, I'm on the mend." She pressed her hand to my jaw, which I knew had clenched at her statement. "Don't be angry."

Stunned, I gaped at her. "Angry? I'm not angry at you, Aoife. Sweet Jesus. As if I could be. I'm mad at myself. We'll never get these months back, baby. I'm so sorry."

Her mouth twitched. "Lena says never to expect apologies from you guys."

"Lena should know when to keep her mouth shut," I grumbled, rubbing her sore bottom lip with my thumb. "When will you be 100%?"

"Another three or so months." Her nose crinkled with distaste for that prognosis.

The idea of being without her for another three months was agony.

"No more sex until she visits again. In nine days' time." This time, she beamed at me. "We'll have to be careful, though. It's still damn sore."

"My angel wants to be treated like a princess, huh?"

Her cheeks turned bright pink. "Not particularly."

I laughed outright at that. "Why doesn't that surprise me?" Tapping her on the nose, I murmured, "You're a dirty little thing."

She winced. "Hardly."

I knew the only thing she was refusing to believe there was the 'little' comment. But fuck that.

"Definitely. There's nothing you wouldn't let me do to you, is there?" When she licked her lips, I knew I had my answer. Groaning, I rubbed my morning wood against her thigh and mumbled, "You're going to be the death of me."

"Just for another week," she said in a delightfully breathy, singsong tone.

"You've been so good, sweetheart." I reached down and began to pat her pussy once more. When she spread her legs eagerly, I grinned at the sight.

When I touched her clit, she clenched her ass and stomach muscles, rocking slightly. In the light of day, I saw the discomfort flicker on her face, the tiny muscles giving her away, and knew that next week, when we finally could be skin to skin, I'd have to be careful like she admitted. But that was okay. I'd treat her like porcelain if I could just get back inside her.

"Don't bear down," I ordered her as I moved to the thick base of the toy and carefully pulled it out. She was a little dry and I winced as she released a sharp gasp—wouldn't be doing that again, but last night, I'd been in a different frame of mind, a dumbass mind, evidently.

In apology, I threw the toy onto the floor. It clunked and somehow switched itself on which had Aoife lifting a hand to cover her face as she burst out laughing. The giggles cascaded from her like a waterfall and they brought so much lightness to my heart, it was a wonder I didn't start flying.

Shaking my head at her as I maneuvered down the bed, I slipped between her thighs and stared at her gorgeous little cunt in the dappled sunlight.

I hadn't meant to spend the night. Had intended on dropping in and then being back at the office by six, but it was just past dawn and through the blinds, the sun sent glittery rays over her creamy form.

From this angle, her hair looked like an intense Douro red wine. And her pussy? Like a Malbec. Christ, I couldn't stop myself from spreading her lips, sucking on her clit, and flickering my tongue over the nubbin. I could taste my seed on her, but more than anything, it was just her. Intense, powerful, *mine*.

I let the stirrings of pleasure flow through her, building her up gently, letting it crest inside her before allowing her to climax. This was for her, not for me.

When she'd come, I pressed my face to her belly, hugging her as much as I could. Her hands came to my hair, and she began to gently stroke it. It felt so good that I stayed there.

"When did you buy the vibrator?"

"You mean the one that's still buzzing around like a demented bee?"

A soft chuckle escaped her. "Yeah."

"A week or so ago." And my goddamn brothers weren't letting me live it down.

"Been planning this, have you?" she teased.

"Well, I was trying not to use it. Then you called me, and we had phone sex, so I decided you needed punishing."

"That was the first time I'd done that."

My lips curved. "Good."

"Good?"

I tilted my head so I could stare up at her. "Those filthy words fall only for me, don't they?"

I watched her bite the inside of her cheek. "Yes, Finn."

God, I loved that breathy tone.

So fucking satisfied with her, I kissed her belly just above her hipbone. A thought crossed my mind, making me grimace.

"Back to the condoms soon. I want inside you more than I want my next breath, but Aoife, condoms suck," I complained with a sulky grimace.

But she tilted her head at me, and her hand cupped my jaw. "You don't mind?"

The morning of the wedding, she'd said she'd stop taking the pill but, in the aftermath, it wasn't like she'd stopped taking it on purpose. Contraceptive medication had taken a back step to all the stuff the doctors had pumped into her to take her pain away, to keep her infection-free, and to make her healthy.

She wasn't ready for kids, I knew that. And after being shot? Her body wasn't either.

I kissed her belly again. "I want this round with my child, angel, but not at a risk to you." My eyes drifted over the special bandages she wore on the incision site. They were made of this silver shit that prevented infection, but gradually, they were decreasing in size and thickness, and I took each graduation as a positive sign. "We'll have them when you're ready."

She grinned at me. "Lena was wrong."

"She often is," I remarked dryly, but I cocked a brow at her, willing to bite. "Why in this case?"

But Aoife didn't say, just looked smug. "I knew you'd be like this."

"Like what?" I asked, confused.

"Considerate."

Clarity hit. "Ah, she thought I'd want you barefoot and pregnant ASAP, hmm?"

I wasn't about to admit that before the shooting, yeah, I'd wanted that with every breath in my body.

"Yup. Thank you for proving her wrong."

Aoife had goals, and I didn't want to get in the way of them. But still... "We could always hire a nanny, you know?"

She tilted her head to the side. "Why?"

I laughed. "For any kids we have eventually."

Her chin tipped up. "I'll consider it."

Amused, because those three words said it would be a cold day in hell before someone else raised her kids, I carefully rolled off her and to the side.

I knew she thought she didn't like kids; also knew she wasn't particularly maternal—she was probably the only woman who complained about the kids being noisy here—but I figured she'd be totally different with her own. She was a nurturer. It would be a crime against nature for her not to have my children.

I was A-Okay with committing crimes, but that one?

Tut. Tut. No way. It would happen at some point, just not as soon as I'd hoped.

"I'm going to shower."

"Are you staying for breakfast?"

I shouldn't, but, fuck it. "Yeah."

"You are?" Excitement leaped in her eyes and I realized how goddamn bored she must be locked up in the damn compound.

Eleven weeks was a record, and I knew all the men were getting shit from their wives, but it wasn't like we had much of a choice.

Just because we thought we had the Colombians on the run didn't mean they weren't about to pull some kind of crazy-assed stunt.

They'd targeted our council on one of the councilor's goddamn wedding day. They were evidently fucking crazy and we weren't about to take any risks.

"I can shower now too." She sounded so proud that I had to smile.

"With Saran Wrap?"

"To be on the safe side." When she climbed off the bed, I noticed the ease in the movement where before, it had been a damn struggle just sitting up.

It was a fucking miracle that she hadn't been taken from me, and rather than kissing her fucking feet since it had happened, earning her forgiveness, I'd spent three-quarters of my time at my goddamn desk.

The room was smaller than I was used to. The bed only a double, with a dresser and a TV on the wall. That was it. It sure as hell wasn't comfortable, and I regretted she hadn't been able to heal at home.

Sadness welled inside me and I tugged her into my embrace. "My miracle," I whispered in her hair, not just for the light she brought to my life but for how she'd survived, how she was healing. Getting better.

She curved her arms around my waist and let me hold her.

I wondered if she knew how much she'd changed my life, how much my goals had veered off course because of her.

Pressing a kiss to the crown of her head, I sighed and just relished the moment, knowing that soon I'd have business to attend to. Something bitter after the intense sweetness of last night with her.

An hour later, I stepped out of the compound and tugged on my shades.

I felt Aoife's eyes on me from one of the living rooms on the ground floor, but I didn't turn back. If I did, I might not leave.

The hotel was surrounded by a fifteen feet high perimeter wall. We had men patrolling the area on a twenty-four hour rotation, and though the place looked and felt like a prison, it wasn't enough in my mind. The place's only saving grace was the safe room in the basement where, if the compound was under siege, the women could hide, and which Aoife could finally reach unassisted.

I hated the necessity of it. Some days, I wondered if we were in the US or some stinking third world country. But this was my life. I'd just never felt the stain until Aoife.

A grim look around the barren yard had me hoping that today's meeting would let the women return home.

Samuel was there, waiting for me with a cheerful grin as he shut the door once I'd climbed in. As we headed out of the industrial estate in Queens and toward Brighton Beach, I dug out my phone and checked through my messages.

There was nothing of any importance. Nothing out of the unusual, anyway.

Was I stressed?

Maybe.

I could be walking headfirst into an ambush, and I might never see my wife again, but I was aiming high and figured that the Russians wouldn't be so stupid as to take Aidan or me out.

We were brokering peace, sure, but we were also bringing a different deal to the table. The Mexican coke was cheaper, after all. Geography made up for one of those reasons, but the cartel we dealt with had tried and tested delivery routes, and I was under no illusion that they'd oiled the bureaucratic wheels too. They'd been at this shit for too long not to. The Colombians, on the other hand, had been easy to hold up. Of the gangs that operated under their colors, they were small fry by comparison.

If the Russians fucked us over, they were idiots.

The risk was still there though, and when I saw Aidan outside the warehouse where we'd met the Bratva before, I tipped my chin at him in greeting and he handed me a briefcase.

Of course, because I was nervous, he was grinning like a Cheshire Cat. We had twenty-five million on the line, but he was so goddamn close to rubbing his hands together in glee, it was a joke.

Still, this was his party. I'd just have to sit through it until the deed was done.

Our weapons were stored by the entrance, but we were greeted with grunts instead of walls of silence like before, as we were guided away from the office where we'd met last time, to a larger space.

I saw the man first.

He was naked and tied to a crucifix of all things.

Had they done that to piss Aidan off? Or to fire him up all the more? I wasn't sure, but Aidan could be so goddamn volatile, I wasn't happy at a potential trigger.

The room was stacked with a variety of different crates, something that put me on edge because only fuck knew what was hiding behind them in the shadows.

The Pakhan and his Obschak were here, looking relaxed, but there was no sign of his Sovietnik—the Bratva's money man. That figured. If Aidan Jr. wasn't laid up in the hospital, he'd be here for the fun and games, not me—as I was Aidan's equivalent of the Sovietnik.

I took their lack of tension as a good sign and dipped my chin at the Obschak when the Pakhan, Vasov, stepped forward to shake Aidan's hand.

"Your gift, as requested," Vasov demurred, and Aidan turned his head to the side.

"Trussed up like a Christmas ham," he murmured, the sound of satisfaction evident in his words. He reached up and tugged at his bottom lip as he turned from the Russian leader and toward the unconscious man on the crucifix.

The sight was outrageous. Even to me. And I'd seen and done some shit in my time.

Aidan either bypassed the crucifix's presence entirely or thought it was fitting. The worst criminals in Christ's time were crucified. That was how Aidan's mind worked. Fucking nutcase.

See, I was the kind of guy who liked shit to be over with. I'd shoot the cunt and that was that. Done. I wouldn't feel guilty because I didn't take a life easily.

Aidan was the sort who liked to play with his food before he indulged. Not that I could add cannibal to his list of oddities, but his nature was definitely reminiscent of a cat with a mouse.

He had the taste for torture, and that was why every Five Pointer knew to avoid the confessional on Thursdays at seven. That was Aidan's time for confession, and he could be there for hours.

Doyle had more dick than most gave him credit for if he had to listen, in graphic detail, to the shit Aidan pulled on the regular. Said shit was why anyone would be insane to get on his bad side.

I had reason to want this man to suffer. He was the guy who'd ordered the drive-by. He was the dumbfuck who'd nearly killed my wife. But if I wanted him to truly suffer, it was best to leave him to Aidan.

The body was so still, the guy might have already been dead. But Aidan disproved that theory by reaching out and shoving his thumb into a weeping wound. When the man jerked awake, a scream tearing from his lips, echoing around the warehouse, Aidan stepped back with a smile as he reached for a handkerchief to wipe off the blood.

"Vas a morir, hijo de puta," Aidan stated gruffly, telling the son of a bitch he was going to die in his own tongue to avoid confusion.

Like there could be any confusion about being fucking crucified.

Still, the Colombians had proven themselves to be idiots, so I guess Aidan felt like he needed to keep things nice and clear to avoid any misunderstanding.

The Colombian's top lip curled in a sneer, but he shot a look at the Russians, men who'd been his allies until recently, and when there was no support forthcoming—no change of heart—he let his head drop.

Pussy.

Aidan stepped back and headed toward the Russians. Then, motioning at me, he said, "As agreed, we fronted you the twenty-five million in exchange for your firepower."

I stepped to a nearby crate and pulled out the laptop from my briefcase. Opening the lid, I stared down at the GPS tracker of a van that was approaching our location. When I showed the Russians the footage, the Pakhan murmured, "Good."

It was a strange deal we'd come to terms with.

We were paying for their first year's shipments from the Mexicans, and we'd split the profits. It came at a high cost, but it had its own benefits. If they decided to screw us over within that year, well, their shipment wouldn't be heading their way, would it? And their profits with it. Not a bad deal on their part considering they'd be earning money with zero paid out, but it was about creating ties that bind, and what better way than through money and blood?

The Pakhan handed Aidan a contract and said, "My daughter is almost fifteen. She can marry in two years."

Aidan scowled. "That's fucking young."

Like the bastard could judge. He'd married Lena when she was seventeen.

Vasov shrugged. "With parental consent, she can marry whoever I choose."

I wasn't sure which of the brothers would be the sacrificial lamb, but it made sense for it to be Eoghan. He was the youngest, after all. At twenty-six, there was an eleven-year age gap. With Aidan Jr., it would be over twenty.

Eoghan wasn't going to like it, but the brothers knew the deal. One of them would be getting married, Aidan Sr. just hadn't outright commanded them.

Even as an outlaw, there was always a boss.

They might be the kings of their own particular kingdoms, but even they answered to Aidan.

With a flourish, Aidan signed the contract that bound the families together. I knew this aspect of the trade didn't irritate him one bit. To his mind, his sons should already be married, and Lena should have a gaggle of grandkids to fuss over.

A cell phone rang and the Obschak pulled it out from his jacket. As he answered the call, a smirk of satisfaction curved his lips. To the Pakhan, he said something in Russian, which had Vasov beaming at Aidan.

"The shipment is here. It is waiting at our gates."

Within five minutes, the laundry truck containing cocaine with a street value of five million dollars drove into the warehouse. We'd only paid out two and a half, and would be earning a million after the profits were split. The other twenty-two and a half million I'd had to sweat to secure in escrow, was just waiting to be transferred over month by month for each shipment.

As the driver jumped out, Vasov wandered over to him. Aidan, having rolled up the contract and shoved it into his jacket pocket, strolled over to the Colombian, bored now the business was dealt with, and wanting to play.

When a horde of Russians appeared from out of nowhere, I tried not to tense. I knew why they were here—to empty the truck—but the Bratva and the Five Points had never been friends. What had just happened was the start of a new era, and trust wouldn't grow overnight.

It would start from this moment, but it would only be truly cemented when Vasov's daughter gave birth to her first son, who would become Vasov's true heir.

I gritted my teeth when a scream ricocheted around the warehouse and avoided looking at the crucifix over in the corner. Accustomed to the noise, no one flinched, and business went on as Aidan's fun and games began.

46

———

AOIFE

EIGHT DAYS LATER

"MY GOD, you're skin and bones!"

In my dad's embrace, I'd admit to feeling like a little girl, which really was the ultimate of ironies considering I'd never known him as a child.

It was good to be in his arms though. Good to be near him again, even if the day of reckoning had come, it was worth it.

I hadn't seen him in over three months. Four lost visits because of my injury and then the lockdown, which, thank God, was finally over. Samuel and Billy were back as my driver and guard though, so some things hadn't changed.

I resented the lost time, even as I accepted what I couldn't change —it was my new philosophy. My PT had me doing yoga to try to improve my flexibility and I was actually getting into it in a big way.

"Hardly, Dad," I chided, staring up at him with a grin.

He frowned. "No, Aoife, you are."

"My appetite's been dicey."

"I can imagine." His jaw clenched, and rather than take the sofa opposite me, he grabbed my hands and urged me over to the one he usually took. His fingers clung to mine as he stared at me. "Why didn't you tell me about him?"

Wincing as he got straight down to business, I ducked my head. "What was I supposed to say to you, Dad?"

"How about 'I'm marrying a thug' for a start?"

I scowled at him. "Finn is not a thug."

"He's a Five Pointer, Aoife," Alan rasped. "What the hell else are they if not that? Granted, he's a rich thug, but—"

I jerked my hands free from his. "Finn makes me happy."

"He got you shot," was his immediate retort.

"I love him." If my tone was flat, it was because I knew that not even that would get around his parental lecture. "And I'm married to him. There's nothing you can do or say that will change that."

He stared at me, aghast. "How can you love him? You can't know him, not what he's capable of, at least."

I knew he was devoted. I knew he was tender when I needed him to be, and rough when those dark urges unfurled inside me. I knew he was neurotic enough to hover over me to make sure I took my meds and felt no shame in siccing Lena on me in his absence.

I knew my next words would be mean, but I didn't come here for a lecture. I knew he'd be angry and bewildered, and I'd expected such talk, but what surprised me was how his denigration of Finn pissed me off.

I knew, more than most, what Finn did. What he was capable of.

I'd heard some of his calls. I knew what he was mixed up in. I think, to some point, all the wives I'd met did. We just never spoke about it.

"Finn didn't leave my side in the hospital unless I was awake and had a visitor so he could go and shower."

Alan flinched, knowing the point I was making. "I'd have been there if I could."

It wasn't in me to be cruel, not willfully anyway, but I was making a point. Sometimes, they had to be hammered home.

I shot him a look. "You weren't though, were you? And Finn was. That's the kind of man he is."

My father ducked his head. I saw his nostrils flare as he gritted his teeth, probably trying to refrain from saying that Finn was the reason I was in the hospital in the first place, but he didn't.

Instead, he turned and reached over to the tea tray that was our custom. I didn't serve, as was our way, he did. The gentle flow of the hot liquid into the cup broke up the charged silence in the hotel room, and I accepted the cup when he doctored mine with two sugars.

"How are you healing up?" he rasped, making me wonder if he was changing the subject for good, or was going to try to blindside me.

He was a military man who had gone into politics upon retiring. He wasn't necessarily a diplomat by nature, but he knew how to fight a battle—even if it was one of words.

"I was lucky," I told him shortly. "I got hit in the abdomen, but the bullet actually ricocheted off the church wall, so it wasn't a direct hit. It ruptured my spleen. I'm not back to normal but I'm getting there."

And tonight, I'd be going home.

I'd told my father I could see him today, and he'd rearranged his schedule to meet me here. As soon as we were done, Samuel was taking me to the penthouse and finally, Finn and I would be together again without having eighty gossiping hens listening to everything we said.

"That *was* lucky," he grated.

It was something to do with reduced velocity, but whenever it was explained to me, the only thing I understood was I should be grateful to be spleenless and not missing half my stomach. Or, ya know, in a casket right now.

Alan reached over and grabbed the hand not holding my cup. His fingers tightened over mine. "You're in constant danger—you have to see that."

"And you're not?" I countered.

"Aoife, you have to see what position this puts me in, dammit!" he ground out, making my eyes widen.

"You don't want to meet with me anymore? Is that it?"

He had visions of being the next President. I guess having a secret daughter became even more of a detriment to his image when she had links to the Irish mob. I'd half expected it, but had hoped it wouldn't boil down to this.

"It's not about 'want,' dammit. You've put me in a very difficult situation."

"I'm sorry I fell in love, Alan."

He winced at my use of his first name. "Aoife, sweetheart, you have to understand—"

"Two years until the election, four years minimum in office," I calculated. "So, I'll see you here, in this room, in six years' time? Or is that ten if you get re-elected?" Coldness pooled in my stomach as he stared at me, and I could see the hurt in his eyes, knew he didn't want to do this, but I was well aware that he would.

He was a pragmatist. Just like I was.

It was funny how alike we really were. He'd had no say in my upbringing, hadn't helped forge me into the person standing here today, and yet, we shared several character traits. That was how I knew why his mind was running down this path, and it was how I figured he'd act, even if it meant cutting ties with someone he cared about.

He had goals, and he wouldn't break them for anyone.

Certainly not an illegitimate daughter.

I wasn't about to beg him to reconsider. Wasn't going to plead with him to keep me in his life. This was on him, not me. But that didn't mean it didn't hurt.

Because it did.

It stung like fuck.

"Why did you have to get involved with a man like O'Grady?"

He half-moaned the question, and it pissed me off more than I could say.

But I had no words. Well, not about Finn anyway.

"How long have you been planning this?"

He frowned at me. "What are you talking about?"

"How long have you been contemplating cutting ties with me?" I stared stoically into my tea. The muddy liquid swirled around the delicate china cup.

"Don't be like this, Aoife."

Somehow, that answered my question. I nodded and carefully climbed to my feet, and placed my tea on the table, untouched. I'd been managing to stand without much pain, but maybe my emotional pain was coming out in the physical, because I winced as I stood.

"I won't bother you again, Senator," I murmured.

Alan released a sigh and grabbed my hand. "Please, Aoife. I have to see this through."

"And I understand that." I pulled my hand from his. I wished I could vocalize what I was thinking, what I was feeling, but the words were stuck.

My marrying Finn had probably been the second catalyst. Becoming Senator had been his original goal, but when his popularity had soared, he'd admitted that he had people around him who were willing to back him all the way to the White House.

As the time approached for him to declare himself in the race, I guessed I was shortsighted in not seeing this coming.

My eyes pricked with tears as I went to walk over to the door, and then my aching heart about broke when he whispered, "Aoife, you won't say anything, will you?"

"When have I ever?" I snapped.

"Does O'Grady know? Did you tell him?"

"No. He asked me why my father wasn't coming to the wedding, and I said we'd argued," I lied. Finn had known about Alan being my father for months. "Alan, I didn't ruin your chance of being Senator, and I won't ruin your prospects now. Just be a better President than you are a father, okay?"

Before he could say another word, I stepped out into the hallway and allowed the tears to fall.

Whatever I'd anticipated today, it hadn't been that.

I'd been waiting so long to meet with him again. I'd missed him. We'd only been able to text infrequently, but now I wondered if that was intentional on his part. He'd been cutting ties all along. And I was so used to not being important to him that I just took it. Accepted the crumbs he gave me.

Fuck. I was pathetic.

Stepping into the lobby, I grabbed my sunglasses from my purse and put them on to hide my pink eyes from Billy. My guard was sitting on one of the sofas in the foyer, and the second he saw me, he was on his feet and heading my way. His hand tucked around my elbow because Finn had informed him I was still shaky on my feet, and I allowed him to guide me out of the boutique hotel for the final time.

Disappointed was an understatement.

Inside, I was devastated. But Alan had always had the potential to act this way. I should have realized that, the higher up the ladder he moved, the less time I'd have with him. I'd been naïve. Then again, this wasn't on me but him. He was my father, after all.

The sun was surprisingly warm as we walked outside. Samuel was waiting, and it was a relief because my legs *did* feel shaky.

I sank back into the comfortable confines of Finn's town car and tried not to feel like my heart had been broken when it most definitely had.

Ironically enough, it had nothing to do with the man my father said would hurt me. Finn hadn't yet, and I had a feeling he never would. But Alan? Nuh-uh. He definitely was not someone I needed in my life.

It was his loss.

Not mine.

But that didn't stop my eyes from welling with more tears as Sam drove Billy and I across town and back home.

47

———

FINN

"THE BASTARD." Then, having made that declaration, I ground out, "Why didn't you call me after it happened?"

She ducked her head dejectedly. "I didn't want to talk about it yet."

"I figured that by the fact you haven't talked about it," I said dryly as I took a seat beside her on the sofa in my office.

Having her back here was a luxury I wanted to become accustomed to. For three months, I'd had to live in and out of my office at work and the compound. For every one night I'd spent with her, I'd had to endure three nights alone.

I had not envisaged married life starting out so shittily, and I knew Aoife hadn't either. Who would?

A wedding reception in the ER department.

A honeymoon in ICU.

The first three months of married bliss separated.

And the gift from the father of the bride to the happy couple? A dear John letter. Well, he'd had the courtesy to reject her in person.

Talk about all heart.

Jesus Christ.

I curved my arm around her shoulders and tucked her close. Pressing my lips to her temple, I whispered, "Aoife, you're supposed to share these things with me. I knew there was something wrong, but you wouldn't say what."

She'd been tense and edgy all evening, totally unlike her regular happy self. Even with cabin fever and being stuck in the compound, she'd been chirpier than this. I'd expected her to be goddamn effervescent—relieved at being away from the other women and their kids, excited about being able to work on the bakery, delighted with the prospect of us being together again.

Instead, she'd been quiet. *Sad.* It had put me on edge until I'd texted Samuel and had asked about Aoife's day. When he'd told me she'd gone to the boutique hotel where she and her father met, I'd had my suspicions of what had occurred.

I knew he hadn't messaged her much over the past few months, and with my ties to organized crime? I'd just been hoping that he wouldn't let her down. But he had.

The cunt.

"It's his loss, sweetheart," I told her softly, sorrow filling me at how hurt she must be.

She turned her face into my side and curled her knees up, so she could hug them. Her next words weren't ones I anticipated, though. "Finn, I've been thinking."

"What about?"

"My mom and her friend."

I blinked at that. Which friend? "What about them?"

"I don't want any secrets from you, and I want to know if you'll do something for me."

"Anything." I frowned. "You know I don't want any secrets between us, either."

She blew out a breath, and her nerves rattled something inside me. "Now, let me just say, there was never an appropriate time to disclose this. And, honestly, knowing what I did helped me get over the rather abrupt start to our relationship. With that being said, the past is in the past, right?"

"I guess," I said, my tone uneasy.

"Do you remember someone named Ellie Donahue?"

I firmed my lips but when she stared up at me, her eyes beseeching, I gritted out, "Yeah. She was a friend of my mom."

"She had a daughter. Do you remember?"

I shook my head. "No. I don't remember much from back then." I'd blanked a lot out—whether that was my subconscious acting defensively or whether I'd done it purposely, I couldn't say. And Aidan had let me stop going to the kid shrink he'd sent me to when I'd threatened to run away again.

"Well, she did. Her name was Aoife Donahue." She ran a hand over her face. "Me. We changed our names to Keegan, her maiden name, after my stepfather died."

For a second, I felt curiously light-headed. "You knew my mother?"

She shot me a look, and I could see her features were tense with wariness. "I did."

"You knew me?"

"No. I was two when you..." She pressed her face to her knees. "Fiona spent half her time thinking you were dead, and the other half hoping you were lost and would be found again. Mom thought you were dead though, and she told me we just had to humor her."

A harsh laugh escaped me. "Deluded as ever. She didn't change at all." I felt tense and on edge, and for the first time since I'd known Aoife, I had no desire to sit close to her. "We both won the lottery when it came to parents, Aoife," I told her, my tone grim as I climbed to my feet.

Feeling her eyes on me, I didn't retreat far. Just as near as the closest drink tray. Pouring myself two fingers of whiskey, I tipped it back, then headed over to the window at the foot of the room.

Leaning against the wall as I stared out at a multi-million dollar view and saw bupkis, I asked, "Why did you bring this up?"

"Because I'm going to ask you to look into mom's death, and by doing that, you may see the truth anyway. I'd prefer you not to think I was lying to you."

That jerked me from the dank pit where I housed memories of my early childhood. "What? Why?"

Aoife reached up to rub her forehead, and it was then I saw how frail she looked. She'd lost a lot of weight over the last few months, but it didn't suit her. She was born to be ripe and curvy, and instead, she just looked emaciated. That, more than anything, tore my heart enough to return to her side.

Taking a seat on the coffee table in front of her, I prompted, "Aoife? What is it?"

She rolled her head on her knees. "I-I can't seem to stop thinking about it."

"About what?"

"The accident she was in."

"It was a car crash, wasn't it?"

She nodded.

It wasn't hard to read between the lines, not when, in my world, the worst-case scenario often came to pass. "You think your father had something to do with it?"

"I-I'd like to think not." She swallowed.

A harsh laugh escaped me. "Jesus, Aoife. You wouldn't be asking me to do this if you more than 'thought' it was a possibility."

"I'm probably just being paranoid," she admitted huskily, her shoulders rounding as she tucked her hands between her knees.

Aoife was the last woman to be taken on flights of fancy, and fuck, did I mention that I hated it when she avoided my eyes? "You think he was tying up loose ends?"

"Sounds like something from a Tom Clancy book, doesn't it?" she whispered, then she lifted a hand and rubbed her eyes. "Forget I mentioned it."

"But mention it you did." I reached for her hand and gripped it in my own. "Why didn't you mention you knew me before?"

It was an abrupt topic change, but I was curious.

"It truly never came up. Until you proposed, I only thought we were hooking up, and after..." She shrugged. "It didn't seem important."

"I think we need to have a discussion on what is and isn't important."

She cut me a look. "Same could be said for you, Finn. Why didn't you tell me how you'd met the O'Donnellys?"

"Because that's a very, very dark part of my past, Aoife."

"And that isn't a secret too?" she replied, deftly twisting things around.

Before we'd married, I'd promised myself that I'd be an open book for whatever questions she had for me. I'd just thought that particular side of my history would forever stay out of the equation.

"My father used to beat us."

Her hand came out to cup my knee. "I know. I saw her bruises when she came to visit Mom. I remember them, even being so young."

My lips twisted. "The old man had no shame. Didn't care if he marked you or not. Arrogant bastard." I swallowed. "He hurt me, Aoife. He hurt me badly. One day, I decided enough was enough and I ran away from home.

"I stayed on the streets for a while, but I was best friends with Aidan Jr. back then. Knew all his family. Brennan and Conor were close to me too. Declan and Eoghan were a bit too young, but the four of us ran around together.

"When I left home, pulled out of school, they looked for me. When they found me, they dragged me to their place and I just never left."

"He disappeared around about the same time as you did," she pointed out softly, and when she caught my eye, her question was, "Aidan Sr.?"

I dipped my chin in agreement. "Said a child molester deserved no other fate than being tossed in the Hudson by his brothers."

She swallowed and her hand clenched around my knee. "Finn?"

As I tilted my head to look at her, our gazes clashed and held for seemingly endless seconds. "Aoife?"

"I'd have pushed him in the river too."

I jerked back in surprise, and though it stunned the shit out of me, I laughed. Fuck, I did more than laugh. It bellowed out of me until my sides ached, my belly twinged, and my eyes watered. When I rubbed at my eyes though, I saw she was pouting.

"What's so funny?" she demanded.

"Just trying to imagine you pushing that bastard into the river."

"I'm stronger than I look." A wince crossed her features. "Well, I used to be. Don't forget I had to heft big bags of flour around."

Raising her hand to my lips, I kissed her knuckles. "Aidan did it so you and I don't have to wish we did." But I was touched. Touched because I hadn't expected her to say that.

I'd expected the usual, "I'm sorry, Finn." Or, worse still, for her to be revolted by the notion that I'd been abused and unable to look at me as anything other than a victim.

Instead, this woman, as was her way, stood firmly at my side. A source of strength, of support and succor.

I squeezed her small hand, loving how hers daintily fit in mine, and said, "I'll look into your mother's death."

"Thank you," she whispered on an exhalation.

"How did she pass?" I clucked my tongue. "I mean, you obviously think there was more to it than just a car accident."

"Hit and run." She cleared her throat. "They never found out who did it."

"It should be easy enough to get the traffic reports." I sighed. "I'm sorry, sweetheart. About her, about your dad, about every fucking thing."

She spread her hand out, unfurling it so she could place it on the side of my jaw. "Thank you for not shrugging off the notion as ridiculous, Finn."

I shrugged. "Crazier shit happens in politics all the time, Aoife."

"That's what concerns me."

Turning my head so I could press a kiss to the center of her palm, I closed my eyes and breathed in her scent.

It was good to be close to her again, close and in our own space. Our own home.

If the Senator had knocked off his ex, then that meant Aoife could be in danger, too. It didn't align with what I knew about the man. I'd always figured he was one of the good politicians—if any of them even existed.

For him to go all Darth Vader on Aoife was just beyond the realms of probability, but she needed closure and I wanted to give her everything she needed.

"Just give me two minutes, yeah?" I asked her, and she nodded, letting her hand slide down to her lap once more. "When was the accident, honey? Where?"

She told me the details and I picked up my phone, I scrolled through to my PA, Paul's number. I sent the text with the information and waited on his reply.

Paul: *On it.*

Me: *Need it ASAP.*

Paul: *Will call our rat at the department now.*

Me: *Thanks.*

Fully expecting to have the report in the morning, I switched my phone to 'Do Not Disturb' mode.

My wife needed me, and I, God help me, needed her.

48

―――――

AOIFE

IT HAD BEEN a shitty day after a row of shitty days, but it was wonderful to be home again, even better to be with Finn, and an absolute joy to be in my own kitchen.

While a great cook, Lena's meals seemed to consist of no other fare than Irish.

For three months, I'd eaten nothing but potato and lamb in a thousand different variations, and sweet Jesus, I was ready for something spicy. I might even have settled for dipping my finger into the wasabi paste in the fridge—that was how desperate I was for something that wasn't bland but hearty.

And for our first meal back at home? Reunited at last? Curry. Yum.

"Are you sure you're up to cooking?" Finn asked as he watched me from his spot at the counter.

I shrugged. "We're about to find out."

He grunted. "Let's not leave it until you're so tired, you're about to fall down."

That had me smirking down at the onion I was chopping. "It's only a quick curry. Fear not."

Another grunt was the only answer I got, but I felt his eyes on me, tracking my color, my state of being. It was like being X-rayed, except Finn's glance wasn't radioactive, just hot enough to make me melt.

Chopped onion, some garlic and ginger paste, a few other veggies then some spices I'd brought from my apartment when I'd moved in, alongside some garbanzo beans and natural yoghurt, and dinner was ready pretty quickly after the basmati rice was cooked.

Finn eyed it. "What is it?"

"It's a chana masala."

"A chana masala? Where's the beef?" He screwed up his nose.

I smirked at him. "You don't have to eat meat every day."

"I don't."

"I'm not talking about fish on a Friday, Finn."

He smirked back at me, appreciating my sass. "I thought garbanzo beans were for vegans."

"They're a good source of protein, but they're not exclusively in the vegetarian section at the store," I told him, rolling my eyes at him. "Jesus. You man, eat meat, huh? Neanderthal."

"Well, meat's good."

"So's this. Try it."

He wrinkled his nose and dipped his fork into the colorful curry. As he took a bite, I watched him carefully, then grinned when his shocked gaze caught mine.

"Good, isn't it?"

"Very," he stated, his surprise evident in his tone.

"I should probably be offended, but I'll hold off on the insult to my cooking skills."

A snicker escaped him, but he didn't deny he'd expected it to be shit. It wasn't the prettiest meal in the world, but it was damn tasty.

"I used to eat this a lot when I was in culinary school," I admitted as I took a bite and remembered that time with some nostalgia. "I was out in Poughkeepsie, doing my Associate's, and it was the first time I'd been away from home. I was scraping by, but I refused to live off ramen."

"How come you just got your Associate's?"

"I should have stayed on for my Bachelor's but..." I pulled a face.

"What?"

"It wasn't where my heart was."

"But you love cooking," he replied, frowning even as he hummed his pleasure after taking another bite of his meal.

"I do. But I like this. Cooking for us. When it's in a professional kitchen, it's totally different. I like the creative process but when you're working as a chef, you make like four new menus a year and the rest is just maintaining standards as you serve the same-old dishes." I shrugged. "It was boring."

"Didn't you feel like that at the tea room?"

I shook my head, wondering how in the same evening we'd gone from talk of conspiracies and murder, to my time at college.

Christ, being married to a man in the Irish Mob certainly changed your conversational skills.

"No. When I was there, there were staples that I had to make every day, but I could create different cakes, whatever was seasonal or whatever I just wanted to eat myself that day. If I wanted to experiment, I could. I loved that side of it.

"But when Mom died and I had to start balancing things between the front of house and the kitchen, that's when I didn't like it."

"Why didn't you sell when we first offered for it, Aoife?" he asked me quietly, tilting his head to the side in that way of his that made the light shine in his ice-blue eyes.

God, he was handsome.

And he was mine.

Before the shitty visit with my dad, my doctor had visited and I'd been given the all clear. Tonight we were going to reaffirm who belonged to who too.

I couldn't fucking wait.

My day might have started out shitty, but it sure as hell wouldn't be ending that way.

Clearing my throat, I admitted, "I wanted to, but I felt like I'd be letting Mom down. It was her dream, and if I'd sold out..." I winced. "After her accident, things were tough. She was in the ICU for over a week, and the bills were just insane. I had a lot of debt, and my dad found out and paid things off for me." That was one of the reasons why my mind had veered down a sharp curve this afternoon. Was it blood money? "When he did that, it gave me freedom in one sense, but it also tied me to the place even more. Every time Acuig offered to buy it, I dug my heels in. Especially because I knew what you were going to do."

"And what was that?" he inquired, brows high.

"Knock it down, build some fancy condo like the one we're eating in, make it so the locals can't live in the area but pumped up city boys can."

He winced. "It's about time the area was gentrified."

I snorted out a laugh. "Finn, pull someone else's leg."

"I'll pull something," he mock-threatened, making me grin at him when he winked.

"Anyway, I just... I don't know, grew stubborn. The unhappier I was, the more I missed Mom, and it just spiraled into my being really focused on not letting you guys get it. The rest, as they say, is history."

He reached for my hand, and as he'd started to do since the shooting, when he was careful not to jostle me too much, pressed a kiss to my knuckles.

"Hardly history. We're still very much in the present."

I breathed out with the joy that made me feel, and yeah, it was weird to feel joy when I remembered how miserable I'd been back then, and when I thought about the ragged shit that had been storming through my mind today.

He squeezed my fingers before tucking back into his meal. After a few moments, though, he asked, "You haven't mentioned Jenny in a while."

I shrugged. "She's been busy."

"Too busy to call?" He cocked a brow at that. "It wasn't like she could visit."

"No. Not too busy to call," I defended. "We talk every few days. She works hard, Finn. She has two full time jobs."

"She does?"

"Yeah. She's trying to put herself through night school."

"To do what?"

"She wants to be a CPA," I told him, curious about what his response would be to that.

He hummed. "Good money to be had there."

I'd almost expected him to say something sexist. That was the response Jenny usually received when she shared her course details with a guy. They either said she was too pretty to be an accountant—because, yeah, no accountants were hot, right? Men were such dicks sometimes—or she got shit for not being able to go out during the evenings. Like her time belonged to them.

Jenny's life revolved around work, school, and her man *du jour*. When work had included me, that meant we'd spent a lot of time together. I wasn't offended that she was too busy to catch up every day.

She had shit she needed to do, and when I got my bakery up and running and could offer her a job again, things would roll back around.

"Jenny hopes so. She doesn't want to stay in the city."

He cocked a brow. "No? Why not?"

"She just doesn't." That was her secret to share, not mine. "Not everyone wants to stay in the city forever."

He quirked a brow. "Since when?"

I grinned at him. "You want to be born, live, and buried here, huh? Well, there goes my dream of being a snowbird."

"Sam wants to go to Florida when he retires."

"*When?*"

"We don't all live and die on the streets, Aoife," he chided.

"If you die on the streets, I'll make you rue the day you were born. I don't intend on losing you now that I've found you."

He grinned at me, looking far too pleased with himself as he purred, "Good to know."

I rolled my eyes at him. "And they say romance is dead."

49

———

FINN

I HAD TO ADMIT, I was curious.

Curious as fuck.

I didn't even mind that even though Aoife got herself all worked up, and me too, she'd done too much today and ended up conking out on me when we migrated our make out session from the living room to the bedroom.

Sure, my dick was aching, but she needed the rest and I needed answers, otherwise I'd get no sleep tonight.

That was how curious I was.

I didn't even mind the hard-on from hell.

When I grabbed my phone and scrolled through the messages and emails for the tenth time this hour, I saw one from an 'Unknown Sender.' Satisfied once more with Paul's efficiency, I opened it and I scanned the contents of the file.

A standard hit and run. A witness had seen the green Jaguar drive off, but she hadn't caught the registration. She *had* noticed that the driver was a woman.

When I saw the picture of Aoife's mom, my breath caught in my chest because it was like looking at Aoife twenty years down the line.

Christ.

They were like twins. The same rich hair and the skin that was almost opalescent with its glorious sheen.

As I looked at a 'future' Aoife, I marveled at how fucking lucky I was, even as I felt sad that I'd never get to meet Michelle Keegan or Ellie Donahue as I'd known her. Seeing her was believing though.

I remembered her vaguely. My mom and her had hung out a lot, but I'd spent most of my time with Aidan Jr., avoiding not only my father, but her too.

My mother's best friend, and my wife's mom, had been crossing the street one day and out of the blue, a car hit her. She'd never have foreseen that, would never have been able to plan her life around it. Wouldn't have said goodbye to her loved ones, to Aoife. Just boom. In an instant, everything had changed.

The witness claimed Michelle had been on her phone before she'd stepped out onto the road, and according to the report, Michelle didn't wake up after the accident so the officers in charge of the investigation couldn't question her to confirm that. She'd hit her head on the way down, and no matter what the doctors did, she never got back up again.

Still, there was something about the report that hit me as odd. Jaguars weren't a common car in the States. Sure, they were here and there, but they were a luxury import, and most people who wanted that kind of status vehicle opted for Mercs or BMWs.

Then there was the color. Something the witness had stated was close to, if not darker than, evergreen.

And I distinctly remember Magdalena's forest green Jag being in the shop back in January.

It was a leap, but, fuck, so was the suggestion that the Senator was behind his ex-girlfriend's death in an attempt to keep his dirty secrets a secret.

I rubbed my temple, disliking how when I carried on reading through the report, my mind kept leapfrogging to Lena. It wasn't like Jags were that uncommon, but that paint job had been custom. It was so dark, it was close to black with green highlights, and from the woman's description, 'an odd black color. In the light, it turned green,' it just hit me on the raw. Then, there was a sketch of the woman behind the wheel.

Those things were usually shit. The illustrations all over the place and hardly accurate, but when I saw the bright red hair that curled into a topknot, as well as traced the similarity in the drawing's features to the woman I knew, I'd admit to feeling faintly antsy.

Aidan had bought her that Jag as a wedding anniversary gift. He'd had it brought over from England as a surprise, and I remember him rolling his eyes and cursing women drivers when she'd had to take it into the shop a couple of months later.

I stared at the ceiling for only God knew how long, wondering what the fuck I was going to do.

I'd gone from being happy that my wife was back home, to learning that she somehow knew my mother, revealing my past, and then her asking me to investigate her mom's death. But that was the thing with these kinds of accidents; they were *accidental*. There was no motive to be found. No reasoning.

Just a split second's inattention and bang. Someone was dead, you were shitting yourself, and rather than hang around and face the music, you tore off out of there.

It was flight or fight at its most basic level.

Though I hoped I was barking up the wrong tree, even though the weird color of the car and that fucking sketch said otherwise, I was left stuck in the middle of a horrendous crossroads.

I stayed close to Aoife as I went through my options. One arm curved around her, one arm behind my head as I wondered what kind of Pandora's box we'd just opened.

If Aoife's mother *had* been knocked down by Magdalena, there was no way I'd be able to hand her over to the police simply by way of who she was. No way I'd even want to hand her over, though. Lena was like my mother, for Christ's sake. I didn't want her to go to jail, but if she'd run down Michelle...

My throat felt thick with concern because even if I betrayed Aidan by reporting Lena, he'd get her off the charge. He'd pay anything to keep her safe. I knew that like I knew my face in the mirror.

Plus, there was every chance that this case had been classified as 'unsolved' for a reason. Aidan might have already paid off the cops in charge of the investigation.

I was, I realized by three AM, fucked.

And not in the way I'd envisaged on my first night home with my wife after a few months.

At four, I gave up on trying to sleep and headed for the gym. After a ten-mile run, I'd killed some time and Aoife was out for the count. I'd intended on waking up with her, on sharing a leisurely breakfast to celebrate her all-clear and our first morning back home, before I got started on work, but I had to know if this leap was illogical—and God, I hoped it was.

Showering and dressing as quickly and as quietly as I could, I sneaked out and saw that it was five-thirty. By the time I made it to Aidan's house, it would be nearer six and he was usually awake by then. He didn't sleep well, and considering he was a sick bastard, it was only right that he couldn't. Not even confession could cleanse a man's soul totally.

I drove myself to the house and felt sick with each mile I passed. Even as I hoped it wasn't Lena, my gut said it was, but discovering the truth would provide no closure to Aoife. It would only bring extra heartache in the long run.

Magdalena, if guilty, had about as much of a shot of seeing the inside of a jail cell as Jesus himself.

Which put me in the shittiest Catch 22 in the universe.

If Aoife discovered the truth, she'd rightfully loathe Lena. Resentment would grow, and it would tear at our relationship because there was no justice for her mother's passing.

In my shoes, if someone hurt Lena, I'd tear down this fucking city to get justice for her, and even then, some bastard moldering away in a jail cell wouldn't be enough.

Which meant keeping all of this from her. *If,* and I prayed it was an if, Lena was involved in this cluster fuck.

Even as I pulled up outside the guardhouse at the head of their drive, I wondered if I should reverse back out, carry on driving, and not stop to answer questions. If I knew the truth, then I was obliged to tell Aoife, but if I did, that could be the end of us. And for what?

Lena would never go to jail, and I could make Aoife happy. Hell, no 'could' about it. I'd make it my life's mission, but that still wasn't enough to avenge her mom's too-early death.

That part of my nature that needed answers though, demanded I smile at Jimmy, one of the runners on guard, and head down the driveway.

I'd always had this need to *know.* Everything and anything. As a kid, when I'd discovered my father had disappeared, I'd gone to Aidan and asked if he was involved. Knowledge brought comfort. It was addictive, and it made me obsessive.

I remembered when, all those years ago, he'd looked at me in that calm way of his, his eyes as gentle as a still lake, and I'd known the answer before he even murmured, "A bastard like that is too vile to walk the same streets as you, Finn. Now, you never have to worry about seeing him again."

Love was something that was slow to grow, slower to form. But I'd loved Aidan from that moment on. As a father, a friend, a confidant, and a mentor. He'd done what nobody else could for me. He'd taken out the threat, had made it so I didn't have to worry about that part of my past.

I wanted to give that relief to Aoife. I wanted to—

As I pulled up outside the house, I pressed my forehead to the wheel.

When the door opened to my left, I jerked in surprise and saw Aidan climbing into the passenger seat.

"You're here early."

His statement had me slouching in my seat. "I needed to speak with Lena."

He cleared his throat. "Got a phone call last night. From a cop on our payroll."

My heart plummeted. "He told you I requested the information."

"Yeah. He did."

"Lena killed Aoife's mother," I whispered, feeling the bottom of my stomach fall at the confirmation of what I'd already figured out.

I wasn't a man who found it hard to accept life could be shit sometimes, but this? I was fucking floored.

"You remember last November when I went to the doctors?"

Frowning, I demanded, "What does one have to do with the other?"

Aidan only went to the doctor when it was serious. The guy could be pissing blood and he'd avoid the clinic. We'd all teased him when he'd made an appointment though, so, yeah, I remembered.

He held up a hand. "Bear with me, son."

I scowled at him but turned back to face the windshield. "Go on, then."

"It was just a physical, but they found something." He cleared his throat. "A lump. I had to have it biopsied. While I was waiting for the results, I—" His hand went to his knee and his fingers clenched as he squeezed down hard. "I've not been a good man, Finn. You and I both know that. I try, but there's the Devil inside me and no amount of confession will cleanse me."

I wanted to call bullshit, wanted to tell him to own up to the crap he did because he *enjoyed* it, but I didn't. This wasn't related to my reason for being here, not as far as I was concerned, so I had no justification for tearing him a new one.

"I was certain it was cancer. I was like a bear with a sore paw as I waited on the results. Each day, time ticked down until I felt sure I was approaching the end, and then I just had to do it. I had to confess to Lena."

"Confess, what?" I frowned at him, saw he was staring at his hands.

"When we got married, I wasn't faithful to her." He pursed his lips. "Have been since, though. That time she hit me with the rolling pin and pressed charges? I knew that she was it for me. She had fire and she was what I needed. Strong and sure, confident.

"I'd married her when she was too young. Naturally, she was nervous, and things weren't great between us for a while. Then, after Aidan was born, things changed. *I* changed. I loved him, and I loved her for giving him to me." He released a breath. "I stopped seeing my bit on the side, but it was too late. When I told her I wasn't coming back she admitted she was pregnant and that she'd need help." Another breath gusted from him. "What could I do? I had a wife and a son of my own. It wasn't like I could help, so I married her off to one of my boys. A good man, I thought. Nothing special, nothing flashy. Just a hard worker. I gave her money to help out every couple of months, made sure he got some of the safer jobs, and I forgot about her."

"What the hell are you talking about, Aidan? I'm here about Lena and Aoife's mother."

"Bear with me, Finn," he repeated, grinding out the words. "Just listen to me, would you? I'm trying to explain."

I gritted my teeth and nodded. "Okay, but get on with it. You're just putting shit off."

"No. I'm not." He ran a hand through his already mussed hair. "I wasn't particularly interested in the kid. Didn't know if it was a boy or a girl, just got on with my life." He sucked down a sharp breath. "Remember that picture of me and Uncle Frank in the hall? Where we're at Coney Island?"

"The one where you're eating hotdogs?"

"Yeah. That one. Well, one day, my son turns up at home with a friend and I thought my eyes were about to fall out. It was like seeing Frank walk through the goddamn door. I almost had a heart attack, especially when Lena told me who the kid's parents were."

My mouth grew dry. "Who were they?"

"His mother was Fiona O'Grady."

Chills shot down my spine. "You're making that up."

"No. I'm not. And to be honest, Finn, I'm glad I'm not. I didn't want to know you when you were born, but when Aidan brought you home, I was happy.

"I had no rights to you. I'd signed those away, and I'd left you to be Gerry's son. But seeing you every weekend? Watching you and Aidan play soccer? It was enough. Then you came to me after he'd done that—" His mouth pursed. "—to you, and I took pleasure in cutting that bastard to shreds.

"Motherfucker thought he could do that to my son?" He shook his head. "Part of me was proud that you knew you could come to me, tell me that stuff, but another part wanted to scream. I could have brought you here. Told Lena she had no say in it. To raise you like you were hers. But I didn't, and when Lena found out what I'd done to Gerry, she asked me why and she was happy when she knew what he'd done to you.

"I never told her you were mine, but when I said you should stay with us, she agreed like I knew she would. We all loved you. You fit in with us so well, and why wouldn't you? You're ours."

A tremor shot through my body. My arms and legs were shaking like I had palsy, and I didn't know what the hell was going on with my head—I wanted to scream, but equally, I wanted to get the fuck out of the car to get away from this. From Aidan. From the story.

I'd come here expecting one thing and had gotten something else.

Aidan seemed to know I couldn't speak because he continued, "So, I confessed to Lena last November. I thought for sure I was dying, and I told her that I had a child with another woman. I confessed. I needed her forgiveness, and I don't blame her, really, but she never gave it to me. She said she would if I told her who the woman was and who the child was, but I couldn't. I couldn't even tell her when or who. Not without her learning you were mine, and I was frightened. All these years she'd loved you, and I didn't want that to change. For either of your sakes.

"So, I refused to tell her, and I didn't think about the vindictive little bitch she can be. When I didn't tell her, she went to the Old Wives' Club," he whispered, referencing the women who'd outlived their Five Points' husbands. "She asked them to help, asked who I'd been seeing back then. But I'd been discreet. No one knew. There was just conjecture. Some fucking bitch told her that it was this woman over on Canal Street. Michelle Donahue. Who just happened to have a daughter."

"So, what?" I asked heavily. "She killed Michelle because someone said you'd had an affair with her?"

"No," Aidan rasped. "She swears it was an accident and from what her guard says, it actually was."

"What do you mean?"

"When Lena knocked her over, Michelle stepped out onto the street without looking where she was going."

"That's no excuse," I snapped.

"No, but it *was* an accident. When Michael called to tell me Lena had knocked someone over and I got to her, she thought she'd hit a man." He shrugged. "Not a justification, just proof to me that she hadn't targeted Michelle as a grudge."

"A big fucking coincidence," I snarled.

"No. She said she'd started going to the tea room every day. Watched Michelle as much as she could."

"Aoife would have recognized her, surely."

"No. She said she tried to see the kid she thought was my daughter, but she never managed to. And I believe her because when you brought Aoife home, she wouldn't have been so nice, would she? Plus Aoife would have mentioned the connection." He grunted. "Lena was obsessed, Finn. Michael says she was too. Confirmed that she was there every day, parked up, watching for hours on end. It ate her up inside.

"There's no wonder she got into an accident. She was irate, erratic, and she stopped taking her meds."

"That's no excuse."

"No, it isn't," Aidan admitted. "But you know they keep her leveled out."

Because I knew it wasn't bullshit, I had to nod. A few years back, Aidan had been stabbed by a rival and Lena had witnessed it. Her shrink said she had a kind of PTSD and gave her meds.

If she hadn't being taking them, then she'd definitely been living on the edge.

I couldn't even think about the revelation that I was his son. My focus was just on Aoife, and what I was going to do, what I was going to tell her.

"What am I supposed to do, Aidan?" I rasped.

"There's nothing you can do," he replied quietly. "I'll never let Lena go to jail. You know that. Let the sin rest on my shoulders."

My throat felt like it was closing in on itself. "She has a right to know."

"Knowing will do her no good, son."

Aidan had always called me that, and now I knew why. I wanted to flinch, wanted to reject the label, but it was too ingrained for him to say it, and too ingrained for me to hear it.

"I'd want to know."

"You're different. Even if Gerry was a cunt, you were raised with the Five Points, and when you moved here, it was natural for you to come in with us.

"One of the proudest days of my life was having you and Aidan come to my office and tell me you were both ready to join up." I heard the emotion in his words but ignored it. I couldn't handle it. It was just beyond me. "Other people are raised to think of law and justice. But we don't live that way."

I swallowed. "We have our own code. If someone had knocked over your mother, you'd have sliced their throat whether it was an accident or not."

"Yeah, but I'm a Five Points man. So are you. Aoife isn't. Aoife would be happy with her mother's killer going to jail, but... Lena isn't going anywhere, Finn. I need her. You need her. We all do."

I did need her. I wasn't going to lie. She was my mother. Fiona had let Gerry do things to me, and though Aoife seemed to think Fiona had loved me, I knew that was wrong. Why had she let him do that shit to me if she loved me? But Lena? Lena would do anything for me. She'd lie on oath to give me an alibi, and had Aidan given her the choice, she'd have helped turn Gerry into fish food. She'd kill for me, *die* for me.

I loved her.

She loved me.

But Christ, what I felt for Aoife...? It consumed me. I couldn't live without it. Without *her*.

"How am I supposed to live with this?" I almost wheezed out the question.

"It's my fault, Finn. I thought admitting the truth would be enough, and when she wanted the details, I was taken aback. I locked down. Didn't tell her shit. Those gossiping old hags gave her the wrong information, and Michelle and Aoife are paying the price for what are *my* sins." He sat forward and the leather seat creaked as he bowed his shoulders, letting his head fall like the weight was too much for him to bear. "Aoife will never get justice for her mother, Finn. You telling her will only wreck what you have."

He was right.

He was only saying shit I'd already thought of.

"What made you look?"

"Aoife asked to see if someone she knew was behind the hit and run."

"Who did she think it was?" Aidan asked, his brow furling in confusion.

I bit off, "Her father."

"He died. Years back."

"No. He was her stepfather." I purposely kept my answer blunt, because I wasn't about to tell him that Senator Alan Davidson was Aoife's biological dad. The man was a bastard, but I didn't intend on burning that bridge. Who knew what might happen a few years down the line? Having a President in my pocket might come in handy.

Aidan ran a hand over his chin. "Why would her father have had her mother killed?"

"It's a long story, and it's irrelevant because he didn't, did he? Michelle's murderer is in the fucking house next to us."

"It was an accident."

Only four words but I heard the warning in them. It was like the low snarl of a lion threatening me with violence if I didn't back off.

I clenched my jaw and turned my head away.

"Does she know I'm your son now?"

"Yes."

That had me whipping around to face him. "What? You told her?"

"After the accident. It was eating her up inside." He shrugged. "It gave her closure."

"She never— I don't remember her changing toward me."

Aidan ran a hand over his face. "Said she was glad. That it was just confirmation of what she'd already known—that you're ours."

My eyes burned. They fucking stung as tears pricked them.

All these years, all these fucking years, I'd been a part of this family in more ways than I'd even recognized.

"Do the boys know?"

He rasped, "No."

For some reason, that made me feel better.

"Do you want them to know?"

I rubbed my chin, regretting not having shaved as the stubble brushed my palm.

"Not yet."

"I understand." He released a sigh. "They're going to be mad at me, and I can't blame them. I cheated on their mother, but it brought us you, so they'll forgive me soon."

"Have you really not cheated on her since?"

He snorted. "She'd have cut my balls off with a table knife, Finn. What do you think?"

That was true. Lena was as bloodthirsty as the rest of us.

"I think I'm confused and..." I shot him a look. "I'm going back home. I'm taking the rest of the week off and I'm spending time with my wife."

Aidan shrugged. "Whatever you need. Was going to suggest it to be honest. You two didn't even get a honeymoon, and these past few months, you and Conor have been running around like flies on shit getting us the financing for the shipments. Both of you deserve a break."

Without waiting, he opened the door. The chill from the early morning sank in and he swiveled on his seat.

Before he could get out, I asked, "You never said. The lump..."

His shoulders stiffened then relaxed. "Benign."

A relieved breath escaped me, and the joke slipped past my lips before I could contain it, "Only the good die young."

As he climbed out of the car, he leaned over to grin at me. "I'll still be around when I'm a hundred." He straightened then, after shutting the door, tapped the roof, and I immediately started the engine and drove back up to the gatehouse.

Whatever I'd expected this morning, it hadn't been any of that.

I'd come here wanting to find answers, and instead, I had more questions than I could ever have anticipated.

50

———

AOIFE

THE BED DIPPED and though it disturbed my sleep, I wasn't about to complain. Not when Finn carefully wrapped himself around me.

When his hand came to rest over my lower belly, he murmured, "I know you're awake."

There was amusement in his voice, and my mouth curved of its own volition. "Not awake," I mumbled sleepily.

"No? You're doing a good impression of it, then."

When he pressed his lips to my shoulder, I released a deep breath and snuggled back into him. "You smell good." Jesus, he really did. Like sex and sin all wrapped together with chocolate—was there a better package?

"I try," he joked, then he fell quiet. Not plunging us into an awkward silence, just into a relaxed one. Where neither of us had to speak. Neither of us had to utter a word. We were in a little bubble, a cocoon of our making, and we were content.

His thumb stroked the seam where my hip met my thigh. It wasn't a sensual touch, just one that sought a connection between us. I loved it. It was intimate and raw, and though he could happily have turned things sexy, he didn't. He just lay there, his eyes closed—I knew because his eyelashes weren't fluttering against my skin.

He lay there so quietly and for so long, I started to realize it was *overly* long.

Finn was usually restless. Incapable of resting or taking a breather. But these past few months had been different. He'd done something to take out the threat from the Colombians, and this was our first morning together in our place, our bed, where he could touch me without me screaming if he accidentally jostled me.

This was, pretty much, our first morning as man and wife in our marriage bed. But he was still. Silent.

"I learned something this morning."

His tone was curiously blank, enough to raise several questions in my head. Was it about my mom?

Clearing my throat as my heartbeat sped up, I asked, "How early was this morning because from the light over the city, it's barely nine now."

"I couldn't sleep," he admitted. "Got an email and had to deal with it straight away."

"What was it?"

He cleared his throat. "Nothing serious but..."

"Finn? What is it?" I asked when he fell silent again.

He burrowed his face into my hair and I stiffened, and then immediately released any tension in my body lest he pull away because I could feel his tears.

Finn was crying?

I tried to move, wanted to face him, but he wouldn't let me. Why wouldn't he?

I wanted to look in his eyes, tell him that whatever it was, every-thing would be okay, but...

"Is this to do with what you told me last night?"

It made sense that talking about his childhood would raise some issues. He'd had a few nightmares in the past, nothing major, though. I'm sure I did too. They were just dreams, after all, except he'd lived a nightmare. Had discussing it brought things back to him?

Shit. I should have left things alone. I should never have told him about my knowing Fiona. I already knew what he'd endured at the hands of his father, thanks to Lena. My selfishness in needing to understand the depths my own father would sink to in order to preserve his reputation had raked Finn's past over the coals.

I'd disturbed something that should never have been mentioned.

Guilt filled me, then he whispered, "Gerry O'Grady wasn't my father."

Whatever I'd expected him to say, it wasn't that.

"*What?*"

"He was..." He sucked down a ragged breath. "I spoke with Aidan. He says Gerry wasn't my biological dad."

"And how the hell would he know?" I snapped, wondering what kind of game the old man was playing.

"*He's* my dad, Aoife. He admitted it this morning."

"Huh?" That was literally all I was capable of saying.

Three letters.

One syllable.

Huh.

It summed up the swirling cocktail of bewilderment, confusion, and the outright 'wtf?' that was this moment.

"H-He had a girlfriend when he was newly married."

After what Lena had warned me about, that all men cheated, that didn't come as a surprise. She'd been bitter enough for me to know that Aidan had fucked someone behind her back.

"That was a shitty thing for him to do," I whispered, dropping my hand to cup his. He'd stopped stroking my belly, was just holding me in place so I couldn't turn around and look at him.

"Yeah. He said things changed after Aidan was born."

Uncertain what to say to that, I stroked his fingers, trying to comfort him, even knowing that there was nothing I could do to ease this burden.

What the hell had made them talk about this all these years later? Hell's bells.

We'd gone to bed at ten! What had happened in the past eleven hours—hours where most people were asleep—to make them raise this topic of conversation?

"Why did he tell you now?"

Finn tensed, then he blew out a breath. "I was handling something else and it came up."

'Came up.' I had to stop myself from snorting out a laugh.

Things like this didn't just come up for no good reason.

Aidan had kept the truth of Finn's paternity for almost forty years, for God's sake. It would take something major for him to reveal all now.

But, I guessed, the why didn't matter. Not in the scheme of things.

Finn had been told the truth, and I was left wondering if he'd have been better off being kept in the dark.

Was it freeing to know Aidan was his father? That the man who'd abused him had no blood tie to him? That news couldn't make anything better, but... Having never been abused myself, thank God, I wasn't sure what was going through Finn's head.

All I knew was that I'd seen Finn's reaction to my raising the topic of his mother. He'd shut down and he'd turned cold on me, when Finn had always been anything *but* cold where I was concerned.

"Finn?"

He tensed. "Yeah?"

The words were on the tip of my tongue. I wanted to tell him I loved him. Wanted them to act as a ward. Those three words would protect him, let him know that he was always safe with me.

But also, I didn't want his brain to connect the dots.

I didn't want him to associate my telling him I loved him when he was loaded down with thoughts of his cruel history.

I'd told him once, when I'd thought I was dying. A second time when I'd known guilt was eating him up. The third time I shared those words with him wouldn't be during a tragic moment in his life.

"I'm here. I always will be."

A shudder seemed to wrack through him. "T-Thank you, Aoife."

I wished I could kiss him, but instead, I whispered, "I was born to be by your side, Finn O'Gr—"

A laugh barked from him, interrupting my words. "Finn O'Donnelly. Who'd have thought it?"

The amusement was cruel and aimed inwardly, and I blamed myself for striking out on my first go.

Fuck!

"You're my Finn," I told him. "Nothing more, nothing less."

Was I surprised when he made no whisper of a reply? Yes. But I was glad too, especially when I heard his breathing even out. He'd drifted off to sleep, I realized.

Had my words brought him some peace?

I could only hope they had, even as I wondered what I could do to make this better.

Was just being there enough?

I wasn't sure.

51

—————

FINN

WAS I up or was I down? That was pretty much the mind fuck I had going on inside my head.

On the one hand, the man I'd loved like a father actually *was* my father.

On the other, the bastard I'd believed had sired me, who'd abused me and beaten me, actually hadn't.

A cause for celebration?

Maybe if the ties that went with it weren't bound to Lena's perfidy—the death of Aoife's mother.

Even if the news was worthy of celebration, it was forever linked with the accident that had robbed Michelle Keegan of her life.

I had no doubt it was an accident.

Aidan had believed it too. And this wasn't some spiritual bypass. He'd asked Lena's guard, who'd concurred. There was no reason to lie when there were no concerns about the consequences.

And there was the rub.

The lack of consequence.

Lena had to pay. Didn't she?

There had to be some reparation made, something done to…

Nothing would bring Aoife's mother back. Nothing. Not even Lena rotting in a jail cell for a few years on vehicular manslaughter. A notion that had my heart pounding in my chest as it was the last place I'd want any of the women in my life to be. If Aoife came to me as Lena had to Aidan, I'd have done everything in my power to cover this shit up.

This was my world.

We ignored society's inbuilt checks and balances as we chose to go to church and confess our sins rather than be punished for them. Going to speak with the Father was far easier than serving prison time, after all.

Had Lena confessed? Had Father Doyle, when he'd said how sad it was that Aoife's mother couldn't be there for her on our wedding day, heard the truth spill from Lena's lips?

I knew he had.

It was how Aidan worked.

He'd have dragged her there, whatever the time. He'd have made her confess and then—and I could see it in my mind's eye—he'd have hugged her afterward, given her a kiss to make it all better, and after she'd worked her penance, they could go on as if nothing had happened.

But something had.

Someone had died.

I knew I was being a hypocrite. What was it? Okay for people to die so long as they weren't related to family close to me?

I'd watched Aidan slaughter the Colombian this week. Had seen so many deaths, it was a wonder the spirits didn't visit me in my dreams. But this one mattered more than any of them, and yeah, it did make me a hypocrite. I knew that.

Aidan wouldn't change. Lena wouldn't change. My brothers wouldn't change, but I could.

I couldn't go far. My life was tied to the O'Donnellys. I loved them. They had been my family before I'd known about the tie of blood. They were all I knew, and all I wanted to know. I wanted to have kids of my own, and even though Aidan and Lena were fucking psychos, I needed them to know my children.

In their heart of hearts, when it came down to family, to those two nutcases, it was all that mattered.

Family and love were what they got out of bed in the morning for.

Retiring from the Five Points was only optional when you had a few years left on the clock. Samuel would be nearing seventy when Aidan let him go, and if he lived to be a hundred, good for him, but even then, Aidan kept his pensioners tied to the mob. He helped them out every Christmas, and their pensions were tied to my hedge fund.

So, not only was I too young to retire, I was an integral part of the gang. I was their money. Conor too, but it was more on me. My father wasn't going to let me go anywhere. Even in these circumstances.

Looking back, I should have realized Aidan would never have let anyone outside the family handle something so vital to the running of our organization. I'd just been floored by his trust in me. But now? It made sense.

I knew more about the Five Points than even Aidan Jr. did, and he was the next in line for Aidan Sr.'s throne.

As the money man, everything went through me at some point. I knew when a drug shipment was slipping through the Canadian border, and I also knew if Eoghan was on a job in the goddamn Congo.

That Aidan had managed to hide a payout to the cops from me, told me he'd gone off the books on this one. I couldn't blame him. In his shoes, I'd have done the exact same for Aoife.

Yeah. I would.

That was the sum of it.

What Aidan had done? I'd do too. So I couldn't bitch and moan about this situation, but what I could do, was change.

And Aidan would listen because this was my leverage.

Pressing a kiss to the back of Aoife's head, I changed gears. Aoife was worth going to war, but it wasn't worth me losing my life in the battle.

I'd get reparations for her. She just wouldn't know it.

In my arms, she twisted over, and I marveled at how much stronger she was. By the end of the first week at home, I fully expected her to be eating better and to have some more motility. Just watching her move in my arms, not seeing the flash of pain cross her features as she wandered around the place, was the best gift I could have asked for.

She huddled into me, pressing her lips to my pec, and I was grateful I was naked when I felt the nudge of her knee against the seam of my closed thighs.

"You slept well," she murmured, the words soft, her breath brushing against my chest with a delicate caress.

"I needed it," I admitted.

She stroked her hand down my side. "How come you don't have any tattoos?"

Whatever I expected her to say, she never said it. Damn woman.

I choked out a laugh—was she disappointed I didn't have any ink? "How come *you* don't have any tattoos?"

She smirked. "I'm not in the mafia. I thought all Five Points had tats."

I'd always been the rebel. "I didn't want one."

"And Aidan let you get away with that?" she questioned, pulling back to stare at me, her surprise evident.

"I managed to wheedle out of it every time it became an issue."

"I thought it was a peer pressure thing."

"It is. Now, I wonder if he let me get away with it because of what I am to him. He said one of his proudest moments was when Aidan and I asked to ascend to the ranks."

Her nose wrinkled. "He makes it sound like you're doing something honorable."

After where my thoughts had been, I couldn't be offended. Two days ago, I would have been though. Crazy, wasn't it? How the world could turn on its axis after one conversation. Her mother's death, the shooting, then news of my true heritage... all of it twined so firmly into a knot of Gordian-like proportions.

A breath gusted from my lips. "To him, it is honorable. We're at war in his mind."

"Explain," she insisted, staring up at me with bright green eyes that trapped me in her snare.

"Aidan's third generation Five Points, Aoife. He was raised with the stories of how we were oppressed by the British. His great-grand-daddy fled to the States to evade arrest." I shrugged. "Every year we send a tithe to the IRA."

A shocked gasp escaped her. "No way."

"Yes way." I found it amusing that I'd shocked her. "Aidan wants to be rich, don't get me wrong. He likes what wealth affords him, and he wants Lena to be comfortable, his sons and grandsons too. But there's a cause he's fighting. Always has been, always will be."

"God, that's..."

When she couldn't seem to find the words, I dipped my head and pressed a kiss to her mouth. "It doesn't have to make sense to you, but it does to him.

"We didn't have a choice about becoming Five Pointers, Aoife. Not in the grand scheme of things. Aidan Jr. especially. But we wanted to. That's the difference."

"Did all the brothers?"

"No. Eoghan wanted to join the army. Aidan let him, but mostly because Aidan Jr. and I worked on him. Said Uncle Sam could train him up for us."

She chuckled at that. "Capitalism at its finest."

I grinned. "I guess. He's one of the best marksmen around though, so it was worth it. His services command a high price," I informed her, well aware of the pride in my voice.

At that, she fell silent. "Why are you telling me this, Finn?"

Seemed she'd figured out my walls were down, and my gates were wide open.

Good.

She'd need to know sooner or later.

"I'm telling you because you're my wife. I trust you."

Her hand clutched mine. "What's changed?"

"Me."

"Because of your dad?"

Aidan was my dad. Fuck, that was never going to be an easy fact to process.

I closed my eyes, shielding them from her, wanting to avoid her perspicacity. "Maybe."

She hesitated a second. "Finn?"

"Yeah."

"If you ever need to talk, I'm here."

She couldn't know what those words meant, and though I wanted her to be my confessor, for her to know all my sins and the secrets I would forever keep from her, I couldn't. I wouldn't. Her soul was clean. Pure. I wouldn't tarnish her. She was the one clean thing in my world, and I wasn't going to sully that.

I'd spend the rest of my life making this woman happy.

That was my new goal.

"Thank you, baby," I rasped, opening my eyes again as I brushed a hand over her belly. "How are you feeling today?"

"Better. No pain."

Now that had my body stirring. Especially when I thought about how we'd made out on the sofa last night like goddamn teenagers. "Really?"

Her cheeks pinkened. "Really."

I bowed my head so I could press a gentle kiss to her lips, and then, when she parted them, I struck. My teeth bit down on the fleshy bottom one and she released a moan that had been created by the devil itself to tempt me to sin.

My cock instantly hardened.

The breathy gasp that entwined itself around the moan was enough to make me want to be inside her.

But not yet. Not yet.

I rolled us so she was on her back. I needed to know she wasn't bullshitting me because she was horny.

The naughty girl had tried to con me several times when she sure as hell hadn't been ready for more, so I knew I needed to keep an eye on her.

However, there was no flash of pain. No darkening of her eyes as she absorbed the strain on her wound.

She truly was feeling better.

Even as relief flooded me, the need to care for her warred with the need to let myself go.

I wasn't a good man.

I never would be.

And with her?

She tempted all the bad inside me. Even though I wanted her pure and untouched, I wanted to tempt her to fall with me and me alone.

On her back, her tits began jiggling as her breathing sped up. She knew what was happening, knew it and wanted it. Her hands clutched at my shoulders, the nails digging into my skin, and she parted her legs, spreading them so I could settle between them. Skin to skin.

We both groaned as my cock settled against her wet cunt, and when she rocked her hips up, rubbing herself against me, I let her. I allowed the move because I knew it would drive her insane before it worked its magic on me.

After a handful of seconds, her nails dug harder into the balls of my shoulders, and a frustrated groan escaped her parted lips as she ground out, "Move! Please. Please."

I smirked at her, keeping my weight off her by propping my fists on either side of her head.

"That's what I like to hear. My girl begging."

Her pupils dilated before sliding into tiny pinpricks. She was a junkie for my cock, and I didn't want her any other way.

I could almost see the creature inside her respond to my words, the beast of her own that needed to be possessed by me. That wanted to be spanked and fucked, used and tormented by me and only me.

She was mine as I was hers.

Forever.

An idea bloomed to life at the back of my mind, but that was for another time. Another place.

"Do you want my cock, Aoife?"

"Yes," she whispered.

"How badly do you want it?"

"Like I need my next breath."

I tutted. "And what if I took that next breath?" I asked slyly, reaching down to cup her throat. Gently, I squeezed, placing pressure there to restrict the flow of air.

Her eyes widened a second before she tilted her head back, giving herself to me, giving me everything she had to give. *God, this woman.*

I wasn't rough with her, not with this. Within my hand, I held her very life, and she didn't shy away from it. Didn't tense or tighten up.

Shifting on the bed, taking some of my weight on my knees, I reached for one of her hands and motioned so she could cup my throat too.

"The air I breathe," I whispered as those slender fingers gripped me, "belongs to you."

Her lips trembled. "The air I breathe belongs to you," she repeated, her thumb stroking my Adam's apple as she said the words.

We stayed like that for endless seconds, and then I gently gripped her hand and tugged it away, even as I moved my own.

"I want that on your skin," I whispered. "On mine too."

"A tattoo?" Her head tilted to the side. "Thought you didn't like them."

I dipped my chin. "I don't. But fair's fair. Everyone will know you're mine then."

She grinned at me. "And they'll know you're mine too. Although,

I think they might know that after the wedding. I don't think it could have been made more public that Finn O'Grady is taken now."

My lips curved. "I was taken the moment I walked into that tea room and I laid eyes on you."

Her breath stuttered. "Really?"

"Truly." Christ, it had happened before then. That first time I'd seen her picture I'd been a goner.

Shit, Conor wasn't wrong. I *was* whipped.

Bending down, I pressed my weight onto her. Covering her for the first time in far too long.

She hadn't lied—she *was* feeling better. Stronger. I could see it on her face, read it in her expression. Her focus was one hundred percent on me. Nothing else.

The doctors had said three to six months, and though I hadn't been there as often as I knew I should, I'd have made changes if I thought she was down or depressed. The doctors told me that made all the difference.

Rubbing my chin along hers, I whispered in her ear, "I'm going to fuck you, Aoife."

A whimper escaped her.

"Do you want that?"

"Y-Yes."

I lifted my hips as I reached for my cock. Settling it at the entrance to her body, I began the long slide home with our eyes united.

Pain flashed now as I penetrated her. She was fucking tight again. Jesus Christ, how had that happened? Sliding into her the first time had been close to painful with how tight she was, but it was like she'd never been mine at all.

Fuck that.

This pussy had better remember who it belonged to.

I rocked my hips, not thrusting like I wanted to, just taking it slow and easy for her first time, and then, when I was back where I belonged, my pelvis flush with hers, I settled there.

And after I grabbed both of her hands and pinned them overhead, I didn't move.

Her pussy clamped down on me, the muscles fluttering in excitable panic as they tried to accommodate the invader. It felt like fucking bliss and by the time some of the tension escaped her, she was panting. Her face was pink, her eyes desperate as she stared at me.

"Need me to move, angel?"

"Please."

"Tell me."

"Please, Finn. Move."

I grinned at her. "You thought that was going to work?"

An exasperated scream escaped her as she bucked her hips, trying to get me to move, but the only thing it earned was a sharp slap on the thigh.

"Tell me why you deserve my cock."

She stilled, and her eyes turned inward as she tried to figure out what I wanted from her.

"I've been a good girl," she whispered, head tilting so she could lick her tongue against my bicep, which was close to her mouth thanks to how I was holding her arms above her head.

"Have you?" I thought back to the phone sex, the ways she'd tried to entice me even though she wasn't ready. "I think you've been bad."

"No!" she cried, her outrage evident—mostly, I knew, because she was aware that I'd punish her for that in a way which would leave her desperate and pleading with me.

"Yes. You teased me, Aoife. You know what happens to dirty little cockteasers?"

She licked her lips. "They get punished?"

"They get no rewards."

A moan escaped her. "No, Finn, please, I need you."

"I'm glad to hear it," I whispered, brushing a kiss over her mouth. When she tried to tug me into a deeper one, I slapped her thigh again, making her yelp. "Who's in charge here, Aoife?"

"Y-You."

"Remember that."

And with that, I began to fuck her.

Not the rough thrusts I wanted, because I was still scared about her wound—three months of being careful was a hard habit to break —but deep and slow, movements I knew she'd enjoy.

As the tight clasp of her pussy worked its magic on me, it was like being reborn as I made love to my wife.

I felt the way my body responded to hers, to her submission, and I felt like I was flying. After the last twenty hours, I needed this feeling. I needed her to help me forget the shit that was on my shoulders. I needed her to remind me that she was mine and I was hers. No matter who or what tried to get in our way. The past, the present, none of it mattered as we raced toward the future together.

Inevitably, my pace sped up, but I did nothing to drag her to orgasm. Her eyes pleaded with me, but I ignored the whispers and whimpers, intent on one thing and one thing alone—getting off.

When I was seconds away from coming, my balls tightening in response, I pulled free from her and reared up. An outraged shriek escaped her, but I motioned to my dick, which was equally as outraged at being left out in the cold. But fuck, I hadn't suited up and I didn't want her getting pregnant so soon—pulling out wasn't exactly a tried and tested method, but it was all I was capable of at the moment.

"Suck me off," I commanded. "Swallow every drop."

She scampered onto her knees, once again showing me how much better she was, and the second her lips slid around my cock, I couldn't hold it. I grabbed her head, took fistfuls of her hair, and began to fuck her face. As I came, spurting long ropes of seed down her throat, she swallowed it all. Accepted every drop.

Even as I roared out my release, I dragged her close. I felt her gag slightly, her hands fluttered around my thighs as she tried to deal with how much cock I was giving her, but she relaxed almost seconds later

—good thing, I really didn't care for being puked on, but I'd needed her to take everything I had to give.

When I let go of her, she fell back against the bed. Panting with exertion and need.

I stared at her, looking at the bright pink folds of her cunt, the way her limbs were shaking, her eyes desperate for everything I'd denied her, and I smiled.

She saw it and moaned. "No, Finn, no."

"Yes, Aoife, yes," I mocked, loving that she couldn't predict my next move. She genuinely feared I'd leave her hanging, and on any other day, I might have. But not today. Not after I'd been so long without her.

"Please," she pleaded, even as I dropped down and positioned my face at her cunt.

"Oh, I'll please you all right." And I did. I licked her clit, slurped and sucked at her. I pulled all the moves that would get her off, and each and every time, I never let her drop over the edge of the cliff I'd taken her to.

Two times.

Three.

I edged her.

And even knowing she hated me for it, it was worth it.

Her pussy was a wet, sloppy mess that I'd made for myself. She was dripping with juices. Her body was a writhing mass of desperation, one that I'd forged.

As she panted her way down from the height I'd taken her to, I studied her throbbing slit.

Sliding a finger in had her squeaking, then releasing a moan. She'd been empty as I tasted her, always empty. Until she was begging me for more. The sudden fullness had her crying out, and I looked up, saw the wide desperation in her eyes.

"Do you feel sorry for teasing me?" I asked her quietly.

A moan was all she was capable of.

I pressed a final kiss to her clit, then reared up onto my knees. I wanted to fuck her from behind, see that juicy ass of hers bounce, but I didn't. Not until I could be as rough with her as my mood required.

Instead, I slid into her once more, then I bridged our fingers and gave her what she needed.

Every downward thrust, I ground down against her clit. Every upward thrust, I almost pulled out until she was gasping with her emptiness.

It took five thrusts for her to explode, and when she did, she took me with her and I barely remembered to jack off onto her belly instead of where I wanted to come. Even so, it was an ecstasy that only she had ever let me feel, an ecstasy I couldn't live without.

52

———

AOIFE

"YOU'RE NOT READY."

Finn frowned down at his paper. But the scowl was odd. More mulish than confused. "Ready for what?" he questioned, when I knew he had to know what I was talking about.

"Church."

His lips firmed. "We're not going today. Remember? I told you, I have some time off."

"I don't think Aidan thought that included church," I teased, but from the glower on his face, the sulky pout, I knew something else was going on.

He'd been weird ever since Aidan had admitted to being his father. Weirder since he'd informed me that my mother's accident had nothing to do with my dad.

It hadn't been a long conversation. He'd just told me that it was unlikely my dad had anything to do with the hit and run. He'd shown me a witness statement that confirmed mom had stepped into traffic, her eyes on her cellphone.

And, truth be told, while I was sad at *why* mom had died, I'd been relieved. I didn't want to like Alan at the moment, but I didn't want to think he was a murderer either.

These past few days, Finn had been inside me more times than I could count, and to be frank, I needed to go to church because my pussy was aching like it had been working out on a jungle gym.

I knew if I asked him to stop, he'd stop, but Christ, denying him was denying myself.

I was a glutton.

Crazy, but true.

Not for cake, but for Finn and that wonderful cock of his. I wonder if the Father would choke if I admitted that at confession. Gluttony was a sin, after all. But how did I phrase it in terms that wouldn't cause the elderly priest to have a heart attack?

Bless me, Father, for I have sinned, I can't stop getting to know my husband in the Biblical sense.

Ugh, just thinking that made me want to take a running leap at him, but I was so-oo-oo-re. If Finn knew how sore, he'd be mad at me, so I figured it was better to go to church. Maybe sitting on a pew would ice my nether regions—I needed some help from somewhere. *Divine intervention, literally,* I thought on an inner snort.

"Come on," I chivvied him.

He shook his head. "We're not going to church," he repeated.

"Since when?"

"Since I decided the other day. I'm never going again."

Taken aback, I frowned at him. "Isn't that like one of the Five Points' ten commandments? You have to go twice a week?"

"Yeah, but things have changed."

"I don't see how," I countered. "Aidan makes all his sons go, he isn't going to make an exception for you. Especially as this is the first Sunday where all the women can go to church after lockdown."

Peering up from the newspaper he was reading, he murmured, "Want to go out to breakfast?"

Bewildered, because the last thing *I* wanted was to go to church, and here I was fighting the cause, I stacked my hands on my hips. "What on earth's going on, Finn?"

He gusted out a sigh. "There are going to be some changes."

"Where?" My confusion was evident. "I know you love him, Finn, but Aidan's a crazy motherfucker. The last change I need is him lopping off your head. I like it where it is, thank you very much."

"He won't argue."

He seemed so sure that I sighed—stubborn man. "If he beats the crap out of you, I'm not going to help you ice the bruises."

He released a mocking gasp. "How mean of you."

"I was born mean," I jibed, grinning at him when he cocked a knowing brow at me.

If anyone was mean in this relationship, it was him, and I was okay with that. Except when he refused to let me come, then I wished him all the way to hell. Of course, I wished he'd come back again because only Finn could make everything inside me detonate. And I needed, quite desperately, to detonate on a regular basis.

Twenty-five years of being a good girl was totally overrated. I was going to be bad from now until the day I died.

"Where are we going then?"

"*Where?*" he asked absentmindedly.

I huffed. "You just said we're going for breakfast. But where?"

"Oh, yeah. I did." He rubbed his chin. "I'll go get dressed."

"We can't eat too much," I called at his back as, with rangy strides, he retreated to the bedroom. Watching him go, I ogled that fine ass of his.

"Why not?" he inquired, turning back and catching me mid-ogle.

"Because there's no way I can eat Lena's Sunday lunch and breakfast too. I mean, I just can't." American portions were big. Irish-American? Gargantuan.

He pursed his lips but nodded. And while I'd expected some kind of teasing riposte for having been caught staring at his ass, he didn't make one. Which immediately told me something was off.

In five minutes, he was back, dressed in a pair of jeans that made that ass of his even fucking finer—how was that possible? He also wore a stone-colored Ralph Lauren sweater with a white tee peeking at the neck. On his wrist, he'd changed watches. From a sleek metal one that was studded with diamonds, to a chunky Rolex that had more of a sporty vibe. He wore dark loafers and a woolen coat in gray.

He looked expensive.

Even in casual wear, he always managed to look dressier than me, and considering my wardrobe was still pathetic, I figured that made sense. His closet was full, and the matching 'her' closet was pretty much like a ghost town.

Still, I felt pretty in the maroon dress I wore. Jenny had encouraged me to buy it when I was on a diet a while back and being shot had one advantage—I'd lost a bit of weight. I had no doubt I'd put it back on soon enough. Finn never seemed to mind my curves, and I wasn't about to deny myself food after twelve weeks of little to no appetite thanks to pain and the meds that had fucked with my stomach.

The skirt swung around my calves but settled neatly against my hips, and the V-neck, while not too deep, revealed a sexy amount of cleavage. The color made it appropriate for church, because if it had been black, I knew Finn would have bent me over the couch and fucked me for that and how much boob I was revealing—black was his dynamite. And in this color, my cleavage wasn't too showy.

Saying that, maroon or black, I'd figured I'd get a comment on how I looked. He always complimented me, and I wasn't offended that he hadn't today. Instead, I was just aware that something was going on inside that beautiful head of his.

When I gathered my coat and purse, he grabbed a firm hold of my hand as we walked into the elevator.

"I'm going to fuck you in here one day," he informed me in a tone that could have indicated it was raining outside for its lack of inflection.

Because of that though, it seemed to make me burn all the hotter. Fuck!

My fingers clamped down on his. "I would be amenable to that."

In the reflection, I watched his lips curve. "I wasn't asking."

Ohh. He was such a shit!

Grumbling under my breath as he chuckled, the doors opened, and he guided me out toward another section of the garage.

Today was a day for firsts, it seemed.

I'd thought there was just the town car. The one that Samuel drove. Apparently not.

He led me to a sleek Maserati that was very low to the ground and had one of those dashes that belonged in a James Bond movie.

He opened the door for me, helped me in like the gentleman he wasn't as getting all the way down there by myself was still a little too much for me, then he rounded the car and got in beside me.

As we drove toward the Upper East Side, I wondered where the hell we were going.

The only time I went here was for my meetings with my dad, and as that wasn't going to happen any time ever, I was surprised he was taking me here.

For all his ways, I knew Finn appreciated simple home cooking. I'd expected us to head for some Mom and Pop joint, but he pulled up outside the Four Seasons of all places.

Giving the keys to the valet who rushed to attend him, I'd opened the door by the time he approached my side of the car.

"I wanted to do that," he grumbled, growling at me.

I laughed. "I think I can manage opening my door, but getting out is another matter entirely."

After he helped me out, I tucked my arm through his as he guided me into the opulent reception area.

Five minutes later, I was seated behind an enormous window that let in the most glorious light. All around me, there were trees too. Huge ones. With large twisting and undulating tree trunks that the waiter informed me were African Acacias.

It was like being outside and inside at the same time.

Finn suggested I try the lemon ricotta pancakes and because that sounded like a good idea, I promptly ordered that.

When I compared the size of my portion of pancakes to theirs, I felt my cheeks burn. Christ, did I overfeed Finn? He hadn't said anything, and he wasn't exactly the shy or reserved type. They were delicious though, and they almost melted in my damn mouth. A part of me was wondering if I could replicate them at home when Finn's phone buzzed.

It was an odd breakfast, mostly because we were eating like we were at home. He'd brought the newspaper with him and I was reading a book on the kindle app on my cell. We weren't talking even though there wasn't any tension between us. It was just nice. Being able to sit together without having to fill the silence. I found I appreciated that more now as a married woman than I ever had when I was single.

So, when his phone buzzed and, shock-horror, he ignored it, I wondered what the hell was going on between him and Aidan.

It didn't take a mind reader to figure out it was his dad, and said dad was wondering why the fuck his son wasn't at church.

Finn switched it off though, and carried on eating and reading like nothing had happened.

He cut me a look when I stared at him in question. For a second, his ice-blue eyes clashed with mine until they softened, turning a warm turquoise as he smiled at me.

"You liked the pancakes?"

I nodded.

"Thought you would." He pinched his bottom lip and rubbed it slightly. "Nice to see you've got your sweet tooth back. I need that ass nice and round when I fuck it."

Of course, he waited to tell me that when I was drinking some of my coffee. Barely refraining from spitting that out, my eyes watered as I forced myself to swallow.

When he shot me a smug look, I raised my hand, and as if I was checking the corners of my mouth for crumbs, I flicked at the edges with my middle finger. Then, after I'd flipped him the bird, I sucked the digit into my mouth, enjoying the tension that invaded his features at the move.

"If you don't want to spend the morning on your knees in one of the suites, little girl, then don't fight fire with fire."

I batted my lashes at him. "Sounds like a promise."

"One your pussy can't keep. What have I told you about teasing me?" he growled, and my eyes widened—he wouldn't do that again. Would he?

Jesus Christ, who was I kidding?

He would.

He'd torment me with ease.

When my cheeks burned, he released a low chuckle and the paper flexed as he returned to whatever had him so engrossed. Of course, now that he'd said that, my brain darted from left to right and wouldn't allow me to focus on my book at all.

By the time we'd paid the check, I was almost wishing he *would* take me to a suite. I'd never stayed in a five-star hotel like this, and it would definitely be a treat. Even if the rooms were as fancy as my own home, it would still be cool.

The car appeared like magic, and I wondered how often Finn ate here for them to know when to bring the car around.

"Did you come here a lot before?"

He shot a look at me as he drove through the traffic. It was Sunday, early too, so it was less manic but still busy. "Before we were married? Yeah. I'll still eat here a lot for business though."

That had me humming under my breath. Finn's business appeared to hover on the brink of legitimacy as far as I could see. I knew he had an office, I just didn't know where it was.

Thinking that was bizarre since I was his wife, and a wife should know where her damn husband worked, I asked him, and he told me with an ease that made me wonder why I'd figured it would be a state secret.

When we made it back to my old neighborhood, I realized I'd

spent half the journey turned toward him because it came as a shock to pull up outside the old salon I was intending on turning into a bakery. As that was on my side of the street and I'd been peppering him with questions, I just didn't notice until we stopped.

"What are we doing here?"

He shrugged. "Thought you'd be chomping at the bit to get this place ready."

When he put it like that...

Of course, he had to surprise me. He had the keys in his left hand, my fingers in his right as we walked toward the salon.

It had a wide shopfront, with large windows that made the place bright and airy, and I could easily envisage a few tables here and there for the people who didn't want to eat breakfast on the go, even if I wanted them to be my principal market.

When he opened the door and we stepped inside, he handed me the keys. "Yours to do with as you will," he murmured, and I released a squeak and rushed at him. He laughed and hugged me tight, dropping a kiss on the curve of my neck before he let me go.

As I stared around, I realized he'd had most of the stuff from the tea room brought here too. A lot of the baking equipment would be used, but I intended on selling the ultra-feminine tables and chairs, as well as the paintings and other tchotchkes Mom had filled the tea room with.

I was more of a minimalist kind of girl, whereas she was maximalist.

"What are you going to do here?" he asked, leaning back against the wall to watch me as I plotted and planned in my head.

I'd drawn sketches of how I wanted the place to be, but seeing it in the flesh brought them all to life.

"Principally breakfast. Which fits considering you get up really early," I told him absently.

"What do you mean?" he asked.

"Well, you're always up at three, aren't you? And I know you only stay in bed sometimes for me. So, when you go to work, you can drop me off here."

He blinked. "You'd be okay with that?"

I had no intention of opening a business and never seeing my husband—I'd work around his hours because he had a shit ton more responsibility than me, and ya know, a customer wasn't going to blow my head off if I didn't serve scones one morning whereas his head was on the line every goddamn day.

Not that I needed to think that way.

Him working for the Five Points was nerve-racking enough as it was without me making it worse.

"Of course," I told him. "I figure the mornings will be the busiest." My thumb rubbed my chin. "But we'll be serving fresh bread until two. After that, I'm going to stop baking and the store will stay open, but I'll go home unless there's a rush."

"That's still a ten-hour day, Aoife, if you work from four until two. That's too much."

I shrugged. "Not to start with. If things take off like I hope they will, I'll hire more staff."

"Hire whatever you need. Most businesses make a loss their first year, but that doesn't matter for us."

"No way. I'm doing this on my own! You've helped me enough by taking the rent out of the equation, so the rest is on me."

I refused to be a drain on him. I wanted to be a productive member of our household, and when/if we had kids, I wanted them to see that their mom was more than just something to prop up their father's arm.

And even as that thought raced through me, I gaped at him.

"What is it?" he demanded, striding away from the wall he'd been leaning against to reach me. "Are you hurting?"

I batted at his hands when he tried to hug me—honestly, the man's hugs were delicious but they weren't exactly a dose of Ibuprofen. "Finn," I whispered, my revelation still powering through me.

"What is it?"

"I just thought of myself as a mother."

He snickered. "Seriously?"

"Yeah. Seriously. I don't even like kids," I wailed. "Jesus." I slapped my forehead with the back of my hand. "This is your fault."

"You want my babies," he teased, grabbing my hips and rubbing our lower halves together.

Shit. I did.

The thought staggered me.

On the few occasions my mom had raised the topic of grandkids, I'd always rolled my eyes at her. And when he'd mentioned my not taking the pill? Yeah, that had been like a knock to the head.

But I could easily see it now. Even in this place. I could imagine having a nursery or something so the baby could be with me while I worked, and I could nurse—

Fuck. This was getting freaky now.

"Hey," Finn murmured, reaching up to cup my chin. "It's okay. No rush, remember?"

I nodded at him, but it was the way I'd gone from never wanting kids, to Magdalena pissing me off by trying to pressure me into having them, and then onto *this*.

He rubbed my bottom lip with his thumb, and urged, "Go on. You were telling me your plans."

I released a sharp breath. "I figure if I'm home by two, then I have a little time to myself. I can make us dinner and then when you're home, we can do... whatever."

If my cheeks burned at that, well, that was because it was still pretty difficult for me to go from New York's oldest virgin to talking about getting hot and heavy with my husband on the regular. Well, outside of the bedroom. In it, my skills with dirty talk were improving.

He laughed, not upset by the notion. "I like the idea of... whatever."

"Hoped you might," I mumbled, then staring at him, I asked, "Is it really over, Finn?"

"What? With the Colombians?" He cocked a brow at me when I nodded. "You think I'd have let you off the compound if it wasn't? We have a new ally. That will keep us safe until the next round of bullshit."

It was that 'next round of BS' that concerned me.

He seemed to sense that though, and whispered, "Aidan's scared of no one, and he respects the Russians, Aoife. There's a reason for that. We'll be tied to them soon enough."

"Tied? How?"

"One of the brothers is marrying one of their daughters."

I gaped at him. He'd mentioned this before but now? It sounded concrete. "It's like something from an episode of Downton Abbey."

He shrugged. "That's the way it works. I'm surprised he hasn't done it sooner. With five boys?" He whistled. "He's in a prime position to secure our streets for a long time."

Even though I was still astonished by the prospect of an arranged marriage, I had to snicker. "An Italian bride, a Latina, a Russian... That's only three."

"Maybe the last two can marry for love like I did," he told me, and my heart seemed to freeze in my chest as he uttered those words, so goddamn nonchalantly I wanted to scream.

"That is not the way you tell your wife you love her," I argued, but because of his admission, I felt so empowered that my chest swelled with confidence.

This man loved me.

This crazy, impossible, *dangerous* man loved me.

"Isn't it?" he argued, grinning down at me. "How about this?" He dipped his head and kissed me. Long, and slow, and wet. Ugh. So fucking perfectly wet. Then, he raked my bottom lip and I waited in breathless anticipation for the bite.

When it came, I moaned low, the sound reverberating through my chest.

The pain was exquisite, and the sensation of his teeth marks as I wiped the sore area with my tongue was even more delicious.

"I love you, Aoife," he whispered, his ice-blue eyes not so icy.

"I love you, Finn," I told him, my heart in my own emerald orbs as we looked at one another as though the sun rose and set on no one else but us.

His smile wasn't cocky like I'd anticipated, instead, he whispered, "I'll spend the rest of my life proving how much I love you, Aoife."

The statement was odd, but Finn was capable of odder.

I reached up and around to hug him. "Thank you for telling me."

He snickered as he cupped the back of my head and held me close. "You're welcome."

53

FINN

THE LAST THING I wanted was to drive to the O'Donnellys'
home.

Not only was I in for a round of shit from Aidan about not
attending church, but it would be the first time I faced Lena knowing
what she did.

After just having heard yet again that my wife loved me, *loved me*
after I'd gotten her shot, almost kidnapped and... well, she didn't
know about the shit with her mom, but *that* too? I felt like the luckiest
man alive to have her heart.

I'd never break it.

Never.

It was a vow most men thought they made when they married
their wives, and it was a vow they broke too. Even Aidan had by
fucking around and siring me. But I wouldn't.

I couldn't.

Aoife had lost so much because of me, and I wanted to give her
the world in return. Not because of a debt, not out of loyalty, but
because she was mine, goddammit, and what the fuck was I working
so hard for if it wasn't to give her the sun, moon, and stars?

What I wanted was to go home and fuck her. But she was sore. She hadn't told me—which I was still pissed about, but it would take time for her to be comfortable with talking about certain things with me. I knew that and accepted it. Didn't mean it didn't piss me off, though.

I'd been on her like white on rice these past few days. Fucking her to forget my thoughts, fucking her because I loved being inside her, and then fucking her because the pleasure she gave me was unique. Honestly, she wasn't the only one suffering. My back was killing me after I'd fucked her on the console table beside the front door. Jesus. Was I getting too old for acrobatic sex with my woman?

I had to hide a snicker—not goddamn likely.

But a rest would do us both good, and though going home for the first Sunday lunch since lockdown wasn't what I wished we were doing, it was what I was going to do.

Tear off the Band-Aid in one go. Shit like that.

As Jimmy opened the gate for me, tipping his chin at Aoife in a respectful greeting, we drove down the manicured driveway that led to the grand house.

It was built like some kind of old English manor. Ironic, considering Aidan hated the English. The place was three stories, a perfect cube with Palladian windows that he'd bought from a wrecker's yard somewhere in the UK.

All around, there were flowerbeds and neatly manicured lawn. Sometimes, when I drove here, it was hard to remember we were in the center of the city.

The driveway was full of cars—my brothers'. Not just in my heart, but by blood.

The concept still had the power to stagger me, even as I felt the ties that bound me to this family grow ever tighter. I couldn't resent or regret that. I just wished learning of my heritage wasn't tied to a secret that had the power to destroy my marriage.

The only consolation was that Aoife would never discover the truth. Lena wasn't about to tell her, neither was Aidan. It was a cover up of the worst kind, but with no alternative, I just had to make sure I gave Aoife the best, the most joyous and contented of lives as an apology to her mother.

Michelle sounded like a good mom, and I knew most mothers wanted nothing more for their kids than someone who would love them and who would stick to their vows.

Even without this dirty black secret on my soul, I'd always intended to have and to hold Aoife for the rest of my life. Not just because I was Catholic, but because she was it for me.

It with a capital I.

When I parked the car behind Declan's, I climbed out and moved around the vehicle to open Aoife's door. Even though she had arms and legs of her own, here? It was old school, and I quite liked it. At the hotel, I'd just glared at her but hadn't said anything, here she knew to follow the unspoken rules.

Aidan had taught all the boys to treat their women like a queen. To open doors for them, to help them out of cars, to ease them into a seat at the dining table.

Little gestures, but ones that were respectful and loving.

When she slipped her hand into mine, she shot me a knowing look. I'd never said that she had to act like a 'lady' around Aidan, but she was remarkably perceptive.

When a throat cleared, my head shot up and I saw Aidan glowering at me from the house. When Aoife was out of the car, I slammed the door shut, glowering back at Aidan all throughout the walk to the front door.

"Why weren't you at church?"

"Because I'll be going when I want to go from now on."

Aidan's eyes flared wide, rage pooling like fire bombs in the orbs that were, I realized, mirror images of my own.

How had I not seen that?

At my side, Aoife tensed, and I knew she was expecting Aidan to blow at any moment. But I didn't. I watched him. Coolly. Calmly. I didn't care if he was angry. I didn't even care if he was outraged. I was going to live by my own rules—just like he fucking did.

Like father. Like son.

I jerked my chin up, telling him to back the fuck off, and his jaw clenched down as he took a step back. His body screamed aggression and I knew, had this been any other Sunday, he'd have probably punched me for my barefaced impudence.

Instead, he conceded to me, and I stepped into the house with my bride at my side.

I could sense her nerves as she approached Aidan. She put her hands to his arms and leaned up to kiss his cheek. All the while he stared at me, and I stared the fuck back. He patted her in the middle of her shoulders in greeting, then murmured, "Leave us, Aoife."

"N-No," she squeaked, turning to look at me, but I shook my head at her.

"It's okay, Aoife. Go on in."

She begged me with her eyes to go with her, but I had to get this off my chest and Aidan needed to hear it.

When she released a heavy sigh and stepped back, heading for the living room that was just off the hall where everyone congregated, Aidan and I were left alone.

"What's your game, son?"

"Don't use the word as a weapon unless you don't want me to call you Dad," I threatened.

He shrugged. "It's time the boys knew."

"When you want to, tell them. But don't involve me in it. I know I'm not fucking happy with a three-and-a-half decade long lie."

A grunt escaped him, and he pointed outside. "Let's talk."

"Sure," I informed him easily, stepping back down the short stone path that led to the graveled drive.

When he joined me, we both strode in tense silence to the back-yard, which was wall-to-wall lawn. Manicured so perfectly, I had to wonder if Aidan had threatened the gardener's life to make it so.

"What's your game?" he repeated.

With my eyes overlooking the large yard, I shoved my hands into my pockets and told him, "I'm not willing to run by all your rules anymore." When he tensed at my side, I carried on, "You're my father. Even before I knew that to be true, I always thought of you that way, and I love you. I will until the day one of us dies. I love Lena, too. She's the mother I wish I'd had since birth.

"You're my boss as well. And I get that, and I will abide by most of your rules. But I'm not as devout as you. I'm Catholic, and I'll go to the special masses, but I'm not going to confess just for the sake of following a rule. I'm not going for communion just because you said so.

"You've shown me that we each have to make our own code. This is mine."

"And what if I say you have no right to have your own code?" Aidan threatened, his voice gravelly with discontent.

"I say you have no choice in the matter." I looked at him, really looked and saw the lines around his forehead and eyes. He wasn't getting younger—neither was I. "I'm not going to rebel. I'm just... making my own way. I don't want to see any of the wet work. I'm tired of the blood. I don't want it on my hands."

"Whether you see it or not, it still happens."

"I know, but that's not on me." I shrugged. "I've never had the stomach for that shit. You know that. I hated it as a kid, just like Conor did."

"You boys always did have your noses stuck in those damn books."

Because I felt like we'd turned a corner, I nudged him in the side. "Those books are why we've got what we've got."

He grunted. "Only some of it. You didn't reinvent the wheel."

"No? I just made us a couple of hundred mil." I glared at him. "You know we're vital parts to the machine. Without us, how would you clean all your dirty money?"

That had him grumbling.

"In this day and age where everything is online? Where everything is monitored... if we'd maintained your old practices, most of us would be in prison serving thirty years. As it is, we're standing in the grounds of a beautiful home you had built a few years ago."

He huffed. "I get your point. You don't have to hammer it home."

"Don't I?" *He* would have. With the afore-mentioned hammer. Shooting him a knowing look, I continued, "By keeping this secret, I'm doing my marriage an injustice. I will live with that, Aidan. I will endure it, because there's no alternative. I don't want Lena to go anywhere, even if that was possible, I wouldn't want that to be the case. So, I have no choice but to be the best man I can be for my wife."

"And that means not going to church?" he cried. "Dammit to hell, Finn!"

"Yes. It does," I countered. "Do you know she's never blamed me for the shooting?"

His brow furrowed. "Never?"

I shook my head. "Never. Can you imagine that? She doesn't blame me at all. It was hard to handle at first. *I* blamed *me*, and the fact she wasn't giving me any shit..." I blew out a breath. "Well, I think I'd have preferred it if she had. It ate at me like nothing else could, so one day, she only tells me to go to confession." I rubbed my chin. "I went, and I couldn't repent for something I felt no guilt for. But I went and I spoke with Doyle and I just felt like it was such a waste of time, Aidan. You can't force someone to seek redemption, especially when I'd kill any bastard who went after my wife again and again."

Aidan stepped in front of me and put a hand on my shoulder. "It's good for you to speak with Doyle. We have no one else to share this with. No one who understands our ways."

"Treat him like a shrink?" I sighed. "Can't you see how stupid it is? I get that it works for you, but it doesn't work for me and I know it doesn't for Conor. Maybe because we're not as active with the wet work as you and the rest, I don't know.

"I'm not saying I'll never go, but I just don't want to be dictated to."

"You wouldn't even be questioning this if you weren't my son," he ground out, anger making his jaw tense.

"I wouldn't be questioning this," I corrected him stonily, "if your wife hadn't killed my wife's mother. There is no justice in our world, Aidan. None at all. We have to make it for ourselves."

"And renouncing the church and stopping getting your hands dirty will do that?" he sneered.

"No," I said truthfully. "But it means I can go home to my wife, who will never receive any justice for what was laid at her door, with a clear conscience. I'll go to confession when I have something I need to confess, not because you order it of me.

"I'm taking back the reins on my faith, Aidan. I'm doing that for me and I'm doing that for Aoife. It's a step forward, one we need to take together, one that lets me steer my future where I want it to go."

Aidan stared at me as he processed that, then he visibly gritted his teeth after biting out, "Leave me and go greet Lena."

I nodded, took a step back and, walking toward the kitchen doors, squinted as the sunlight peeked over the roof.

She was standing there in the doorway, watching me leave Aidan behind. She was ringing her hands and I knew Aidan had told her that I knew the truth.

When I stepped onto the stone patio where she liked to have tea in the morning on the white filigree table and chair set, she stepped out and approached me.

I let her hug me, and I curved my arms around her back and embraced her.

She'd done wrong. There was no righting what she'd perpetrated, but, and it was a big but, I loved her.

In my world, that had to be enough.

"Promise me something, Lena."

"What?" Her voice was husky with emotion.

"Promise you'll never tell her."

She stiffened then sagged. "I won't."

"If you do, you'll destroy everything she and I build together."

"I know." She leaned back, and I saw in her eyes a world of guilt. "I didn't mean to... It really was an accident."

Whether it was or wasn't, Michelle was dead.

I just nodded, then kissed her forehead.

She wasn't the only one who'd have to live with what she'd done that day.

54

AOIFE

"AIDAN WILL BE HOME SOON," Lena told everyone as, from the head of the table, she began to pass around dishes in a circle.

As I spooned out potatoes, I cast a look around the boys. Everyone was faintly subdued, and that was probably because of Aidan's scowl. It wasn't aimed at anyone in particular—not even the source of his mood, my husband—but it was like a thundercloud was hovering over the table, and we were just waiting for the rumbles in the atmosphere to start.

"He'll be miserable," Conor predicted with a sigh. "You know what he's like. He won't even wear Ace bandages because he says he looks like a pus—weak," he quickly corrected when Lena glowered at him. "How's he going to cope with a cane?"

"We can't think that way," Lena chided him. "We have to make sure he knows it's not forever."

With my meal dished out, I started to eat. It tasted good but inside, I was nervous. The morning hadn't started out like I'd imagined, and though I'd enjoyed it, I was still staggered by the ease in which I'd imagined myself as a mother. Combine it with the reason for Aidan's bad mood, I just felt on edge.

It was nuts that I could remember, weeks before, when Magdalena had asked me when we'd be having kids. I'd felt like snapping at her boldness for asking me something so personal. Something I hadn't figured I was ready for. But something had changed. What was that? Finn? Was he the reason why I could suddenly see myself having a family with him?

It wasn't like the world had changed since we'd married, so did it mean my faith in him had?

"I've seen Aidan's PT trainer. She's even cuter than yours, Aoife," Eoghan said, tongue-in-cheek as he prodded me from my thoughts. "I think he'll manage to be *up* and about for her."

The men snickered and Lena growled. "No talk like that at the table."

Eoghan shrugged. "Didn't say anything dirty, Ma."

"The implication was there. She's there to help him get back on his feet."

"No better way for a man to get back on his feet than by—"

"Don't even go there," Aidan snapped at Eoghan, who grinned at me. Totally unaffected by his father's temper. Conor was edgy because of it, but I realized Brennan and Declan were untouched by the storm brewing around us as well.

Were they just so used to it they didn't care?

I shot Lena a look, saw she was scowling into her dish as she ate. "Do you have to do anything to the house?" I asked.

She glanced at me. "We'll need to put a ramp in at the back. He'll still be in a wheelchair for a few months until he can use his leg more." Her head tilted to the side as she looked at me. "How are you?" She dropped her gaze to my belly.

"It's fine. Getting there. Yoga is helping."

"Can you do the splits?" Eoghan asked, mischief in his eyes.

"Whether she can or can't is for me to know and for you to have a broken nose if you find out," Finn told him curtly, a warning in his narrowed eyes as he pointed his fork at Eoghan.

"Now, brother, I'm just worrying after your wife's flexibility. No shame in that."

"No coveting allowed at the table," Conor mocked, making me laugh.

I grinned at him. "Eoghan doesn't covet me, Conor. He just wants to get into the practice himself. I can see him in head to toe Lycra, can't you?"

"A leotard? Even better," Conor crowed.

Eoghan curled his arm and tensed his bicep. "I'd snap Lycra."

"Superman fits into Lycra, bud. If it can stretch around him, it can stretch around you."

He pouted at me. "Are you saying I'm not special?"

"I'm sure you're many things, but special isn't one of them," I told him with a grin.

Finn's hand came to rest on my thigh as he began to eat with just his fork, and as he did, I felt something settle inside me at the connection.

I loved when he did this. When he joined us with a simple touch, and it seemed all the more poignant now since he'd told me he loved me.

I smiled at him, knowing my heart was in my eyes as we stared at one another. The table could have disappeared, the bickering people around it too. For a moment, it was just him and me, and that was how I wanted it to be forever.

Finn and I against the world.

"You'll never guess who I saw last week, Dec."

Declan was the quietest of them all, and he rarely spoke to me. Not because he was rude, I thought, but because he didn't say much to anyone.

"Who?"

"Guess," Brennan joked.

He grunted. "Not interested enough to guess."

That had Brennan rolling his eyes. "Aela O'Neill."

For the first time, I saw Declan react to *something*. His fork clattered as he dropped it on his plate.

"Aela O'Neill? I thought she fucked off to Ireland?"

Lena tutted. "Language, Declan."

He cut his mother a look. "Sorry." Like a laser, he pinpointed his brother with his stare. "Conor?"

"She did, but she's back. She's an artist now. Glass, I think."

"How do you know?" The intent in his voice had everyone around the table looking at him, but he didn't seem to notice, his focus utterly zoomed in on Conor.

"I saw her getting coffee and walking into a gallery. On the side, there was her name. Splashed all over it with these weird statues." He jiggled his shoulders. "She hasn't changed all that much. Still like a pixie."

A grunt escaped Declan. "Which gallery?"

Conor frowned at him. "I don't know. I didn't write it down."

"Where was the coffee shop then, idiot?" Declan snapped.

"Calm down, Declan," Lena murmured, her brows high as she took in her son's reaction. "Conor, where was the coffee shop?"

"It's just by Eighth Avenue."

The minute he'd finished speaking, the sound of his chair scraping against the tiles shrieked throughout the room.

Aidan scowled at him. "Where do you think you're going?"

"I—" For a second, he was wordless. Then he shook his head, cut his mother a glance and said, "I have to go. Sorry, Ma."

Because Lena was as bewildered as the rest of us, she tilted her head to the side as a prompt. He leaned over to kiss her cheek.

"Thanks, Ma. Great meal as usual."

And like that, he was gone. No longer than two minutes later, his engine boomed in the yard and with a screech, he took off.

"Idiot will kill himself if he drives like that all the way to Eighth Avenue," Aidan groused. "Who the hell is Aela O'Neill?"

The skin around Finn's eyes pinched. "Deidre's best friend."

Lena's hand tightened around the glass. "Oh."

"Deirdre was Declan's childhood sweetheart," Finn explained softly.

"Why was he so eager to see her friend?" Eoghan queried. "It's not like him to be excited about anything anymore."

That was why he was so quiet?

He was still grieving?

My opinion of the dour brother instantly changed, and I felt guilty for just thinking he was a miserable bastard when his misery was forged from grief. If anyone could understand that, it was me.

Until Finn, I'd been at a complete and utter loss after my mom's death. But with Finn, it was like he was my rudder. The pain was still there, her loss would never leave me, but at least he was at my side, and I wasn't alone anymore.

Any amusement or humor died the second Declan left. We were all curious about what he was doing, all wondering why he'd run off the way he had. It was a relief when Lena hadn't made dessert, and Finn excused us early, saying I still needed to rest.

Liar.

As we drove off their estate, I asked, "There a reason you wanted to get out of there so quickly?"

He shrugged. "I'm ready to go home."

"Aidan was mad at you."

"Aidan's mad period."

My lips curved at that. "But you love him anyway."

"I do," he said on a sigh, one that sounded like it was dragged from the depths of his soul.

"Hey, that's okay. Love works in funny ways. Who'd think I'd love the man who was bribing me into his bed?"

His nose crinkled at the bridge. "Big difference."

"Is there?" I laughed. "If you'd been crap in bed, I'm not sure I'd have fallen head over heels for you."

"You'd have fallen for something, angel," he said teasingly. "It's how I roll."

55

———

FINN

"SO THE THREAT from the Colombians is off the table?"

I shrugged at Aidan Sr. "As off the table as it can be." Watching as he rubbed his chin, I asked, "What's wrong?"

"Don't you think it's too easy?"

I had to snort. "No. If you'd seen how much work Conor and I—"

"Not saying anything about the work, Finn."

"What then?" I demanded, unsure why he was raising this particular topic so many weeks after he'd put an end to the leader of the gang.

"Things have changed. The Colombians would have come at us with fucking rocket launchers back in the day."

My lips curved. "Thank Christ then that we aren't back in the day."

He shot me a look. "I'll forgive you the blasphemy only because I'm thankful too." Sinking back in his desk chair, he murmured, "Why haven't they come at us with rocket launchers, Finn?"

Crossing my legs at the ankle, I slouched back in my seat. "Because they don't have any money to fund them. Currently, at any rate. On top of that, the only people who genuinely don't fear the

Russians are us, and that's only because you're a crazy motherfucker."

If my tongue was far laxer now that I knew he was my father, so be it. It wouldn't save said tongue from being sliced out, but I guessed I was going through a rebellious phase. The kind most kids endured through their teenage years? Well, I was experiencing it in my late thirties.

He didn't seem angered by the condemnation though. More than anything, he seemed resigned. "I'm old, Finn," he said sadly.

"We're all getting old," I countered.

"We're not as much of a threat as we were because of that though."

"You're talking to the wrong son about recruitment and defense," I informed him, aware that it was getting easier to think of myself as his 'son' around him. "But, if you're scared about the Russians going back on their deal with us, don't.

"You and I both know that Vasov wants to cement ties with the next generation. If he doesn't, his family is fucked. You know what his lot are like. The next Pakhan that isn't related to him will slice his widow and his daughters' throats to make a point."

That had Aidan grunting. "True."

I tipped my chin at him. "He's like you in that."

"Like what?"

"Loves his wife."

Aidan rubbed his chin again. "That Sunday after lockdown... Lena said you hugged her."

"I did."

"Said that was the last time you hugged her too."

I huffed out a breath. "Aidan, why do you do this?"

"Do what?"

"Bring me here on business then make it personal?"

"We're at the house. You should know that the two mix when we're here."

I had to concede to that, but still, it pissed me off. "Look, the

Colombians have no funds to do fuck at the moment. We didn't just hit the New York branch, Aidan. We hit them at the core. They're going to take a while to come back from that."

"And they're going to be pissed when they do," he pointed out.

"If you didn't like the tactic back when I came up with it, then you shouldn't complain now."

"Not complaining, just saying."

Heaving a sigh, I continued, "It could take them fifteen years to recoup what they lost. Never mind the ties. And by then? Fuck knows what could happen. Fifteen years is a long ass time. Yes, we're borrowing trouble, but when aren't we? When don't we have shit from rivals?"

"These rivals are going to be more than pissed at us."

I snorted. "Rivals always are. Look, we *are* borrowing trouble, but we're also trying to protect ourselves from that. Eoghan and Brennan are working on recruiting and training.

"By that point, we'll also have more funds because projects like the Heights will be up and running. We're going to make a couple of hundred million on that alone, Aidan. Whatever happens, the money will protect us."

"Until it doesn't. What if they hack us like we hacked them?"

"We're protected."

"They thought they were."

I sighed. "If you want to talk about firewalls, again, you're talking to the wrong son."

"At least you're talking to me."

That had me narrowing my eyes. "Huh?"

He shrugged. "If you'll only talk to me about business, then talk about business we will."

For a second, I could do nothing less than gape at him. "You're being serious, aren't you?"

His grin was dry, and fuck, how was it the first time I noticed the similarities in our grins? "When aren't I serious, Finn?"

I studied him, hard. Looking for similarities between us, looking for the shared connection our genetics gave us. Then, I blew out a breath. "I love you, Aidan."

"Dad."

Narrowing my eyes at him, I murmured, "Dad?"

He shrugged. "Waited a long time to hear it. We're alone. The boys aren't here," he pointed out.

"That mean you're going to tell them?"

"At some point in the future. I'd prefer to keep them focused on the active threats."

"Things never calm down," I retorted, unsure why I was pushing the issue when I didn't particularly want my brothers, by blood *and* choice, to know about my heritage.

Mostly I was concerned about it changing shit between us. That was the last thing I wanted.

"No. They don't," Aidan replied calmly. "I'll choose my moment."

"Would you have ever told me?" I didn't realize that had been gnawing at me until right that second.

"Yes."

"On your deathbed?"

Aidan grunted. "Maybe."

"Fuck," I bit off, and couldn't help myself when I got to my feet and started striding from one side of his office to the other.

He didn't stop me though, seemed to sense that I needed to do this. That I needed to work off some of my frustration.

How long I paced, I wasn't sure. I just did it. Just carried on because damn, I needed to. I was mad. Infuriated. So fucking outraged that only by discovering Lena's perfidy had the truth been revealed to me.

"Did you love Fiona?"

Aidan snorted. "No." He drummed his fingers on the desk. "She was a good girl though. Didn't deserve that cunt of a husband. I thought he was a good man, thought he'd do right by you both. I was wrong. That's the only reason I let her live."

That had me braking to a halt. "Huh?"

Aidan tilted his head to the side. "You think I'd have let her live after what he did to you? After what she let happen?"

Everything inside me froze. It twisted, morphed, until I remembered being in this office twenty fucking years ago, admitting to what had been done to me. Why I'd had to run, why I refused to go back.

The memories staggered me and I was too old to be so weak, so fragile where this was concerned.

Either Aidan didn't notice, or he wanted to carry on regardless because he said, "I let her live but I made her suffer. I made sure no one knew about where you were. It helped that you weren't on the streets long," he admitted. "I wanted you in the back offices, anyway. That brain of yours, just like Conor's. Didn't want it wasted on the streets. Just had to get your hands wet enough for you to be respected by the rest of the Points. You did your duty, then I got you away from that shit.

"Everyone knew that I'd slit their throats if they spoke a word about you."

I gaped at him. "How the fuck did you do that? We're talking thousands of wagging tongues!"

"You said it yourself—I'm a crazy motherfucker. People knew not to mess with me back then. Apparently, I've grown soft if the Colombians thought they could come onto my turf and..."

I held up a hand. "Everyone knows you're insane, Aidan. I wouldn't worry that opinion has changed on that score. It's more like they know we're morphing into different ventures, and that leaves gaps. We know now where we need to focus, and we will. The Colombians saved us, really. At least now we know where to plug the holes."

Aidan shrugged. "I guess. Fucking waste though." And I knew he was thinking of the girls who'd been killed and tortured as the Colombians pissed on our turf.

"Yeah. A damn waste."

"I helped their families, but it's never enough. More guilt on my shoulders," he murmured, tipping back his head to rest it against his chair.

I'd never seen Aidan like this, and if I was being honest, I didn't like it. Aidan was never introspective. It just wasn't how he rolled.

"I handled Gerry personally," he said out of the blue, almost like I was Doyle and he was in the confessional. "Enjoyed it too. Took me five years before I could atone, so I understand more than you think about that. Sometimes, it's hard to repent for shit you wanted to do."

I narrowed my eyes at him. "Why are you telling me this? Are you sick again?"

"No," he said with a snort. "I don't always have to be at death's door to be telling you this shit. It's shit you should have known a while back. I'm just making up for lost time, and also, I want you to —" He blew out a breath. "I don't want forgiveness because I don't deserve it but I want you to look at me like you did before."

"Look, Aidan—"

He held up a hand. "Not just me, but Lena too."

"How can I? I'm a dirty fucking secret," I snarled.

"You were never a dirty secret, Finn." Lena's soft voice startled me—she never entered Aidan's office. Not without knocking first.

"Wasn't I?" I snapped, turning around to glower at her. "You went on a fucking rampage because of Aidan's secrets, and that means I'm going to have to lie to my wife for the rest of my life."

She flinched but took a step into the office. "That's on me, not you. I wish I could go back, Finn. I do. I wish, every damn day, that I'd been concentrating more. That—" A harsh breath escaped her. "It will weigh on my conscience for the rest of my life. Sometimes, the fact that Aidan covered it up is more than I can stand."

"Boo fucking hoo," I snapped, aware that Aidan tensed at that but I didn't care, Lena hadn't driven into a damn fire hydrant. "My wife is without a mother because of you."

"And I'm going to go out of my way to be the mother she needs, even if I know I'll never replace hers."

My jaw turned to stone at that—couldn't she see that wasn't enough?

I shook my head, words escaping me as I tried and failed to process how fucked up this was. Was it any wonder I preferred to deal with business rather than this? Speaking of this shit just gave me heartburn and later on, when I was with Aoife, I felt like such a fucking piece of crap because I was lying to her.

Endlessly fucking lying.

"I know it's not enough," Lena whispered, then she raised her hand and rubbed tiredly at her face—I saw there were tear tracks down her cheeks, and knew she'd been crying quietly. "Every time I look at her, I'm aware of what I did, but I know this is God's way of punishing me, making sure I don't forget what I did. She's my penance, and I'll do what I must to make sure that she's not only safe but that your children are too."

"And what about the fact that I'm Aidan's son, Lena? That has to be gnawing at you?"

"No. You're mine," she snapped, and her tone was so ferocious that I almost took a step back. She pushed forward into my space, her finger prostrate as she prodded me in the chest. "*She* gave birth to you, but you're mine. I'm the one who made you better. I'm the one who fixed what she broke. You're mine, Finn."

My jaw clenched because I'd always fucking wished she was my mom. When I was little, when I'd come over and stayed with the boys after school, she'd bustled around us like a fly, feeding us, patting our shoulders, encouraging us as we groaned about homework. When Gerry had started on me, I'd wanted, so fucking badly, to tell her, and only knowing it would upset her had stopped me.

Yeah. Nuts.

I'd known she would believe me. Had known it implicitly. I'd never, I realized, had any fear that Aidan or Lena would doubt my word. Gerry had told me as he tormented me that nobody would believe me because I was scum, but I'd known they would, and I hadn't said a fucking word out of pride. It had been easier to run, easier to get away—until my brothers had come for me.

A shudder washed through me and before I knew it, Lena had slipped her arms around my waist, and she was tugging me close. "I love you, Finn. I can never make up for what I did to Aoife, I know that. But I'll love her like I love you."

She was so short, so small, but packed as much of a punch as Aoife did. She squeezed me so damn tight it almost hurt, and she did so until I wrapped my arms around her and kissed the crown of her head.

I jolted when Aidan slapped me on the back and half-hugged me too. "Son, I'll tell the boys soon."

I was like a fucking woman with these goddamn mood swings, I knew, but I said, "No. We'll figure out when to tell them. Together."

We looked at each other, then nodded, and that was that.

56

AOIFE

"WHAT'S WRONG?"

I winced because I couldn't exactly tell Jenny that I was missing a father she thought had died years ago. But I *was* missing my dad, and this was the Tuesday when we were supposed to meet.

Dads fucking sucked.

"Nothing," I told her as she licked cookie dough from a bowl on the counter. We were in the penthouse, and Jen was staying for dinner.

"Bullshit."

I snorted. "Fuck you."

"Fuck me? Why, yes, I would too."

Despite myself, I grinned. "Good thing I love you."

She winked. "I love me too."

"I know. You're terrible."

"Nah. I'm luverly," she mocked the movie we'd been watching while I baked and she caught up on some of her studies—*My Fair Lady* with the Queen that was Audrey Hepburn. She winked at me again. "Love you too, sugar. Especially love this place."

I grinned. "It's the bomb, right?"

"It totally is." She whistled. "If the package wasn't fine enough, he has this place too."

"That's right, Jen, she wants me for my penthouse."

Warmth unfurled inside me at Finn's voice and I turned around, saw he was standing there and rushed over to him to hug him. Tight.

Fuck, he always smelled so good, and I loved when he hugged me back as though he never wanted to let me go.

"Why do you always smell so good?" he grumbled, his train of thought so tightly aligned with mine I had to grin.

"Because she bakes all the damn time," Jen retorted, her eyes on her books. Not because she was embarrassed by the PDA—she was getting used to them. Finn did this shit all the time at home. Hugging me, kissing me, fuck, he'd have done it in public too but he'd told me that he wouldn't because then his enemies would know I was a weakness.

It was both touching and terrifying to know that.

"It's because you smell like mine," he whispered in my ear so Jenny couldn't hear.

I grinned as I tipped back to stare at him, but my grin slowly died and I asked, "Are you okay?"

He closed his eyes. "Rough meeting with Aidan."

Nodding my understanding, I told him, "I have cookies."

"You have a great cookie," he replied, and I laughed.

"I have two different kinds. The one down below which is not for public consumption, then I have quadruple chocolate chip."

"Quadruple?" He cocked a brow at me. "How's that even possible?"

"Because she's a demon," Jen retorted, again, without looking up.

Finn rolled his eyes, but he urged us toward the counter where my concoctions were cooling. "You doing okay?" he asked quietly, and I knew he'd remembered that today was when I should have been meeting Alan.

"No. Not really. It sucks."

"*He* sucks," he countered.

"This is true." My lips curved. "It will be okay. He didn't deserve me."

"No, he damn well didn't."

I reached up and kissed him for that.

"I don't deserve you, either," he admitted on a sigh, and there was a sadness in his eyes that upset me.

"What's going on?"

He shook his head. "Nothing. Just wish there was more I could do."

"You did enough. I-I asked something of you that—"

He hushed me. "I wish I could give you more answers about your mom."

"I think I was crazy to think he was involved in that."

"No. Nothing's crazy in this world." He pressed his forehead to mine. "I love you, Aoife. It will never be enough, but I do."

When he said shit like that, it made me fucking melt like my gooey quadruple chocolate cookies that I intended on making me Insta-famous. I knew something was weighing on him, but then, something would always be weighing on him. I just had to accept that I wouldn't always be able to alleviate the strain, but I could ease the burden by being his haven.

Jen grumbled, "You two have a guest, you know? Jeez, if you can't keep your hands off her, then—"

"Shut up, Jenny," Finn grumbled, shooting her a glower over his shoulder.

I couldn't say my husband and my best friend actually liked one another, but that was because Jen was brassy and crass—exactly how I liked her.

She gasped. "Aoife, are you going to let him talk to me like that?"

I snickered. "Yup." My eyes were sparkling as I peered around Finn's arm. "After all the PDAs I've endured from you, you can deal with me hugging my husband."

A scoff escaped her. "He looks like he wants to devour you. There's a difference," she informed us with a sniff.

"Ah, but you see, that's exactly how I like him to look at me," I told her, winking up at said husband, and meaning every goddamn word.

57

FINN

FOUR MONTHS LATER

AS I WATCHED the words being inked into her skin, I loved the feeling of possession it gave me.

I had the same ones tattooed on me, but it was in Gaelic, and no one could read the language all that much now. Hers was in English, and there was no doubt it was a declaration about me.

The air I breathe belongs to you, it said, the words arced over her shoulder and down to her arm. It was surrounded with roses that were colored in bright red ink.

She'd had the etching for a few weeks now, and today was the color section. She didn't cry out, not once, whereas I'd had to bite my fucking cheek throughout the agonizing two-hour session.

If anything, she looked so zen, it made me want to fuck her to see the sleepy sloe eyes brighten and widen, to shock her awake. But even as the tattoo artist cleared away the ink, even as he applied gauze and Saran Wrap and informed her to use the same cream I had to put on mine, she was dopey on endorphins as I guided her out of the store forty minutes later.

Relieved we'd gone to the gun range before the tattoo parlor, I drove us through the busy Saturday morning traffic.

Aoife was getting quite good with a gun, and I'd be relieved when she could carry. I hated the necessity, but it was better to be safe than sorry. Mostly, I was glad I wasn't having to force her to do it. When Aidan had asked Lena to carry, she'd outright refused. Aoife being Aoife? She'd come to me when I'd been fucking *fretting* like some kind of old hen about approaching the topic.

I was, as was confirmed every single day of the goddamn week, fucking lucky.

And did I mention that the sight of my wife with a gun gave me the worst hard-on? The minute we got home, I was going to be on her faster than red sauce on spaghetti.

It took an hour longer than usual to get toward our side of town. We stopped off at the bakery to check up on things.

Jenny was there, managing the troops as they scrubbed the place from top to bottom. Aoife had spent the past few weeks running herself ragged with the opening next Saturday, and I'd thrown my weight around and made her take this weekend off.

I let her check in with the place though, because I knew how much of a control freak she was about her baby, and because I was the same, I didn't want her stressing out over something that could be resolved with a quick glance at the place and a short chat with Jenny.

We grabbed some food from the store and I knew Aoife wanted nothing more than to test drive some cookies this afternoon. I was totally down for that since I got to be her judging panel. Declan, Aidan Jr. and Conor were coming over for that hardest of tasks too.

The penthouse was blessedly quiet after the chaos of the city, and I knew we both were relieved to get home.

That was the craziest thing about being married, I'd realized. I'd called this place home for years, and I'd done my best to make it comfortable and apt for my every need, but it never had been.

Now, Aoife was home, and I knew that sounded like a phrase from a Hallmark card, but it was true.

True enough that it made me shake my head at myself because if the guys knew where my brain went some days, they'd upgrade me from pussy-whipped to... well, whatever was worse than pussy-whipped.

I shrugged off my coat and grabbed hers. When she headed for the kitchen and I diverted to the bedroom, I let her, but I stopped off at the nightstand to grab a condom and to shove the bottle of lube I stored there in my pocket.

It was about time I worked on another fantasy I'd had, and I wanted to do it while my words were still drying on her skin, and the sun was still high in the sky.

When I made my way to the kitchen, I found her mumbling about brown sugar. Smirking at the sight, I headed on in and grabbed her hand. When I tugged her, she stared blankly at me, then I waved the condom and she narrowed her eyes at me.

"Don't tease."

I laughed. "I'm not teasing."

She pouted. "You know I have my period."

"I do. And that's why we've been playing with your ass for the past few months." I'd taken to fucking her with a butt plug every now and then, but I'd just been waiting for the right moment to take every one of her holes.

Her cheeks burned hotly. "N-Now?"

"Yep." My tone was cheerful—and why the fuck wouldn't it be?

I was about to be two for two with every virgin orifice this woman possessed.

Yum.

I watched her focus switch from brown sugar to me, and boy, I could see the molasses-like crawl as desire swarmed through her veins.

Grinning, I tugged her hand and dragged her to my office.

"Do you know how badly I've wanted to fuck you in here?"

She snorted. "Of course. You bent me over the desk the other night."

"Ah, but that was different."

She cocked a brow at me. "It was? Why?"

"Because it was nighttime, and I want to do this in the daylight."

Her cheeks burned hotly, but she didn't argue with me, and even if she had, I'd have kissed her into forgetting any and all arguments.

Instead, I carried on, heading for the window at the base of the room where I looked out when I was working at my desk.

I wanted to replace that image with her, and I had a plan.

There was a window seat in front of it, so I hauled her into my arms, laughing when she released a squeal. She landed as she always did—her thighs around my hips, her pussy to my cock. Fuck, that felt so good.

As I walked her over to the window, I murmured, "I have devious plans for you, my dear."

She snickered. "How very wicked of you."

"I try my best," I teased as I bowed my head and connected our mouths.

I sighed into the kiss immediately. Everything about her welcomed me in, her mouth, her arms, her body. She was what I'd always been waiting for and hadn't even known.

Pressing her into the wall beside the window, I just enjoyed the kiss. We had no reason to rush, even if my dickhead brothers were coming over later on, and I just wanted to enjoy this moment. This purely innocent moment, as we shared a kiss that united us in more ways than one.

Her sighs, her breathy moans, as always, worked me into a ravaging need. There was something about those sounds, it just fucked with my head, made me want to rip into her, to make her remember who those sounds belonged to. But I didn't need to force that memory, she'd never forget. I'd marked her in so many ways, there was no way anyone could be confused over who this woman belonged to.

Pulling back, I watched her lick her kiss-sore lips. They were pink and puffy and the bottom one was just screaming at me to bite it.

I didn't though, I was withholding that particular caress until I was ready.

She reached for me again, her tongue thrusting into my mouth the instant we touched, and I let her play the aggressor for once, let her explore my mouth, let her taste me.

She was delicate where I was rough, hesitant where I had no shame. The contrast had the hairs at the back of my neck standing on edge and I was determined to let her kiss me like this more often because it felt so fucking good.

When she was panting, I murmured, "Are you ready to be mine, angel?"

"Always," she whispered back, her eyes like crystalline pools I wanted to drown in. If I did, I'd die a happy man.

Even as I pushed her into the wall, supporting her like that, I pulled back so I could reach between us. I dragged off my shirt first, and then unbuttoned hers—she'd worn it so she could cover herself up some at the tattoo parlor.

I'd managed to work on her body confidence to the point where she didn't give a shit where I fucked her now, in the bright sunlight or in the shadows the moon cast. But the prospect of some fucking tattoo artist gaping at *my* tits had her snickering while she covered up to soothe my possessiveness.

I knew she loved it though.

She never got mad when I growled at some bastard checking out her ass—an ass that was about to belong to me in more ways than one. She didn't grumble if I glared at a fucker for gaping at her tits. She seemed to blossom under it, like petals spreading under the rays of the sun.

With the shirt unbuttoned, I stared at the front clasp of her bra, thanking God for the minor miracle that was this technology. With one brush of my finger and thumb, it was open, and her heavy tits spilled free.

Fuck!

Each and every time, they had me wanting to worship at the altar that was Aoife O'Grady.

With a grunt, I dipped my head and pressed a kiss to the upper swell of her ripe curves. Using my lower body to keep her pinned in place still, I cupped her tits and pushed them together then dove into them.

She giggled, as she always did, before she moaned and her fingers came up to cup my head, to run through my hair and drive me wild with the pressure of her nails against my scalp.

Goddammit, I was sick of almost coming in my pants every fucking time I had denied her. Her periods were my idea of hell.

I rocked my cock against the warmth of her pussy, loving that she'd be as slick for me as I was hard for her.

She clung to me, writhing against the wall as I made her body beg for me, and then, I knew enough was enough. I needed in her. Stat.

With one hard grind that had her moaning, I pulled away from her entirely, helping her stand when she looked like she'd sink to the floor.

Any other time, I'd have loved her mouth on my cock, but I had other ideas for this little adventure.

I tossed her shirt and bra to the ground and pushed her pants and panties down to her ankles, grateful she'd left her shoes in the kitchen —the woman walked barefoot in front of the stove, I only had to knock her up to complete the image. When she toed out of them, I kicked them aside with a smirk, delighting in the sight of her.

With another smile, I helped her onto the seat, and said, "Spread your legs and curve your toes around the edge."

She obeyed, and I took a step back to look at the pretty picture she made.

When I carried on stepping back, her shoulders dropped. "You said you wouldn't tease," she whined, and I grinned at her over my shoulder as I headed across the room to my desk.

Sitting there, I reached for my phone in my pocket and opened up my camera. She swallowed, aware of what I was doing, but she didn't argue—for that alone, I was determined to give her an orgasm that she'd feel for days. Well, until I could give her another one after she'd finished shark week.

I sat there for a few minutes, tormenting us both as I looked at her and she looked at me. I wanted this sight imprinted on my retinas. I wanted to see this image in my head for the rest of my life when I sat behind this desk.

She stayed remarkably still. Remarkable because she was a fidgeter when she was horny, but I took several snapshots for prosperity, zooming on her tits and pussy a few times.

My tongue cleaved to my mouth with need for her and when I'd finished torturing us both, I stood and returned to her.

With little ado, I shucked out of my jeans, saying, "Hold out your palm." She did as told, and I passed her the bottle of lube and the condom. She kept them high, like she was holding a platter, and I smiled at her, so fucking satisfied with my angel that I could feel the joy beaming out of me like a spotlight.

When I grabbed the condom wrapper, tearing it and sliding it on my cock, she released a breathy sigh that told me she loved watching me as much as I loved watching her.

Once sheathed, I grabbed the bottle of lube, splashed some on my dick, then dropped to my knees.

Her cunt was clean, thank Christ. She used one of those Diva cup things, so her pussy was perfect as usual. All pink and red thanks to her pubic hair. It was torture though. Looking at it made me forget what was going down, and then when I remembered, I wanted to sulk.

Yeah. I knew I was approaching forty, way too old to sulk, but what this woman did to me was unprecedented.

If I wanted to sulk, I'd fucking sulk.

With a groan, I leaned over and pressed a kiss to the top of her pubic bone. She wriggled, and I knew she was uncomfortable with my being so close to that area when she had her period. But I ignored her, moving down to swirl my tongue around her clit but going no further.

As I teased her, I slid a single digit down her perineum, and she tensed as I began to tease the tight pucker. When she shifted with another moan, I smirked against her clit.

She slurped my finger in with no problem, and I thanked God for Lelo because, hell's bells, I wanted in her and that naughty little plug was going to make it happen.

Within a few minutes, I had three blunt fingers inside her. I scissored them a few times, trying to stretch her out, but every time I did, she clamped down around them so tightly, I knew I might pass out when I finally got my cock inside her.

"Oh, God, Finn. Please. *Screw me.* Please." Her begging worked its wiles on me. Those words had the same effect as her sucking on my cock would.

It was awkward doing it this way, but I didn't care. I wanted her eyes on me when I came inside her. I wouldn't get as deep as I'd like, but that was for another time.

With her lubed up and ready for me, I gave one final kiss to her clit, then moved up to the banquette. It was deep so she could lie back comfortably, and I covered her writhing form with a delight I couldn't hide.

Reaching between us, I pressed my cock to the tight rosette and began to sink home.

Each inch was a battle worth fighting as I finally managed to slide inside her. She was tight and hot and it was another hole of hers to torture me.

I rested my elbows on either side of her head and dipped my chin so I could kiss her as I fucked her slowly.

I wanted to enjoy this, wanted to savor every moment inside her tight ass.

Knowing I wouldn't last long, not when I'd been denied access to her for three days, and knowing she was on the brink of implosion, I leaned on one arm so I could slide a hand between us. When I reached her clit, I began to thrum it with my thumb, giving her the touch she needed without the fast speed she liked.

Within seconds, she was panting like she'd run five miles. She was gasping for air, almost pulling away from my lips to breathe, but I didn't let her. I gave her my air, let her breathe my oxygen.

When she came, she ripped her mouth from mine. The scream that burst from her lungs would have hurt my ears if I hadn't readied myself for it. It was hot and sharp and so fucking sexy, I felt the cum boil in my balls as I spurted long and hard.

With a roar of my own, I clenched my eyes to process just how awesome that had been.

Christ, what this woman did to me.

I slumped over her, our breathing ragged as we panted in time. Then, I felt her lips, soft and gentle on mine and she whispered, "The air I breathe belongs to you."

Smiling, I kissed her back and repeated, "The air I breathe belongs to you."

Resting my forehead against hers, I took a few seconds to appreciate what I had in my arms.

This woman, if she only knew, was my life.

My fucking everything.

It was time I proved that to her.

Sucking down a breath, I whispered, "Aoife?"

She hummed an assent, but her eyes found mine again.

"Marry me?"

Her head tilted to the side. "We're already married."

"Marry me properly this time." My mouth suddenly felt dry and I realized I was more nervous now than I'd been the first time I proposed. "I want you to have the white dress and the bridesmaids. The bachelorette party and the honeymoon. I want you to have it all. I want to make a memory we should be proud of, one we can tell our grandkids about."

When her eyes filled with liquid diamonds, my nerves sank away like they'd never existed.

I knew her answer before she whispered a word.

Yes.

Forever, yes.

58

___

AOIFE

"I THOUGHT DECLAN WAS COMING TONIGHT."

Conor shook his head. "He canceled. I got the message on the way up in the elevator."

"Again?" Aidan shook his head. "What's up with him? I know Dad's going nuts about him missing Sunday lunch last week."

Finn rubbed his chin. "Don't think it's to do with that Aela chick, do you?"

Aidan snorted. "After Deirdre? Nope. If that bitch didn't burn him enough, he's fucking insane if he goes looking for more scars."

Aidan's words had me braking to a halt. I'd been sliding cookies onto plates, and I didn't even care that some fell onto the counter as I turned and asked, "I thought Declan and Deirdre were childhood sweethearts."

"They were," Finn confirmed as he forked up some pie I'd given the guys to try out first.

"So, what do you mean? How did she burn him?"

Aidan chuckled and he stabbed the fork my way. Finn, spotting it, walloped the back of his hand with his own fork. As he rubbed at the sting, he glowered at Finn before lowering the piece of cutlery, turning to me and saying, "She was insane."

Conor winced. "That was never proven."

Finn laughed. "How do you prove it? Have her committed?"

"Well, yeah. Or her shrink does."

"She should have been committed. She was nuts. She followed him, Aoife. Can you imagine that?"

"She followed him?" My eyes widened. "What on Earth... why?"

"Because she was crazy," Aidan repeated, like him saying it over and over again would make me believe it.

"Well, did she think he was cheating or something? It seems a tad extreme, but women have done nuttier things around the men they love."

Conor nodded and moved onto his second piece of pie. As he chewed, he groaned, "Fuck, Aoife. This is *good*."

I beamed with pleasure, so happy they were enjoying my creations. It was corny but I was looking to create the next big Instagram fad. It would put me on the map, I just had to settle on what that fad would be.

There'd been rainbow bagels and black soft serve, I was trying to figure out what my big break should be. I'd thought that my quadruple chocolate cookies would do the trick, but they were beyond rich and really expensive to produce.

"Thanks, Conor."

"I told you before. She makes stuff so good the devil's jealous."

Aidan snorted. "Try not to say that around Dad next time, yeah? He's let up on you going to church but the rest of us still need our asses on those pews at nine AM sharp."

Finn pulled a face but didn't argue. Things were still weird between him and Aidan, although every time I saw them together on a Sunday, they were relaxing around each other again.

Men. Too stupid to breathe sometimes.

"Anyway," Conor interrupted. "You know Declan works around the docks, yeah?"

That was code for 'deals drugs.'

It still boggled my mind that Declan did shit like that. He was so softly spoken, and in comparison to the rest of his brothers, gentle.

"Yeah, I know," I replied, amused by his phrasing. They wanted to keep me in the dark, but they also treated me like one of the guys. It was odd, but fun. I'd never had friends that were guys before, and Conor and Aidan liked shooting the shit with not just Finn, but me too.

"So, one day, Deirdre gets it into her head that Dec's cheating on her—like he would. His cock was in knots for that bitch, and she made him pay for it every single time."

"She charged him for sex?" I choked out.

Finn snickered. "He means metaphorically. She had him on a very short leash."

"Oh, okay."

"Well, she follows him to this place by the water. He doesn't know, starts to do the job. The dick he's with is antsy. Probably hopped on the product himself. The guy sees something at the back of the warehouse, is paranoid as fuck it's the cops. Gets trigger happy and the rest, as they say, is history."

My mouth dropped open at that—considering my own history with being shot, Conor was pretty cavalier about his retelling of the story.

"She died?"

He nodded. Finn's mouth was curved down and I knew he didn't appreciate the topic.

Aidan, however, was the one who spoke next, "That's why we keep business and family separate, Aoife."

I got it then.

They were warning me.

"Fuck, guys, you think I'm going to follow Finn around the docks?" I squeaked in outrage. "If you don't think I have better things to do than sneak around spying on you—"

Finn laughed, got to his feet and hauled me onto his lap. I settled with a pout, and as he rested his chin on my shoulder, he turned and pressed a kiss to my throat.

Refusing to shiver, I folded my arms across my chest and demanded, "Did that really happen? Or was it like a fable? Were you trying to teach me something?"

"Well, yeah," Conor admitted. "I was trying to teach you a lesson but unfortunately for Dec, it's true. He can't live with himself because of it."

Finn sighed. "Connor's right, Aoife. Her death is a huge weight on his conscience, and he'd done nothing wrong. I think, by that point, he hadn't even slept with anyone other than her, for Christ's sake. Yet there she was, following him around like he was a dog." He shook his head. "If she'd trusted him, stayed at home, she'd still be alive, making him miserable."

I elbowed him in the belly. "That's not nice."

"The truth doesn't have to be." Aidan turned the counter stool to look at me better. "Jen coming around tonight?"

I smirked at him. "Thought you didn't like her."

"I don't. But she's pretty to look at." He smacked his lips. "Her ass is almost as fine as this pie."

A laugh escaped me. "I'll be sure to tell her that. I think she'll appreciate the comparison."

He wrinkled his nose. "Better keep it between us, Aoife. You ladies are very particular where your asses are concerned."

Finn chuckled softly at that, and my cheeks burned because I knew he was thinking about what he'd done to *my* butt that afternoon.

I cleared my throat and told him, "Your secret's safe with me."

"That's why you're the best sister-in-law in the world."

With a grin, I moved off Finn's lap even though he tried to cocoon me there, but the oven timer went off and he relinquished his fierce hold on me—more's the pity. There was no better place to be than his arms, after all.

When I went to retrieve the second batch of cookies, the men went back to talking about shit I shouldn't, by rights, know about.

But as I went about my baking, I tuned in and out of their conversation.

Aidan had called me his sister-in-law even though none of them were aware of that truth. It filled me with warmth though, to know that they truly did consider me family without being aware of their father's behavior all those years ago.

In less than ten months, I'd gone from being utterly alone to having more family than I knew what to do with.

Today, Finn had proposed to me. We were in such a different place compared to the last time he'd asked me to be his wife. I'd only had Jenny in my life. With just her, I didn't know enough people to have any bridesmaids, and things like flower girls and ring-bearers had been out of the question. Now, I had Mary-Ellen, and she could be my matron of honor especially as she'd popped out her twins and was no longer waddling—I wouldn't have minded, but I figured she would.

By bringing me into this nutty family, Finn had given me more than he knew.

Not only did I have his love, I had theirs too.

There wasn't much I needed in this life. My business was opening soon and I was excited as I sought that signature dish which would make my name on social media. Finn was at my side, and who knew, in the next year or so, we might even start a family of our own...

The contrast was enough to have tears stinging my eyes.

Because of one man whose intent had been to screw with my life, I'd been brought into a world that was filled with highs and lows.

There was danger, yes, but in Finn's arms? I knew there was no safer place on this Earth.

THE CROSSOVER READING ORDER
WITH THE FIVE POINTS

FILTHY
FILTHY SINNER
NYX
LINK
FILTHY RICH
SIN
STEEL
FILTHY DARK
CRUZ
MAVERICK
FILTHY SEX
HAWK
FILTHY HOT
STORM
THE DON
THE LADY
FILTHY SECRET
REX
RACHEL

FILTHY KING
REVELATION BOOK ONE
REVELATION BOOK TWO
FILTHY LIES
FILTHY TRUTH

RUSSIAN MAFIA
Adjacent to the universe, but can be read as a standalone
SILENCED

FILTHY RICH
NOW AVAILABLE ON KU!

EOGHAN

Two Years Later

I HATED CHURCH.

And that wasn't something I said lightly.

I hated it with a passion, and as a Five Pointer, that sucked, because part of the position of being in our exalted brotherhood was that we attend church and confessed our sins.

Of which there were many.

On a daily basis.

Really, we should have had a hotline to the confessional with how much sin we perpetrated, but as much as my father, the head of the Five Points—the biggest Irish Mob family in the United States—donated to St. Patrick's, it wasn't enough for his entire crew to be outfitted with their own personal priests to service them.

My lips twitched at the thought, even as Father Doyle glared at me for daring to be amused within these hallowed walls.

While my father thought the sun rose and set on the old fuck, I didn't, so I glared back at him, amused even more when his cheeks blanched and he stared straight ahead.

The day my father died was the day when this old fuck was being sent to wherever they sent old priests off to.

And yeah, I saw him outliving my father, mostly because of the life Aidan O'Donnelly led.

The lives we all led.

That Da had hit the grand old age of sixty-six was pretty much a fucking miracle. I wasn't sure if I'd live that long, and maybe with a Bratva bitch as my bride, I wouldn't last the fucking week.

The enmity between the Russians and the Irish wasn't as bad as it was with the Italians—fucking hated that scum. Jesus, everyone did. They were cocksuckers who made the Albanians look trustworthy, and let's put it this way, I wouldn't trust an Albanian to look after a sandwich from Subway, never mind my territory—but the hostility between us was still bad.

Never the twain shall meet, and all that shit.

And personally, I didn't appreciate playing Romeo to a fucking Muscovite Juliet, but it wasn't like I had a choice.

Today was my wedding day.

Yeah, I was getting married, and I wasn't fucking happy about it.

It was also my bride's goddamn birthday.

Fucking eighteen.

Jesus.

I had about six hundred of New York's elite at my back, we even had the Deputy Attorney General of the state in the pews, and the hypocrisy within these walls which, ordinarily, would have amused me, instead, irritated the fuck out of me.

The place stank of shit.

I didn't give a fuck if these bastards were wearing eight hundred dollar an ounce scent, all I could smell was crap.

A lot of it.

The place was decked to the nines, both families' wealth out on display in the way it was decorated, but also, with the level of protection we had on this event—most of which I'd arranged because security was my jam. For every two guests, we had one detail covering their asses because this wedding meant something.

It was a way of formalizing ties between the Bratva and the Irish Mob, a way of securing them too, but I knew it was also my father's way of trying to take us up to another level. The number of famous faces, of political figures in the pews, spoke clearly of both families' spheres of influence, and he wanted that—wanted his greedy mitts all over those spheres. He'd long been playing the property ladder in the city, and with our money man and close friend to the family, Finn O'Grady, working the figures, we were starting to take over shit, owning the biggest skyscrapers, holding controlling stakes of the best plots of land in space poor Manhattan.

I already knew my father was a whack job, but if I hadn't known it, this wedding proved it.

He wanted my kid in office.

Or, at least, one of his sons' kids in office.

That was the end game, and fuck, I wanted nothing to do with it and didn't have a goddamn say in it either way.

My mouth tightened as the organ started playing the *Bridal Chorus*, and the slap of my brother Declan's hand to my shoulder had me glaring at him in irritation—did the fucker think I didn't know what that meant?

We'd already dealt with Pachelbel as two kids, a boy and a girl, had traipsed down the aisle, and a herd of fucking bridesmaids had soon followed.

Even in midsummer, St. Patrick's was goddamn cold, so the *Bridal Chorus* came as a relief—my dick was about to fall off from the chill within the old stone walls.

"You look at her like that, she'll have a heart attack," Dec muttered, as he twisted around to stare at my bride.

Disinterested in the proceedings, I shrugged. "Will save me the trouble of having her as a ball and chain."

His lips twitched. "She looks hot."

"She's eighteen. I don't go in for kids."

"She's legal," Declan replied, "and, let's face it, you can't not consummate it. Da won't allow it."

"What's he going to do? Put fucking cameras in the bedroom to make sure I fuck her?"

A hissed, "Quiet!" had me glowering at Doyle.

Declan snorted. "Just bone her. She's beautiful. You should have gone to her birthday party yesterday, man. That was fucking rude. She looked banging."

My mouth tightened at the mention of the early birthday/rehearsal dinner I'd refused to attend.

Before now, I'd seen pictures of her, but every time the Bratva Pakhan, the leader of the Russian Mafia, tried to get me to meet his spawn, Inessa, I'd managed to be out of the country.

It had taken some fucking calculated risks, but I'd achieved it. Sure, there was more blood on my hands as a result, but I liked honing my skills, making sure that my abilities with a rifle were as hot shit as ever.

Plus, I had a couple of million in the bank which my father couldn't touch, and that was always a bonus.

The prick had a habit of tithing us when we displeased him.

Beneath the organ, the throbbing notes that signified a death knell for every man's freedom, under the low hum of the crowd's oohing and aahing at my child fucking bride, I heard the hushed murmur of her skirts against the floor—that was only because my senses were honed.

I also heard her father's tapping footsteps, and knew my fate was sealed.

I mean, I'd known that earlier, but still. This was it.

It was really fucking happening.

Those tapping footsteps, the shushing skirts, they signed my death certificate.

I twisted around when the scent of lilies invaded my nostrils, and though it wasn't displeasing, I hated it instantly.

Because I wasn't a schmuck, and I knew Inessa had to be as unhappy with this situation as I was, I didn't glower at her, but I kept my face expressionless as I nodded at her father and accepted her hand.

I wasn't sure how Da had managed to wear Vasov down and had gotten him into a Catholic church and out of an Orthodox chapel, but from the look on his face, he was as happy as Aidan Sr. was with the upcoming nuptials.

I knew why, of course. Women were a commodity to the Bratva. Children were property to be bought and sold, and while that was the case with the Irish Mob too, we didn't tend to pimp out our kids to the enemy.

I cut him a look, more interested in him than my bride, and when our eyes met, his flashed slightly, a flicker of something I couldn't read surging to life inside them.

Maybe he saw my lack of fear, something that probably surprised him, maybe he saw that I was so beyond over this I'd moved into a different stratosphere, whatever it was, he muttered something in Russian to Inessa, then scuttled away like the pond scum he was.

He'd fucked off to his pew where a woman I assumed was his wife—not Inessa's mother, because she was definitely too young—had taken a seat, dressed like some kind of colorblind whore in a bright green dress that was more fitting for a nightclub than a wedding. Her hat looked like she had a nest of parrots on her head, so I knew Vasov hadn't married her for her taste in clothes, but for the tits that were spilling out of the dress. Tits were thirteen a dozen in my world, especially falsies, so, disinterested once Vasov was seated, I turned to Inessa.

The first thing I looked at was her hand trapped in mine. Her fingers were slender, delicate. The skin white and soft against my callused digits. The proof of my trade was written into the rough flesh of my hands, and there'd been so much blood shed by them that it should have marred her purity in a flash. The ring my father had procured for her sat on her finger. It wasn't gaudy, which told me Ma had helped purchase it, and the clear emerald was a dark, rich green that throbbed with life.

I had to think that, with her involvement, the emerald would suit Inessa's character—Ma would know my bride more than me. She'd met the bitch, after all. That was more than I'd done. So, for whatever reason, she sported an emerald instead of a diamond, and the heavy stone suited her delicate hand.

Letting my gaze drift over her fingers to her wrist, I took note of the thin sleeve that covered her forearm, and when I saw no sliver of skin, her face held more interest to me. Only, her head was covered with a veil, a thick one. The lace so dense that it was a wonder she could see through it without tripping.

The cream color reminded me of paper that had been aged with tea, and it draped over her, covering her from head to waist, revealing only a tight bodice that was decorated with what were probably diamonds, and the flared skirt that was like fancy netting that flounced with each step. It was large, enough for the skirts to get in my way and to put a few feet of distance between us.

Her other hand was primly pressed in front of her belly where she held the offending bouquet of lilies. The sight filled me with relief, even if I knew lilies were usually funereal flowers, not wedding. That she didn't use a lily-based scent actually perked me up.

What didn't?

Why her father hadn't raised her veil.

Why her maid of honor hadn't darted forward to do the same.

I wasn't a man who appreciated weddings, but I was Catholic. Weddings, funerals, and fucking baptisms were our stock-in-trade.

I knew the score.

And I knew that, even if the Orthodox rituals were different, they weren't that different.

Even if they were, I knew my father. He'd have micromanaged the shit out of the ceremony, and he liked things done just so. He wanted the world to know the father was giving up the daughter, handing her over like a virgin sacrifice. He'd want Vasov to raise the veil, to look at Inessa, for the girl to know she was a commodity her father was willing to trade, before handing her over to the buyer.

Yeah, sick, but that was daddy dearest for you.

That was how I knew something was going on.

Something that set my nerves on edge.

I stared at her so long, I heard Dec whisper, "What's the hold up?" I could easily foresee Da cutting him looks, glaring at him and waving his hands in an effort to get him to do something, but that wasn't going to work now. Not here. Not at this moment.

Behind me, people started to murmur too, wondering why I wasn't moving. I could imagine my father's face had gone from jubilant at a successful plan coming to fruition, to infuriated as he wondered what I was waiting for.

I just knew my mother was having to calm him down, and behind me, I could feel Doyle shuffling, his cassock whispering against the altar, and the bridesmaids starting to grow uneasy as my pause went to extreme lengths.

I ignored it all, focused only on her, on the puzzle that I was about to uncover, because all my instincts were telling me something.

Something I didn't fucking like.

They were hiding her away like she was some ugly bitch, where Declan had distinctly told me she was beautiful. He wouldn't lie. Not to me. Not without knowing I'd castrate him if he lied about that.

So what the fuck were they hiding?

Whether I wanted Inessa or not, she was my property. Had been since my goddamn father had tied me into this fucking engagement.

And I knew, fucking knew what I was about to see.

So my stillness?

It was me trying to prepare myself.

Me trying to calm myself down, because if I didn't, I would slice Vasov up like a motherfucker, and I didn't care who was watching.

Deputy Attorney Generals, Lieutenant Governors, and five hundred and ninety other witnesses be damned, blood would stain the altar of St. Patrick's for an eternity if I didn't get a handle on my temper.

The bouquet trembled, and I knew I was frightening Inessa—unfortunate, but it couldn't be helped. Not now.

The sight did stir me into action a minute later, because I didn't want her fear to encompass me, didn't want her to associate me with fright. So, I reached out, noticing she flinched at the movement, and slowly began to unveil my prize.

They'd done a skilled job of it.

I'd give them that.

The makeup was pretty flawless, but my trade was blood. Broken bones. Bruises.

I knew a black eye when I saw it.

I knew a busted jaw too.

My own popped out to the side as I processed the beating she'd taken, and I stared at her wedding dress, taking in all the covering, from the wrist-length sleeves to the way that not an ounce of her chest was revealed to me.

Sure, they might have been going for the demure look, but I'd seen nuns show more skin.

My mouth tightened, and I stopped looking at her flaws, and instead, looked at her.

My bride.

She was beautiful.

Dec was right.

She was a fucking stunner.

Her face was delicate, the bones strong, but somehow fragile. Like she was a fairy. Her blonde hair was in a fancy topknot, and tiny curls bobbed around her cheeks—it was a neat updo, but the way it teased and bounced with the faintest movement reminded me of the way a woman would raise her hand to grasp a hold of her hair during a blowjob when shit got real and she got down to business.

The thought, surprisingly enough, had my dick twitching when my mind's eye switched Inessa into that role, but I pushed thoughts like that aside and focused on my future wife. Her ears sported heavy emeralds that complimented her engagement ring and her clear green eyes, and her mouth was made for sinning.

At my unveiling, the congregation hushed down, evidently thinking the show was about to start, but when I reached for her bouquet, more whispers stirred.

She frowned at me, her brow puckering at the move, and I appreciated the push and pull as she tried to evade my grasp on the bouquet, but I ignored it. And the second our hands collided, she did too.

Her eyes transmitted her confusion, but I wasn't confused.

She was just registering the truth.

She was mine now.

Tossing the godawful lilies at the flustered maid of honor, who caught them with a gasp, I tugged her forward, being more gentle than I usually would have been, because rage was filtering through me with the purity of distilled vodka—and these fucks knew what that tasted like—and I didn't stop until we were standing opposite Doyle. I'd curved an arm around her waist, bringing her into me.

The move was not traditional, and Doyle's lips parted to scold me, but my scowl was evidently deterrent enough, because he instantly intoned, "Dearly beloved, we are gathered here today—"

As he got on with the ceremony, I tilted my head to the side. "I will make them pay for beating you."

She stiffened. "I-I...they didn't."

"Bullshit."

Another flinch.

"Don't lie to me, Inessa," I warned, and as Doyle droned on, I whispered, "They did a good job, but not good enough. You'll dance in their blood if you want."

She didn't reply, and while she was tense from the unusual hold I had her in, she relaxed somewhat at that.

If there was any consolation to marrying Bratva scum, it was that she'd been raised in the life.

She knew aggression and bloodshed were the universal language. Aoife, who was married to Finn, wasn't of the life, but she knew about the Five Points, had been raised in one of our neighborhoods, and the violence of our world still surprised her.

Not Inessa.

She was as used to it as I was, even if I doubted she'd ever gotten her hands dirty.

I twisted my fingers about said hand, surprised by the daintiness of it against mine.

My father had beaten the shit out of me just over a week ago when I'd raised hell about the upcoming wedding, but I was a man.

More than that, I was used to a beating.

Inessa?

She looked like a china doll, and while I'd never found that sexy in the past, had never found virginity or fragile women attractive, this was different.

She was mine.

I'd never put those pieces together until now.

She belonged to me.

This marriage would see to that.

She was mine to protect, mine to defend, just fucking mine.

Unlike every other aspect of my life, I wouldn't have to share her.

Not with my brothers, not with the family, not with the Five Points.

She belonged to me, and Eoghan O'Donnelly protected what belonged to him.

That was a fucking fact.

INESSA

HE KNEW.

Even as terror had filled me that he'd reject me, break off the wedding I knew he didn't want—probably even less than me, considering he'd managed to evade every single one of my father's invitations for us to meet—he'd raised my veil.

And he'd seen.

He'd seen what few men would.

He'd seen what I was supposed to hide, what fantastic makeup had tucked away, but he'd noticed. Had witnessed the truth of what had gone down a few days ago.

My heart had been beating like I'd been working out for hours on end, and by the time he'd tucked my hand into his, I wasn't sure if I was going to pass out or not. Whether it was from discomfort at his focus, fear of his rejection, or terror of being returned to my family... The latter was a fate worse than death.

I would die if I failed in this, if I shamed the family name.

So, when he tugged me toward the altar, the sweetest relief filled me, and I took a second to gape at him and take stock of the man who'd avoided me for so long. My first impression? That Eoghan was like all the O'Donnelly sons—wickedly handsome.

But the term wicked came in two definitions. Everyone in our circles knew what he, in particular, was capable of.

An expert marksman who'd been dishonorably discharged from the army, his skills were renowned—even by my father.

And Antoni Vasov didn't approve of anyone or anything.

The asshole.

But Eoghan's talents were undeniable. As a sniper, he was famous in our circles. A dubious fame, of course, but then that was the world I lived in. A shitty one.

My mouth tightened as Father Doyle—a man I'd met more times than my fiancé—began to start the service in earnest.

Undoubtedly, Aidan O'Donnelly Sr. thought he'd won some kind of boon by having the wedding ceremony in a Catholic church, and by being able to hold a traditional Catholic wedding when, really, it was a sign of my father washing his hands of me.

There'd be none of the traditions my sister would get at her wedding.

No special ceremonies like the crowns brides and grooms were given on the day, the earrings a bride received during the ceremony— Eoghan's family had given me a set that matched my ring as part of a bridal trousseau. There'd be none of the games that were played between a couple who was in love for the entertainment of their family.

This was a business transaction, and Father had made that very clear by not having a thing to do with the ceremony.

Not even to save face among our people was he willing to lower his disregard of me, and though I didn't want to be married at eighteen, I did want to be out from under his thumb.

There were only so many times an animal could be beaten before they decided to bite back, and each and every time he hit me, each and every time Svetlana slapped me and I was expected to do nothing other than take it, I was finding it harder and harder not to fight back.

Gritting my teeth was almost as painful as the bruises they inflicted upon me. Things had gotten worse recently, and it had culminated in the beating I'd 'earned' three days ago.

My entire face was numb. I was a little high on Tylenol with codeine from the pain—not just from the wounds themselves, but from the fact I'd had three makeup artists flittering around me, torturing me with beauty blenders on delicate skin.

I wasn't sure how I hadn't cried my makeup off, but it stuck. Somehow. And here I was.

Somehow.

Maybe I shivered, I didn't know, but Eoghan's hand tightened about mine, and it brought me back to the here and now.

A here and now where I was getting married.

To a man I didn't know.

To a man I didn't want to know.

To a man who had killed only God knew how many people for cold, hard cash.

I bit my lip at the thought and forced myself to think of anything other than the clusterfuck of this week, and how I'd endured my worst beating ever because I'd dared to tell my father that Eoghan was, essentially, a serial killer and that I didn't want to marry him.

Instead, I concentrated on the vows.

There was no divorce in our world.

Only death.

Either through the freedom of illness or violence.

My mother had died that way, when our house had been infiltrated by the *Famiglia*, and she'd been raped first before she'd been slaughtered like a pig.

I'd always thought that would be my fate, had always thought...

Despite myself, I turned slightly into Eoghan, curving my body toward his warmth.

He was a stranger, the aforementioned serial killer, but the people I knew had beaten me like I was a dog, so I had no place to go for safety.

And while his words weren't comforting, they sure as hell stuck with me.

"You'll dance in their blood if you want to."

My vision blurred as I contemplated that, then I thought about the fact I no longer had to answer to my father.

He wanted me to listen out for things, keep him in the loop, but I didn't want my new, relatively safe haven to be tarnished by my being a spy, so there was no way in hell I was going to do that.

And if I avoided him like the plague, there was no way he could ever expect that of me.

Well, that was naïve.

He could expect it of me, but I didn't have to give it to him.

All week, loathing for him had burned in me like a fever. It had distracted me from the upcoming marriage, and I'd focused only on getting away from him, on getting out of the house that was my prison in Brighton Beach...and after that, when I was wed, to getting away from Eoghan. To running and starting a new life for myself.

But now?

I could dance in Father's blood?

I tightened my hand around Eoghan's, turned my attention to Father Doyle, who was glowering at Eoghan over something—I didn't know what. Eoghan didn't seem the most reverent of people. Far as I could tell, he didn't give a damn for rules, which meant he either wanted this wedding—which I highly doubted—or someone had some power over him.

Having met my future father-in-law, I knew who that someone was.

I couldn't blame him.

Aidan Sr. was scary, and I said that when I was a Pakhan's daughter.

When I was the daughter of a woman who'd been slain for being married to said Pakhan...

Scary and me were friends.

But Aidan Sr.'s eyes said it all. He was insane. I wondered if his family knew it, and if they did, if they were as terrified of him as I tried not to be.

Like any predator, they distrusted fear, respected strength. The second I lowered my guard, showed Aidan Sr. I was scared, was the second he'd pounce. I just didn't know what that might entail.

Eoghan tugged on my hand once more in the silent communication I was slowly getting used to, and I realized I had to get involved in the ceremony.

I'd read up on the Catholic ritual, so I repeated the words the priest intoned, then I headed to a pew to the side of the altar where Father Doyle began a sermon about the power of marriage and how it could bring peace to a world filled with strife.

Fitting, but I highly doubted most of the congregation knew just what kind of peace it was bringing to the city.

A truce.

Between the Bratva and the Irish Mob.

Sure, they weren't the only players in the city. There were the Albanians, the Triads, and the *Famiglia*, but today's union bound the separate brotherhoods together in a way that would reap misery on the other factions.

Even though I was kept out of the business, I knew that much.

I wasn't an idiot, even if my family treated me like I was one because I had issues with the violent world I lived in.

"Who did it?"

His voice was like silk, whisper soft as it slid over me. I jolted in surprise because my focus had shifted when Doyle had started droning on—I knew my concussion wasn't helping me appear lucid—and quickly shot him a look. I just realized he hadn't let go of my hand, and his fingers tightened—not punishingly, but enough for me to feel his grasp.

"Why is it important for you to know?" I half-mouthed, not wanting to disturb the ceremony.

"It matters to me."

I knew I was his property, knew what my father had done was

essentially like giving Eoghan a backhanded slap, even if I was an unwanted bride, even if the beating was the only reason I was here today, but...

A united front, a merging of the Bratva and the Mob, would make us stronger.

Safer.

And I really didn't want to die like my mom had.

I didn't want to be raped by scum who hurt me just because they hated my husband.

I didn't want to be butchered like an animal, even though I'd had no say whatsoever, just like she hadn't, in whom she married.

Tears pricked my eyes at the thought, and I dipped my chin, whispering, "They can't touch me anymore."

He stiffened at that. "You're damn right they can't."

I froze, a little horrified at how loud his voice had been. A hush fell over the church, and Doyle stopped mid-sentence and twisted around to glare at Eoghan again—this was getting to be a theme of the day—before he flared his eyes in warning and returned to the full lecture.

Despite myself, my lips twitched, and I whispered, "Your irreverence is showing."

He snorted. "That's one word for it. Doyle can't stand that I don't give a shit about this crap."

"Why are you here then?"

"Because, like your father, mine rules with an iron fist. He might be an old bastard, but he's handy with them."

"You were beaten too?" My mouth rounded at that, and I gaped at him, unable to believe it.

Eoghan was...

He was, well, like a warrior of old.

I could see him in a kilt with a claymore on his back, could see him on horseback with armor covering him.

Sure, his features were a little baby faced, but his eyes? Those dark brown orbs held a multitude of secrets, and I got the feeling most of them were terrifying. His body was taut and trim, and the tails he wore—a long suit jacket with a 'tail' at the back—fit him to perfection. He gave off a slender appearance, I guessed, but there was something coiled about him. Like he was just preparing to spring into action.

And from his response to my very well hidden, expertly concealed bruises?

I figured that was pretty apt.

He had dark hair, so dark it was almost black, and his brows matched. They hooded gleaming eyes that, I got the feeling, saw everything and missed nothing, and his jaw was clean-shaven but, judging by the faint tan on his cheeks, he usually had a short beard.

The notion intrigued me, as did his handsomeness.

I'd known, at some point, I'd be married off to someone. Sure, I'd never thought it would be when I was eighteen, and I'd never thought I'd be married to a goddamn Irish man, but to be wed to a handsome guy who wasn't thick around the waist, smelled of potatoes that had been lost in the back of the kitchen cabinets, and drank more vodka than water?

Yeah, technically Eoghan was a dream.

A technicolor one.

"You're staring."

His lips twitched, the dusky peach flesh moving, enticing me to smile with him.

I hadn't expected any kindness from him.

If the Russians hated the Irish, that was nothing compared to what they felt for us. I'd known I was walking into enemy territory today, but, of course, life was full of surprises.

My 'home' camp had treated me worse than Eoghan who, the second he'd seen me, had stopped glowering at me, and had started glaring at the world like he was pissed at it and not me.

I couldn't even begin to describe how much of a relief that was.

Not to be in his crosshairs? Bliss!

And the truth was, if he could keep me safe?

I'd do anything, be anything he wanted. I'd even stay, I wouldn't run.

I just wanted away from my family, I just wanted a life of my own, even if it was still curtailed by being a wife to a high-ranking lieutenant in a crime family.

"You're very handsome," I whispered, my voice husky.

He arched a brow. "Thank you." His voice was toneless, but his eyes gleamed with humor.

I felt gauche, very young and stupid, until he leaned into me, pressed a kiss to my temple, and whispered, "A handsome groom for a beautiful bride. We're going to make the congregation weep."

It was my turn for my lips to twitch, and I grinned at him, liking the softer side he was showing me, and hoping and praying, even though I knew both were stupid and dangerous, that maybe we could have something together.

Maybe we could take this arrangement and make it work for us.

Even if we led shorter lives thanks to our affiliations, we still had a long time on this earth to be tied together. I didn't want to spend every day miserable, and that kiss? His tenderness? While surprising, they filled me with dreams I shouldn't have.

That I was foolish to have.

AFTERWORD

Guys, how are we feeling?
Are we ready for more from the O'Donnellys?

I hope so!

FILTHY RICH is now live on Amazon!! You can find it here: www.books2read.com/FilthyRich

Don't forget, if you want updates on when new books in the series drop, then you have several options because, I promise you, these Filthy Feckers are so worth dropping everything for—your panties included. ;)

FACEBOOK READER GROUP: www.facebook.com/groups/SerenaAkeroydsDivas

BOOKBUB: www.bookbub.com/profile/serena-akeroyd

NEWSLETTER: www.serenaakeroyd.com/Newsletter

Thank you so much for your support, guys,

Love you all,

Serena <3

FREE EBOOK ALERT!!

Don't forget to grab your free e-Book!
Secrets & Lies is now free!

Meg's love life was missing a spark until she discovered her need to be dominated. When her fiancé shared the same kink, she thought all her birthdays had come at once, and then she came to learn their relationship was one big fat lie.

Gabe has loved Meg for years, watching her from afar, and always wishing he'd been the one to date her first and not his brother. When he has the chance to have Meg in his bed—even better, tied to it—it's an opportunity he can't refuse.

With disastrous consequences.

Can Gabe make Meg realize she's the one woman he's always wanted? But once secrets and lies have wormed their way into a relationship, is it impossible to establish the firm base of trust needed between lovers, and more importantly, between sub and Sir...?

This story features orgasm control in a BDSM setting.

Secrets & Lies is now free!

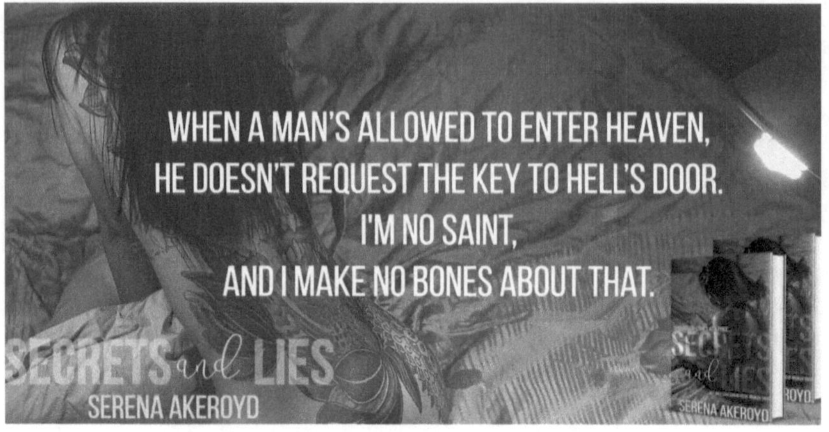

CONNECT WITH SERENA

For the latest updates, be sure to check out my website!

But, if you'd like to hang out with me and get to know me better, then I'd love to see you in my Diva reader's group where you can find out all the gossip on new releases as and when they happen. You can join here: www.facebook.com/groups/SerenaAkeroydsDivas. Or, you can always PM or email me. I love to hear from you guys: serenaakeroyd@gmail.com.

ABOUT THE AUTHOR

I'm a romance novelaholic and I won't touch a book unless I know there's a happy ending. This addiction is what made me craft stories that suit my voracious need for raunchy romance. I love twists and unexpected turns, and my novels all contain sexy guys, dark humor, and hot AF love scenes.

I write MF, Menage, and Reverse Harem (also known as Why Choose romance,) in both contemporary and paranormal. Some of my stories are darker than others, but I can promise you one thing, you will always get the happy ending your heart needs!

facebook.com/SerenaAkeroyd

x.com/SerenaAkeroyd

instagram.com/Serena_Akeroyd

amazon.com/Serena-Akeroyd/e/B00EC76REA